KISSING CAITLIN

"I'm not one of your pupils, Caitlin. You don't intimidate me. If we are to play out this charade, then we will play it out as man and wife, and that means on my terms. In case you haven't noticed, it's the man who calls the shots in a household."

"But we aren't really—"

"Do you want all of Mineral Point to know that? Let me remind you that this was all your idea and I've done everything you asked of me. Well, it's time to pay up, Caitlin."

She pushed herself free of him and headed for the bedroom. "We'll discuss this in the morning when you have better control of your reason," she said with a haughty toss of her head.

"We'll talk now," he said. "I'll start." Before she could react he pulled her hard against him and kissed her. He was determined to make her feel the desire she roused in him. He could not make her love him, but he could make her want him the way he hungered for her.

The unexpectedness of his kiss took Caitlin by surprise. Her first reaction was to fight him, but within seconds she found herself yielding. Her heart and body betrayed her as she tried to wrestle with the impropriety of the situation. But the truth was, she had longed for this, dreamed of it to the point of physical pain. In spite of her determination to remain in command of the situation, she found herself relinquishing the control that was her only weapon against her love for this man. . . .

BOOK YOUR PLACE ON OUR WEBSITE AND MAKE THE READING CONNECTION!

We've created a customized website just for our very special readers, where you can get the inside scoop on everything that's going on with Zebra, Pinnacle and Kensington books.

When you come online, you'll have the exciting opportunity to:

- View covers of upcoming books
- Read sample chapters
- Learn about our future publishing schedule (listed by publication month *and author*)
- Find out when your favorite authors will be visiting a city near you
- Search for and order backlist books from our online catalog
- Check out author bios and background information
- Send e-mail to your favorite authors
- Meet the Kensington staff online
- Join us in weekly chats with authors, readers and other guests
- Get writing guidelines
- AND MUCH MORE!

Visit our website at
http://www.zebrabooks.com

COURTING CAITLIN

Willa Hix

Zebra Books
Kensington Publishing Corp.
http://www.zebrabooks.com

ZEBRA BOOKS are published by

Kensington Publishing Corp.
850 Third Avenue
New York, NY 10022

Zebra and the Z logo Reg. U.S. Pat. & TM Off.

First Printing: December, 1998
10 9 8 7 6 5 4 3 2 1

Printed in the United States of America

One

Dylan Tremaine sat in the single rickety wooden chair outside the tavern on High Street where he and the other miners had spent the better part of the past two days blowing off steam. They'd all settled in western Wisconsin for one reason—the hills were rich in lead. The men, or their ancestors, had come from Cornwall and other parts of Europe to mine the rich deposits of ore to be found in those rolling hills. The lead deposits had pretty much been worked out or bought up by the time Dylan arrived, but he knew the old ways of getting that last bit of ore from the ground and he'd set up his stake near an abandoned mine just outside town.

Lazily, he watched as the schoolmarm sashayed past him on her way to the Methodist church where she'd set up a school in the basement. Not that she was aware of the interesting view she afforded as she came his way. No, her shoulders and back were as rigid as those of a raw recruit trying to impress his captain. She looked neither left nor right as she performed her no-nonsense strut past Heathcote's Tavern. Her features were shaded by the ridiculous and completely unflattering bonnet she'd worn the few times he'd seen her. Her chin thrust forward, accenting the tight, thin, determined line of her mouth. But he had a glimpse of high pronounced cheekbones tinged with the faintest touch of pink beneath creamy unblemished skin.

"Morning, ma'am," Dylan greeted her as she lifted the hem of her skirt and made the necessary detour to miss his long outstretched legs. "Glorious morning, I'm thinking it is, too." He caught a glimpse of unexpectedly bright red curls framing her face before she deliberately turned her head a fraction of an inch farther away from him and kept on walking.

Once she'd passed, Dylan watched the side-to-side sway of her hips, appreciating the way her long legs set a stride and pace that set those hips in motion in the most provocative way. Respectfully, he placed his battered hat over his heart and sighed. The lady had definitely lifted his spirits on this dreary late October Monday.

"You're wasting your time, Tremaine," Gar Heathcote commented as he paused before dumping a bucket of sudsy water into the dirt street and followed the young miner's gaze. "Them Pearce women have been raised to see themselves as too good for the likes of you. You might have had a chance with the younger one, Molly, but she's got her sights set on that blueblood lawyer from out East—the one running for the state legislature? Problem is the ol' man holds to the old school that says the younger sister can't marry 'til the elder is hitched. Poor little Molly. She'd do a sight better to wait for her pa to die than for that one there to marry." He jerked his head in the general direction of the woman striding purposefully down the street.

"The schoolmarm don't look so bad to me," Dylan observed. "Of course, she's always so buttoned up and wearing those silly bonnets hiding her face and all. I mean, she's not homely, is she?"

Gar laughed. "There was a time when she coulda had her pick," he continued as he set the bucket aside and bit off the end of a fresh cigar, spitting the tip into the street as he narrowed his eyes at Dylan. "But none was good enough for her. Too proud, she was. Set your sights on something easier, son. There's plenty who'd be happy to satisfy your needs while you're in town. That's my advice." He patted Dylan on the shoulder as he headed back inside his establishment to finish cleaning up from the previous night's celebration.

Dylan put his hat back on and brought the chair to rest on all four legs. He leaned forward, resting his elbows on his knees and continued watching Miss Caitlin Pearce until she turned the corner. He knew Gar was probably right, but he'd never in his life been able to resist a challenge, and the one set of words guaranteed to set him on a new path were those that said something couldn't be done. Dylan stood and sauntered into the tavern.

"Then you'd be saying I can't spark with the school-marm, is that it?" he asked as if the conversation with the saloonkeeper had not missed a beat.

Heathcote looked at him, then continued sweeping the scarred wooden floor as he chewed thoughtfully on his unlit cigar. "Why trouble yourself with somebody as stuck up as her? I've seen the way the young ladies in this town watch you. Lord above knows when you get yourself cleaned up, you strike one fine picture of a man. Why not make it easy on yourself and choose from the menu that's already on the table? Besides, why start something when you're not planning to stay?"

"Then you'd be saying I couldn't win the fair Miss Pearce," Dylan pressed.

Gar sighed and leaned on his push broom. "Look, you've only been over here a few months. It's different here in America than back in Cornwall—or maybe not so different, depending on how you look at it. The Pearces are British. John Pearce is a nice enough fellow—a little prissy for my taste—but he has certain ideas about how his girls should behave and what they should have in this life. The man wants the best for them, and, sorry to say, a Cornish miner who hasn't even got a roof over his head ain't exactly his idea of the perfect match for his daughter. Now if you was to have a title—"

"I've got better than that," Dylan objected. "I've got prospects. I've already gotten a good start here—good enough that before too long I'll have the stake I need to head out West. Someday I'll have more than enough to dress old man Pearce's precious daughter in all the finery any duke or earl could provide."

Gar shook his head "You oughtn't believe all them wild stories about gold out there in California—or wherever it is you're thinking of heading. One prospector finds a couple of nuggets and you'd think there was gold lining the hillsides."

"The stories are true, Gar. I've checked 'em out. Just last week I had a letter from my brother about a strike. He was heading there himself. You wait and see. Some day . . ."

Gar grinned and resumed his sweeping. "That brother of yours is a dreamer—you said so yourself. Fact is, you don't even have a roof over your head, and *someday* don't impress the likes of John Pearce or his daughter. Heed my words and go for something easier. You want something to scratch your itch? Even if you've got your sights set on someone proper, there's more to pick from here than just the Pearce girl."

Dylan leaned against the bar and stared out the window. It was true about not having a roof over his head. It wasn't that he couldn't afford it. Heathcote was right about his lifestyle, but the fact was he just liked the idea of doing things the old way—the way the Cornish who'd settled the area had gotten their start. After watching practically every male member of his family work themselves to death digging through rock and stone deep in the bowels of the earth, he'd sworn he would find another way. Even now, he spent part of every day working above ground rather than going down into the abandoned mine. And he chose to spend his nights outdoors, under the stars, breathing free.

"You badgers are all the same," Gar observed. "Digging into the hillside to make your camp. That was fine for them that came early on when there was no town, no houses. You, you're just being stubborn. They're building houses around here faster than you can count, and I know for a fact you've taken enough ore over to the smelter to more than pay for a house to suit your needs."

"Maybe, then again maybe it's better to sleep in a badger hole than to spend money you can use to better purpose on bed and board when it's just you by yourself," Dylan replied. He'd never minded the brand of *badger*. He'd liked the idea that he was as ferocious and strong as the animal that roamed the area. Dylan pushed himself away from the bar and walked across the freshly swept floor.

"I may be nothing more than a badger, Gar," Dylan said with quiet resolution, "but I'll wager I can kiss Miss Caitlin Pearce in full view of most of the town within thirty days and she'll not only accept it, she'll be a willing partner in that kiss."

Gar halted his sweeping and stared at the young miner. "You ain't even met her," he protested.

Dylan shrugged. "Easily remedied. Do we have a wager?"

Gar squinted as he considered what could possibly be the drawbacks of taking this bet. "How much?"

"Name it," Dylan answered with a confident grin.

"Ten bucks says you can't get her to kiss you willingly in front of the town by thirty days from today," Gar dared.

Dylan flinched involuntarily. It was a good chunk of his savings if he lost. If he won though, it was enough to leave Mineral Point and have a head start on a proper stake for him and his younger brother, Ty. It was one kiss, for mercy's sake. There hadn't been a time in his life that he'd been unable to make his charm and wit work to win him any girl he set his sights on. He thrust out his hand. "Done," he agreed.

Gar shook his hand and also shook his head. "I like you, kid, but you're one cocky son of a gun. I'm gonna hate taking your money. I'll give you one last chance to rethink this."

Dylan grinned. As if any man from Cornwall would ever back down on a bet. "How about double or nothing?"

"You ain't got that kind of money, son, and we both know it."

Dylan adjusted his hat and clapped the older man on the back. "I ain't gotta worry about that, ol' man, cause I ain't gonna lose," he said cockily as he headed for the door.

"All right, I'll take your bet on one condition," Gar called after him. "Miss Caitlin can't know what you're up to. You have to get her to kiss you for real, not so you can win the bet."

"Agreed. And while we're setting the ground rules, no-body in town's to know about our little wager—even when it's over and paid. I won't have the lady getting her feelings hurt by hearing she's been the prize in a bar wager."

Gar nodded. "Thirty days. Double or nothing. And son? I expect to be paid," he said as he struck a match against the side of the bar and finally lit his cigar.

Dylan paused for a moment. Everybody in town knew Gar Heathcote had the biggest heart around. No miner ever went hungry or without a bed for the night if Gar could help him, but he had no patience with foolishness and no doubt he thought Dylan had just made a foolish wager. He would indeed expect to be paid.

Ordinarily Caitlin Pearce loved teaching. Ever since the town fathers had spent all of the school funds to add that expensive addition to the school building and then had to shut the place down for lack of money to run it, Caitlin had dedicated herself to teaching. She had persuaded her father to provide funds for the establishment of a school in the basement of the church.

"I can't pay you a wage, daughter," he'd told her.

"As long as I live at home there's no need," she'd replied. "Perhaps the children's parents will pay a modest fee."

Her father had frowned at that. He wanted her to marry and settle down and raise children of her own. "I'll put the cottage on Shake Rag in your name—that can be your pension," he told her. He had meant it as a joke, but she had held him to his promise and talked often of the day she might move into *her* cottage. The congregation had insisted on setting aside a portion of the collection in order to pay her for teaching their children. Suddenly, she was an independent woman.

The truth was Caitlin had no intention of marrying—ever. She was content with the life she had made for herself and happy to be rid of the need to play silly games of courtship and flirtation. She excelled at finding ways to challenge the children's curiosity. On a good day, she could even get through to the recalcitrant Rob Heathcote and the half-dozen young boys who idolized him.

This was not one of those days, Caitlin realized. Rob had arrived at school late, his eyelids heavy with the need for sleep, a surly sneer curling his lip. Clearly he'd been up half the night. He made a great show of interrupting the lesson in progress as he paraded lazily to his desk in the front of the room and noisily cleared his throat and yawned as he pulled out his books and settled in. Just when she thought ignoring him had had the right effect and continued the lesson, he launched a fake coughing attack complete with flailing arms and offensive gagging noises for effect. His followers were enthralled by his antics while Caitlin's patience was being tested to its limits.

"Mr. Heathcote, one more disgusting noise and you may

take your place in the cloakroom," she warned, then turned her back to the class to make notes on the chalkboard.

The belch echoed throughout the room.

"Mr. Heathcote, please remove yourself to the cloakroom immediately," Caitlin ordered as she pivoted and glared at the smirking boy.

"Ma'am?" he replied, his face suddenly a mask of innocence.

"You heard me. Go." She stretched out her arm and pointed toward the narrow walled-off closet at the back of the room.

He glared at her in defiance. The rest of the students seemed to hold their breath.

"Mr. Heathcote," she repeated, her eyes never wavering from his. "Take your slate with you and finish the sums you were to do last night and which I assume you have not completed."

"I had to work," he protested.

She knew it was true and hardly the boy's fault. He probably had been up until who knew what hour helping his father in the tavern. After his mother died in childbirth, Rob's father had taken the boy with him to the tavern. Over time he'd started depending on the boy more and more to help him with the business. In spite of Caitlin's efforts to convince Gar Heathcote that Rob's education was also important, there was little support for making Rob do his homework or attend class. "I appreciate that you had to help your father last night. I am giving you the opportunity to complete your homework now." Again, she extended her finger toward the cloakroom.

Rob Heathcote curled his lip in a dismissive sneer and stood up. He sauntered toward the cloakroom, clearly making faces or muttered comments to his classmates as he passed. Just before he entered the cloakroom, he gave forth with one final defiant belch. Every student in the classroom released the giggles they'd held in check throughout the ordeal.

"That's enough!" Caitlin shouted and hated the shrillness of her own voice as she pounded her wooden pointer against her desk and adjusted her spectacles. When order was instantly restored she turned back to the lesson at hand, but her heart wasn't in teaching today. The truth was, she hadn't had much sleep herself and she was as anxious for the day to end as were her students.

Her younger sister Molly had kept her awake most of the night. Caitlin's mother liked to say that Molly had inherited her great-grandmother's Irish temperament, along with her name. Caitlin's sister was desperately in love with Geoffrey MacKenzie. They wanted to marry as soon as possible. There was just one stumbling block. Their father, John Pearce, was a firm believer in the old traditions. His greatest fear about raising his family in America was that they would lose touch with the heritage of their ancestors in England. There, eldest sons inherited titles and properties—as John Pearce's older brother had; younger sons entered the ministry or business world—as John Pearce had; and eldest daughters married before their younger siblings—as he was determined Caitlin would.

The hitch was that Caitlin refused to marry simply for the convenience of maintaining tradition. She would marry for love—the kind of grand passion expressed in her favorite novels—or not at all, and the latter choice was holding increasing appeal for her with each passing day. To be sure, there would be lonely times in choosing not to wed, but from what she had observed, there could be lonely times even within a marriage—especially if it was loveless. She'd noticed that often enough in dealing with the parents of her students. She'd also seen what that could mean to the children themselves, and she was determined no child of hers would know that kind of unloving household. Once she had accepted that there was no man in Mineral Point with whom she cared to spend the rest of her life, Caitlin had come to terms with her decision. She had been con-

vinced that Molly could win their father over once he realized her own determination to remain single.

But Molly was young and impatient and completely in
love, all of which made her more than a little desperate.
The night before she had sobbed out her misery and threatened to take matters into her own hands. She would run
away with Geoffrey, she had declared dramatically. When
Caitlin had reminded her that such an action would force
their father to take a stand and possibly even disown her,
Molly avowed that she didn't care. She would do *anything*
to be with Geoffrey. When Caitlin had suggested that such
a rash action might jeopardize Geoffrey's political career
and he might end up resenting her, Molly had burst into
fresh gales of sobbing, chastising Caitlin for caring only
for herself and nothing for Molly. At one point she had
even accused Caitlin of being jealous of the love she had
found with Geoffrey.

Caitlin sighed and turned her attention once more to the
students. The day crawled by. Rob Heathcote slipped out
of the classroom and church at lunchtime and did not return. The other children fidgeted and fussed through the
long hours of the afternoon, perhaps caught up in the same
restless impatience for the day to be over that their teacher
fought to hold in check. Determined to salvage something
from the day, Caitlin insisted on continuing lesson after
lesson.

"Miss Pearce?"

Caitlin blinked and paused in the middle of her lecture
on the arrival of the first colonists and turned her attention
to the class. She had been determined to teach the children
something of value before they left for the day, and history
was her favorite topic. She had just warmed to the telling
of the story of the *Mayflower* when Elizabeth Pembrooke
interrupted. "Yes, Elizabeth?"

"I promised my mother that I'd come home right after

school and help her with the baby." The girl looked meaningfully at the large clock on the wall over the door.

It showed fifteen minutes past the end of the school day. Caitlin had continued to teach with no thought for the time, her mind preoccupied with thoughts of Molly. "Very well, then. Of course. Everyone, remember to do your homework, and don't forget to ask your parents about how your ancestors came to America. I'll expect your reports tomorrow. Good day, children."

"Good day, Miss Pearce," the children chanted in unison, and then bolted for the door. Their shouts of exhilaration echoed through the suddenly deserted church hall as they scattered in all directions. Caitlin busied herself with the process of setting the room to rights before leaving herself. She was not looking forward to going home. Molly would be there, across the dinner table, casting her alternately accusing and pleading looks. Caitlin sighed and erased the chalkboard.

There was no doubt that Caitlin must do something to help her sister. In pouring out her heart the night before, Molly had admitted that she and Geoffrey had moved well beyond hand-holding and chaste kisses. With eyes glowing at the memory, Molly had described that evening's meeting. Geoffrey had opened her dress to the waist, he had touched her breasts, even kissed them. Molly had not only permitted it, but encouraged it, and she informed Caitlin, there would be no going back—she would not, could not.

Caitlin had been shocked. "What if you become pregnant?" she had asked.

"Then Father will have to permit us to marry," Molly had answered and had smiled. "That's it," she'd announced excitedly. "It's the answer."

"No, Molly. There has to be another way," Caitlin had protested.

"Then find it," Molly had retorted sullenly before turning her back to Caitlin and refusing to discuss the matter further.

Caitlin had lain awake the rest of the night trying to come up with a solution. By dawn she had decided the answer lay in leaving town herself. She could take a teaching post somewhere out West, then write after a decent interval to say she had married. That would leave Molly free to wed Geoffrey. The problem was that such a plan would take weeks—even months. She would have to find a position, convince her parents to permit her to move, and allow for the time necessary to pretend to meet someone, be courted properly, and marry. It was clearly an impossible solution, but what else was there?

She turned to place the pile of books she'd been gathering on the shelf in the cloakroom and gave a startled shriek. The books went flying, and she and the man who'd been lounging in the doorway watching her for who knew how long cracked heads as they both bent to retrieve them.

She was well aware of his identity. Certainly Dylan Tremaine had been the talk of town since his arrival in late summer, insisting as he did on reverting to the old ways of the first Cornish miners to settle in Mineral Point. It was ridiculous for him to live out there in that hole he'd dug into the side of the hill, yet she admired his stubbornness, his determination to live life on his own terms. Local gossip had it that Dylan Tremaine was a man with ambitions and a plan for achieving them. Caitlin could not ignore that. She was also quite aware of the effect he had on the other single women in town. They tittered like silly schoolgirls about his dark good looks, his bewitching smile, his tall muscular body. Local gossip had it that he had inherited his dark good looks from his mother's Irish side and his talent for extracting ore from the ground from his father. And while she refused to participate in such drivel, Caitlin could not deny that she had observed him when she was certain no one would notice and had found him most appealing. To her, he was at least the physical embodiment of those heroes she admired most in her beloved books.

She was also aware that he had observed her as she went about her business in town. She hated the telltale color of embarrassment that rose to her cheeks as she felt more than saw him watching her long after she'd passed him. This morning had been a prime example. He'd been mocking her with that greeting of his, commenting on the loveliness of a day that promised rain even as he refused to move his long, outstretched legs from her path. Dylan Tremaine was nothing more than a grown-up version of Rob Heathcote. Rob had an excuse—he was fourteen. What was Dylan Tremaine's excuse? No, Caitlin did not approve of this stranger one bit, no matter how tall and handsome he might be.

"Can I help you?" Caitlin asked in her firmest schoolmarm voice.

"Yes, ma'am, I'm hoping you can do just that," he answered with a twinkle in his deep-set blue eyes that belied his expression of abject sincerity. He held the pile of books he'd retrieved and waited for her instruction.

"There, if you please," she said, indicating the shelf in the cloakroom. She headed back to the front of the room and took her place behind her desk, rearranging papers. "Thank you, Mr. Tremaine, for assisting with the books. Now, how may I help you?"

Dylan was momentarily taken aback that she knew his name. He hadn't expected that. He moved down the narrow aisle toward her, considering the best approach. "I was hoping you might be willing to give me lessons."

As he'd expected, that got her attention. She looked up at him and then immediately away again. But there was time to see her eyes, bright, probing, missing nothing. "Lessons, Mr. Tremaine?"

"Yes, ma'am, and you could call me Dylan."

"What kind of lessons, Mr. Tremaine?"

"Reading," he answered quickly. He'd been planning to ask for tutoring in arithmetic, but when he'd shelved those books, he'd noticed the range of titles. Dylan had been reading all his life, and he recognized a lover of good books by the diversity of her selection here in the classroom. In that moment he knew she'd be unable to resist giving the gift of great literature to another.

"You can't read?" Now she looked at him with interest.

"No, ma'am," he lied.

"At all?"

He shrugged. "Enough to get by with signs and such, but my dear mother gave me a love for poetry, reciting it to me when I was a lad. She was Irish, you see. She always hoped . . . Well, she died before she could teach me proper." It was only the smallest lie. His mother was indeed Irish and had died, but not before teaching him the rudiments. The rest he'd picked up with practice. "I can see that if I'm to make anything of myself here in America, I'll need to read and write. After all, I don't want people taking advantage of me," he added.

"I don't give private lessons, Mr. Tremaine," she said. "Perhaps there's someone else in town. You may have heard that a number of citizens have established private schools."

"No, that won't do, ma'am," he protested, then hastened to explain. "You see, I don't want it known that I need the lessons. The fellas out there in the mines would think it strange, like I was putting on airs and such. I guess you could say I'm a bit proud that way," he added with a shy grin.

"How do you propose to pay for the lessons, Mr. Tremaine? After all, if you can't afford a proper roof over your head . . ." She saw that she had touched a nerve.

"I choose to live the old way," he snapped, then once again took up the charming demeanor with which he'd entered the room. "To tell you the truth, I can't pay, but I'd be willing to strike a bargain. I could do some chores around here. Or perhaps you have something else in mind?" There was pure devilment in his eyes as he added that last.

His smile made her heart race. There was something about the way it occupied every feature of his face, especially his eyes. He looked at her as if they shared some wonderful secret. Suddenly she wanted very much to know what that secret might be.

"Chores?" she managed to force the word past the dearth of breath in her lungs. He had leaned across the desk toward her, his palms flattened on her papers, his surprisingly clean fingers no more than an inch or so from her own, his face closer than any man's had been in a very long time.

"I could build a fire," he said softly, his eyes wandering to her lips. When she gave a little gasp, snatched up her papers, and moved away from the desk, he grinned and moved to the stove, opening the door to examine the fire. "Or whatever you'd be needing. I only ask that we keep this little bargain just between the two of us. I don't want to be the brunt of jokes around town, you know."

"I don't believe I agreed to your bargain, Mr. Tremaine," Caitlin reminded him as she distributed the marked papers to each desk.

Dylan frowned. This was not going at all the way he'd planned. The only way he had a chance of winning the wager was to spend time with her. His plan had been to exchange chores for lessons, making it natural for him to be with her at odd times of the day.

"I can understand your reluctance," he said as he half sat on the desk and turned his hat nervously in his hands. "You must treasure your time away from your teaching duties. I expect some fortunate young man takes up a great deal of it." He watched her back stiffen and smiled.

"You see the thing of it is," he hastened to add, "I haven't much time. As soon as I've put together enough for a stake, I'm leaving Mineral Point. My brother Ty is already out West, and I plan to join him. There's gold out there—maybe lots of it by the reports. I think we stand a good chance of striking it rich, but I'd like to be ready. I've heard tell of other miners making their strike and then losing everything in some unscrupulous deal. If I can read, write, and do my own figuring, chances are we'll be able to hold our own. But I need help, and I don't know who else to turn to."

"You could go to Pastor Evanston," Caitlin suggested, but her mind focused on the information that he planned to leave town. She was beginning to see a way of helping Molly by helping Dylan Tremaine.

"To tell you the truth, Pastor Evanston makes me nervous." He grinned charmingly.

Caitlin resisted the urge to answer with a smile of her own, for Pastor Evanston made everyone nervous with his shock of white hair, his bushy unkempt eyebrows, and his thunderous voice delivering messages of fire and brimstone. "Why did you not join your brother out West to start with?" she asked.

"He's my younger brother and headstrong. Set out all alone, determined he was going to strike it rich before I could get there. Me, I'm a bit more practical. Back in Cornwall we knew of the opportunities here in Mineral Point. Friends of my father's came here when the lead deposits were first discovered. I figured if I could come here and apply the methods I learned in the old country, working what was left of the lead, could earn enough in leftovers to pay my passage West and make sure Ty and I had enough to live on while we prospect. Whatever Ty started out with, I'll wager all my savings it's gone by now. He'll be needing my help." He'd never talked at such length about his family or motives for coming to America before. He wondered why he was doing it now. He watched as she placed the last paper on the last desk. "Do you have younger siblings, Miss Pearce?"

She nodded and gave the first hint of a smile. "A sister—Molly."

"Then you understand how it is."

"How much longer do you think it will take for you to raise the money you need to head West and go into partnership with your brother?"

Dylan relaxed. She was considering his idea. "Four weeks—maybe eight. I've got a pretty good start."

Caitlin mentally calculated the time frame. It might just work. "And then you'll be leaving Mineral Point for good." She said it as a statement, but as if mulling the news over in her mind for her own purposes.

"That's right." Dylan felt distinctly uncomfortable with the direction the conversation had taken. Why all the interest in his leaving town?

"You have no plans to return? Even if your venture with your brother doesn't work out?"

"I expect not. We'd probably just settle there or head on up the coast to Oregon—do some farming, most likely."

Caitlin's head was spinning with the possibilities. What if instead of her leaving and sending word she'd married, she pretended to marry Dylan Tremaine right here and then he left? What if after a respectable time word came that he'd been tragically killed in a mining accident? Molly could marry as soon as everyone thought she and Mr. Tremaine had wed, and once she was "widowed" no one would ever expect her to marry again. She could settle into her cottage on Shake Rag Street without raising any eyebrows. She could surround herself with her books. She could live out her days teaching the children of Mineral Point and enjoying the bliss of a solitary life. It was the perfect solution for everyone.

"I'll do it, Mr. Tremaine," she announced, "under the following conditions. . . ."

She watched him visibly relax and realized that this had indeed been quite important to him. That realization endeared him to her in the same way having Rob Heathcote successfully recite his multiplication tables did.

"Name your terms, ma'am," Dylan said with a cocky grin.

"I want you to marry me," Caitlin replied as she moved to the windows and reached high to slam each shut in quick succession. Warm weather or cold, she was a firm believer in the importance of fresh air. The noise helped to cover his sudden speechlessness.

TWO

Dylan shook his head in disbelief. He could not possibly have heard her right. *Marry?* Perhaps she'd said *carry* her, but where and for what purpose? Either he hadn't heard her right or she was as loony as she was prim.

"I didn't quite get that last, miss," he said as she slammed shut the last window and turned to him, her cheeks high with color. Was that from the exertion of closing the windows or something more personal?

She seemed to take a moment to gather her courage; then she looked him straight in the eye and repeated herself. "I said that my terms for giving you lessons are that you will marry me," she said quietly.

Dylan swallowed, then swallowed again. "Well, you see, that's a pretty dear price for a few reading lessons, miss. Not that you wouldn't make a man a fine wife," he hastened to add.

Caitlin released a sigh of relief. At least he hadn't laughed at her and gone running from the building. He was still here. "Permit me to explain, Mr. Tremaine."

"Of course, marrying you might be one way of getting you to call me Dylan," he said with a smile. *What on earth is going on here?* Dylan wondered if Gar might not have misjudged the fair Miss Pearce. After all, a woman alone with no prospects . . . He moved closer so he could see her face in the waning light. She certainly didn't look desperate, but a fella couldn't be too careful.

Caitlin was quite sure that the increased beating of her heart was purely a scientific reaction to the extraordinary plan she was about to share with him. It certainly could have nothing to do with this uneducated miner. "As I was about to explain, Mr. Tremaine, ours would be a marriage in name only—not legal or binding in any way once I have achieved my purpose."

"Which is?" His voice was soft. His breath fanned her heated face, but offered no relief.

When had he moved so near? When had the sun gotten so low and cast the room into shadow? Caitlin found herself more aware than she ought to be of his size, his scent, his face looking down at her.

"I . . . uh . . . that is . . ."

"Your purpose, Miss Pearce," he said huskily as he used two fingers to lift one errant strand of her hair and move it to one side.

Caitlin took one step back and found herself against the wall of the cloakroom. "My sister wishes to wed," she began.

" 'Twould appear that wish runs in the family," he teased. "Is it to be a double wedding then, or am I perhaps expected to marry the both of you?"

"Mr. Tremaine, this is serious," Caitlin announced in her finest schoolteacher reprimand. "Are you interested or not?"

"Oh, I'm very interested, Miss Caitlin Pearce. Wild horses couldn't drag me out of here at this moment."

"Then sit down and listen," she ordered, and brushed past him to head back to the front of the room where she lit the lantern on the edge of her desk. "Sit," she said again when she turned and found him standing just behind her. To her relief, he sat on the edge of Rob Heathcote's chair and waited.

"My younger sister Molly wishes to marry. Our father is a believer in old traditions and insists the elder daughter must marry first. Thus, we have the dilemma—Molly wishes to marry and I do not. You can see the problem."

"Why wouldn't your sister and her beau simply run off and marry? Surely your father would come to terms with that in time."

"Molly's beau is a rather prominent young attorney who has great ambitions of a political nature. He cannot have a hint of scandal, and frankly I don't want that for Molly either."

"But you're willing to jeopardize your own chance at a happy marriage by hitching yourself to the first available man and possibly being miserable for the rest of your life?"

"Please try to pay attention, Mr. Tremaine," Caitlin said wearily. "I have no intention of marrying at all, much less tying myself to someone who would make life miserable for me." She saw him bristle at that and hastened to add, "I'm not speaking of you now. I'm sure you're quite a wonderful man and will someday make a wife very happy."

"Thank you," he said sarcastically. "I'll try to remember to tell the lucky lady she has your blessing when I finally meet her."

"Do you want to hear this or not?" she snapped.

He stretched his legs out and leaned back in the desk seat, placing his battered hat over his eyes. "I'm listening," he said.

"Last night I was thinking that I could help Molly by finding a teaching post in some other community far from Mineral Point. My thought was that after a decent interval I could write to say I had met a wonderful man and we had wed. You see, that would leave Molly free to marry."

"Go on," he said with obvious suspicion.

"Well, when you came here today and asked for lessons, my first instinct was to refuse. But then you spoke of leaving town in the near future which, of course, was something of a coincidence since I, too, had been contemplating leaving Mineral Point—though for different reasons, of course, and—"

"Are you getting to the point sometime before daybreak?"

"There's no need to be rude, Mr. Tremaine. The point is if you are planning to leave Mineral Point within the next several weeks—leave forever—then perhaps I have no need to go away."

Dylan sat up and pushed his hat back with his thumb. He stared at her in total confusion. "Miss Pearce, I know you're a very smart lady, but the fact is you aren't making any sense at all right now."

Caitlin sighed miserably. It was a stupid idea and ridiculous to think Dylan Tremaine would have any reason at all to make it work. "I thought that in exchange for lessons you might be willing to pretend to . . . to . . . court me and in a few weeks to marry me, then leave as planned and I would stay here. Molly, of course, would marry her true love." She glanced at him and saw that she had his full, if dumbfounded attention. She rushed to complete the details of her sketchy plan. "After a time you could have your brother send a letter telling of your untimely death— not that you would actually need to die, of course."

"That's a relief," Dylan muttered.

"I would be the grieving but respectable widow—never expected to marry again. You would be off in wherever it is you're headed, a man well educated to handle his fortune and business." She paused for breath.

"We wouldn't actually marry—no ceremony at all?"

"No. While I haven't yet worked out the complete details, I believe it might be best if we simply went somewhere one day and pretended to marry, then returned a day later, after our . . . after staying the night . . . after—"

"Celebrating our wedding night, Miss Pearce?" Dylan asked as he stood and once again moved toward her. "And where will we live once our blissful but ill-fated marriage has taken place? With your parents or in my badger hole?"

Caitlin frowned at him. The subject was not one to be made light of in her view. "I have a cottage that my father has deeded me as a part of my teacher's salary," she said. "I've never lived there because as a single woman with family right here in town it seemed improper, but if I were married it would be perfectly reasonable."

Dylan noticed that the idea seemed to give her a great deal of pleasure. "It's still a stiff price to pay for a few reading lessons," he argued.

Caitlin shrugged, but he saw the way she nervously bit her lower lip. "I believe you will find the rewards substantially more than simply learning to read, Mr. Tremaine, though that in and of itself is wealth beyond measure."

Dylan smiled. "Really? And what might those rewards include?" he asked with a bold perusal of her tall erect body from head to toe.

To her credit, she neither shied away from him nor flinched. Instead she stood more erect and spoke in the voice she must have perfected for teaching her most unruly students. "I have a stipend, Mr. Tremaine, a savings I've accumulated as a result of my living at home while teaching. It's yours if you deliver your part of our bargain." She rushed to press her point. "You would have the stake you need to make sure you and your brother have success out West."

"What if I refuse?"

"That is, of course, your choice. Please remember that you came to me, Mr. Tremaine. It was your wish to find a method for hiding your need for lessons. I am simply providing a solution for you." She turned back to her work as if she didn't care one way or the other.

"What if I leave and head over to Heathcote's saloon and tell the whole town about your crazy idea, about how you propositioned me?" He was determined to call her bluff.

To his surprise she turned and fixed him with a steely look that must have surely struck terror into the very souls of her students. "If you are foolhardy enough to try such a thing, Mr. Tremaine, I will be forced to inform my father that you have begun spreading vicious rumors because I spurned your romantic advances. Trust me, sir, there isn't a person in this town who would take your word over mine."

She turned on her heel and began gathering her books and papers into a worn cloth satchel. "Besides, winter is coming. I've no knowledge of winters in Cornwall, but I suspect you spent them indoors. Here in Wisconsin, I am quite sure that your *badger* hole will prove quite uncomfortable in the weeks to come as the rains and snows of late autumn set in." She looked up and smiled. "My cottage is quite comfortable, if a bit small. The sooner we get on with our courtship, the sooner we can wed, and the sooner you will be spending your evenings stretched out before a warm *indoor* fire."

"And once you are *widowed?*"

Her face brightened immediately. "Oh, then I can live there without question. Everyone will understand my choice to remain in the one place I had shared with my beloved. It's a lovely cottage with plenty of room for my books and even a small study."

The lamplight highlighted her flawless skin and made her face glow. Dylan had to restrain himself from stroking her cheek as he stood next to her. "You're certain that it has room for a husband?" he asked softly. "Even if only temporarily."

Caitlin's pulse raced as she realized that he was actually considering the idea. "Are you saying you'll help me?" she asked breathlessly.

Dylan smiled. There wasn't a question in the world that Gar Heathcote was about to lose the wager and soon. Miss Caitlin Pearce had not only agreed to permit him to call on her, she had set the courtship in motion herself. " 'Twould be my pleasure to assist in such a finely crafted plot, Miss Pearce," he said and punctuated his words by taking her hand and kissing her fingertips as he delivered a courtly bow.

Caitlin was fascinated by the softness of his lips touching her hand. She was keenly aware that propriety dictated that she pull her hand away, but instead she permitted Dylan Tremaine's light brush of her fingers with his lips and wondered how those lips might feel if he gave her a real kiss.

"Caitlin, may I see you home?"

Her heart hammered at the question and all that it implied about the bargain they had just struck. Dylan Tremaine was going to be a part of her life for the coming weeks. He would come here to the school, see her home, sit with her in the family's parlor in the evenings, take her for long rides in the country on Sunday afternoons. Her head spun with the realization of just what she had set in motion. "That would be nice," she replied briskly as she moved quickly to retrieve her cloak and tie on her bonnet. "On the way we can discuss your lessons."

She did not permit him to come all the way to the house with her. When they reached the corner of her street she insisted that he take the lantern and a slim book for the beginning reader and head back to his camp. "You can return the lantern tomorrow afternoon when you come for your first reading lesson. Bring the book." She seemed anxious to be rid of him, nervous that they might be seen together.

Dylan waited until she had turned the corner for home before calling after her. "You know, Caitlin, your parents will have to know soon enough. We can't keep meeting like this—in secret." He knew they were completely alone on the street. The people of Mineral Point were home eating their suppers and finishing their evening chores. He watched with satisfaction as she paused for half a moment and then squared her shoulders and continued marching up the hill as if he had not spoken.

Dylan continued to watch until she entered the gate of the large lighted house and climbed the stairs of the porch. Still, she did not glance back at him. He felt his temper flare. *We've a bargain, Miss Caitlin Pearce, and it's one of your own choosing. You'll have to understand there's a cost to that.* Once he heard the front door close he turned and headed for home—the cramped campsite in the side of the hill that had seemed perfectly adequate to him until now. It did not even amuse him to see that she lived on a street aptly called Virgin Alley.

Caitlin could not concentrate as the family's chatter swirled about her throughout the evening meal. Father had received the wrong supply of fabric at the store and customers were clamoring for him to fill the orders they had left weeks earlier. Mother had spent the day calling on her friends and gathering castoffs for the church charity box. Molly had had a letter from Geoffrey and wanted to share his description of the building of the new state capitol in Madison with anyone who would listen. Caitlin's brothers, Edward and Charles, interrupted with stories of their own work—Edward at the bank and Charles at the hardware store.

"You're very quiet, Caitlin," John Pearce commented. "Was there trouble at school today?"

"Nothing unusual," Caitlin answered.

"I saw that Heathcote boy on the streets at mid-morning," Charles said.

"He was late for school," Caitlin admitted.

"Again?" Mary Pearce shook her head in distress. "John, you really should have a word with Mr. Heathcote. Surely, he needs to understand the importance of educating his son if he expects the boy to take on the saloon one day."

"He's a regular hooligan, that one," Molly added disdainfully.

"He has a hard life," Caitlin said in Rob's defense. "He's actually quite intelligent."

"All the more reason he needs to apply himself," Edward insisted. "Gar Heathcote keeps him up until all hours working in that saloon. Last night I understand there was some sort of celebration among the miners."

"I heard about that," Charles rushed to add. "Seems the badger made a strike."

"The *badger?*" Mary Pearce asked and looked to her husband for an explanation.

"The young Cornish fellow," John explained. "Tremaine, I believe his name is. A nice enough young man, polite and keeps himself clean in spite of working in the mines and living there on that hillside."

This is not going to work, was all Caitlin could think as she looked around the table and tried to see things through Dylan Tremaine's eyes. The table was beautifully set with her grandmother's china, silver, and crystal. The family members were dressed in what for most families would be their Sunday best. Two silver candelabra held half a dozen flickering candles each to light the room. Through the door behind her father, Caitlin could see the formal parlor with its imported furnishings polished to a high sheen and upholstered in rich damask.

She refocused her attention on the members of her family. What could have possessed her to think she could bring Dylan Tremaine to this table? Not that her family would not be perfectly well mannered and welcoming, but Dylan would be lost here where the conversation could turn in a moment from discussion of the mundane to a lively debate about the philosophy of Plato or the true meaning of *King*

Lear. The man could not read, for heaven's sake. He would be hopelessly lost at this gathering.

"Caitlin, dear, you look quite pale," her mother said, reaching out to place the back of her hand against Caitlin's forehead. "Yes, I believe you may be coming down with something."

"It's nothing, truly, Mother. I've just had a long day. May I be excused?"

Her father and brothers stood as she left the table and practically ran up the stairs to the sanctity of the room she shared with Molly. *No, this will not work at all,* she thought as she closed the door and leaned against it. She would just have to tell Mr. Tremaine that she had made a terrible mistake—or perhaps she should pretend it had all been a joke, then offer to tutor him in exchange for chores as he had first suggested. Either way, there could be no more thoughts of a courtship and certainly not of a marriage. No one would ever believe such a thing.

Caitlin.

Dylan wrote her name once and then again on the blank page of his journal. He mulled over her startling proposal as he stared at the letters of her name. He thought about how he'd been as surprised by his physical attraction to her as he was by her astounding plan.

Caitlin with the flaming hair, he wrote, then scratched it out. He often tried his hand at poetry or lyrics for a song. It was a way of entertaining himself as he passed the long hours alone. He thought about her eyes and the way they had sparkled with excitement as she'd warmed to the details of her plan. That led him to thoughts of her lips. There'd been a moment when he had thought about kissing her.

Dylan muttered an oath and slammed shut the diary that to date had only held the recordings of his finds in the field. The woman had gotten under his skin. She hadn't been at all what he'd expected. Not that he wouldn't win the wager. Truth be told, it should be easier than before, with her needing his help in playing this ridiculous ruse she'd dreamed up. He extinguished the lantern and stood outside his campsite, staring up at the clouded sky. It would rain tomorrow. He double-checked his supply of candles to be sure they were protected from the elements. The mine shaft would be pitch black no matter what the weather. He'd need good light for his work sixty feet underground.

He closed his eyes and relived the strange meeting with the schoolmarm. He'd waited for the children to leave, then waited longer, thinking to approach her as she left the building. After a while he'd gone inside the church to see what was keeping her. She'd actually seemed reluctant to leave the schoolroom. He understood that. Sometimes his camp became a sort of refuge for him, a place for him to sort through thoughts without outside interruption.

Unseen by her, he'd watched her putting everything in order, murmuring to herself the whole time. She was certainly meticulous about things, stacking the papers on her desk just so, lining up her pens and other tools with precision.

He hadn't gotten a good look at her at first. Every time she turned in his direction, he'd stepped away from the door. His first impression had been pretty much what he'd anticipated—a spinster who took solace from her lonely life in her teaching. From some of the comments he'd heard from young Rob Heathcote and his cronies, she didn't share much of that pleasure with her students. Dylan had caught a glimpse of wire-rimmed spectacles and a full view of hair pulled into a bun so tight it gave him a headache just looking at her.

He'd decided there was no choice but to either make his presence known or plan to stand out in that darkened hallway half the night. When she turned and he got the first real look at her, he'd been stunned into speechlessness. For one thing she was younger than he had imagined. But the most astonishing thing about her were her eyes—deep emerald green and they caught the glint of the light from the setting sun the same way precious metal might catch the faintest light deep in the mines. He had the sudden sensation of having struck great wealth—a lode beyond comprehension. That was when she'd given a startled shriek and dropped the books.

The rain pelted the drilling of his makeshift shelter, and Dylan checked the bushy framework he'd built to protect himself from the elements. Satisfied that he was as dry as he was likely to get, he pulled his mackinaw around his shoulders and tried to sleep. Lying there listening to the rain, he imagined the sound a downpour would create hitting the tin roof of the church. Would its echo carry all the way to the basement schoolroom? He thought about Caitlin sitting across from him at her desk, the lantern their only light and the rain a shield that kept the world at bay as she tutored him in reading and they set the plans for the next phase of their staged courtship.

On the walk to her house, she had said she wanted to marry within a month, for she could not be certain of keeping her sister chaste much longer. He recalled how she had struggled to find the words to share that last bit of information with him and knew instinctively that her cheeks had flamed with embarrassment at such intimate talk. That was when he had realized that Caitlin Pearce, for all her bravado, was as astonished by what she had suggested they do as he was. That was when he had relaxed and decided the next several weeks were going to be more fun than anything he had known since leaving Cornwall. He and this unlikely partner were about to perpetrate a prank of wondrous proportions.

Back home in Cornwall, he and his brother had played many a practical joke on friends and family alike—and been the recipient of such tricks in return. But what Miss Caitlin Pearce had proposed was nothing short of extraordinary, and the beauty of her plan was that in the end, everyone would have exactly what they wanted. A man could respect a woman who could come up with something so complex and clever as that.

"Caitlin?" Molly sat on the side of her bed performing the nightly ritual of brushing her luxurious blond hair. "Who was that man who saw you home tonight?"

Caitlin paused in the act of changing into her nightgown. "What man?" she asked, her voice muffled by the voluminous folds of the gown as she pulled it over her head.

"The man who walked with you to the corner. You were so late coming from school that I was worried. I watched from the window there." She indicated the windowseat both girls had found a wonderful refuge throughout their youth.

Caitlin considered her options and decided to tell a partial truth rather than blatantly lie to her sister. "Oh, that was Mr. Tremaine. He was on his way to his campsite. We walked along together for a bit."

"Isn't his campsite near those mines to the east of town?"

"I've no idea," Caitlin replied.

Molly stopped brushing her hair and turned to study her sister. "Of course, it is. I heard Gar Heathcote talking about it one day. Why would he come this way when he's set up his camp east of here?"

Caitlin feigned a yawn and shrugged as she turned back the covers. "Good night, sister," she said.

Molly wasn't so easily dismissed. She came and sat on the edge of the bed, continuing to brush her hair. "I didn't know you knew Mr. Tremaine."

"Molly, I have a full day tomorrow. I must be at school earlier than usual, and I really need to get some rest."

"He's very handsome," Molly continued as if her sister had not spoken. "All my friends think so. That smile of his is just so . . . so . . . full of mystery."

More like full of mischief, Caitlin thought and suppressed the memory of the nearness of that smile to her own face earlier in the day. She punched her pillow and hoped her sister would take the hint. "Good night, Molly."

"He would be a wonderful catch," Molly mused. "I heard Charles saying that he's made quite a success of that abandoned mine Mr. Hayward used to own. Besides that, Edward says he can find lead in rocks lying right on the ground—rocks others walk over every day on their way to the working mines. He must have a great deal of money, though Edward says not a penny of it has he brought to the bank."

Caitlin pulled the covers over her head.

"You know, Caitie, you knowing Mr. Tremaine is a little like . . . fate. I mean he's nice-looking and everybody says he's . . . well, not dumb as a stick like some. Do you think there might be a chance . . . that is, could you perhaps see the possibility of . . ." Suddenly Molly began to cry.

Caitlin sighed and sat up. "What's the matter? Why are you crying?"

"Oh, Caitie, I'm sorry. I'm reduced to clutching at any straw. I saw you with Mr. Tremaine, and in the time it took for you to walk up the street and into the house I had the two of you madly in love and announcing your nuptials. The truth is, if I can't marry Geoffrey soon I shall simply die." Dramatically, Molly flung herself into the comforting arms of her older sister and sobbed uncontrollably.

"Sh-h-h," Caitlin crooned as she gently rocked Molly. "Everything is going to be fine. I promise. Now, let's get some sleep. Things will look better with the morning."

Molly sniffed loudly and wiped her nose with the back of her hand. "You've said that before," she accused.

"This time I mean it," Caitlin assured her.

Three

Somehow Caitlin made it through the day. It probably helped that Rob Heathcote did not come to school at all. Without him to set a poor example, the rest of the children were dull but well behaved. Caitlin gave the children more than the usual amount of deskwork to complete—columns of sums to add for the older children, numbers to copy for the younger ones. Finally the day ended and she dismissed her pupils with a dual sense of relief and foreboding. The children were gone, but now she had to face Mr. Tremaine and she had no idea what she would say to him.

On the one hand, she had decided to return to her original plan of leaving town and pretending to find someone to marry. It had been pure folly to involve the miner in her scheme. On the other hand, Molly was becoming increasingly desperate. Long after Molly had cried herself to sleep, Caitlin had lain awake, weighing her choices and wondering if she could trust Dylan Tremaine. After all she knew nothing about him.

She restacked the papers the children had left and resisted the urge to take a few minutes to rest her head on the desk. She'd gotten precious little sleep the night before, and she would need to be at her best when Tremaine came—if he came.

"Good afternoon, Caitlin."

The object of her musings stood in the doorway, the unlighted hallway behind him casting him in shadow. He held a box with both hands and seemed hesitant to step over the threshold. Caitlin sighed. Perhaps he, too, was having second thoughts.

"Come in, Mr. Tremaine." She pushed her glasses back from the tip of her nose, folded her hands to hide her nervousness and waited for him to approach the desk. She still had no idea what she would say to him.

"I brought you this," he said and placed a hatbox on the desk in front of her. "Open it," he urged when she stared at the box as if it might bite her.

She recognized the box as coming from the millinery shop of Tillie Polkinghorn. She fingered the cord that held the lid in place. "Mr. Tremaine . . ."

"Dylan," he said softly, covering her hand with his own. "You're Caitlin, I'm Dylan—and this is a present." His gaze was locked on hers as he slowly removed his hand and waited for her to untie the cord.

She stood up, as much to give herself a moment to recover from the intimacy of his hand on hers as to better handle the hatbox. "You shouldn't be bringing me gifts, Mr.—Dylan." She fumbled with the knot.

"Why not?" He leaned toward her, resting his hands at either side of the box, his face close to hers. "That's what a suitor does."

His smile brought a flush to her cheeks that seemed to race through her body all the way to her toes. The cord finally gave and she lifted the lid and pushed aside the tissue.

"Its a new bonnet," he said proudly.

"I can see that," Caitlin said as she examined the most beautiful and frivolous green velvet bonnet she'd ever seen.

"Try it on."

"It's much too . . . Mr. Tremaine, this is . . ." She touched the soft velvet and ran her fingers the length of one long satin tie, unable to resist indulging herself for the moment. "I can't possibly accept this," she said firmly, and replaced the hat in the box.

Dylan pulled the hat from the box and came around the desk. "Try it on, Caitlin." His voice was soft, not hurt or angry as she might have expected after her refusal to accept his gift. "No one's here except the two of us. Aren't you curious?" He placed the bonnet on her head and began tying the long satin streamers. She was mesmerized by the soothing tenderness of his voice and the hands roughened by years in the mines tying the bow as if he did such things every day. "There," he said and stood back to admire his handiwork.

Tentatively Caitlin touched the bonnet's brim. She looked at Dylan and did not need a mirror to know that the hat suited her. "Dylan, it's lovely, but it must have cost a pretty penny, not to mention it's much too personal a gift. We barely know one another."

"Caitlin, we're to be married and soon. It seems to me that an impetuous gift is exactly what is called for here." He smiled and then frowned. "Don't tell me you've had second thoughts."

Slowly, and with regret, Caitlin loosened the bow and removed the hat. She stroked the crown, then resolutely replaced the hat in its box and pressed the lid firmly into place. "I'm just not sure this is wise," she said firmly.

"The bonnet or the courtship?" Dylan asked. He perched on the edge of her desk and waited for an answer. It was disconcerting to see that he was as handsome when he frowned as when he smiled.

His physical presence was overpowering. She found herself more aware than ever of his muscular shoulders and arms, and thought of the labor he performed daily as he built his future through sheer physical strength and perseverance. When had he had time to shop for the bonnet? More to the point, what had he told the milliner? Tillie was a notorious gossip, and only the quality of her handiwork kept the women of Mineral Point patronizing her shop.

Caitlin sighed and plunged ahead. "I'll admit to having second thoughts. I suspect you have had ample time to rethink the lunacy of this idea yourself." She moved around the desk and walked the length of the schoolroom and back as she ticked off each reason why their plan could not possibly work. "Consider if you will the difference in our backgrounds."

Dylan shrugged. "I know nothing of your background and have told you nothing of mine. Perhaps I am the son of a nobleman who is determined to make my own fortune in this world."

Caitlin ignored him. "A courtship between us would cause gossip under the most normal of circumstances. The fact that we plan to complete each phase in double time makes the entire situation ripe for scandal."

"Oh no, not that," he replied throwing up his hands in mock horror.

"This is no laughing matter," she said testily. "Suppose we are successful at convincing people of an attraction, there is a great deal more to this than simply a few assignations. In order for Molly to be free to marry—"

"I have a few thoughts if you'd care to hear them." There was a hint of temper in his words, enough so that she stopped her pacing and faced him.

"All right. I'm listening."

"In the first place, your sister's marriage is the least of this. Whether we carry through with the plan or not she will marry, and begging your pardon, Caitlin, but there's nothing like a prenuptial pregnancy to make your father see the wisdom of permitting a union."

"My sister is not—"

"Not yet anyway," he interrupted. "In the second place the two people who really stand to get what they want out of all this are you and me. For reasons I cannot fathom you appear to set quite a store by the idea of spending the rest of your days in solitude. As one who has spent a fair amount of time alone my advice would be to at least consider some other possibilities. Still, you seem to have your heart set on settling into that cottage with your books, and far be it from me to question another person's dreams."

Caitlin folded her arms across her bosom and tapped her foot impatiently. "And you, Mr. Tremaine, what about the gains you stand to make?"

Dylan nodded. "I was coming to that. I'm facing the opportunity to shorten by a considerable margin the days I need to spend living out there on that hillside. As you pointed out, with winter coming on, my badger hole is losing some of its appeal."

"And, of course, there's the money—my stipend which will make your trip West a great deal easier." She was deliberately trying to provoke him now. The man's perpetually calm demeanor was exasperating.

"Yep, there is the money." He agreed affably as he turned and took the bonnet from the box and perched it on his forefinger. "And I won't for a minute deny the appeal of the money." He grinned as he walked toward her twirling the hat. "But you know the best part of all, Caitlin? We could have so much fun."

"Fun?" she croaked as she focused on the bonnet in order not to focus on his proximity.

Once again he placed the bonnet on her head and tied the ribbons. "Fun," he repeated. "No one will know what's really going on but the two of us. We'll be changing lives, and they won't even know it." He pulled her glasses off, folded them and handed them to her. "Come on, Caitlin, we both work hard. Let's have a little fun, what do you say?"

What do I say? The entire situation had somehow gotten completely out of control. Suddenly Dylan was in charge— her plan had become his plan. This would never do. It simply was not proper, no matter how handsome the man was.

"Are you ready for your reading lesson, Dylan?" she asked as she turned and walked back to the desk, removing the bonnet and replacing her glasses as she went. "You did remember to bring the book I loaned you?"

Dylan watched her march back to the safe haven of her desk. There had been a moment when he put the bonnet on her for the second time that he had thought of kissing her, not to win any wager, but simply because he wanted to—a lot. Now as she peered at him over the tops of her glasses, he wondered what he'd been thinking.

"Got it right here," he mumbled, pulling the book from his coat pocket and holding it up for her to see.

"Very well then. Come along and let's begin."

If she sat any straighter in that chair, she was in danger of having that ramrod spine of hers snap like a dry twig, Dylan decided. He moved toward her with deliberate slowness, his eyes riveted on her face. He had noticed that his watching her made her nervous and was gratified to see by the color that reached her cheeks that he had not misjudged that.

The lesson was tedious for him because he could read every word of the book, but had to pretend he knew none at all. She was a patient teacher and whenever he pretended to understand and recognize a new word, her delight at his success was genuine. She would reward him with one of her rare smiles.

"I believe we have done enough for today, Dylan," she said, closing the book. She was determined to be home at a reasonable hour so as not to raise questions within her own family. "You are a quick learner. I don't think it will take long at all for you to learn the fundamentals. After that, it becomes a matter of practice."

She turned to retrieve another book from the small bookcase next to her desk. He could not help but notice the pull of the fabric across her back, drawing his eyes to her slim waist. He had a sudden image of his hand on her waist, spanning it, urging her closer.

"There's a dance two weeks from Saturday," he said taking the book from her and placing it carefully in his coat pocket. "Perhaps we should plan to go."

"Together?" Her voice was a whisper of surprise.

He pretended to consider, stroking his chin and staring at something she'd written on the board. "Well, let's think this through, Caitlin. You want me to pretend to court you and then one day in the not-too-distant future marry you. . . ."

"Pretend to marry," she corrected.

"Either way, it seems to me that we'd best get this thing on track. Now for the dance I could either call for you officially or simply monopolize you at the dance. Either way folks will be talking and speculating by Sunday morning. And then when I come to church and you wear that hat, well . . ." He raised his eyebrows in a mockery of what the local gossips would do and grinned.

"Oh, dear," Caitlin murmured as the enormity of what she planned to do hit her. "Oh, dear," she repeated as she walked to the door and stared down the hallway without seeing anything. *He is right, of course,* she thought and the thought irritated her. *I have no choice but to pursue this if Molly is to be saved from certain scandal.*

"Caitlin?"

The nearness of his voice as always startled her. He had come to stand behind her, his voice no more than a whisper next to her ear. "If your sister and her young man are as much in love as you say, they will convince themselves of the rightness of giving in to those feelings. You have devised a foolproof plan for saving her, Caitlin. Don't lose your nerve now."

Caitlin bristled at the insinuation that she might fail her only sister. She turned and brushed past him. "We should go," she announced, moving to retrieve her cloak and ser- viceable bonnet from the cloakroom. "Budding courtship or not, it's unseemly for you to be here with me for so long." She walked back to her desk and picked up the satchel of work she carried home each night.

"You carry this," Dylan said, handing her the hatbox and relieving her of the satchel in one smooth motion. Then he offered her his arm as an escort would. "Shall we?" he asked.

"Let's get one thing straight from the outset, Mr. Tre- maine. This is my plan and I will determine what is ap- propriate and what is not."

He snapped to attention and saluted her. "Aye, my cap- tain. I await my orders."

With an indecipherable exclamation of her frustration she marched ahead of him, down the hall and up the narrow stairway, exiting by the side door of the church. Dylan hur- ried to catch up, matching her stride for stride as together they headed toward town.

Because of the early hour the stores were still busy as they neared High Street. Caitlin could see customers going in and out of her father's mercantile. Mr. Heathcote was passing the time of day with a patron in front of his tavern. Tillie Polkinghorn was helping Mrs. Filbert load her pur- chases in her buggy.

"I can leave you here and head back to the mines if you'd rather," Dylan said as if he could read her mind.

Caitlin glanced at him and realized he was sincere in his offer. She hesitated for only a moment. "No, Mr. Tre- maine, I believe we have come to an understanding, and to postpone acting on our plan until another day makes no sense at all. Let us proceed."

Once again she took up the gait that reminded Dylan of a prisoner being led to her doom. "You might try not to look so grim," he advised.

"Yes, of course, you're right," she mumbled, and he

watched in amazement as she made a conscious effort to relax the tense muscles of her face and neck and failed miserably.

"Just act natural," he coaxed, gently taking her elbow as they stepped off the boardwalk and waited for Mrs. Filbert's buggy to pass.

"Good afternoon, Caitlin," Mrs. Filbert greeted her, but her eyes were on Dylan. To Caitlin's relief, he tipped his hat to the older woman and offered a slight bow of respect. "Lovely day to you, ma'am," he said and smiled broadly.

Caitlin was not surprised to see that Mrs. Filbert was as affected by that smile as she was.

"That was a start," Dylan said softly. "Now for Heathcote." His fingers tightened on her elbow, and she wondered why the saloonkeeper would be a cause for worry.

"Good afternoon, Miss Pearce." Heathcote stopped his sweeping and greeted the teacher with respect. "Tremaine," he added with a sly grin.

"Mr. Heathcote, Robert was not in school today, and he was unprepared for his lessons yesterday. I trust I will see him in class tomorrow on time and prepared?"

Both men gazed at her as if she had suddenly begun to speak in a foreign tongue. They had been thinking of their wager, and the schoolmarm's lecture caught them off-guard.

"Robert has the potential to be an excellent student, Mr. Heathcote," she continued. "What is needed here is a firm hand and encouragement at home. Do I make myself clear?"

"Yes, ma'am," Heathcote replied through gritted teeth.

Dylan suppressed a smile and gently took Caitlin's elbow once again. "Miss Pearce," he said, "I believe your sister is coming this way." He nodded in the direction of the Pearce family mercantile which Molly was just exiting. "Good day, Heathcote," Dylan added as he urged Caitlin toward her sister.

"Cait," Molly called out and waved. Her eyes like everyone else's were riveted on Tremaine.

"Ah, finally, I get to meet the family, my dear," Dylan said softly and lifted his hand in greeting to Molly. "Smile," he added as he took Caitlin's elbow and ushered her down the street. "Try to look as if you're enjoying my company."

It was Caitlin's turn to grit her teeth. The man was impossible. He'd taken to their pretended courtship as if it were the most normal thing in the world to be engaged in a ruse so elaborate that it must involve the entire citizenry of Mineral Point. Caitlin pasted on a smile just as Molly joined them.

"Hello," Molly said as she smiled winningly up at Dylan.

The miner tipped his hat and returned her smile. "Good afternoon."

Then both of them glanced at Caitlin and waited for the necessary introductions.

"Molly, this is Mr. Tremaine," Caitlin said, and felt suddenly as if she were a character in a farce. "Mr. Tremaine, my sister, Miss Molly Pearce."

"What a charming hat, Miss Pearce," Dylan said as he nodded politely in greeting. "It suits you perfectly."

Molly smiled and self-consciously touched the ribbons of her bonnet. "Why thank you, sir," she replied with a coquettish smile and a lowering of her lashes.

Caitlin could not explain the emotions that rushed through her in that moment. It was impossible that she could be jealous of the little flirtation being played out here in broad daylight between her sister and her . . . her . . . Mr. Tremaine. It certainly wasn't the least bit proper. She would need to speak to Molly when they reached home. It was unseemly for her to—

"I was just escorting your sister home, Miss Pearce. Perhaps we could have the pleasure of your company as well?"

Caitlin glanced up at Dylan to assure herself that this was the same man. Suddenly the uneducated miner was conducting himself as if he were the picture of manners and civility. Molly's Geoffrey could certainly learn a thing or two from Dylan about wooing the voters. "I'm sure my sister has other errands," Caitlin said and was shocked to hear the petulance in her tone.

"No, I've finished them all," Molly said. "I'd be honored to join you, sir," she said with a slight curtsy.

Stars in heaven, Caitlin thought.

The three of them proceeded through town, Dylan between the sisters. Caitlin could practically feel the eyes of shopkeepers and customers alike watching them. By morning Tillie Polkinghorn's interpretation of the scene would be all over town.

"Your sister tells me you and Mr. Geoffrey MacKenzie have been keeping company, Miss Pearce. May I say that I admire Mr. MacKenzie's politics and I sincerely hope he wins election to the new legislature?"

"Thank you, Mr. Tremaine," Molly gushed. "Geoffrey and I are to be married—someday." She eyed her sister, and then turned her attention back to Dylan. "Would you care to meet him? We'll be at the dance two weeks from Saturday. He has to be in Madison until then I'm afraid." She pouted with disappointment.

"That would be nice. Your sister has graciously accepted my invitation to the dance, haven't you, Caitlin?" He turned the full force of his smile on her.

So once again he has taken matters into his own hands. Caitlin fumed. "Now Mr. Tremaine," she said with an exaggerated flapping of her own lashes as she gazed up at him, "I only promised to consider your invitation."

"Oh, Cait, you must say yes. We'll have such fun—the four of us. How wonderful it will be. Please say yes. Now, Caitie, now," Molly insisted, practically leaping up and down in her excitement.

"I promise to be on my very best behavior," Dylan said solemnly, but his eyes twinkled mischievously.

"In that case, how can I possibly refuse?" Caitlin replied, giving him a look she hoped could be translated by her sister as one of adoration and by him as one of warning.

"Oh, goody." Molly clapped her hands, then turned her attention back to Dylan. "I'll tell Geoffrey to pick you up in his carriage and the two of you can come to the house together. Perhaps you should come early. Geoffrey always does. I sometimes think he only calls on me so he can engage in political debates with my father and taste my mother's baking."

"I doubt that, Miss Pearce. Any man would have to be daft not to realize how lucky he was to have your affection"

There it is again, Caitlin thought. *That same sensation of missing something, wanting something that Molly has. Wanting to be more like her and to hear a handsome man like Dylan say such things about her.* She pressed her lips together in a hard line and trudged on, trying in vain to ignore her sister's chatter.

"So it's settled. Geoffrey will call for you and then come to the house and we'll all go to the dance together. Where do you live, Mr. Tremaine?"

It seemed to Caitlin as if the world stopped for an instant. For the first time she saw that Dylan was unsure of himself. He glanced at her, and his eyes sought her help. At the same time Molly must have recalled the previous evening's dinner conversation.

"My stars, you are the badger," Molly blurted, and then her face flushed a most unbecoming shade of red. "I had forgotten. That is, you're so . . . different from what I expected."

To Caitlin's surprise, Dylan relaxed and laughed heartily. "That I am, Miss Pearce," he said, and then seeing Molly's extreme embarrassment at her blunder, added, "Please don't concern yourself. Trust me when I tell you I've been called much worse than the noble badger. The fact is I'm proud to live in the manner of my ancestors who came here decades ago. They found a good life for themselves. I'm hoping to do the same."

Caitlin noticed how kind his voice was, and she was touched that he was trying so hard to ease Molly's discomfort.

"I'm so sorry," Molly said again. "It was stupid of me. Please forgive me."

"Miss Pearce, I believe we were discussing the upcoming dance?"

Immediately Molly's face brightened and she nodded eagerly. Caitlin wondered if the man had a similar effect on all women—making them absolutely willing to do his bidding.

"Suppose I simply come to the house and we can all wait for Geoffrey together. Would that be agreeable, Caitlin?"

Caitlin had been so caught up in observing the interaction between her sister and the man that when he addressed her directly it took a moment for her to react. "Why? I mean why that would be lovely, Mr. Tremaine."

"Oh, this is going to be such fun," Molly squealed, twirling around them and grabbing her sister's arm as they turned the corner to their house.

With each step that brought them closer to the gate, Caitlin found herself praying her mother would not suddenly appear. She and Dylan had caused quite enough of a stir for one afternoon. Molly was sure to keep her up half the night seeking details—details Caitlin would need to construct and fill Dylan in on when he came to the school the next day.

"Well, I'll leave the two of you here," Molly said with a twinkle in her eye. "Mr. Tremaine, it was a pleasure to meet you, and I look forward to seeing you often." She turned to go, then turned back. "I have the perfect plan.

Why don't you come to church the day after tomorrow and join us for Sunday dinner afterward? That way you can meet our parents."

"I wouldn't want to impose," Dylan replied.

Caitlin was still caught up in Molly's proposal that Dylan actually sit down and break bread with the entire family. Their parents . . . their brothers . . . Oh, heavenly stars, what had she set in motion here?

"I'm sure that Mr. Tremaine—" she began but Dylan cut her off.

". . . Would be delighted to accept such a kind and thoughtful invitation," he put in. Then he grinned at Molly. "After all, I have to meet your parents sometime, don't I?"

Molly nodded. "Definitely before the dance. Father would not think it at all proper if you simply showed up on the night of the dance."

"Then church and Sunday dinner it is," Dylan said with a wink.

Once again Caitlin struggled to subdue the sudden rush of undefined emotion that roiled through her. It had all the earmarks of envy, but that was ridiculous, of course. *You're being childish, Caitlin,* she admonished herself silently. *What on earth do you care if the man flirts with every female in town?*

She did not see him at all on Saturday, though she found herself looking for him as she and Molly did their shopping. Molly had insisted on finding the perfect fabric for a new gown for Caitlin to wear to the dance. "Something that sets off your eyes," she announced. "And we'll have to do something with your hair," she added.

"I will do something," Caitlin replied. "I'll put it up the way I usually do."

Molly made a face. "Caitie, you may be smarter than most any man that ever lived, but when it comes to your looks you are absolutely dull. Now I want you to trust me, give yourself over to me entirely. Your Mr. Tremaine will need help keeping his eyes in their sockets when I am done with you," she announced proudly and marched straight into their father's mercantile.

On Sunday Molly orchestrated Caitlin's preparations for church. "Where is that hatbox you were carrying the other day? I've surmised that it was a gift from Dylan, for heaven knows you would never do anything so frivolous as to purchase a hat for yourself. Where is it?" She opened Caitlin's wardrobe and peered at the top shelf.

"Never mind that hat," Caitlin argued. "It won't match my dress."

"Ah, here it is." Molly stood on tiptoe to retrieve the box. She opened it and held up the beautiful green velvet bonnet. "Oh Caitie, it's perfect. You must wear it."

Caitlin looked at the hat. She had tried it on a dozen times when no one was around. She felt foolish for liking it so much, liking the way it framed her face and made her look almost pretty, certainly softer, somehow.

"Put it on," Molly urged.

"I'll wear it on one condition," Caitlin said sternly as she briskly tied the ribbons into a no-nonsense bow. "You cannot tell Mother and especially not Father who gave it to me."

Molly came to her, undid the bow and retied it, fluffing out the loops until she was satisfied. Molly was the only person Caitlin had ever known who was absolutely unintimidated by her. Caitlin had tried every tactic that usually worked with her students, all to no avail. It was as if Molly saw something in her no one else did. "I mean it, Molly," she said warningly, jerking away and putting on her gloves.

"All right," Molly agreed. "Your secret is safe with me, but you may as well prepare yourself. Dylan will be invited for Sunday dinner."

"Not if he doesn't show up for services," Caitlin muttered under her breath as the sisters hastened to join the rest of the family.

But he did show up. In fact he was there when John Pearce pulled the team of horses to a halt in front of the church. Caitlin had spotted him from a block away. He was wearing a ready-made suit that fit his lean frame surprisingly well, though he looked quite uncomfortable in it. He kept running two fingers beneath the stiff starched collar as he paced a short path near the entrance to the church.

Caitlin knew his habit of pacing well. In the short time she had worked with him on his reading lessons, he had often gotten up suddenly and paced the length of the room and back as he digested the words she had written on the board, pronouncing and spelling them again and again, and then insisting he use them in a sentence. The pacing seemed to help him relax. He was clearly a man well suited to living in the outdoors. Walls seemed to make him uncomfortable.

"He's here," Molly whispered gleefully, then turned to accept her father's helping hand as she stepped from the carriage. "Mr. Tremaine," she called gaily.

"Molly, please, a little decorum," her father admonished, but there was no sting in the rebuke. Instead he turned to assist Caitlin from the carriage. "Do we know that young man?" he asked.

So. The moment has come, Caitlin thought. "He is——"

"Isn't that the badger?" her brother Charles asked, squinting against the morning sun for a better view.

Caitlin flinched. There was no call for insulting the man. "That is Mr. Dylan Tremaine," she said stiffly. "Mr. Tremaine will be joining us for services today, and with your permission, Father, I should like to invite him to join us for Sunday dinner."

The normally animated family fell silent. They could not

have been more shocked if she had suddenly announced her intention to ride through town in her underwear. Only Molly seemed unperturbed. "Come meet him, Mother," she urged. "He's truly lovely. Mr. Tremaine, may I present my mother and father?" Molly glanced over her shoulder at John Pearce. "Mother, Father, this is Dylan Tremaine."

"It's very nice to meet you, ma'am," Dylan said, politely smiling down at the petite woman who was an older version of her youngest daughter. "Sir," he said to John Pearce and offered his hand in greeting.

John acknowledged the introduction. "Mr. Tremaine. Our sons Edward and Charles."

Caitlin stood watching the exchange of introductions and greetings as if she had no part in this at all. Dylan's confidence and ease stunned her. Her father could be a bit aloof and off-putting. Most people needed time to warm to him. Dylan gave him just the perfect amount of respect while at the same time conveying a sense of equality. Caitlin saw that it was her father who was momentarily at a loss, an emotion he hid behind the bluster of ushering everyone inside.

The Pearce family had occupied the second pew on the left every Sunday since the family had arrived in Mineral Point. They had filed down that narrow aisle ever since Caitlin could remember. Their mother followed by Molly, then Caitlin, then Edward, then Charles. John Pearce brought up the rear—always. Until today. On this Sunday Dylan followed the family to their place, stood respectfully until all had seated themselves, then took a place on the aisle in the row just behind them. If Caitlin turned her head just slightly to her right, she could see him.

The organist pumped the organ and then struck up the first hymn, and as a unit the congregation stood and sang the familiar tune. Caitlin was keenly aware of Dylan's strong baritone. It surprised her to feel relief that he sang so well. *Why should it matter to me how the man sings?* she wondered.

The sermon was long and rambling. Caitlin was anxious for it to be over and at the same time praying it would go on forever. She had noticed the looks the other members of her family cast her way when they thought she wasn't looking—the mild curiosity of her mother, the shock of her brothers, and the probing stare of her father. Each of them expected an explanation. Caitlin stiffened her spine and squared her shoulders. *Well, why should it be so surprising that a young man might show an interest? It isn't as if it were the first time.* Of course, she'd driven all the others away with her exacting personality and refusal to pretend she found them more fascinating than any man she'd ever known.

She tightened her jaw and narrowed her eyes. She might not be as pretty as Molly, but she was far from homely. *Handsome* was probably the best word for her—a handsome woman. It suited, and it was good enough. She pursed her lips and concentrated on the cross above the altar. It might have been some time since any young man had called, but that was no reason to think no one would ever come. After all, Mineral Point was a small community. Eligible men did not actually grow on trees. She expected her family to understand that and be happy for her, not judge her.

"Caitie," Molly whispered urgently, poking her sister with her elbow and nodding to the rest of the family, their heads bowed as the minister delivered his final prayer.

Caitlin quickly folded her hands and bowed her head, glancing quickly over her shoulder to see who had observed her lapse. Her eyes met those of Dylan Tremaine, his head partially bowed. He smiled uncertainly, and Caitlin turned quickly away.

Lord, she is one proud and haughty lady, Dylan thought as he studied the schoolmarm. Even the bonnet couldn't soften that way she had of drawing herself up so resolute and prim. When the services began he'd noticed how unsure she'd looked, almost vulnerable, and his heart had gone out to her. He wouldn't cause her embarrassment for the world, and yet the curiosities of the family and the rest of the congregation were something to be endured.

Then as time went on and she had intercepted the glances of her family, and probably felt the curious stares of others, it was as if she had willed herself to construct a defensive position. First the shift in posture, followed by the narrowing of her eyes and the hard tight line of her mouth. He'd seen it more than he cared to recall in the brief time they'd known one another. For reasons he could not fathom his reaction was always the same. He had the urge to grab her and kiss her until she literally melted in his arms and that damnable unyielding attitude of hers was completely demolished.

By the time the service finally ended both Caitlin and Dylan were on edge and not in the mood for the banter of Molly or the probing looks and thinly veiled inquiries of Caitlin's brothers and parents. Dylan cast about for a way to refuse the invitation to Sunday dinner officially proffered by Mrs. Pearce as they waited outside the church for Mr. Pearce to bring the carriage. His intention to decline must have been plainer than he intended, for Caitlin suddenly interrupted.

"I'm not sure Mr. Tremaine is available for dinner, Mother. He has a great deal of work to attend to. After all, he must make certain his mining stake is secure at all times."

On the one hand Dylan was pleased that she had paid attention when he'd talked about his work. On the other, she had this annoying way of taking over and making decisions before other people had a chance to open their mouths. He smiled at Mrs. Pearce. "Actually, ma'am, I'd be delighted to accept your invitation. Rumor has it that

you make some of the best pastries in the state." The blush
that spread across Mrs. Pearce's face told him he'd made
one more conquest among the Pearce women. He glanced
triumphantly at Caitlin.

Four

When they arrived at the house the women disappeared into the kitchen while the men gathered in the parlor to await dinner. Dylan could not remember a time when he was more uncomfortable. The clock on the mantel seemed to move at half-speed and thunder each tick. The chiming of the quarter-hour echoed through the silent room. Caitlin's brothers stood like bookends to either side of the mantel and watched him. Dylan sat stiffly on the edge of the fanciest settee he'd ever seen. Across from him sat Caitlin's father, puffing a pipe and studying him intensely as if daring him to make a wrong move.

Dylan glanced at the clock. It was exactly one minute later than the last time he'd looked. For the twentieth time, he studied his freshly polished boots.

"How did you and my daughter meet, Mr. Tremaine?" Caitlin's father appeared relaxed, but his eyes gave him away. His eyes were wary, suspicious, concerned.

"We . . . uh . . . that is . . ." Stick close to the truth, Caitlin had advised. "I stopped by the schoolhouse—that is, the church schoolroom—one afternoon."

"You just decided one day to stop by the school?" Pearce sucked on his pipe. The clock ticked. The brothers didn't move.

"The truth is, sir, I was hoping to pick up some extra work. I thought there might be a need for someone to come and start a fire in the mornings what with cold weather setting in and all."

Pearce narrowed his eyes, whether because of the smoke from his pipe or his dissatisfaction with Dylan's response it was impossible to guess. The clock chimed the half-hour. Somewhere in the bowels of the house there was feminine laughter.

"Are you looking for extra work then?" One of the brothers spoke, which one Dylan couldn't have said.

"I was thinking of it. Mining can be feast or famine." He knew by the sudden tightening of Pearce's mouth around the stem of his pipe, that this was not the best answer.

"Dinner is served," Mrs. Pearce announced from the doorway, and Dylan leapt to his feet.

In the spacious dining room, he was seated as far from Caitlin as possible, next to Mrs. Pearce, while Caitlin sat next to her father. Dinner conversation was stilted and spare, and the strange thing was, Dylan suspected this was fairly normal. He supposed he should take it as a sign of acceptance, but the truth was, it made him uneasy. He could practically hear himself chew.

"Have you known Caitlin long, Mr. Tremaine?" Mrs. Pearce asked as she passed the side dishes.

"They met at the school," one of the brothers said.

"He was looking for extra work," chimed in the other.

Dylan felt Caitlin watching him. He glanced at her just as she was about to put a forkful of green beans in her mouth. She missed and the beans fell to her lap.

"As you well know, Mrs. Pearce, your daughter is highly respected in the community. The truth is I used looking for work as a ruse to have the opportunity to meet her." Wrong answer, he realized at once as he saw the startled look that passed between husband and wife.

"What does it matter how they met," Molly said, leaping

in to save the day. "The point is they did, and they have found interests in common."

"What would those interests be?" Pearce inquired as he carved another slice of beef for himself.

"Poetry," Dylan said.

"Reading," Caitlin said at the same time. "Reading poetry," she hastened to add, and glanced nervously at Dylan who smiled with relief.

"There's also history," Molly added. "Don't forget that."

Dylan and Caitlin both looked at her. History? their expressions asked. Molly shrugged.

"History," John repeated, clearly waiting for an expansion of the topic.

Caitlin sighed. "Well, yes, Father. You know history has always been a love of mine. Dylan . . . Mr. Tremaine shares that interest. He tells me about Cornwall, while I tell him about America." She gave both Dylan and Molly a look that dared them to say anything more.

"You have chosen a unique lifestyle, young man," John said later as he waited for the women to clear the table and serve dessert. "I trust that is due to some allegiance to tradition and not because you can afford no better."

So here it is at last, Dylan thought. He looked at Caitlin's brothers and saw that they were as interested to hear his answer as was their father. His native pride surfaced. The truth is it's none of your business, he wanted to say. He was aware that Caitlin had paused in her clearing duties and was watching him anxiously.

"It's not my custom to speak of my finances, sir," he began, and saw Caitlin's hand tremble as she set a piece of apple pie in front of her father.

"Father, please," she entreated softly.

"Your father is only doing his parental duty, Caitlin," Dylan assured her as she served him. "I would expect no less from a man of his stature in the community. He's only protecting you."

"You didn't answer the question," Caitlin's brother Edward noted.

Dylan ignored the young man and turned his full attention to John Pearce. "Sir, I will not discuss my finances with you. I will assure you that I have elected to live as I do for reasons that are rooted in practicality rather than necessity. As you may recall, knowing some of the earlier Cornish who settled this community, we choose to live as we do in order to put aside as much as possible as quickly as possible. My needs are few, sir. That may change when the day comes that I choose a wife." He looked directly at Caitlin and both Molly and her mother gasped with delight.

"Eat your pie, Mr. Tremaine," Mary Pearce urged as she and her daughters resumed their places at the table.

Dylan took a bite and smiled broadly. "Your reputation as one of the region's premiere bakers is well-deserved, ma'am," he said lifting a glass to her in a toast and in so doing forcing her husband and sons to do likewise.

"Here, here," John Pearce agreed, determined to regain control of his position as head of the table. "Mr. Tremaine, when you have finished your pie perhaps you would join me for a cigar?"

"Actually, sir, I was about to ask permission to take Caitlin for a ride in the country. I'd like to show her some of the landmarks established by my predecessors."

"I think that's a lovely idea," Mary Pearce said before her husband could respond. "Molly and I can take care of the dishes, dear. You and your young man go along now." She ignored her husband's clearing of his throat in an obvious attempt to get her attention.

"Mother, I—" Caitlin began.

"He doesn't have a carriage," Charles said. It was clear the brothers were not sold on this new beau of their sister's.

"I arranged to borrow one from a fellow miner," Dylan replied. "It's liveried just down the street behind Mr. Heathcote's establishment."

"Then it's settled," Mary said and ushered Dylan from the table, signaling clearly that the meal had ended. "It's a lovely day for a drive. Who knows how many more we shall have before cold weather sets in?"

"I'll just get my cloak," Caitlin said, rushing up the stairs before her father could speak up and change the plan her mother had so skillfully set in motion.

"I'll go get the carriage and come back for you," Dylan called after her.

"That's not necessary," Molly insisted. "Caitlin loves to walk. She'll come with you." She made a shooing motion to her sister who had paused on the stairway. "It was so nice to see you again, Mr. Tremaine," she said graciously.

"Yes, I do hope we can plan on your being a regular guest in our home," Mary added.

Dylan turned to John Pearce. "Sir, with your permission I would like to call on your daughter and accept your wife's kind invitation to return to your home."

"It would appear that I have little to say in the matter," Pearce replied sternly, but then he offered his hand to Dylan. "My daughter is of age, sir. If she chooses to have you call upon her, then you are welcome."

"Thank you, sir."

"My brothers didn't like you," Caitlin said as soon as they had left the house.

"I'll grow on them," Dylan replied. He could not help but take note of the worried tone of her voice, and for some reason he couldn't fathom, that irritated him. He thought about reassuring her, in a sarcastic tone, that despite outward appearances he came from decent stock and could indeed hold his own with the likes of her brothers.

They said no more all the way to the stables. Dylan hitched the horses while Caitlin paced. Clearly something was worrying her. He helped her into the carriage and wrapped a laprobe around her knees, then climbed aboard and snapped the reins.

"Where do you want to go?" he asked as they headed down the deserted main street and out of town. She noticed he took the road toward the mines where he worked and lived.

"We have to be gone at least an hour but no longer than two," she said as if calculating a formula. "Let's just ride out for twenty minutes, then we can work your lesson, and return. That should be perfect." She rummaged under the neckline of her cloak and retrieved the watch she wore on a chain around her neck.

Her exactitude irritated him. In fact, it had been an irritating day. The brothers didn't like him, the father didn't like him, and from all appearances Caitlin didn't like him much either. "You'll let me know the exact moment I'm to halt the horses," he said tersely and snapped the reins to set the team into a canter.

The sudden thrust forward caused Caitlin to reach for something to keep from being pitched out of the carriage. Dylan's arm was the handiest thing so she grabbed on, then immediately released her hold as soon as she had regained her balance. "There's no need to rush," she said.

"Don't blame me, honey, I'm just a lovestruck guy out for a few stolen moments with his woman." Dylan knew he was being deliberately crude, but he really didn't care. He was tired of the whole Pearce clan and their haughty better-than-thou attitude. He'd agreed to help her with this absurd scheme of hers. Was it too much to expect a little gratitude and respect in return? He set his jaw and stared straight ahead as the horses headed up the dirt road that led to the mine.

"May I ask what the matter is?" Caitlin said in a prudish schoolmarm voice after a short pause.

"You may. You may even take a wild guess if it fits into your almighty master plan."

"Mr. Tremaine . . ."

He reined the horses hard bringing the carriage to a sudden stop. They had reached one of the open hilly areas where the miners plied their trade. She knew this was near where he worked. She was loath to admit that she had stood in the doorway and watched him head off for work on more than one morning.

He turned to her and grasped her shoulders. "Let's get one thing straight, Miss Pearce. I have agreed to help you in return for some lessons. Well, the price just went up." The horrified look in her eyes gave him a great deal of pleasure.

"Unhand me, Mr. Tremaine," she said quietly. "If you have it in your mind to . . . to . . ."

He loosened his grip slightly. "Dishonor you? You see that's the problem—you think I'm capable of such a thing, and heaven knows I've never in my life met a woman more in need of a good kissing than you are. But I am an honorable man, Caitlin. I may not live in some fine house or hold what to your family would be a proper job, but I have plans and dreams, and I am someone who has never willingly harmed another person. I deserve some respect." He dropped the reins and got down from the carriage.

"Where do you think you're going?" she asked, and her voice shook with a different sort of alarm, the fear of abandonment.

"Don't worry, I'll be back. You just sit there and think about whether you can meet my terms for our little bargain." He stalked off.

Caitlin watched him go. At first she was astonished at his outburst. Who would have thought the man could have such a temper? He'd always appeared to be so mild mannered, as if nothing phased him at all. That was partially why she'd felt she could trust him with her plan. And she had trusted him. Didn't that show respect? What on earth was he getting so upset about? Why was he taking this whole thing so personally? She threw back the laprobe and climbed down from the carriage. "I want to discuss this," she called to his retreating back, then gathered her skirts and followed him. He kept going, his long strides covering the rough terrain far more easily than she could manage.

When she finally caught up with him, it was because he had reached his destination, the rudimentary campsite where he kept all of his worldly possessions. He looked around, obviously assuring himself that all was as he had left it. When she finally topped the rise that surrounded his camp, he was rummaging through a worn knapsack. She was out of breath and out of patience. "Mr. Tremaine. . . ."

"I'm going to say this one more time, Caitlin. You either start calling me by my given name or the deal's off. Now sit." He pointed to the tarp and blanket he'd spread out for her. Without a word, he gathered some wood and started the fire; then he pulled the book she'd given him to study from under the knapsack and handed it to her. "So, teach me," he ordered, "before we run over your precious time schedule." He turned his back to her and busied himself tending the fire.

Caitlin cleared her throat and set the book aside. "I'm sorry to have offended you, Dylan. It's been a trying day for both of us. The truth is I didn't want my father or brothers to hurt your feelings. I knew that they were doing so, and I was completely at a loss as to how to stop them. I do apologize, but you must keep in mind that they don't know what we know—that this is all a pretense. They think it's real, that you are a serious suitor. I assure you they have put others through the same tests."

She saw the tension in his shoulders begin to ebb and kept talking.

"You see my mother and Molly are so anxious for me to marry that they are determined to find the good in any man who happens to look my way. The men of the family take the opposite point of view. In their minds no man has been interested for so long that they are suspicious of your intentions. Why on earth would you be interested in me? They are no doubt thinking that perhaps it's the family's money or business that has caught your attention, for how could it possibly be me?"

Dylan turned in time to see her daintily wipe one tear from the corner of her eye. These rare moments of vulnerability never failed to touch him. They were so out of character for her and, therefore, could not possibly be attributed to a deliberate attempt to use feminine wiles to work her will. He tossed a small branch on the fire and sat next to her on the blanket.

"Are you warm enough?" he asked softly.

She nodded and he knew that she was willing herself to regain control of her emotions. "We should get to your lesson," she said matter-of-factly, turning to retrieve the book. "I believe you had gotten through the first four chapters. You're making remarkable progress, Dylan."

He reached over and took the book from her, laying it aside. "Caitlin, are you sure you want to go through with this scheme of yours?"

He watched the determination return to her features. "Yes," she said firmly, but she did not look directly at him. "I have no other choice. I can't stand by and have my sister ruin herself or see my family torn apart should she and Geoffrey do something foolish."

"But why not use this time to seek someone who could love you and marry you for real? You're a fine-looking woman with much to offer."

She laughed mirthlessly. "I'm afraid we haven't that much time, Mr.—Dylan." The firmly set jaw trembled slightly. *Fine-looking is nearly as bad as handsome,* she thought.

"And so you will settle for me," he said.

She looked at him then, turning so that she could be

face to face with him. "My stars no, Dylan. It's you who must settle for me, at least for the duration of our ruse. I know I have not said this directly, but I am extremely grateful that you are willing to assist me in this. It is you who must give up the opportunity to . . . to pursue others while we pretend—"

"Caitlin," he said gruffly as he leaned in to kiss her, "shut up."

Caitlin was so surprised by the brush of his lips on hers that she kept her eyes wide open for the duration of the kiss. It was unlike any kiss she had ever known—not that she was so experienced, but there was a heat to it even though he made no move to deepen the kiss. His lips were soft and firm at the same time. Moist but not slobbering. Caitlin recalled the boy who had first kissed her and how disgusted she'd been by his drooling all over her. She rather enjoyed kissing Dylan.

"Caitlin," Dylan said as he moved a fraction of an inch from her, "stop analyzing and kiss me back."

"I couldn't. This isn't—" But his lips were on hers again before she could finish the thought.

This time he put his arms around her. It seemed only appropriate to put hers around him if for no other reason than to place herself in a defensive position should he try to take the matter any further. Of course, it was difficult to understand who was doing what. Certainly she had the opportunity to break the kiss, and yet her natural inclination was to lean into it. His fingers cupped her face and slanted it slightly so that there was a better fit.

She became aware that he had loosened the streamers of her bonnet and removed it and his breathing had accelerated. Or was that her breathing? "I think that's enough, Dylan," she said, pulling away as she flattened both palms against his shoulders and pushed.

He released her at once and turned to bank the small

campfire. "We'll have to show signs of affection if we're to pull this off, Cait," he said.

Caitlin was still trying to deal with the differences that had taken place in her in the span of a few short moments. Her lips felt different, her body burned with a kind of liquid heat, and she found herself studying the stretch of his coat over his broad shoulders in a decidedly unscientific manner. He seemed unmoved by the entire encounter.

"Did you hear me?"

"Yes, of course, you're right. I suppose from time to time we will need to hold hands, cast longing glances, that sort of thing." She stood up and brushed off her skirt. "Still, I don't think it would be proper for us to kiss in that manner, Dylan. On the cheek perhaps."

"Lovers are rarely proper all the time, Cait," he observed as he retrieved her bonnet and handed it to her. He kicked dirt over the embers. "We should head back. It's time." He fingered the watch that hung between her breasts, and it seemed like the most intimate thing any man had ever done.

"Of course," she agreed and finished tying her bonnet in place. "Will you come for your lesson tomorrow afternoon as usual?" she asked suddenly unsure as to whether or not they had resolved his initial protest.

"I'll be there." He held out his hand to steady her as they walked the rutted path back to the road where the horses snorted and stamped impatiently.

When Caitlin arrived at school the following morning the fire was made and on her desk was a bouquet of bright red and gold fall leaves. Perhaps affected by her own mellow mood, the children were remarkably well behaved for a change. Even Rob Heathcote could not provoke them into mischief, though he certainly tried.

The pattern continued every day that week. She would come to school to find everything in readiness and a small token on her desk. One day it was the feather of a bluejay, another it was a multicolored stone, smoothed by years of rushing water. In the afternoons Dylan would come for his lesson. Then he would walk her home. By Saturday when she and Molly went shopping the town was abuzz with speculation about the suddenly blossoming romance between the schoolmarm and the miner.

She had to admit that he was doing everything he could to live up to his end of the bargain. She might be flattered if she didn't suspect that his real goal was to earn the promised money so he could head West to be with his brother. He talked of little else, and told her stories he had heard at the mines or at Heathcote's tavern of the amazing wealth to be had there.

On Sunday he once again joined the family for church and for Sunday dinner. Caitlin's father and brothers continued to view Dylan's intentions with skepticism, while Molly and her mother championed his cause. Once again the couple rode out into the country on a Sunday afternoon. They were observed walking across the hilly terrain by several of the housewives on Shake Rag Street. On Monday those same housewives speculated across the low stone walls surrounding their cottages about the intentions of the miner and the potential for his success in wooing the elder Pearce daughter.

Their husbands—miners themselves—teased Dylan unmercifully about his courtship of the prim and proper schoolmarm. Dylan took the good-natured ribbing in stride whenever he met the other miners at Heathcote's or near the mines, but most of his time was spent alone these days. The time he spent courting Caitlin had to be made up for in increased hours spent at his stake. As the sole miner who camped on the hillside at night, he had a lot of time to think, and what he thought about most of the time these days was Caitlin Pearce.

The woman was a mystery to him. One minute she was

all spit and vinegar, unapproachable, untouchable. The next she let down her guard and revealed a softer more vulnerable side. At such times everything about her would change—her posture, her facial expression, her voice. The frustrating thing was that regardless of her mood his basic reaction was increasingly one of wanting to touch her, hold her, kiss her into silence or submission.

Over the past week and a half he had become far too aware of the shape of her, lying awake nights to speculate about what would be revealed if he could peel away those layers of stiff clothing. When he was with her he devised new ways of touching her hand, brushing against her. He had not lost sight of his wager with Heathcote, and that was the confusing thing in all of this. He should have been pursuing her with a vengeance, taking every opportunity to woo her, to touch her, to kiss her. If he made her believe she was irresistible to him he stood a far better chance of pulling off the public kiss. He knew how to make a woman feel desired and he knew the payoff, even from a woman like Caitlin—especially with a woman like Caitlin. For it was the women like her who were the most susceptible, the ones who had given up on ever attracting a man. Women like that would do anything a man wanted eventually.

So, it should have been easy. It was the perfect situation. They both understood the rules, so no one would get hurt in the long run. They might as well have a little fun. *Surely there's no harm in that,* Dylan thought, then wondered what kept him from pursuing the idea. *Damn the woman.* She had gotten under his skin, made him want to protect her at the same time he wanted to bed her.

Between losing sleep at night, having little success with his prospecting during the day, and trying to figure out the effect Caitlin had on him when they sat together in that empty schoolroom every afternoon for his lesson, Dylan's patience was running thin. The good-natured teasing of his friends began to wear on him, especially when their comments came too close to the truth.

"Tremaine," one burly miner called out across the crowded room at Heathcote's on Thursday night, "how goes it with the schoolmarm? Have you gotten into any *advanced* studies yet?" The other patrons snickered as they sipped their beer. "I'd wager them long legs of hers would require a lot of homework. A man would need to get all wrapped up in that lesson."

Everyone turned to Dylan expecting his usual goodnatured retort. Instead he walked across the room and punched the miner in the face, sending him staggering to the floor, his nose pouring blood. Instantly, the room erupted into a brawl. By the time it ended, shattered glass and broken chairs littered the saloon. Heathcote ordered everyone out, saving his parting words for Dylan. "You'd best hope you win our wager, Tremaine. You'll be needing that extra cash to pay off the damages here."

On Friday morning the stove was cold when Caitlin arrived at the schoolhouse, and there was no token from Dylan on her desk. She overheard some of the older boys quizzing Rob about an altercation in his father's saloon the previous night. She paid little attention wishing the boys would show as much interest in their studies as they did in such scandalous behavior.

". . . broke his nose," she heard Rob say to one friend as she urged the children back to their places following recess. "Just walked right up and punched him in the face," he added. "I saw it myself."

"That will be enough, Mr. Heathcote," she said. "Now take your seat." She knew by the muffled snickers that the saloonkeeper's son was mocking her behind her back as she walked to her desk. It would be a long difficult day, she knew. The attention of her pupils was far more fixated on the brawl that had taken place the night before than on their sums or spelling. Finally, after everyone had left for the day, she waited for Dylan to come for his lesson—and waited.

When he had not arrived after an hour she became concerned. What if he'd been hurt? He worked alone. If he had fallen or encountered some sort of accident in the abandoned mine he worked, it could be hours before someone discovered him. She envisioned him lying there, injured, in pain. She considered her options. She could continue to wait or alert someone in town to her fears or go out and try to find him herself. She decided to confide her fears to Mr. Heathcote. In the days before she and Dylan had met, she'd often noticed him sitting outside Heathcote's Tavern, and that day when he'd walked with her through town and encountered Gar Heathcote, they had seemed to know one another. Perhaps Mr. Heathcote would send someone to Dylan's campsite to check on his welfare.

"Mr. Heathcote, I've come to ask your help," Caitlin said as she stepped inside the dim and nearly deserted tavern.

Heathcote remained seated, and to her surprise, it was Dylan who stood up and turned to greet her. Seeing him safe and sound, her first reaction was relief. Her second was anger. She had been so concerned, and here he was lounging about a tavern as if he hadn't a care in the world. Before he could cross the room, Caitlin turned on her heel and left.

"Cait," he called, doubling his pace to catch up with her. "I had to handle something with Heathcote here," he said quietly as he fell into step with her and nodded at a passing shopper. "The matter took more time than I anticipated. I just lost track. I'm sorry, but it pleases me to see you might have actually been concerned enough to cross the doorstep of a saloon." He grinned, hoping to lighten her mood.

Caitlin marched along, keeping her eyes firmly focused on the ground before her. "I have no doubt you were unaware of the passing hours, Mr. Tremaine. Spirits will do that to a person," she retorted. "I had not thought you needed to fortify your courage in order to come for a simple reading lesson."

He tipped his hat at Tillie Polkinghorn who peered out from her shop window at them as they passed. "I'd like the chance to explain," he said through gritted teeth.

"I'll expect you at the normal time tomorrow, Dylan, assuming you can fit that into your busy *work* schedule." And with that Caitlin turned the corner and headed for home. She had not looked directly at him the whole time. If she had she might have wondered how he'd got the cut that split his upper lip and the black eye.

That evening Dylan called at the house. "Caitlin forgot her book satchel at school," he told Mrs. Pearce. "I'm sure she'll need it before tomorrow's classes," he added as he handed the satchel to Caitlin's mother.

"Why don't you come in?" Mrs. Pearce said kindly. "My heavens, son, what on earth happened to you?"

Dylan shrugged and gave Mary Pearce an embarrassed smile. "I was in the wrong place at the wrong time, ma'am."

"Well, I should say so. Caitlin is just finishing some work in the kitchen. Why don't you take her the books yourself?"

"Thank you, ma'am. I don't want to disturb you and Mr. Pearce."

"Oh, Mr. Pearce is at the store working on the ledgers, and I'm just finishing some mending." She gave him a little nudge. "Go on now," she urged.

Dylan walked through the dining room and into the pantry that led to the kitchen. Caitlin was humming softly to herself, a nice melodic voice she had. He'd noticed that in church. He stood in the shadows of the pantry for a moment, observing her.

She was scrubbing the last of the pans. Everything else was stacked on the counter next to where she worked. She wore a shirtwaist with the sleeves rolled back, exposing her arms. Her hair was up but coming loose from its usual disciplined bun, tendrils curling around her face in the heat of the kitchen. But the most appealing thing of all was that she was barefoot—no shoes or stockings, just her small bare feet planted firmly on the floor. Dylan smiled as he stepped back to the pantry door that led to the dining room and opened it, deliberately letting it close hard to announce his coming. Clearing his throat, he entered the kitchen.

"I brought your books," he said without preamble. He placed the satchel and his hat on the square wooden table already set for breakfast, then picked up a dishtowel and began drying the pots she'd just washed.

"That wasn't necessary," she said, not looking at him as she continued to scrub the last pan.

He shrugged trying to keep his attention from focusing on the undone buttons at the neck of her blouse. He'd never once seen Caitlin Pearce so undone, and it gave him pause. He took the pan from her. "It's clean enough," he said when she resisted giving it to him. In the minor tug of war that ensued she accidentally splashed soapy water on him. A dollop of suds landed right near his eye.

"Don't rub it," she warned, but he did anyway and then gave a muffled cry at the sting. "I told you not to rub it," she chastised. "Sit down here and let me get some cool water for you."

"I don't need a drink of water," he said testily as he sat and held his hand over the affected eye which also happened to be the one bruised and blackened in the bar fight. He winced again and muttered an oath under his breath.

"The water is to wash the soap out of your eye. Possibly I should have aimed the suds at your mouth. I don't tolerate swearing, Dylan," she announced sternly as she gently pulled his hand away and prepared to cover his eye with a cool wet cloth. "Good heavens, what happened to you? You look as if you've been on the losing end of a fight."

"Actually, the other guy looks a lot worse," he replied. She seemed oblivious to the fact that she was standing between his legs and that his view of the bare skin beneath the open neckline of her blouse had improved considerably. "Is that better?" she asked as she gently lifted his chin and squeezed the cloth, releasing a few drops of the cool water directly into his irritated eye.

"Better," he agreed huskily and wondered what her reaction might be if he placed his hands on either side of her slim waist and pulled her onto his lap.

She lifted the cloth and leaned in to inspect his eye. "I think it's going to be fine," she said.

Was it his imagination or was her voice a little shaky? Was she as aware as he that they were in the perfect position to kiss? He'd thought a lot about the kiss they shared at his campsite that day. He'd thought a lot about repeating it. "Caitlin," he said softly and reached up to stroke her cheek.

Immediately she stepped away and busied herself rinsing out the cloth and folding it efficiently over the edge of the counter. "Thank you for bringing the books," she said.

Dylan stood up and went to stand behind her. "Cait, look at me." Gently, he took her by the shoulders and turned her to face him. "I did not skip out on my lesson today. There was a fight at the tavern last night. I was in it, and I'd gone there to try and soothe Heathcote's ire by paying part of the damages. But when I got there he was upset about his son. He thinks the boy has been taking money from the till. He's at his wit's end. We got to talking—or rather he was talking and I was listening. It's hard for him, raising the boy alone and all." As he explained the whole situation to her, her expression softened.

"You're a good man, Dylan," Caitlin said looking up at him as if really seeing him for the first time. "Please accept my apology for doubting you."

Lord above, the woman has no idea what those big green eyes can do to a man when she looks at him that way, Dylan thought. Her scent surrounded him. Her body radiated warmth and a heat that he sorely wanted to explore. "Caitlin, I'm going to kiss you now," he said. "Would that be all right?"

She nodded, and he noticed that she did not close her eyes as his lips met hers. He also noticed that in spite of his desire to deepen the kiss and let it take its natural course to actions more primal, something held him back. This was different. She was different—not at all a woman to be trifled with, and the fact was, there was something inside him that prevented him from doing anything that might eventually cause her pain or embarrassment.

"Caitlin . . ." He murmured her name against her parted lips. Her eyes were closed now, and she swayed unsteadily as he broke the kiss. He placed his hands on her shoulders until she'd regained her balance. "Such slender shoulders for such a strong lady," he said and smiled down at her.

Caitlin stared up at him. She wondered if he had any notion what effect his kisses had on her? Did he know that they made her think about things no proper unmarried woman should? Did he know kissing him made her aware of so many things she'd never even considered before? Things like the strength of a man's back beneath her flattened palms, the mingling of breath as his lips met hers, the natural urge to open to him, draw him closer, feel him touching her? Was this what was meant by *becoming as one,* she wondered?

"I think you should go now," she said, deliberately stepping away from him and smoothing invisible wrinkles from her skirt.

"I'll call for you tomorrow?"

"It's Saturday," she replied thinking he meant to walk her home from school as had become their pattern.

"For the dance," he replied.

Suddenly the image of being in his arms, dancing with him, having him hold her for a prolonged period of time seemed unnerving. "Oh, yes, the dance," she said softly.

"You still want to go?" he asked, and there was the slightest trace of uncertainty in his tone.

"Yes, of course. It's part of our overall plan, after all. To not go would seem . . . unusual."

He reached for the hat he'd placed on the table. She saw that he was frowning. Perhaps he had hoped that she would refuse to attend the dance with him. Then he would not have to be seen in quite so public or intimate surroundings with her. More to the point, she would not have to be seen with the likes of him. "I'll be here at seven o'clock," he said and headed for the back door.

"I'll walk you out," she said, indicating with a gesture that they should retrace his original path through the pantry and dining room and back to the front door.

"That's not necessary. The back door has always been good enough for my people," he replied stiffly.

He was out the door so quickly that Caitlin had no chance to reply.

Damn the woman. One minute she made him feel as if he wanted to protect her from his baser self. The next minute he wanted to wring her pretty neck for being so all-fired arrogant and haughty. It was clear to him that she'd forgotten all about the dance and that once reminded, she was less than thrilled with the idea of going with him. It was clearly an ordeal to be endured in her mind. He, on the other hand, had allowed himself to look forward to the occasion, to indulge in fantasies of holding her as they whirled around the dance floor. He'd actually dug into his hard-earned savings to buy a new shirt and vest for the occasion. The woman was going to drive him to financial ruin if he didn't stop buying clothes to make himself presentable, first for the Sunday services and family dinner afterward and now this dance.

Five

"Are you sure you wouldn't care for some refreshment, Mr. Tremaine?" Mrs. Pearce asked for the third time since he'd arrived promptly at seven to call for Caitlin.

"Thank you, no, ma'am. I appreciate the offer," he assured her and wondered what could be keeping Geoffrey MacKenzie. Dylan had been sitting there on the edge of his chair for what seemed an eternity, enduring the anxious fidgeting of Mrs. Pearce and the thinly veiled and silent scrutiny of her husband.

As if in answer to his prayers, carriage wheels rattled on the drive.

"That'll be Geoffrey," Mrs. Pearce said with an expression of relief as she raced to open the door for their visitor.

"You don't own a carriage, Mr. Tremaine?" Pearce asked.

"I haven't found it necessary, sir." *Where is Caitlin? What could possibly be taking the woman so long?*

"Geoffrey's here, dearest," Mrs. Pearce announced unnecessarily as the powerfully built young man strode into the room, bringing a breath of the cold night air with him.

"Mr. Pearce, sir, how are you this fine evening?" He approached the older man as an equal, offering his hand in greeting, then turned his attention to Dylan. "And Mr. Tremaine, my apologies for my tardiness. There was a legislative matter that needed my attention, though I can see by their absence that Molly and her sister are completely unaware of my delay." He laughed heartily, and to Dylan's shock, so did both Mr. and Mrs. Pearce.

"Come have some refreshment," Mr. Pearce urged the young man. "Something to take the chill off." It was clear to Dylan that Geoffrey was already viewed as a member of the family.

"Geoffrey . . ." Molly's voice rang out from the stairway in the large foyer. She fairly flew into the room and Dylan wondered if she ever moved at less than breakneck speed. She was a vision in pale blue, her blond curls bobbing saucily with each move of her head.

Dylan was struck by the way Geoffrey moved instantly to her side. He had never really known love or even observed it, but surely there were never two people more devoted to one another than this handsome couple. Molly's eyes glowed as she looked up at her beloved and Geoffrey appeared struck dumb by the beauty before him. No wonder Caitlin was so determined to help them find happiness.

"Ah, Caitlin," Mr. Pearce said, and Dylan turned his attention to the schoolmarm who stood just outside the doorway in the shadows of the hallway. "Come in, my dear." Pearce crossed the room to escort his daughter within.

Dylan was stunned by the transformation. Caitlin was dressed in a deceptively simple gown of taffeta, the deep blue green of pine trees on the hillside at sunset. The neckline was cut wide and accented in heavy white lace, revealing the creamy perfection of her neck and shoulders. Her flaming hair was done up in an intricate twist with ringlets that framed her face and just grazed her cheeks. When she raised her eyes and met his gaze, he thought his heart would hammer its way straight out of his chest.

"Mr. Tremaine has been keeping Mother and me entertained while you two girls dawdled about," Mr. Pearce announced.

Caitlin shot a startled glance at Dylan. He shrugged and smiled at her.

"Father, don't start. We're late already," Molly protested when Mr. Pearce appeared prepared to have his daughters take their seats and join the family circle.

Pearce laughed. "That's hardly my fault, little one. For it is not I who has taken nearly an extra half-hour to appear." There was no doubt the man adored his daughters.

"Never mind. We must be off. I haven't danced in weeks. Come along, Geoffrey," Molly said, and coming from her it was more an invitation than a command.

"Mr. Tremaine, I leave Caitlin in your hands and Molly in Mr. MacKenzie's. Good evening, sir." Pearce offered his handshake.

Dylan accepted it. "It's been my pleasure as always, sir. I look forward to more opportunities for us to talk." Then he turned to Mrs. Pearce. "Ma'am, thank you for the hospitality of your beautiful home." Finally he turned to Caitlin. "Shall we go?" he asked, and reached for the cloak she held clutched in both hands.

Outside the cold night air was a welcome relief from the stifling atmosphere of the parlor. Molly kept up a lively chatter all the way to the dance, making it unnecessary for Dylan or Caitlin to do more than nod and smile and occasionally express appreciation for one of Molly's witticisms.

The hall was bustling by the time they arrived. Molly and Geoffrey took charge, disposing of coats and insisting they all head for the refreshment table and a glass of punch. The two lovers were immediately joined by several friends who dragged them away to visit with more friends on the other side of the room. The musicians had just struck up a waltz.

Without a word, Dylan took the glass of punch from Caitlin's trembling hand and led her to the center of the dance floor, where only a few other couples had begun the dance.

"We're here to be seen, Caitlin," Dylan said as if reading

her mind. "It wouldn't matter if there were a hundred other couples dancing, everyone would be looking at you and the way the lamplight catches the color of your hair and makes your eyes shimmer."

She felt as if she were bewitched as she found herself held tight in Dylan's arms and spinning around the floor while he showered her with compliments. Suddenly the room that had seemed so crowded before seemed empty. There was no one dancing except Dylan and her.

"You're a wonderful dancer," she said.

He flashed the smile she was coming to expect. "Why, Miss Pearce, I do believe you're flirting with me," he teased.

Caitlin laughed. She felt young and beautiful and not at all like her normal self. It was a night for fantasy. "Would you mind that so much?" she teased back.

Suddenly his dark eyes sobered. "Only if you didn't mean it, Caitlin," he replied.

His sudden shift in mood confused her. She stumbled over a step and his hand tightened on her waist. She was aware of the perfect match of their bodies as they continued the dance. His hand was large enough to span her small waist, powerful enough to keep her from falling. "Where did you learn to dance?" she asked, searching for safe conversational ground.

To her relief he smiled. "My mother insisted my sisters learn, and I was their partner. Ma used to say that a man could get by being clumsy on the dance floor, but a woman needed to be graceful, and she also needed to be nimble enough to keep from being trampled by a clumsy partner."

"How many sisters do you have?"

"Four. Four very good dancers," he added with a smile just as the waltz ended.

They were approached by people who knew Caitlin, mostly parents who pretended concern over a child's lessons but who clearly wanted a closer look at the school-marm and her beau. Tillie Polkinghorn needed no excuse.

"Well, Caitlin, I see your romance with the badger is no passing fancy," she commented when Dylan had gone to get them a fresh glass of punch. "He's very good-looking, and I understand he's been most fortunate with his prospecting."

Caitlin opened her mouth to answer, but Tillie kept right on talking.

"Of course, he comes from that good Cornish stock. Hard rock miners I've heard them called, but that one seems to personify the epitaph, if you take my meaning. I mean did you ever see such shoulders on a man? And that broad chest of his—my stars, he is powerfully constructed wouldn't you say?" The woman was practically drooling as she gazed at Dylan. "I did hear that he was thinking of heading West. You know he must have heard the rumors of gold in California. Even the papers are just full of stories about it."

"I'm sure—"

"How long he stays in a dreary little town like Mineral Point is anybody's guess. If I were you, Caitlin, I'd—"

"Ah, but you aren't me, Tillie, and if you'll excuse me, I believe Mr. Tremaine and I have another waltz to dance." She walked away from Tillie as fast as she could and went in search of Dylan.

"Let's dance," she said tersely as soon as she had downed the punch with a most unladylike gulp.

Amused at her obvious fury, Dylan followed suit, then led her to the center of the floor. "Why do you let Miss Polkinghorn get under your skin?" he asked.

She told him the gist of the conversation, still fuming at the audacity of the woman—a peer of hers and a spinster as well—daring to offer advice for the lovelorn.

Dylan threw back his head and laughed. It was a won-derful sound and attracted the attention of other couples surrounding them. He tightened his hold on Caitlin and spun her around the room until they were both breathless but giddy with the exertion. "Let's get some air," he said as soon as the music ended. He led her toward the door.

"Everyone will think we came out here to spoon," she said as they walked a few yards from the entrance to the hall and stopped next to a row of parked carriages. She felt nervous and shy with him, unprepared for what might be expected of her under such circumstances, and yet strangely hopeful that he might kiss her again.

"Then let's don't disappoint them," Dylan replied, pulling her into his arms and kissing her before she could utter a word of protest.

Her hands were flattened against his chest, and she could feel the steady pounding of his heart. She knew she should use her hands to push him away, but his kiss was so inviting, so intoxicating. The soft rush of his breath tickled her nose. And this kiss was unlike the others. This time there was no hesitation, no waiting for permission. The man was kissing her with all the passion and desire she'd read about in her favorite novels.

"Dylan," she murmured.

"Kiss me back," he commanded.

She slid her hands up around his neck. It seemed the most natural thing in the world to entangle her fingers in his thick dark hair as she met his kiss instead of simply accepting it passively.

Silently, he instructed her. First, his tongue traced the tightly clenched opening to her mouth. Gently his teeth tugged at her lower lip. When she opened her mouth to call his name, he smothered any protest she might be prepared to make with a searing kiss, his tongue sweeping the inside of her mouth in a bold statement of desire and possession. Caitlin's limbs turned to liquid, as a heat began where his kisses ravaged her mouth and oozed slowly but with overpowering force through her body, filling her with a need, a desire she had never thought possible.

Even when he broke the kiss and she drew a ragged breath, he did not release her. Instead he moved his open mouth over her face, her eyelids, her cheeks, her ears, where he breathed her name even as he traced their outlines with his tongue. Without thought she turned her head to give him better access, inviting him to continue. And he did. Next he traced a path of hot wet kisses down the slim column of her throat. She became aware of his hands touching her bare skin at the place where the wide neckline of her gown rested on her shoulders. Gently, he was tugging one side of the dress lower, his mouth following the path his fingers blazed.

If she did not stop him she would be undone, for she seemed powerless to protest something that made her feel so desirable, so alluring. Suddenly she understood Molly's desperation, for if what Molly shared with Geoffrey were anything like this, how could she not give in to it?

"Dylan, we can't," she managed to say in breathless protest. "Someone will come. They will see us," she pleaded.

"I thought that was the idea," he replied as he once again covered her mouth with his own.

If he had doused her with a bucket of cold water, he could not have created the momentous shock those words did. She had permitted herself to believe that the message of desire his kiss delivered was genuine—that for the moment he felt what she did. She pushed hard against him and turned away to readjust her gown and straighten her hair. "We should go in, Mr. Tremaine," she said, and without waiting for a response headed immediately back to the dance.

Dylan stood in stunned silence for a long moment, trying to figure out what had just happened. Then it dawned on him. "Cait, I didn't mean that the way . . . Cait, hold on a minute." But she was already inside. He shook his head and followed her, wondering if there would ever come a day when they didn't wallow in misunderstanding just at the moment when they seemed finally to have made some progress. Then he wondered why on earth he should care.

It took several minutes before he spotted her among the whirling dancers and onlookers. She was standing in the shadows in the corner of the hall farthest from the door, a glass of punch clutched in one hand as she stared without expression at the dancers. He took his time working his way through the crowded room toward her.

"Cait, listen to me," he said in a low voice when he reached her side.

"I'm ready to go home," she said tersely. "Please see if you can find Molly and Geoffrey. They aren't in the room."

"Cait, look at me." He regretted the request as soon as she turned the full fury of her emerald eyes in his direction. Her cold expression froze any explanation he might have been inclined to offer. "I'll take you home," he said quietly. "Let's go find your sister and Geoffrey."

He collected their coats and helped her with hers. When he rested his hands on her shoulders in a conciliatory gesture, she pulled away. She tied on the bonnet he had given her and shoved both hands deep inside her muff. "I'm ready," she said without looking at him.

"You go wait in the carriage while I find them," Dylan said when they were outside. "You'll be warmer there."

She nodded and headed off toward Geoffrey's carriage. Dylan watched her stiff back as she walked away from him and thought how much in contrast that was with the woman who only moments before had been so pliant and willing in his arms. Thrusting his hands in the pockets of his jacket and hunching his shoulders against the suddenly chill wind, he went off to find the young lovers.

Caitlin was so lost in thought and miserable that she had reached Geoffrey's closed carriage and pulled open the door before she realized the carriage was occupied. Light from the dance hall spilled into it. So stunned she could not bring herself to turn away, Caitlin took in the sight of her sister lying across the carriage seat, naked to the waist, her skirts bunched high exposing her to Geoffrey who was poised over her, his own clothing in disarray and his hands touching Molly in the most private places possible.

"Molly!" Caitlin cried out. "Oh, Molly, what have you done?"

Geoffrey gave a low moan of distress and attempted to cover Molly's nakedness. Molly responded by languidly pushing herself to a half-sitting position and fixing her sister with a defiant stare. "It's not what you think, Cait," she said as she adjusted and refastened her gown. "Although had you not come along it might have been." She touched Geoffrey's face tenderly. "It's all right, darling," she told him. "Really, it's all right."

Geoffrey excused himself and stepped out of the carriage, disappearing quickly into the shadows. The young man mumbled apologies as he brushed past Caitlin.

"Molly, anyone could have come along," Caitlin said as she searched for exactly the proper way to respond to this situation.

"Is Dylan with you?" Molly asked as she finished fastening her gown and began expertly repairing her coiffure. She paused and glanced at her sister, her eyes sparkling with excitement. "Were the two of you hoping to find the carriage available?"

"Heavens, no," Caitlin replied, glad that her sister could not see the flush that covered her cheeks as she remembered how Dylan had kissed her not ten feet from this spot.

"Is everything all right, ladies?" Dylan's tone was one of nonchalance and something in it told Caitlin he had heard and perhaps even seen everything.

"Could you get Geoffrey, please? I believe he stepped over there for a moment," Caitlin nodded toward the wooded area just past the carriage. At that moment she realized that Geoffrey had selected this place to halt the carriage deliberately. It was sheltered by a grove of trees even though it was close to the hall. Only one carriage could fit in the small space. He had known that his tryst with Molly was unlikely to be noticed or disturbed.

"Molly, we are going home this minute," she said, climbing into the carriage and taking the seat next to her sister.

Molly responded by drawing herself as far as possible from her sister, folding her arms sullenly across her chest and pouting. When Geoffrey and Dylan returned they climbed into the other seat without comment. Dylan drove the carriage, while Geoffrey sat beside him, occasionally glancing miserably at Caitlin as if pleading for her cooperation.

When they reached the house, Caitlin climbed down from the carriage first. "Come along, Molly," she ordered. When Molly appeared on the verge of defying her, she added, "I don't think you want to oppose me, Molly. It would be very dangerous to make me any more upset with you than I am at the moment."

With a muttered comment no one could decipher, Molly left the carriage, but she turned back for a moment to reach a hand out to Geoffrey. "Don't worry, darling," she said softly. "Caitlin understands."

"Good night, gentlemen." Caitlin said firmly.

It was still fairly early for a Saturday night as Dylan followed the rutted path to his campsite after being dropped off by Geoffrey at the edge of the trail that led to his camp. He had considered stopping at Heathcote's for the duration of the evening, but everyone knew he'd taken the schoolmarm to the dance. His appearance at the tavern while the dance was still going on would cause comment and questions he wasn't interested in answering.

Geoffrey had been completely cowed by Caitlin's discovery of him making love to her sister. He told Dylan that things had not gone as far as it might have appeared and had sworn that there was no danger Molly was pregnant. Clearly, he hoped Dylan would carry that message to Caitlin. His greatest concern was for Molly and the reaction of her parents when Caitlin told them what she had seen.

"I doubt Cait will say a word," Dylan had assured him, and had wondered why he should believe that. Somebody as straitlaced as Caitlin was sure to believe that the best way to save her sister's reputation was to tell John Pearce so he could put a stop to his daughter's unchaperoned outings with the young politician.

Dylan stirred the fire at his campsite to life and went about his nightly routine of checking his stake for any signs of intruders or tampering, laying in a supply of wood to keep the fire going through the night, setting up his lean-to, and changing out of his "courtin' clothes" as Heathcote called them. He would not be going to church the following morning. He had no interest in being a part of the Pearce family scene on the day Caitlin revealed Molly's behavior to her parents.

He pulled out his journal and settled back to write down his observations of the day. At first his nightly entries had recorded his success in flushing out the valuable lead left behind by other miners. He took a lot of pride in his native ability to work the mines more deeply than other miners. There was an old saying that wherever there was a hole in the ground, you'd likely find a Cornishman—a *Cousin Jack* as they were often called—at the bottom of that hole.

Dylan faithfully recorded the day's work. He was at sixty feet now in a main that had been left for dead by others. He licked the tip of his pencil and considered what else to write. Occasionally he would include a commentary on the evening's entertainment at Heathcote's or some wrestling match he'd won at a contest sponsored by the mine owners. More recently he'd recorded his observations of Caitlin and her family, actually more of Caitlin than anyone else.

As frustrated as he was with her, he could not help writing about the way she had looked when she'd first appeared in her father's parlor to be escorted to the dance. That led to recording the details of holding her and dancing with her, and that led to writing page after page about the feelings that had engulfed him when he was kissing her outside the hall. He could not for the life of him understand what there was about the woman that drove him to such desire and need. She was bossy and haughty and a royal pain in the rear. The chances were better than average that she would only grow more shrewish with age, and yet every time he kissed her, all he could think of was what it might be like to bed her, to be wrapped in those long legs as he poured himself into her.

He paused, his senses on alert. Heathcote had said someone was stealing from the till at the saloon. Maybe the thief had decided this would be a good night to rob Dylan. Had he heard someone coming? Was that the crunch of a dried leaf or simply the wind? He eased his pen inside his journal to mark the place and reached for his gun. Pulling his blanket over some of his belongings to create the illusion of a body sleeping, he slipped away from the campsite into the darkness to await the intruder.

Caitlin kept her eye on the small glow of Dylan's campfire as she stumbled along the rocky terrain and rutted path. She'd dressed in her brother's old pants and shirt and had taken one of his jackets along with a cap that allowed her to tuck under all traces of her hair. It was the middle of the night, and the good citizens of Mineral Point had been asleep for hours, still she didn't want to take any chances on being seen.

"Dylan," she whispered as soon as she reached the edge of his campsite. He appeared to be sleeping like a baby. *Men,* she thought with disgust. Her sister had nearly ruined herself earlier, yet he was sleeping as if there were nothing to worry about. No doubt Geoffrey was sound asleep as well. "Dylan," she whispered louder. When he didn't move, she continued, knowing full well he was faking being asleep just to annoy her. "As much as it pains me to ask," she continued, "I need your help. So wake up and give me your full attention."

"Why are you whispering?" Dylan asked in a normal voice, and Caitlin gave a startled shriek and whirled around to find him leaning nonchalantly against a tree, a rifle cradled in his arms.

"Heavens above, you startled me out of ten years of my life," she said.

He ambled into the camp and put the gun away. "A man can't be too careful. Now what can I do for you, Miss Pearce?"

"We will have to accelerate our time schedule," she said without preamble.

"Our time schedule?"

She sighed impatiently. "For being married—pretending to marry."

He rubbed one hand thoughtfully over his jaw and studied her. "I see. Now you would be the same woman who was so mad at me a couple of hours ago that she could barely stand the sight of me."

"This is business, Mr. Tremaine."

"Oh, that's different. Please, be seated." He indicated the ground next to the fire. "By the way, that's a stunning outfit you're wearing, my dear."

She hitched up the pants that were two sizes too large and held up only by a length of ribbon she'd found on Molly's dressing table. "Will you please be serious? My sister's entire future is at stake."

"So, you have no concern at all about what this evening has done to your plan. This is about your sister."

"Well, of course. You saw and heard everything. I know you did. How can you be so calm?"

He sat on the ground and waited for her to join him. "Perhaps because she's not my sister. Perhaps because I know all too well how passion can carry young lovers away. A kiss that begins innocently enough, then turns into a hunger for more. And for a time that, too, is satisfied by certain concessions—the mingling of warm breath, the whispered confession of need, the taste of exposed skin, the full ripe heaviness of—"

"Stop it," she whispered, her face revealing her own shame at knowing exactly what he was saying.

"What do you want, Cait?" he asked after a long moment.

"I think we must be married as soon as possible. If we left tomorrow while everyone is at church, we could drive up to Madison, stay the night, send a letter to say we had eloped and return on Monday. I don't want to keep you from your work, of course, and this seems the most sensible plan."

"You know that nothing happened between Geoffrey and Molly tonight."

"How can you say that?" she cried. "You saw them, saw her . . . her nakedness."

"But there was no consummation. Geoffrey assures me of that, and I believe him. There is no danger your sister is pregnant."

"But what if someone else had opened that carriage door?"

"But they didn't. I expect that sort of lovemaking has been going on for some time between the two of them. They know what they are doing and when to stop. Geoffrey is not going to allow anything to compromise Molly's reputation. He loves her."

Caitlin turned to him, her eyes aglow with alarm. "Geoffrey is not the problem. Molly confessed to me tonight that had I not shown up and spoiled it for her, she had intended to have Geoffrey impregnate her. That way they could be married immediately."

"It doesn't work that way—she can't just decide that tonight's the night," Dylan said, trying to find a way to calm her.

"If not tonight then tomorrow or next week. I tell you she is determined, and she told me that if I reported what I had discovered tonight to our parents, she would say there was every chance she was pregnant so that Father would have to agree to their marriage." Two large tears spilled down either side of her face.

Dylan reached over and removed the cap, permitting her hair to spill over her shoulders. She had never looked more beautiful or vulnerable. He felt the increasingly familiar desire for her swell within him. "So, you want us to marry?"

She swiped at her tears impatiently with the back of her hand. "Yes. The plan I have devised is perfect. No one knows us in Madison, save for Geoffrey, and I've no doubt he'll be at church with the others tomorrow. We can drive up there, take rooms at the hotel for the night, send the message to say we have exchanged vows and return. Molly and Geoffrey will then be free to announce a proper engagement and plan the wedding I know she has always dreamed of having."

"And what about you, Caitlin? Have you never dreamed of a proper wedding?" he asked softly.

She shifted uncomfortably, but her jaw was set in its stubborn thrust. "Don't talk foolishness, Dylan. Will you do this or not?"

"I said I would," he replied testily. She was the most exasperating female he had ever encountered. Her need to always be the one in control irked him. Her refusal to admit her own feelings irked him. He felt the urge to teach her a lesson, to call her bluff and see what she might do. How far was she willing to go for the best interests of Molly?

"I will help you," he repeated. "However, the price has gone up."

"That's the second time you've threatened that, Mr. Tremaine," she said primly.

"This time I mean it—if you want this deal to work, then you'll pay the price I ask."

"What does that mean?" she asked with alarm.

"I haven't decided," he admitted with a wicked grin. "But if you want this enough, it won't matter what I ask of you. Do you want it that much, Caitlin?"

She stood up and walked a few feet away from him. He knew she was thinking about the challenge he had just thrown before her. Her quick mind would consider it from every possible angle, turning the thing around and around, thinking of the very worst he might ask of her.

After several long moments she turned and faced him defiantly. "Yes, Dylan. Regardless of what you may demand, I will hold you to our bargain."

"Then you'd best think about what it is you're getting out of this aside from saving Molly's reputation, Cait, because nobody is that selfless. There's something in this for you. I just haven't yet figured out what it is."

"But you'll keep your word?" she asked.

"Yes. I'll meet you tomorrow behind your father's store after everyone is in church. I'll have a buckboard and team waiting to take us to Madison. If you aren't there by the time church let's out, I'll assume you changed your mind."

"I won't change my mind," she said obstinately as she crammed her hair under the cap once again.

"And neither will I, Caitlin," he assured her. "Now let me at least see you to your street. You could fall and injure yourself stumbling around in the dark."

She accepted his offer to walk with her and waited while he lit a lantern to light their way. For most of the time they walked in silence, each lost in thoughts of what the new day was to bring. Occasionally he would take her elbow to help her over the uneven terrain. Each time she wondered at the rush of pleasure she felt at his touch and the distinct sensation of disappointment when that contact was broken.

"Thank you, Dylan," she said when they reached her street at last.

"I need you to know something before you go, Cait," he replied.

She looked up at him, but his face was in shadow. "What is it?"

"What I said tonight about people supposed to see us, I didn't mean . . . That is, I don't want you to think that. . . . It wasn't that I was kissing you because I was setting us up to be seen."

"Then why were you?" His words had hurt her deeply, reminding her that her days of being the eligible, pursued maiden had passed.

He chuckled. The low rumble she had come to recognize and enjoy. She knew he was smiling that cocky smile of his. "I was kissing you because I find I like kissing you, Cait. I like it a lot." And before she could make any reply or protest he lifted her face to his and kissed her. It was the same kind of knee-buckling, take-no-prisoners invasion of her mouth and senses that he'd delivered outside the dance, and it ended much too soon.

She stood there, her eyes closed, her lips pursed and swollen, her body and mind screaming for more. What she got was another of those infernal, all-knowing chuckles.

"And if you'll be truthful with yourself, Miss Pearce, you like being kissed by me almost as much as I like doing it. Good night, Caitie." He turned and started back down the deserted street, the lantern swinging at his side. He was whistling.

Six

It was easier than she thought to feign illness the following morning. After being up most of the night, she certainly looked ill. Even Molly put aside her anger in the face of her concern for Caitlin's health.

"Oh, Caitie," she cried when she saw Caitlin's drawn face and the dark circles beneath her eyes. "I'm so sorry. I didn't mean to worry you so. Now you've made yourself ill worrying over me, and that's just not necessary. Let me get you some tea and toast. I'll sit with you while the others go to church."

"No," Caitlin protested, and it came out a croak of panic.

"Now just listen to you. You're hoarse and your throat is raw. I'm sure it was the night air. I'll put honey in the tea." She ran off to the kitchen.

Caitlin sat up in bed and threw back the covers. *Now what?* she thought glancing toward the small carpetbag she'd packed the night before and hidden behind the door. She slipped out of bed and pushed the bag farther out of sight. She had to think of some way to assure that Molly would not stay in the house to play nursemaid.

"Here we are," Molly announced as she came down the hall. "Mother had the tea all made and toast as well. I told her you were ill and we would be staying in this morning." She balanced the tray on the edge of the dressing table, then poured a cup of tea from the steaming pot. "Try this."

Caitlin dutifully sipped the sweet brew. "Molly, you

should go. It's only a little sore throat. I just need some rest and I'll be fine. There's no need for you to sit with me, and what of Geoffrey? You really cannot leave the poor man to imagine all sorts of horrors when you don't appear for services."

Ah, the magic word—Geoffrey, Caitlin thought as she continued sipping the tea and watching her sister. Molly wrestled with loyalty to her sister and the need to reassure her true love that all was well.

"Well, perhaps you're right. After all, Geoffrey must think the worst has happened. You were so upset last night." Molly moved about the room, already beginning to groom herself for attending services. "If you'll promise to stay right there and not try to get up or do anything," she added.

"I'll be fine. You go along."

Relieved to have been given her sister's blessing, Molly smiled and refilled Caitlin's teacup. "Have I ever told you how glad I am to have you as my sister, Caitie? I don't care what anyone says about you, you're the sweetest, most understanding person I know—next to Geoffrey, of course."

"Of course," Caitlin said wryly. "Now hurry or you'll be late."

Molly blew her a kiss and raced down the stairway, calling out to the rest of the family, "Wait for me."

Caitlin rushed to the window and lifted the lace curtain just enough so that she could see the whole family get into the carriage and head toward the church. The house was silent and empty. She dropped the curtain and hurried to dress. She'd never had so much trouble selecting a traveling costume or accessories. Her hair seemed to have a mind of its own, and in the end, she left it down, pulled back at the nape of her neck with a clip. As she bent to retrieve the carpetbag from behind the door she caught sight of Molly's bottle of cologne set precariously on the edge of the dressing table. She reached to push it back before it fell to the floor, then on a whim she lifted the stopper and applied a bit of the scent to her wrists and neck as she had watched Molly do a thousand times. Immediately she worried that she had been too heavy-handed and Dylan would notice. She grabbed a handkerchief and scrubbed at her wrists to remove any excess scent. That was when she heard the bells peal. Church was in session.

She grabbed the bag and headed out the door, looking back once to make sure she hadn't forgotten anything. She paused in the act of closing the bedroom door and really looked at the room. It would never be the same again, this room she and Molly had shared since they were infants. It would not be *her room*. The next time she came here it would be as a visitor, for the family would think of her as a married woman living with her husband in the cottage on Shake Rag Street.

The last church bell chimed, and Caitlin hurried from the house and down the narrow streets and alleys to her father's store. As promised, Dylan was waiting. He had borrowed a rig and a team. The horses snorted and tossed their heads impatiently. They seemed as anxious as she was to be on their way. When he spotted her, Dylan hobbled the horses and jumped down to relieve her of the bag and help her aboard. He was relaxed and smiling. "Good morning," he said cheerfully as if he pretended to elope every Sunday morning.

They didn't pass a soul on their way to Madison. Caitlin kept up a constant chatter throughout the trip, and it seemed that the more she talked, the less cheerful Dylan became. She went over every minute detail of the plan—how they would need to secure hotel rooms the minute they arrived, for Geoffrey had mentioned something about a constitutional convention meeting and rooms were sure to be scarce. Then they needed to go right away and send a message letting her parents know that they had married. Caitlin knew the pair would be frantic once they returned from

services and found her gone. She'd closed the bedroom
door in the hope that they would think she was sleeping
and not want to disturb her.

"Do we get a chance for a meal anywhere in there?"
Dylan asked. Her constant need to plan everything to the
last detail annoyed him. He'd been looking forward to their
little adventure before she'd managed to take all the fun
out of it. Every time he allowed himself to think that maybe
what was happening between them went beyond a simple
business arrangement, Caitlin Pearce made sure to remind
him that what they had was a simple bargain, no more.

"Of course." She reached for her reticule and pulled out
a roll of bills. She saw Dylan's astonished expression. "As
I explained, I've been able to save quite a bit living at
home as I do," she explained. "Here."

She thrust the money in his direction.

"I don't want your money, Caitlin," he said and focused
on some distant horizon, refusing to acknowledge the
money.

"It's to pay for the rooms and the food," she explained.
"It will look odd if I pay the bills."

"I'm paying the bills," he said through gritted teeth.

"Oh, no, Dylan. That's not acceptable. I mean I cannot
allow you to—"

"Caitlin, could you just for once shut up and trust somebody else to handle things?"

It was clear he didn't expect or want an answer, and that
ended the conversation for the rest of the trip.

Madison was under construction. The state's capital city
was bustling with activity, but had a long way to go to
match the glory of other, more developed communities in
the state. Caitlin glanced around at the rutted and muddy
streets, the hastily constructed shops and business establishments. If Geoffrey maintained his political career, he
and Molly would likely live here. Caitlin wondered if her
sister knew what she was giving up in order to follow her

true love. Madison seemed downright primitive compared to Mineral Point.

Dylan pulled the team to a halt in front of a hotel that appeared to be one of the more respectable establishments along the street. "There's a livery across the street," he commented as he helped her down from the carriage. "Might as well see to boarding the horse. Maybe we can hire a youngster to carry word back that we're married. There's no sense worrying your folks unnecessarily."

Caitlin nodded, surprised that he would think at all about carrying out the details of her plan. He had given the distinct impression that he was harboring second thoughts about his part in this fiasco. Actually the silence he had enforced had given her time to think. She didn't like doing things on the spur of the moment and was grateful for at least a little time to gather her thoughts and consider the details of her plan.

"That would be best," she agreed as she struggled to follow him across the street made treacherous by several days of rain and by the amount of traffic rumbling by. The mud sucked at her shoes, and she paused to gather her skirts in one hand in a futile attempt to rescue them from being completely ruined.

"For heaven's sake," Dylan huffed and lifted her high in his arms just as a buckboard pulled by two wild-eyed horses narrowly missed trampling them both. He strode the rest of the way across the street, not looking at her or seeming to be at all aware of the close contact of their bodies. Unceremoniously he set her down just inside the entrance to the livery.

"Thank you," she said curtly as she adjusted her bonnet and clothing and attempted to scrape some of the mud off her shoes.

"Have you got some paper and a pencil? You'll need to give the kid a note to carry."

Caitlin rummaged through her purse and retrieved the

required pencil and paper. "What should I say?" she said more to herself than to him.

"Just tell them we're married," he answered as he beat his hat against his thigh to remove the dust of the ride. His statement immediately caught the attention of the blacksmith.

"Well, newlyweds, is it?" The barrel-chested, bearded man grinned at them. "Congratulations, folks."

Dylan ignored the congratulations. "We'll need to board our team for the night. And, I wonder if you could recommend a lad to carry a message to . . . to my wife's family down in Mineral Point?"

The blacksmith squinted at each of them in turn. "Your folks gonna be upset, are they?"

"We're of age," Dylan said dryly and watched Caitlin start and reject several versions of the message.

"Just say—Married Dylan. Home tomorrow," he dictated impatiently.

Caitlin gave him a look intended to silence him and kept working, writing a few words, then scratching them out and beginning again. She ignored the arrival of another customer until she heard the clerk greet the man.

"Ah, Mr. MacKenzie, what brings you in on this fine day? If you'd be wanting to send another note to that sweetheart of yours over in Mineral Point, these two are fixing to hire my boy to run a message for them. You could split the cost." The clerk winked broadly, then added, "You ought to do what these two did—just take her away and marry her."

Caitlin slowly turned to face Geoffrey who stood just inside the wide door looking from Dylan to her to the blacksmith and back again.

"Hello, Geoffrey, I thought you were still in Mineral Point," Caitlin said.

"I . . . that is, I was so . . ." He glanced at the curious blacksmith who was clearly eavesdropping and lowered his voice. "I'm sorry for what happened last night, Caitlin. I was so upset that I rode up here. I didn't want to put Molly in an awkward position at church this morning if you had . . . that is, if her parents. . . ."

Caitlin took pity on the man who would soon be her brother-in-law. "I didn't tell my parents," she said. "This gentleman is right. You should indeed send Molly a message. She'll be beside herself with worry when you aren't in church."

Geoffrey nodded and smiled. "Is it true then?" he asked. "You're married?"

"Well," Caitlin began, attempting to stall for time in order to come up with the best possible answer.

"Yep, just tied the knot," Dylan answered immediately with a huge grin.

"Well, that's just wonderful," Geoffrey said, shaking Dylan's hand heartily and hugging Caitlin. "Just wonderful. Does the family know?"

"Well, we just left the justice of the peace. We're about to send word now," Dylan replied, and Caitlin wondered at how easily the lies rolled off his tongue. "Do you think they'll approve?"

"Of course. Molly is going to be thrilled. I must get word to her immediately—when you're done, of course, Caitlin," he added politely. "Are you staying here in Madison then?"

"Just for tonight. Can you recommend a place?"

"I can do better than that." He searched his pockets until he discovered a piece of paper and dashed off a quick message to Molly. "Here, Willie, have your boy deliver this as well as Miss—that is, Mrs. Tremaine's message. Cait, you take your time here. Dylan and I will go across the street and make all the arrangements. No, no, I insist," he added when he saw that Caitlin was about to protest. "We'll come back for you in a few minutes; then I want to treat both of you to a celebratory lunch."

Before Caitlin could respond, Geoffrey had wrapped his arm around Dylan's shoulders and was leading the way back across the street to the hotel. "You old sly dog," he teased as the two men left the shop. Dylan was grinning broadly.

When they reached the hotel, Geoffrey took full charge. Dylan stood to one side thinking about how upset Caitlin was going to be when she realized that Geoffrey had arranged for them to stay in the bridal suite—together. He began to dread the time they still needed to spend together. He had noted that her defense when she could no longer control the events around her was to resort to her role as teacher. *Lord almighty,* Dylan thought, *she probably brought along those infernal readers of hers and she'll insist we work on my lessons.* He knew that Caitlin would do this in order to show her appreciation for his help, but he really didn't think he could stand spending the night with her and playing student to her teacher.

"They'll take care of everything," Geoffrey said as he handed Dylan the key. "Let's go get Cait and have some lunch while they prepare the room and unpack your things. I took the liberty of ordering a tub and plenty of hot water."

The image of Cait naked in the bath flashed across Dylan's mind. Of course, it was wishful thinking. She'd never in a million years go for getting undressed with him around. She'd probably sit up all night in her traveling clothes, waiting for daylight, once she realized they'd be sharing a room. Of course, that didn't mean he couldn't enjoy the bath. An idea began to form, one that gave him enormous pleasure. "Yes, let's go get Cait," he said to Geoffrey. "Suddenly, I'm famished."

By the time the trio went to lunch at a private club for legislators and their guests, Caitlin noticed that Geoffrey and Dylan seemed to have become the best of friends. Geoffrey insisted on a champagne toast, which he shared with everyone in the club by standing, raising his glass, and toasting them with, "To two wonderful people who I hope very soon will be able to call me family." To Caitlin's chagrin everyone in the club stood and raised a glass in their direction. Dylan grinned and lifted his glass to her, then leaned in to kiss her cheek, an action Geoffrey and the others applauded heartily. Caitlin forced a smile.

After lunch, Geoffrey kissed her cheek and hugged Dylan. "I have a meeting with some colleagues, and I suspect you would rather be alone. I want you both to know you have made me the happiest man alive today," he enthused, so emphatically that Caitlin was afraid he might actually start to weep. "Molly and I have waited so long for this day. God bless you." He hurried back inside the club, waving one last time as he closed the heavy oak doors.

"Shall we walk back to the hotel, my dear?" Dylan said with a grin as he offered her his arm with a courtly bow.

She took his arm, but did not reply. *How much champagne has he had?* she wondered. She risked a glance up at him. He was gliding along beside her, tipping his hat to everyone they passed, smiling broadly as if he had the most wonderful secret.

At the hotel, they were warmly received by the desk clerk. "Everything is arranged, sir," he said with a conspiratorial wink at Dylan. "We have placed all of your luggage in our bridal suite." He handed Dylan the pen and turned the guest register so he could sign it.

"The bridal suite?" Caitlin whispered, her eyes wide with shock.

"Geoffrey insisted," he replied innocently. "Besides, the hotel is full," he lied.

"Mrs. Tremaine, please be assured that you and your husband have done us a great honor today. You are our first wedding couple, and we hope that once you have experienced the hospitality of our hotel, you will tell all of your friends."

"In other words, it's on the house . . . free," Dylan said

with a charming grin. "Thank you, sir. Please see that we aren't disturbed," he added as he pressed a coin into the desk clerk's hand. "Come, my dear," he said as for the second time that day, he swept Caitlin high in his arms.

This time he headed straight for the wide curved stairway that led to the upper floors and the bridal suite. "Put me down," she whispered. "You're making a spectacle of yourself." She glanced around at the hotel staff and the other guests gathered in the lobby. All eyes were on them. Everyone was smiling.

He gazed at her with lowered lids as he paused on the landing. "They love it, my dear. It can't hurt to make these people happy," he said, then kissed her full on the mouth.

Because her own mouth had been open to voice yet another protest, he took full advantage. His kiss was aflame with passion. It was as if all of the frustrations of the day were released in that kiss. She felt vanquished, entranced, and utterly captivated. She wanted more.

She was barely aware of the hoots and cheers from the people gathered in the lobby until Dylan broke the kiss and favored his supporters with a triumphant grin. Then he took the remaining stairs two at a time, strode down a long hallway to a door separated from the others by a small vestibule and standing slightly ajar. He pushed it open with his foot, carried her through a small sitting room and straight into the bedroom where he deposited her in the middle of the softest bed she had ever known.

"It's time we discussed my fee for helping you, Caitlin," he announced casually as he removed his coat and hat, then strolled around the room, closing the drapes on each of the windows. When he had completed the task, he lit a lamp on the bedside table and sat on the edge of the bed. The lamplight cast his features in shadow, and she could not read his expression.

Caitlin immediately pushed herself higher against the multiple pillows as she considered possibilities for escape.

"If you scream, no one will come," he said softly as he began removing her muddy shoes. "They will think you have been caught up in the passion of our lovemaking. They will smile and shake their heads in amazement at my stamina, but they will not come." He dropped the shoes on the carpet and moved so that his face was very close to hers. He fingered the ribbons on her bonnet.

"What are you going to do?" she asked, her eyes wild with fear. *How could I have misjudged him so?*

"I am going to do you a favor, Cait. In the next twenty-four hours before we return to Mineral Point, I am going to be the teacher. I am going to teach you about lovemaking." He loosened the ties and removed her bonnet. "I am going to give you the look only a woman who has been loved repeatedly can have." He began slowly opening the buttons on her suit jacket. "I am going to leave no doubt in anyone's mind—including your father's—that our love was so overpowering that you could no more have waited out the time of a proper engagement and nuptial than you could fly," he finished with a whisper as he leaned in and kissed her lightly on the lips.

She fixed him with a look of complete control. "Let me up from this bed, Dylan," she commanded.

"No," he replied.

Caitlin was unsure of her next move. Her students never defied her. Dylan had never defied her. Until now, he had gone along with everything she'd wanted. "No?" she repeated incredulously. "If you think for one minute . . ."

He eased her jacket off her shoulders, an action that pinioned her arms to her sides and effectively left her powerless to strike out at him as he pulled her hard against his chest. "Trust me, Cait. I won't do anything to compromise you," he replied just before kissing her.

She knew she should turn her head, fight him, but something inside her wanted to show him that she was unafraid, that he could not win. She forced her own tongue past his and invaded his mouth. With satisfaction, she felt his surprise as he let down his guard for a moment. Taking advantage, she bit him hard on the lip and scampered off the bed. By the time he had recovered she was halfway to the door.

"It won't work," he said thickly as he nursed his tender lip. "If you leave the room, everyone downstairs will know. They'll talk. It'll get back to Geoffrey and eventually to Molly and your family. Your father will be convinced you have done the one foolish thing you ever did in your life. In his zeal to save you, he will pull strings to have the marriage annulled and you and your sister will be right back where you were before I came on the scene. Only this time your father will be watching you like a hawk. You will not only not have saved your sister's virtue, you will have sacrificed your own precious independence." He shrugged and lay back on the bed, his hands folded behind his head, one ankle crossed over the other.

He's right, Caitlin thought. *His logic and analysis are perfect. For someone who can't read and write, the man has an uncanny sense of people.* "Be reasonable," she said, easing back into the room and taking a position next to the dressing table where she noticed her things had been unpacked and laid out for her. "I am not likely to sacrifice my own virtue in order to save my sister's."

"No one's suggesting you should," he said.

"But you are," she argued, advancing a step toward him as she pursued her point. "You said . . ."

He swung into a sitting position, causing her to retreat a step. To her horror and fascination he began removing his boots and then his shirt. "I said I was going to teach you how to *look* like a woman who had been loved. It's the price I'm asking and believe me, it's a most generous offer. You'll thank me for it in the end," he said with a cocky grin as he stripped off the shirt and stood to hang it on the bedpost.

"What do you get out of it?" she asked, curious in spite of herself.

"Trust me. We both come out winners. Now, if you'll excuse me, I asked the hotel staff to prepare a hot bath. The water should be just the proper temperature." He strolled to the bathroom, leaving the door open.

Caitlin needed to think, and she thought best when she was active, so she began bustling about the room, hanging his shirt in the wardrobe, picking up his boots and discarded socks. When she stood up from retrieving the socks, she caught a glimpse of his naked backside as he stepped into the tub and eased himself into the hot water. She was momentarily spellbound as she drank in the beauty of his hard muscular body.

"Have you ever seen a naked man, Caitlin?" he called as if reading her thoughts.

She moved quickly to the other side of the room and began hanging up her own jacket in the large wardrobe.

"Have you, Cait? You'll need to know things. The women will talk to you now. They'll expect you to know. If you look shocked or surprised, they'll know the truth. Are you ready for that kind of gossip?" He didn't seem to expect an answer. "Lesson one . . . the differences between the male and female form," he announced.

"Will you be long?" she asked as if she hadn't heard a word. "I'd like to freshen up and change for dinner."

"Change away," he called grandly and punctuated his command by sliding down into the tub until he had dunked his whole head, then surfacing with a hoot of satisfaction.

Since it appeared he would be occupied for at least a few minutes Caitlin thought this would be an excellent time to change out of her traveling clothes. She removed her blouse and skirt and hung them in the wardrobe. She reached under her petticoat to unfasten and remove her stockings.

"Cait, come scrub my back," Dylan called startling her

as she stood before the mirror, examining herself in her camisole and petticoat.

"Scrub it yourself," she replied haughtily.

"If you don't come, I'll be forced to come get you," he answered. "And I won't bother covering myself with a towel." She heard noises that sounded as if he were prepared to deliver on his threat.

"All right, I'm coming, but you are to keep your back to me at all times and your eyes averted. Is that clear?"

The answer was a low chuckle of victory.

The bathroom was hot and steamy, and she was relieved to see that the surprisingly large mirror was fogged over. He could not see her. She relaxed and sat on the edge of the tub behind him. She kept her eyes averted from any possible view of his nakedness as she reached for the long-handled scrub brush and the soap. "I believe, Dylan, that the purpose of the extended handle on this brush is to allow a person to scrub his own back."

"But where's the fun in that?" he said huskily as he hooked one arm around her waist and pulled her into the tub so that she was lying across him. Water sloshed over the edges and onto the floor. In seconds she was soaked. The more she struggled, the wetter she got and the more aware she became of his body beneath hers.

"Lesson one—the differences between male and female forms," he said, his mouth next to her ear, his tongue tracing the path of the interior of her ear. "A man grows harder in lovemaking while a woman becomes softer, fuller." He brushed his thumbs across the tips of her nipples, plainly visible through the wet linen of her camisole as he continued his intoxicating exploration of her ear.

"Don't," she whispered, her eyes closed against the desire she felt seeping through her. It was less a plea to him than to herself. She felt a cool dryness on her chest and opened her eyes to find her camisole open. She gasped and reached up to cover herself.

"Leave it," Dylan commanded gently. "You need to understand the beauty of your body, the power of what it can do to a man." His voice came from just next to her ear, steady, soothing, hypnotic. "See how your excitement is exposed through the heaving of your breasts, the deepening red of your nipples as they swell with desire and need. If I touch them like this, see how they pucker, begging to be kissed."

The liquid heat that had seemed lodged in her breasts flowed freely now, pooling in her loins as she pressed her legs tightly together to prevent its release. "Dylan," she pleaded, tears of frustration and shame wetting her lashes. Frustration because she seemed powerless to stop him, shame because deep down she really didn't want him to stop. How could she willingly permit him to humiliate her so?

The night before he had asked her what she got from all of this, suggesting that her motives were not entirely related to Molly's welfare. She wondered if he could be right. She had never known the love of a man. This might be as close as she could come to understanding the magic Molly had found with Geoffrey, and try as she might to deny it, she had not been able to think of anything other than the sight of Molly and Geoffrey half-naked and entwined and to imagine Dylan doing that with her.

She glanced at Dylan and saw that he was watching her intently. With a heavy sigh, he reached for one of a stack of towels and covered her with it. "The water's getting cold," he said as he helped her extricate herself from the tub. "Go, dry off and change." Cait clutched the towel to her exposed breasts and hurried from the bathroom.

Dylan watched her go, taking note of her obvious relief to be away from him. He'd been fooling himself to think he could woo her, to think she would permit herself to get caught up in a moment of desire and passion. By the time Dylan had dried himself and dressed, all was quiet in the next room. He wondered if she had slipped out. The bedroom was unoccupied, although the drapes had been opened and the lamp extinguished. The rumpled bedding had been straightened. Caitlin was not in the room. He quickly pulled on his boots, grabbed his jacket and hat and headed for the door. There was no telling where she might have gone, and Madison was no place for a woman alone.

He never made it to the door. She was in the sitting room, reclining on a chaise lounge as she calmly read a book. Her hair, freshly brushed, was framing her face. She was wearing a heavy brocaded dressing gown, and she looked good enough to eat.

"Are you going out?" she asked as if nothing had transpired between them in the bathroom.

"I was . . . I thought . . . No. I'll wait for you to dress, and we'll go out for dinner together." He put his hat and jacket on a chair and walked over to the window. Suddenly he felt shy with her. He could feel her studying him over the tops of those infernal glasses she wore.

"I've been thinking that perhaps you were right. Perhaps we should have dinner served here," she suggested. "It plays so well with the rest of our ruse. Surely the hotel staff will talk in detail about how we were so in love that we disappeared into the bridal suite and did not emerge until the following day?"

Dylan studied her. She was up to something, he was sure of it. That quick mind of hers had been working away ever since he'd relented and let her leave the bathroom. Once again she had somehow regained the upper hand.

"My price stands," he said through gritted teeth.

She closed the book and removed her glasses. "Yes. I've been thinking about that. I believe it's a fair offer you've made, Dylan. I only want to make certain I have considered it from every angle."

Now she had his full attention. "You've reconsidered?"

"Yes. I'll admit you took me by surprise, but then I

realized that the sort of thing you did in there, pulling me into the bath with you and all is exactly what impetuous lovers do, isn't it?" She strolled to the standing full-length gilded mirror and studied herself intently. "And I see that you are right. There has been a change due no doubt to a process of discovery I have begun about my own body." As if she had forgotten he was in the room at all, she gently cupped her breasts and kneaded them. "Amazing," she whispered, then turned to him with a smile. "We shall look on this as a scientific experiment, Dylan."

His face turned beet red. "Ex-experiment," he managed to stammer.

"Yes. Now that I've had time to think of it, I'm really quite anxious for us to continue." She came across the room and stood close to him, reaching up to caress his face. "You see, I could never understand what Molly was babbling about when she said that she must think of Geoffrey and his *needs.* She would say it just that way— *needs*—as if it were quite a serious condition."

He caught her hand at her wrist and slowly lowered it to her side. "If you think you can shame me into changing my mind, Caitlin, think again. My terms stand," he said. "Nothing you can do will change that. I plan to take something more from this than a few reading lessons."

She turned and strolled the length of the room and back, the same way he'd seen her pace the length of the schoolhouse a dozen times. "Of course. Although, frankly, Dylan, you have no idea of the wealth the ability to read offers. But I understand that in your shoes, that might seem like meager repayment for what I've asked you to do." She paused and studied him for a moment from head to toe. "This is what Molly spoke of, isn't it? The *needs* of a man. It doesn't matter then whether you love the woman or not. It's purely of a physical nature, is that right?" She did not seem to expect an answer as she returned to her pacing. "Interesting," she said to herself.

He wanted to wring her neck, but he also wanted to kiss her senseless and then make her lie on that ridiculous fancy lounge while he showed her just what need was all about.

"So when we kiss," she continued, "something happens. Each of us changes in some minuscule way. And if the circumstances surrounding the kiss are sufficiently risky, that heightens the excitement for both parties. That would explain why couples long married do not exhibit that same passion seen in lovers like Molly and Geoffrey. Molly and Geoffrey are indulging in something forbidden."

By this time he had surrendered and taken a seat on the edge of the chaise to wait out her little charade. He was certain she thought she had come upon a solution that would make him back away and keep his distance. What, in fact, she had done was strengthen his resolve to call her bluff, make her his one way or another, before they ended this little exercise and he headed off for the gold fields of California.

"So, how do you want to handle this?" he asked as if he didn't really care one way or another.

For the first time since he'd entered the room, she hesitated. "Handle this?"

"The lessons? Do you want me to go through the whole thing now before we eat or after supper or what?"

"Well, let's see. I'm not clear on what exactly is involved. You did say that you would do nothing to compromise my virtue."

"I said I would do nothing to compromise your reputation. We're married as far as the world is concerned, Cait. That in itself opens a lot of *forbidden* doors." He had the satisfaction of watching her swallow hard and nervously play with the sash of her dressing gown.

"I was thinking we could exchange lessons. We would read for a while and then you could explain the art of . . . you know."

"Making love? Well, it's a little more complicated than

that. You see you'd be hard put to explain how you teach a person to read. You just have to do it. Teaching you to make love isn't all that different. It'll take some time. It'll also take some showing," he added, and was pleased to see her blush.

"I see."

"Hey, here's an idea." He moved close to her, lifting one curl of her hair and twisting it around his finger as he explained his plan. He spoke in a low seductive voice. "Why don't we go downstairs and have dinner in the hotel dining room? What you said about staying locked up here for the whole time is good, but what if folks were able to observe us dining out, eyes only for each other, our passion boiling beneath the surface to the point we can barely keep our hands off each other." He tucked the curl behind her ear and trailed his finger down the side of her neck. "It'll be good practice for when we return to Mineral Point," he added seductively. When she looked up at him, then immediately lowered her lashes, he knew she would offer no protest if he kissed her. Instead he gave her a sharp smack on the fanny. "Go on now and get dressed. I'm starving."

Seven

The dining room was crowded when they arrived. The low buzz of gossip that had followed them as they made their way to the table through the crowded room told Caitlin that they had been recognized as the newlyweds. The proprietor led them to a small table near the front window. His actions made it clear that he saw them as good advertising for his establishment and he wanted to place them at the center of attention. He held the chair for Caitlin as Dylan seated himself, then handed them menus.

Dylan immediately laid his menu aside. "You look lovely, my dear," he said reaching across the small table to cover her hand with his. The waiter smiled as he filled the water goblets, then disappeared. "Put down your menu and look at me, Cait," Dylan said in a low voice meant for no one but her. "That's it. Now think about something that excites you, that makes your eyes sparkle, your breath quicken."

"Dylan, I—"

"I'm thinking of you with me in the bath, the way the water soaked you, exposing you to me, the way the buds of your nipples flowered under my touch." He smiled. Her breathing had escalated noticeably and her face glowed in the candlelight.

"That's enough," she rasped. "Someone will hear you."

Dylan raised his eyebrows. "I thought you wanted me to teach you, to help you achieve that married glow." He shrugged as if it didn't matter to him one way or another and picked up his menu.

The waiter returned to take their order, which Dylan took charge of giving. He ordered a full meal of dumpling soup, chicken, potatoes, squash, and various other side dishes he found to his liking.

"You can't mean to eat all of that," Caitlin said incredulously when the waiter had left.

"Nope. You're going to eat some of it," he replied with a charming grin. He buttered a roll and held it out to her.

She reached to take it, but he pulled it back. "Let me feed you," he said.

"Are you mad?"

"Trust me, Cait. Just take a bite of the roll." He brought it to her lips and watched with satisfaction as she took a small bite; then he deliberately smeared a little butter on her lower lip. Before she could attend to it with her own napkin, he reached over and corrected the offense with the tip of his finger.

By the time the waiter brought their meals, Caitlin was a nervous wreck and hardly in the mood to eat. She noted that nothing seemed to affect Dylan's appetite. He attacked the food as if it might be the last food he saw for some time.

"Are you a good cook?" He used a crust of roll to soak up the gravy that had covered everything on the plate.

"I can cook," she replied defensively. She wasn't sure she would be able to manage the volume of food he evidently required, but she certainly knew how to cook.

"Aren't you going to eat?" he asked as he wiped his mouth and pushed back his own plate—a plate wiped so meticulously clean that Caitlin wondered if the kitchen staff would bother to wash it.

"I'm not that hungry," she replied, and pushed her own barely touched plate back an inch.

Dylan frowned. "Are you feeling all right?"

"I could use some air," she said. *Anything to buy some time before going back to that room where we will be alone. Somehow once again Dylan has managed to turn the tables, using my strategy to his advantage.*

"Let's go for a walk," he suggested and signaled the waiter. When he had paid the bill, he made a show of escorting her from the dining room. Once in the lobby, he ushered her to a chair. "Wait here and I'll go up and get your wrap."

She watched him climb the stairs. He really was a thoughtful man, and so graceful in the way he moved. She watched his long legs take the stairs two at a time as if they were too shallow to take singly. She noted the easy rhythm of his hips as he moved away from her. She recalled the glimpse she had had of him naked as he stepped into the tub and closed her eyes against the rush of memories that followed.

"Caitlin, are you sure you're all right?" He was back, holding her cloak, a look of sincere concern lining his brow.

"Of course." She stood up and let him place the cloak on her shoulders. She wondered if he felt any of the tension she did whenever they were near one another, even in such routine and public circumstances. *Of course, he doesn't,* she chided herself. *Honestly, you think more like a love-starved spinster every day.*

The night air was bracing, with a hint of winter to come. They could smell wood fires from the chimneys of the dwellings that lined the side streets. They walked for several blocks in silence, but there was nothing strained about it. Caitlin had thought more than once that she had never known someone like Dylan—someone with whom she could simply be herself.

Gradually Dylan began to talk about the building of the capital, commenting on things Geoffrey had told them about the political battles behind the choice of Madison, shaking his head and laughing as he considered the ridiculous egos of powerful men. Caitlin would occasionally insert a comment, mostly aimed at keeping him talking. She had never had such a conversation with him, had not known his views of politics and the world in general.

"Ah, there's the lake," he said, pointing ahead as he took her hand and headed for the shore. "Lake Mendota. Beautiful, isn't it?"

"Geoffrey says it will freeze in another month and we can all come ice-skating," Caitlin told him. "Do you ice-skate?" *Tomorrow, I shall tell everyone we are married and yet I know so little about you,* she thought.

Dylan laughed. "I can stand up on skates—when I'm not falling down."

Caitlin smiled. "You're a nice man, Dylan Tremaine," she said at a loss to put into words what she was really feeling.

"And you're cold," he observed. "Here." He took off his coat and wrapped it around her, then pulled her into a hug intended to warm her rather than start anything amorous. "Look at the way the moon shines on the lake there," he said, his chin resting lightly on top of her head. "It looks like a street you could just walk out on and get lost in the stars, doesn't it? I used to go down to the sea at night back in Cornwall. I'd stand there at the crest of a cliff, dreaming of coming here, finding my fortune."

"And here you are," she said, lifting her face so that she could get a better look at him.

He stared down at her for a long moment. "We should go back," he said huskily.

"Yes," she agreed. "You must be cold." She was reluctant to let the moment pass, but forced herself to step away from him and turn away from the moonlit lake.

Their walk back to the hotel was silent, but this time the air between them was charged. When they reached the suite, Caitlin waited for him to resume the advances he had begun earlier. In the walk back from the lake, she had determined that she would permit him certain liberties—after all, this counterfeit marriage might be her only chance to ever know what being with a man was like. On top of that, he had needs and she was asking a great deal of him. It would be wrong not to make him as comfortable as possible, she reasoned, without compromising her own virtue in the process, of course.

"You go along and get ready for bed," he said as he lit the bedroom lamp. "It's been a long day, and tomorrow will be a full day as well." He handed her the dressing gown from the hook in the wardrobe. "Go on now," he urged.

She took her time in the bathroom, paying careful attention to the brushing of her hair, the drape of her nightgown and the dressing gown that covered it. Finally she knew she could stall no longer. Like a sacrificial lamb, she opened the door of the bathroom.

The bed linens had been turned back and the lamp lowered. Dylan's shirt and vest were neatly draped over a small chair, his boots were on the floor. "Dylan?"

He appeared at the door leading to the sitting room. He was naked to the waist and barefoot. Caitlin swallowed hard, but did not turn away. "I'm ready," she said softly.

"Get into bed," he directed, coming all the way into the room. "Go on," he urged when she hesitated. He held the covers back for her as she removed her dressing gown and sat on the edge of the bed.

"Do you usually sleep with a bunch of pillows like this?" he asked.

She shook her head. "One. I use one," she answered.

"Okay. Then I'll take one for myself, and we'll get these others out of your way."

To her surprise he lined up the extra pillows on the side of the bed next to her—the side where she had assumed he would take his position. "Sweet dreams," he said as he kissed her lightly on the forehead and headed for the sitting room. "I'll be right out here if you should need anything." He gave her one of his engaging grins. "Anything at all," he added and chuckled as he softly closed the door.

Caitlin lay looking at the ceiling long after he had stopped moving around in the other room. The man's constantly shifting moods tormented her, and never was she more distressed than at times like this when he showed such tenderness.

The following morning Geoffrey sent word that he wanted to meet them for breakfast in the hotel dining room. His note implied that he had a surprise for them. Neither Caitlin nor Dylan had gotten much sleep, though neither would admit it to the other as they took turns packing and dressing. When they met Geoffrey in the dining room he made no bones about the fact that they looked exhausted. "My heavens, did you get any sleep at all?" he teased.

Caitlin's face turned scarlet as she realized he was implying they had spent the night making love. *Good heavens,* she thought, *do people really do that?*

As usual Dylan responded to Geoffrey's teasing with a good-natured grin. "None of your business," he said. "What's this surprise?"

"We're taking the stage back to Mineral Point—the three of us. Molly is to have everyone at the station to greet you and take you immediately to a celebratory party at your parents' house, Cait." He seemed very proud of himself. "Molly sent word back by the blacksmith's son last night," he admitted with a proud grin.

"We have a wagon and team here," Caitlin protested. "There will be plenty of time for a party once we're back and settled." *A party! With everyone I know congratulating me, watching me with Dylan, studying us for the telltale signs of newlywed bliss.*

"I've already arranged for that," Geoffrey said. "A friend is headed that way today and he'll return the rig for you—it saves him having to rent one himself. He's delighted to do it."

"What time do we need to be at the station?" Dylan asked as he leaned back to permit the waitress to serve him another stack of pancakes. Clearly he saw no problem with the plan. Caitlin nudged him with her foot and gave him a look of warning. He glanced at her and smiled. "You can take a nap on the stage, sweetheart," he said.

Sweetheart? How could he not see the problems this presented for them?

"Then it's all set," Geoffrey said gleefully. "The stage leaves at one. I'll send a porter for your bags and we can all meet at the station. Now I must bid you farewell until then. I have some business to attend to before we leave. Good-bye for now." He kissed Caitlin on the cheek and shook hands with Dylan.

As soon as he was out the door, Caitlin turned to Dylan, prepared to give him an earful about the foolhardiness of Geoffrey's plan. But Dylan had stood up and put on his coat. "I have an errand to run myself, Cait," he said. "I'll come back for you in time to get to the station. Are you all right? You're looking a little pale."

"I'm fine," she said. *Just not used to men running my life—something I assure you will not continue, Mr. Tremaine.*

"Why don't you go back to the room and rest for a bit? You really should eat something. No wonder you're so small—you don't eat enough to keep a bird alive." He picked up a piece of bread from her plate and took a bite of it as he left. "I'll see you around noon," he assured her. He seemed in a terrible hurry to leave.

Caitlin lingered over her morning tea as she gazed out the window and observed the activity on the street. The waitress had seated them at the same table they'd shared the evening before. If they were truly lovers, this table would hold significance for them for years to come, but it was an artifice just like everything else about their relationship. She suddenly felt sad, for she realized that under other circumstances she and Dylan might have shared something special—a friendship that would comfort them into their later years at the very least. Growing up Caitlin had always gravitated toward the boys in her circle of friends. She enjoyed their games and conversation more. She felt out of touch with things that interested the girls. Yes, in another time and place, she and Dylan might have been the best of friends.

When Dylan returned she was back in their room, perched nervously on the edge of the chaise. The porter had come for the luggage as promised, and there was nothing more for her to do than wait for Dylan to return.

"This is hopeless," she said the minute he entered the room. "We can't possibly pull this off. I had counted on the time we would have together on the way home to get our stories straight. Now Geoffrey will be with us every step of the way, and then Molly will make certain the entire town is there to welcome us. There's Mother and Father to deal with. Father is sure to be upset—"

"It'll work out," Dylan said as he sat down beside her. "Here. See if this fits." He handed her a small box. The label indicated it was from a jeweler.

Momentarily surprised into silence she slowly opened the hinged lid. Inside was a plain gold band.

"I thought folks might be looking for that—you know, on your finger. Try it on," he urged.

She pulled off her glove and slipped the ring on. It fit perfectly. Suddenly she was overcome with emotion, the stress of the past few days coupled with Dylan's surprising knack for thinking things through and doing exactly the right thing. She started to cry.

"Ah, Cait, the hard part's over for us. From here on out, it just gets easier, you'll see. The thing you need to do is relax and enjoy yourself. You've done nothing wrong, and no one is going to be the wiser. We're right on schedule here, and you can see how happy you've made Geoffrey. Why, Molly is liable to bowl us both over with her relief and gratitude the minute we step off that stage today. Everybody's going to be happy for you because they want you to be happy. They'll think you've found what every girl's supposed to want."

As he talked he awkwardly stroked her back. It was the most tentative he had ever been with her, and it made the moment all the more special. She cried harder.

"Come on now," he coaxed, a bit of genuine panic in his voice, "this won't do. Geoffrey will think I've been mean to you or something. Dry your tears." He thrust a kerchief toward her. "I'll just wet a washcloth with some cool water." He was back in seconds gently dabbing at her face with the cool cloth. "There now. I didn't mean to upset you. I just thought the ring was a detail you might have overlooked. I can return it if you'd rather not use it."

"It's perfect," she managed to gulp out, which started a fresh stream of tears. "Thank you, Dylan," she blubbered.

"You're welcome, I think," he replied lifting her chin to study her face. "Cait, you've got to get into the spirit of this thing and have some fun with it."

"I don't know how," she said, her eyes more luminous than usual through the tears.

He smiled at her. "Yes, you do. You have fun when I kiss you. I know you do." He kissed her. "See?"

She nodded.

"And yesterday you had some fun with me when you were parading around in that dressing gown, remember?"

She smiled shyly. "You were being impossible," she said.

"Maybe. But it was fun, wasn't it?" He kissed her again.

"You're being impossible now," she whispered when he broke the kiss.

"It's part of my charm," he said, and kissed her once more. "Caitie, we have to go," he whispered, continuing to kiss her cheeks, eyelids, and temples. "Geoffrey will send out the state militia if we miss that stage."

She laughed. "You're right about that." She cupped his face with both her hands and looked at him. "Thank you, Dylan. For the ring and everything it stands for—I mean, your willingness to help me pull this off so Molly and Geoffrey can have what they want."

"I'm not doing it for Molly and Geoffrey," he replied, and kissed her so thoroughly that she had trouble regaining her balance when he stepped away. "Ready?" he asked as if they hadn't just shared the most devastating kiss of their short relationship.

"Ready," she replied in a voice that was no more than a croak.

The stagecoach ride was dusty but uneventful. Geoffrey and Dylan discussed business and politics most of the trip. Ordinarily Caitlin would have been right in the thick of the conversation with opinions of her own, but all she could think of was Dylan. She fingered the thin gold band beneath her glove a hundred times, as if to reassure herself it was really there. She tried to imagine Dylan making the selection, determining the right size and design. Upon closer examination, she had discovered the ring was not plain after all, but engraved with intertwined vines.

She watched Dylan as he and Geoffrey talked. She liked the way he listened and then made his point. She liked the way he wasn't intimidated by Geoffrey's position and education. She liked the way he talked with his hands and glanced over at her from time to time as if to include her if she chose to be a part of their discussion.

She touched the coat he had removed and placed on the seat next to her. It was the coat he had placed around her shoulders as they stood looking out at the lake. Had that been only last night? It seemed a long time ago. In fact, it seemed a lifetime since they had left Mineral Point.

Dylan laughed at something Geoffrey said, and his laughter sent a thrill of recognition through her. She loved his laughter. She loved the way he moved and talked and especially the way he kissed her. The fact was, she was falling in love with Dylan Tremaine. The realization stunned her. It wasn't possible. It wasn't appropriate. It . . . was the truth.

"There they are," Geoffrey said excitedly when he spotted the gathering of townspeople. "Leave it to Molly to have practically the whole town there," he added with pride.

Geoffrey leapt from the stage the moment the driver reined the team to a halt. He held the door open with a flourish while Dylan put on his coat and Caitlin checked her hair and the angle of her bonnet. "Ladies and gentlemen," he announced with a hint of fanfare, "may I present Mr. and Mrs. Dylan Tremaine."

A cheer went up as Dylan helped Caitlin down the steps and onto the boardwalk in front of the hotel. They were immediately surrounded as everyone seemed to want to be the first to say how thrilled and surprised they were and how wonderfully happy the couple looked. Caitlin found herself in an impromptu receiving line of people who wanted to offer their best wishes and hug her while they congratulated Dylan. At last she saw her parents, standing a little apart from the others, their smiles looking tentative and tainted by worry.

"Can you be happy for me?" she asked as she hugged her mother and looked up at her father.

"I had no idea you and Mr. Tremaine had such serious

intentions," her father said. It was hardly the answer she had hoped for. "Do you love him?"

"Yes," she replied and prayed he wouldn't ask her if Dylan returned that love.

"He's a good man, John," Mary Pearce said. "Hardworking and polite. He's good to Caitlin and from everything I hear he can provide for her."

"Where will you live?" John asked, cutting his wife short.

"In the cottage you gave me on Shake Rag."

"Molly and her friends have already been there to clean and get everything set up for your arrival," her mother told her. "Your father is simply upset that he was robbed of the opportunity to walk you down the aisle," she whispered.

"Mary, I do not need you to speak for me," John chastised. He then turned his attention back to his eldest daughter. "In inquiring of your plans for where you will make your home, I am asking in what town you plan to do that. It seems to me that Mr. Tremaine had talked at length of plans to head for California."

"And if that is his plan, it is my plan as well," Caitlin snapped. But she softened immediately. "Father, this is what I want," she said, giving her father a quick hug. "Please try to see that it's the very best thing."

"I'll take good care of your daughter, sir," Dylan said as he joined the group. "You have my word on that." He offered his handshake as proof of his good intent.

John Pearce accepted the handshake, and everyone seemed to breathe easier. "I thought you and Molly had some big shindig planned," he said gruffly to his wife. "Hadn't we best get on with it?"

Caitlin's brothers let out a cheer and led the parade down the street away from the Pearce house. Caitlin was momentarily confused as she and Dylan got caught up in the crowd headed down High Street. Then she spotted the low wall surrounding her cottage. The door and deep window wells

were decorated with greenery and flowers and a bright pink
piece of cloth was tied around the doorlatch.

"It's your rag," Molly explained, untying the fabric and
handing it to Caitlin. "After all, this is Shake Rag Street,
and all the miners' wives wave a rag to let their husbands
know it's time to come in from the mine fields for supper."
She waved the colorful bit of fabric at Dylan.

"I believe traditionally the rags are white, Molly," Caitlin
commented dryly.

"I know, but this one is very special," Molly replied
with another flirtatious wave of the cloth in Dylan's face.

Everyone laughed. Dylan grinned at Caitlin. Come on.
Have some fun with this, his expression told her.

"Give me that rag," she teased as she playfully grabbed
it from Molly and gave it a good shake. "No one is to
shake a rag at Dylan but me, understood?"

"Here, here," her brother Charles shouted, and the crowd
roared its approval.

"Carry your bride over the threshold, Tremaine," called
one spectator and the crowd murmured its agreement,
pressing forward so they might have a better view of the
small cottage's interior once the door was opened.

Dylan held out his arms to Caitlin, and she walked to
him. He swept her high in his arms and then kissed her
long and hard. When he broke the kiss, she was blushing
but smiling. Dylan bent to lift the doorlatch. "Welcome
home, Cait," he said and pushed the door open.

Two small animals raced from the cottage as if their
lives were in danger. The stench that assailed everyone was
foul and repulsive.

"Skunk," someone warned and everyone beat a hasty
retreat. Molly started to cry. Geoffrey tried to comfort her
at the same time he covered his own nose with a clean
white handkerchief. "It's ruined," Molly wailed. "Look at
it—everything is ruined."

Stunned into immobility Dylan and Caitlin stood at the

door and looked at their new home. Aside from the foul odor, everything inside was in disarray. Apparently the two animals had led one another on a merry chase during the time they'd been locked up in the house.

"How did a skunk get in there?" Caitlin wondered aloud.

"A skunk and a badger," Edward added. "That's pretty strange. It seems somebody's played a very mean trick on you, sis."

"Come, everyone. Let's go on to our house," Molly said, recovering enough to take charge of the moment once more. "Mother has prepared a veritable feast. Somebody has to eat all that food."

"I'm sorry, ma'am," Rob Heathcote said as he passed by the stricken couple.

"If he's so sorry, why is he smiling?" Molly muttered as they walked up the hill to her parents' house.

Then Caitlin stopped dead in her tracks. "Oh, my stars," she murmured.

"What is it?" Dylan asked, motioning for the others to go on ahead. "Cait, we'll get the cottage cleaned up. It's a little smell and mess. It's nothing we can't fix."

"Rob Heathcote," she said.

"You think Rob is responsible for that?"

"He's been threatening to get back at me for weeks now. He feels I've embarrassed him in front of his friends, and then when I spoke directly to his father that day—well, apparently Mr. Heathcote's idea of encouraging his son to attend school is to beat the living daylights out of him. Rob was furious with me."

"I don't know, Cait. The beating he got was because he'd been lifting money from the saloon's take, not anything you did. Besides, this was pretty well thought out to be the work of one boy, not to mention the nerve it would take to actually be there when you discovered it and then walk right past you."

"But I've told you how bright and creative he is. He's

perfectly capable of coming up with such a plan—and on the spur of the moment. His best friend is Timothy Filbert whose father works at the mercantile. No doubt Tim heard about our news and couldn't wait to be the first to tell Rob. It's so seldom he can outdo his friend by knowing something first."

"What are you going to do?" Dylan asked. He was beginning to feel sorry for the Heathcote kid.

"I'm going to go to school tomorrow and wait for Mr. Robert Heathcote to show up. Then he and I will have a little chat." Having decided on a course of action, she seemed perfectly satisfied to continue on to her parents' house and the party that awaited them there.

"I'll take care of getting the cottage cleaned," Dylan said as he hastened to catch up with her.

"No. Rob Heathcote and any accomplices he may have enlisted will be cleaning the cottage," she replied as they stepped through the front door and into the waiting throng of well-wishers. If he lived to be a hundred, Dylan thought, he would never understand this woman's ability to be completely distraught one minute and totally in control of the situation the next.

The one thing Caitlin had failed to think through was where she and Dylan would spend their first night back in Mineral Point now that the cottage was unusable. She had known Molly would set up the cottage for her. How many times had they talked about that late at night as they spun their fantasies. Molly, of all people, would know that was exactly where Caitlin dreamed of living.

But thanks to Rob Heathcote, that was impossible, at least for the time being. As their guests said their good nights, Caitlin tried to determine a workable plan.

"I'm spending the night with Sarah," Molly announced. "That way you and Dylan can have our room." She accepted her cloak from Geoffrey and leaned down to kiss her sister's cheek. "Push the beds together," she whispered.

"That isn't necessary," Caitlin protested.

"Of course, it's necessary," Molly replied looking at her strangely. "And try and get at least a little rest," she said with a teasing grin. "You look completely done in." She kissed her again and left with Geoffrey.

"I put some extra linens in your room—towels for Dylan," her mother said. She seemed almost as nervous as Caitlin felt. "The boys also put your luggage up there. It's only for a few days, darling," she said, looking apologetically at Dylan. "And Mr. Pearce and I sleep like the dead. We hardly ever hear a thing."

"Mother," Caitlin protested, her cheeks pink with embarrassment.

Dylan smiled at her mother. "I think everyone will sleep well tonight, ma'am. Thank you so much for taking such trouble to make me comfortable."

"You're part of the family now, Dylan," Mary replied. "You're my son." She stood on tiptoe and kissed his cheek. "Good night, children," she said and headed down the hall to the bedroom she shared with her husband.

It gave Caitlin some satisfaction to see that her mother could make the usually unflappable Dylan Tremaine blush.

Eight

"Will you light somewhere?" Dylan said as he watched her flit from one task to another once they had retired to the assigned sleeping quarters. "Sit down and tell me what the problem is."

Caitlin glanced at him, wringing her hands as she looked back toward the door leading to the hallway. "My brothers will expect . . . that is, they'll be eavesdropping. . . . I mean, there are surely certain . . . sounds they anticipate hearing."

Dylan started to laugh.

"Not your laughing," she said, horrified at what interpretation the boys might place on that.

Dylan smothered his guffaws in a pillow until he could get control of himself. "Okay," he said with an attempt at seriousness. "How can we not disappoint them and keep you chaste and pure? Is that the assignment, teacher?"

"Stop making fun of me," she hissed. "This is serious."

"Then let me take the lead. Lesson two: how to fool all of the people who might be listening and think they know what they are hearing. We begin by pushing the beds together." Noisily he dragged Molly's bed across the floor until it was lined up with her own.

"Sh-h-h," she warned, casting an anxious glance toward the door.

"No. We've just given them exactly what they want for an opener." Next he sat on the side of the bed and pulled off his boots dropping each to the bare wood floor with a decisive thud. "That's a big old tree outside your window there, Cait," he said getting up to study it. "Did your brothers ever climb out there and spy on you girls—watch you undress or anything like that?"

"Oh, my stars," Caitlin whispered, and rushed to the window to look. "Do you think they'd . . . ?"

Dylan shrugged. "You tell me. They're your brothers."

"They might," she confessed miserably.

Dylan shook his head and looked at her with a worried frown. "We'd better make this look good then," he said. "Come over here." He lowered the lamp so that there was only enough light to cast them in shadow. "Come on," he said. "I'm not going to hurt you."

"What are you going to do?" she asked as she came to him.

"Undress you," he said. "Just keep in mind that it's dark and I won't see anything I didn't already see when we were in the tub yesterday." He began opening the buttons of her dress. "You can't sleep in your clothes, Cait, so just stand still."

In an amazingly short time he had the dress completely opened. "You're very good at this," she commented nervously.

He pushed it off her shoulders at the same time he pulled her close against him. "I'm going to kiss you now while we take the gown to your waist. Ready?"

"Are you sure this is necessary?" she asked shakily.

"We can take a chance they aren't looking, but from what I've seen of your brothers they like to play pranks. My guess is they can't help themselves and they're out there this very minute."

He was right. They had spied on Molly and Geoffrey numerous times, not to mention each other when one of them was seriously courting a young lady. "All right," she said and lifted her face to his.

He kissed her, distracting her so much with his mastery of her lips that pushing her dress off her shoulders seemed only one more element of the kiss. "Okay. Now unbutton my shirt and let's do the same thing in reverse," he coaxed. "That's it. Go ahead and pull it free of my pants. Good. Now push it open and kiss my chest while you push it off my shoulders and arms. Let's give the boys a good show."

She couldn't help herself, she started to giggle. She buried her face against his bare chest and shook with laughter. This was utterly preposterous.

"I must admit that's not the reaction I was hoping for," Dylan said.

"Oh, Dylan, I'm sorry, but don't you see how ridiculous this is?"

He gave a low chuckle. "Maybe. But it's also a lot of fun. Think how smug you'll feel at breakfast knowing you've fooled them completely."

The idea of finally putting one over on her brothers was too delicious to contemplate. Dylan had proven more than once that he would not hurt her. Certainly at the hotel the night before he had had every opportunity to attack her and yet he had given her one chaste kiss on the forehead and sent her to bed.

"All right, tell me what to do next," she asked, eager to continue.

"Well, let's see. Can you take off your gown completely and let it fall in a kind of heap?"

Eagerly she obliged, relishing the soft thud the voluminous fabric of the gown made as it hit the floor. That was followed by the distinct clink of metal. "What was that?" she asked.

"My belt," he replied. "Let them chew on that for a few minutes."

"What next?" Caitlin asked eagerly, now fully engaged in their game.

"Let's get on the bed," Dylan said. When she hesitated,

he led the way, bouncing gently up and down to show her the distinctive squeal of the springs.

Now it was Caitlin's turn to smother her giggles with a pillow. She laughed so hard, she had to sit down on the bed and once she had, she could not help joining him in the gentle bouncing rhythm.

"That's it," Dylan instructed. "Now harder and faster. There, like that."

The bed squealed in protest to their actions. Caitlin was laughing hard now and so was Dylan. They had joined hands and sat bouncing away. He interspersed the squeaking bounces with guttural grunts which she decided not to mimic. "Okay, stop," Dylan ordered, and suddenly all was silent. Then he flopped back on the bed with a loud sigh.

"What was that for?" she asked.

"Satisfaction," he said. "That is the sound of a man whose needs have been well satisfied," he added, then pulled her down next to him cradling her against his chest to cover the sound of her giggles.

They stayed that way for some time, both listening to the sounds of the sleeping household and thinking their own thoughts.

I wonder what it would be like to really make love with him, she thought.

God help me, I want her, he thought.

She shifted slightly and realized her mouth was only a fraction away from his bare chest. Kiss me on the chest, he had instructed before. She wondered what he would think if she did it now.

His fingers itched to close around the firm ripeness of her breast, just inches from his reach. What would she do if he touched her, caressed her?

"Dylan? Are you sleeping?" she whispered and the warmth of her breath fluttered across his skin.

"No."

"Tell me what it's really like . . . I mean between a man and a woman . . . I mean . . ."

"Making love?" *Glory be, the woman had no idea what she was asking.*

"Yes. I mean is it always so . . . noisy."

He chuckled and she felt the sound of it deep in his chest. His fingers wound their way into her hair. "There are different ways—sometimes it gets pretty boisterous."

"And other times?"

"Other times it's quiet but intense," he said.

"I see," she said and raised herself onto one elbow to look at him. Her hair fell across his face and chest, and he thought he would explode from the sensation of it covering him if only for a moment. "Which is better?" she asked. "Boisterous or intense?"

Dylan gave a low moan of frustration. "Cait, I'm going to teach you lesson three which is actually a review of lesson one. Remember what I said in the tub about a man growing hard while a woman gets softer and fuller?"

She nodded and pushed her hair back with one hand.

He reached up and took her hand, placing it gently over the press of his erection against his pants. "This is what happens when a man wants to make love to a woman. Now you decide, are you ready for lesson four where I demonstrate exactly how that comes about or would you like to lie back down and get some sleep?"

He released her hand and she slowly pulled it away. "Good night, Dylan," she whispered and moved to the far side of the bed.

"Good night, darlin'," he replied.

Dylan was already up and out before Caitlin awoke. She told her parents he had had to get an early start with his prospecting to make up for the time they had taken for the wedding. It gave her a great deal of satisfaction when one of her brothers commented that Dylan must not have gotten much sleep the night before. "There were all these strange noises coming from somewhere in the house," they teased.

Caitlin gave them what she hoped was a satisfied look and gathered her satchel for school. "I expect we'll need to stay here for a few more days, Mother," she said as she tied on her bonnet and pulled on her gloves.

"Stay as long as you need to, Caitlin. You know you're both welcome, and Molly is thrilled to be spending time with Sarah. I think they are planning Molly's wedding dress. She's asked Sarah's mother to make it for her."

"That's wonderful," Caitlin said and left for school feeling good about what she and Dylan had accomplished for her sister's happiness. But her mood took a decided downturn as she passed the cottage she had dreamed of occupying since the day she'd first played there as a child. In those days it had served as an office and storage for her father's store. That was before he had moved the business to larger quarters and no longer needed the cottage. How many times she had fantasized about placing the furnishings and filling the shelves with her precious books. Thank heavens, Molly had understood her need to place each volume in exactly the proper order. The books were still packed in boxes at her parents' house, as were those linens and treasures she had dutifully collected, at her mother's and sister's urging, in a marriage chest.

She arrived at the school in time to see Rob Heathcote sneak around the back of the church building and head down Dory Street toward the outskirts of town. She suspected he had gone off to the wooded area there to have a cigarette before ambling into school an hour late as was his habit. But she had no doubt he would show up in class sooner or later. He would not want to miss an opportunity to torment her in front of the others.

What Rob didn't know was that Caitlin and her brothers had played in those same woods as children. She knew them as well as she knew any place in Mineral Point. She gave her book satchel to Amy Bryant and asked her to have the children start working on their sums. As soon as the older girl had entered the church and herded the younger children down to the schoolroom, Caitlin set off to have a talk with Rob Heathcote.

As she had suspected he was perched on an outcrop of rocks smoking a cigarette. He appeared to be lost in thought. He was smiling as he practiced blowing smoke rings into the crisp fall air.

"You're feeling pretty proud of yourself, I imagine," she said, and was satisfied to see she had taken him completely by surprise. "Tell me, Robert, since Mr. Tremaine is known as the badger, am I to assume I was to be known as the skunk?"

For the first time in her experience, Rob Heathcote looked scared. "You got no proof I had anything to do with that," he blustered.

"With what, Rob?"

"You know. Everybody's talking about it."

"You mean the willful destruction of my property? You're right. I have no proof. Of course, Timothy Filbert is bound to talk once I mention to his father that I suspect he was the instigator of the whole thing. I mean, it's only logical that he heard people talking about my marriage and wanted to help you, his good friend. What do you think his father will do to Timothy, Rob?"

"I don't know," Rob said sullenly. "How would I know?" He tossed the cigarette aside in a practiced way.

"Well, you've been in trouble before, so I would think you'd have a pretty good idea. Chances are even before he tells on you, his father will give him a good whipping. Of course, Tim's younger than you and not as strong, but his father is going to be very upset. He might hit harder than he means to. Sometimes fathers do that when they don't know how else to handle a boy and his problems."

To her utter amazement Rob Heathcote's eyes welled with tears. "I don't want nobody taking my beating," he said. "So go on. Tell my daddy what I did. Tell him I'm no good. He'll believe you. Everybody believes you." He spit the words out bitterly, then wrapped his arms around his knees and hid his face so she wouldn't see him cry.

But she could see the shaking of his shoulders, and she realized how very young he was. A boy in the body of a man, big and gangly and strong—and expected to live up to his father's needs. Suddenly she had no idea how to reach him so she resorted to the only thing she was certain of—instruction.

"Now you listen to me, Robert Heathcote. You are one of the most gifted students it has ever been my privilege to teach. That may help you understand why I demand a great deal of you. I have expected you to set an example for the younger children. I have tried to respect the need for you to help your father in his business in addition to attending to your studies, and admittedly I have sometimes become frustrated when work took precedence. On those occasions I have spoken to your father, but make no mistake, my reprimand was for him. He needs to understand that you have certain abilities which, if property honed, could make life a great deal easier for both you and your father. If you are telling me that your father has turned around and taken out his own frustrations on you, then we will have to attend to that."

Rob had stopped crying and was looking at her with suspicion. "How?"

"I will make a bargain with you. I will not confide my suspicions of your masterminding this entire fiasco to a soul. You in return will organize a team of your comrades to prepare my cottage for proper habitation."

"Huh?"

"You clean up the mess and I won't say a word to anyone," she translated.

"If I go down there to clean, everybody'll know it's a punishment and they'll know why," he reasoned. "Pa will hear about it, and I'll get a good whipping."

The boy had a point. Caitlin squatted next to him, resting her elbows on her knees and her chin on her fists as she considered alternatives. "You have to make this right," she said.

"I know."

Well, that's something. Her heart swelled with pleasure at the headway she had made. "What do you suggest?" she asked.

Rob frowned. Then he smiled. "Here's an idea. Why don't you have Mr. Tremaine say he'll pay somebody to clean the place in short order. Everybody knows I'll take any odd job to earn the money I need to repay what I took from the saloon. It wouldn't look funny at all. He could stop by the tavern and hire me right there in front of my pa."

Caitlin smiled. "It's perfect," she said and reached over to ruffle his hair. "You see, I said you were a smart young man. I'll tell Mr. Tremaine this afternoon. You make certain you're at the tavern this evening."

Rob nodded and grinned. He really was a handsome young boy.

She stood up and brushed off her skirt. "Now I'm going to school. Are you coming?"

"Ah, Miss . . . that is, Mrs. Tremaine, how would it look if I came walking in with you? I got a reputation to take care of here." He grinned. "I'll be along," he promised.

There was no repeat of the night games to keep Caitlin's brothers amused. When Dylan heard of the plan to have Rob and his friends clean the cottage, he insisted on overseeing the job. He told Caitlin and her parents that he would not sully their home with the stench of the cottage.

His complete dedication to Caitlin's happiness gradually won over John Pearce and his sons. The men helped out with the renovation of the cottage in the evenings after they'd finished their own day's work. A week later Dylan presented himself at their door. He was freshly scrubbed and wearing his Sunday clothes.

"I've come to take Caitlin home," he said to John Pearce when the older man answered the door.

John smiled and opened the door wide. "She's more than ready to go," he assured Dylan. "I think one more day without spending time with you would have been her undoing."

Dylan smiled, wishing it were true.

"Well, go on up and get her," John urged. "You know the way by now."

Dylan took the stairs two at a time and paused for a second outside Caitlin's bedroom to check his hair by spitting on his hands and slicking back the sides. Then he knocked softly and opened the door.

She was curled on her side on the narrow bed. Her everpresent book open. Her eyes were closed, and her breath came in soft even puffs. He stood next to her, watching her sleep, thinking of the nights he'd spent trying to erase the image of her lying next to him that night they'd spent in this room, trying to work out his feelings and fantasies by writing about her in his journal, describing her to some unseen muse. Last night as he'd walked through the newly whitewashed and scrubbed cottage to assure himself that all was in readiness, he had imagined her in every room. And every time he thought of her, he saw himself there with her. That's when he'd understood that he was falling in love with her.

"Cait?" He shook her shoulder and held his breath as she slowly opened those gorgeous emerald eyes. "It's time to go home."

She blinked and then stared. Then she sat up. "You mean

the cottage is finally ready?" She seemed hardly able to believe it.

Dylan suppressed his disappointment that her thought was only of the cottage and not of his return after days of absence. "Ready for you to cook our first meal there. Fortunately, I'm starving."

"As usual," she teased. "Is the cottage really all right?"

"It's fine," he assured her. "All it needs is you to make it a real home." It was more than he had meant to say. It had slipped out. The last thing he wanted to do was scare her off. He had some time. Maybe she could learn to love him.

"Oh, Dylan, thank you." She threw her arms around him and kissed him hard on the mouth.

"Do you need some help moving things?" John Pearce asked after clearing his throat loudly to announce his presence. "I'll have the boys bring over your books and that chest there," he added, nodding toward her marriage chest.

"Thank you, Father. As soon as we're settled for a few days I want you and Mother to come for supper."

Her father smiled. "Just be happy, Caitie," he said softly.

"I am," she replied and kissed his cheek. "Well, are we going or not?" she asked Dylan, impatient to see her cottage.

"Lead the way."

In many ways their first night alone in the cottage was more stressful than staying with her parents. Since there was no longer the need to satisfy the imaginings of her brothers, the mood in the small house was capricious. One minute they were working in tandem, unpacking Caitlin's books and other belongings, and the next they were each wandering from the small sitting room to the kitchen and back on the pretense of needing to attend to some minor task. Neither of them strayed near the first-floor bedroom everyone in town thought they would share.

After supper, Caitlin insisted on continuing the reading lessons. Dylan thought he would explode from the need to touch her as she stood behind him reaching over his shoulder to point out a word as he pretended to struggle with the passage she'd prepared.

"That's very good, Dylan," she praised.

"And that's enough for tonight," he said, standing up and moving as far from her as possible in the confines of the small parlor.

She didn't argue the point. Instead she picked up the book of poetry she'd been reading and took his place at the desk, reading to herself. It was too early for bed. The evening stretched before them.

Dylan paced the room. Normally he would have pulled out his journal or worked on his accounts, but he could do neither in front of her. "Read aloud to me," he asked after several restless moments.

She selected a volume of poems by Elizabeth Barrett Browning. She put on her spectacles and cleared her throat. "This selection is called 'A Romance of the Ganges,' " she said, then began to read:

> "Seven maidens 'neath the midnight
> Stand near the river-sea
> Whose water sweepeth white around
> The shadow of the tree.
> The moon and earth are face to face,
> And earth is slumbering deep;"

Dylan had paused in his pacing to stand behind her and watch her as she read aloud to him. " 'The wave-voice seems the voice of dreams,' " he quoted, " 'That wander through her sleep; The river floweth on.' I always loved that," he said. " 'The wave-voice . . .' " he repeated to himself.

"How did you know that?" she asked, astonished that he'd apparently been able to read the end of the verse.

His cheeks reddened as he realized his error in reading over her shoulder. "It was a favorite of my mother's. She taught it to me when I was a lad," he lied. He feigned a yawn. "I have to be at the mines early tomorrow," he said and leaned down to kiss her cheek "Good night, Cait."

"Good night," she replied and watched him climb the stairs to the loft, where they had set up a pallet for him. She heard him moving around preparing for bed and then all was quiet. She felt the increasingly familiar bile of disappointment as she put out the lights and headed for her own bedroom—the room they would have shared had they truly been married, had they truly been in love.

The next day, she woke early and made him breakfast. The sky was still dark as he watched her prepare a meal of cheese and bread to pack in his tin lunch bucket.

"Do you know how to make pasties?" he asked, referring to the pastry filled with meat, potatoes, and onions that was the staple recipe the miners had brought with them from Cornwall.

"No. I suppose I could learn," she said.

He nodded. "They're filling and I can carry them in my pocket."

She closed the bucket and handed it to him. "I'll see what I can do," she said tightly. It was obvious she thought he was criticizing her attempt at preparing his meal.

"I won't be able to call for you after school," he said. "I've been away from the mine too much lately. I need to make up for lost time."

Once again she bristled. *So, it was lost time that he had spent with her.* "I don't expect you to call for me now that everyone assumes we are married. We no longer need to keep up appearances of courting," she reminded him. "We can work on your reading lessons in the evenings after you come back from your work if you aren't too tired."

Her comment rankled. He had thought she enjoyed having him call for her and walk her home each afternoon. He hadn't come for the lessons. He realized that in moving into the cottage their relationship had changed. There was no longer any need for pretense. The townspeople would expect them to settle in fairly quickly and co-exist as man and wife. The spirit of adventure they had shared during their feigned courtship and the trip to Madison, and even the night they had spent with her parents, was over. Now they were simply marking time until he left to join Ty in the gold fields.

He felt like a fool for daring to hope that in time she might come to care for him. Clearly, she felt they had played their parts and she had achieved her purpose. How relieved she would be when he could finally leave after a decent interval and she would have the cottage to herself. "Don't wait up," he said tersely. "I'll probably stop in at Heathcote's."

By week's end the atmosphere inside the tiny cottage was charged with tension. The two of them had settled into a routine of sorts. She insisted on rising every morning before daylight to make his breakfast and pack his lunch. Most days he came home to find her reading by the fire or working on her lessons at the desk.

They ate supper together and made polite conversation about her day at school and his down in the mine. He told himself that it was his imagination that made him see a flicker of concern when he talked about going deeper and deeper into the bowels of the earth. She was a good cook so the meals were appetizing and filling. By the third day she had mastered the art of the pasty, and on the occasions when he'd shared a meal with a fellow miner while taking a break from the exhausting work, he'd been proud to see that Caitlin's crust had the thickness necessary to stand up to the test of being carried in his pocket and containing meat, potatoes, and onions.

After supper she insisted on continuing the lessons. By the time that was finished, Dylan was so wired with the need to melt that ramrod straight posture of hers by kissing her senseless and making love to her that he could not wait to escape to his pallet in the loft. There he would ease his frustration by pouring out his desire and love for her on page after page of entries in his journal.

Occasionally Molly and Geoffrey would stop by or Caitlin would invite her parents or some of her friends for dinner or an evening of poetry reading or music. She never asked if Dylan had people he'd like to include, and while she was cordial and pleasant to the wives of the other miners, it was clear that she was uneasy in their company.

As the days passed, the two of them had less and less to say to one another. Caitlin was miserable. She missed the times they had shared when plotting the details of their bargain. She missed his gentle teasing, his laughter, and the charm of his smile. She missed having him hold her and kiss her, and wished fervently that she could think of some reason why he should continue the lessons in the art of lovemaking. These days he was often distant and moody. His goal seemed to be to spend as little time as possible with her at the cottage. He performed his duties by maintaining the house, attending church with her on Sunday, and being his usual charming self with her family and friends. It seemed to her that he talked constantly of the reports of gold discoveries. When they were alone it was as if he couldn't wait to escape from her. More than once Caitlin cried herself to sleep in the large double bed she slept in alone each night.

"I'm going out to the mine," Dylan announced late one afternoon.

"It'll be dark soon," Caitlin replied.

"Daylight or night—it's all the same when you're underground. I'll be back. Don't wait supper. I've packed something for myself." He held up the battered tin pail.

Outside he took a long deep breath. The cottage had become confining to him in a way he hadn't expected. The more time he spent there, the more aware he'd become that this was her place, not his. He was a temporary boarder. In her excitement to have everything just so, Dylan saw that moving into this cottage and setting up a life of her own was what she had hoped to gain from the bargain. Now that she had achieved that, as well as the safe engagement of her sister, she clearly couldn't wait for him to pack up and head West.

In an effort to work through his frustrations, he brought his pickax down on a rock he'd leaned against a thousand times as he wrote in his journal and updated his ledgers. The rock split and one large chunk broke away. Dylan picked it up and examined it closely; then he smiled. A thin vein of ore snaked its way through the heart of the large section of the boulder. The strike boosted his confidence. He certainly didn't need Caitlin's money to head West now. If his calculations were right, this single boulder along with his winnings from the wager with Heathcote could yield enough to pay his way. He climbed out of the shaft and perched on top of the boulder as he looked back toward the row of small miners' cottages that lined Shake Rag Street. He focused on the one at the end of the row, where Caitlin no doubt sat before a fire, reading one of her precious books and hardly thinking of him at all. *Well, Miss Pearce, I don't need your help anymore. It appears we all got what we set out to win in this bargain, after all.* The problem was he had begun to think things might turn out differently.

Finding the vein brightened his black mood and made him want to celebrate. He decided to stop at Heathcote's to share the news of his good fortune with his friend. While he was there he would collect his winnings.

Heathcote's saloon was rowdy with men blowing off steam from the day's hard labor. Dylan relaxed and smiled as he entered the tavern and was greeted by several other miners.

"Whoa, look who got away from the old lady to sneak out for a little brew," called one friend.

"Does she know you're out on the town?" asked another.

"If I had to go home to that schoolmarm every night, I'd need a little fortifying myself," chorused a third.

Ordinarily Dylan would have taken exception to that last remark, but tonight he felt completely in charge. He'd have his beer, talk to Heathcote and the others, and go home when it damned well suited him. He'd establish right now a pattern with Caitlin that would show her and the rest of Mineral Point who was the boss in that house.

"Where's my money?" he asked Heathcote as his friend pushed a mug of beer topped with two inches of foam across the polished bar. The bartender had put off paying off their bet, protesting that Dylan had never said he planned to marry the woman and besides he owed him for the damages the night of the brawl.

"I have to admit when you kissed her there at the train station, the lady definitely was not protesting a thing. Of course, you never said you'd planned on marrying her," he grumbled. "That tends to make a lady more cooperative in most cases."

"I'll settle for the original wager and we'll call things square on the damages."

Heathcote considered the offer then turned to open the cash register. "If it'll get you outta my hair, Tremaine, I'll pay you," he grumbled.

Dylan grinned and pocketed the stack of coins the bartender pushed his way with the beer. "Thank you, Heathcote. It's been a good day."

"So, with that pretty little lady waiting at home, what

are you doing here?" Heathcote asked, wiping a glass and eyeing his friend suspiciously.

"Celebrating." Dylan downed the beer and handed it to Heathcote for a refill. "I made a strike today."

"Congratulations," Heathcote said sincerely and handed him the second beer, which Dylan chugged immediately. "Another?"

"Nope. Time to head for home. As you mentioned, there's a pretty little lady there just waiting for me." He tossed payment for the beers on the bar and headed for the door.

A lamp burned in the window of the cottage as he opened and then relatched the gate. He could see her sitting in the small rocker they'd brought from her parents' house and placed near the fireplace. She was fully clothed and reading. He knew she'd heard him coming. He'd been whistling as he came down the street, and their gate had a distinctive squeak she'd asked him to fix, but she gave no sign of welcome. Dylan's temper flared. After all, he'd played his part to perfection. She had everything she'd wanted. The least she could do was show a little appreciation.

She did not look up from her reading when he entered the house. Her lips were pursed, and her jaw was set in that stubborn way she had. He knew she was angry and that fueled his own temper. "Are we not speaking, my love?" he asked as he sat down and pulled off his boots, letting them fall noisily to the floor, unmindful that they were covered with clumps of mud from walking back across the hills.

She gave him a look, closed her book, and got up. "So nice of you to decide to come home," she said. "Good night." She brushed by him without looking at him.

He caught her by the wrist and pulled her down onto his lap. "Were you worried?"

"Let me go," she ordered, her eyes flashing with anger.

"No. Tell me what you're so angry about."

"What do you think? We've been married less than a month and you go off for hours without so much as a word of explanation . . ."

"I told you I was going to work," he said reasonably. "I did that. Now I'm home."

"You've been drinking," she accused.

"I had a couple of beers. It was a good day in the fields. Would you like to hear about it, Cait? Would you like to know one damn thing about my life, what I'm doing, what's important to me, what I think? What I dream about at night lying up there above you?"

His anger took her by surprise. It was unexpected and unexplainable. "There's no need to swear," she said, automatically resorting to the reprimand she would have used with an unruly student.

"I'll swear if I want to, Cait. I'm not one of your pupils. You don't intimidate me. If we are to play out this charade, then we will play it out as man and wife and that means on my terms. In case you haven't noticed, it's the man who calls the shots in a household. You should have learned that much from your father."

"But we aren't really—"

"Ah, do you want all of Mineral Point to know that? Let me remind you that this was all your idea, and I've done everything you asked of me. Well, it's time to pay up, Caitlin. I hold the winning cards now, and I expect you to dance to my tune for a change."

She pushed herself free of him and headed for the bedroom. "We'll discuss this in the morning when you have better control of your reason," she said with a haughty toss of her head.

Her assumption that simply by walking away she could end the discussion infuriated him, and he leapt from the chair and caught her just at the doorway to the bedroom. "We'll talk now," he said as he pinned her against the frame of the door. "I'll start." Before she could react he pulled her hard against him and kissed her, his mouth open over hers, his tongue demanding that she open to him. When she did, the tone of the kiss went from violent to passionate. It had been days, and he had imagined kissing her so many times. He was determined to make her feel the desire she roused in him. He could not make her love him, but he could make her want him the way he hungered for her.

The unexpectedness of his kiss took Caitlin by surprise. Her first reaction was to fight him, but within seconds she found herself yielding to him. Her heart and body betrayed her as she tried to wrestle with the impropriety of the situation. The truth was she had longed for this, dreamed of it to the point of physical pain. In spite of her determination to remain in command of the situation, she found herself relinquishing the control that was her only weapon against her love for this man.

Kiss for kiss she matched him. Their tongues dueled, then settled into a slow sensuous dance. He pulled the pins from her hair, freeing it to cascade down her back. She furrowed her fingers into his thick locks and pulled him closer. He trailed kisses across her jaw and down her throat. She arched her neck to give him access. He covered her breasts with his hands, making the layers of her clothing seem suddenly a barrier. She responded by pulling his shirt free of his pants and stroking his bare back with her open palms.

"Caitlin, I want you," he growled as he grasped her hips with both hands and pulled her tight against his erection. "Do you feel that? I want you." He was breathing as if he'd run a race, and his eyes were bright with fervor. "I want to make love to you."

Caitlin recognized it as her last chance to gain control of the situation. If she said no now, he would do the honorable thing, of that she was certain. The problem lay with her—she did not want to say no.

"There are ways, Cait. I won't defile you. Trust me."

Her mind raced. She looked into her future and saw
years of nights alone, her only comforts her teaching, her
books, and her memories. Once, that was what she'd
thought she wanted. Once, that would have been enough.
But that was before Dylan came into her life. What if she
let him make love to her? For the rest of her life everyone
would believe she had been married to him. For the rest
of her life she could live on the memory.

She met his look, then slowly began opening the buttons
of her dress.

"Are you sure?" he asked, clearly surprised at her decision.

"Are you backing out?" she said with a shaky laugh.

And there it was—the smile she had come to love. The
charming twinkle in his eyes, the lopsided grin. "Not on
your life," he said and carried her to the bed.

He sat her on the edge and pushed her dress off her
shoulders, then he knelt before her and removed her shoes.
The sensation of his hands under her skirts cradling each
calf as he stripped off her stockings made her stomach
tighten and her breath catch. "Stand up," he said softly.

She could no more have denied him than she could have
flown. She watched in fascination as he lowered her dress
to the floor, then sent her petticoat following. She stood
before him in her camisole and pantaloons. He was still
on his knees, his hands slowly working their way up her
body as if trying to memorize each detail. She felt wor-
shiped and, for the first time in her life, she felt beautiful.

"Dylan," she whispered just to hear the sound of his
name on her lips.

He got to his feet and began kissing her again. His hands
and mouth were everywhere, touching her, massaging her,
bringing her fully alive. She longed to make him feel the
same intense throbbing that he had initiated in her. She
pressed herself against him and relished the low moan of
desire he had no power to control. She used her fingernails

to draw patterns over his back and stomach, tunneling her hands under the fabric of his shirt to do so. She noticed his breath quickened the closer she drew her patterns to the waistband of his tight trousers.

"Cait," he gasped, and it was a warning.

She smiled and arched to receive his kiss.

This time he lowered her to the bed and lay beside her. He opened her camisole, and when he trailed kisses down her throat he continued until his mouth covered one engorged nipple. Caitlin went absolutely still as a whole roster of new sensations rocketed through her. When he abandoned her breast she gave a whimper of protest, but then realized he was not done. Now he opened her pantaloons, pulling them slowly down her legs. She realized that her face was lit by the lamp in the parlor and he was watching her. She was completely exposed, yet she felt no shame, only the necessity to please him.

Dylan got off the bed and undressed. "You're sure?" he asked once more, and his voice shook.

She nodded and reached out her arms to him. She could see only the outline of his magnificent body, and she longed to experience the sensation of his skin next to hers. She swallowed the words of love that rose naturally to her lips.

Dylan gave a low moan and lay down beside her, pulling her against his side as he buried his face in her hair and held her for a long moment, stroking the length of her in a rhythm designed to comfort and assure. After a time, he feathered his fingers across her thighs and then between her legs. Her instinct was to close around his fingers, but he urged her to relax with whispers and tender kisses.

"Touch me, Cait," he whispered.

She could feel the press of his sex against her. "I don't know how," she murmured, ashamed at her ignorance of such matters.

"Just touch me," he whispered.

Tentatively she stroked him. His reaction was exciting and immediate. She recalled how he had held her breasts and encircled him with one hand. He bucked and swore softly, his breath coming in hard gasps.

Before she realized what had happened, she felt his fingers slide inside her. Then he was stroking her with a slow steady rhythm. She thrashed about trying hard to control the sensations that overpowered her. She closed her legs tight on his marauding fingers, and this time he did not urge her to open. Deeper and deeper he probed, increasing the pace until she thrust her hips upward in time to the rhythm he set.

She had no awareness of time or place only that she needed him in a way she had not imagined possible. She clutched at his back, urging him closer. He straddled her and lay on top of her, rubbing his hard erection against her hip in tandem with the magic of his fingers inside her.

His body was covered with a light sheen of sweat. His breath was warm and moist against hers. His tongue imitated the action of his fingers, probing, filling her, bringing her to the edge.

"Let it come," he whispered. "Let go, Caitie. It's okay. I'm right here with you."

It was unlike anything she could have imagined. One minute she felt ready to explode, the next she was engulfed in a sensation she could not describe. This was why poets wrote sonnets, she decided. She felt both exhilarated and exhausted.

Dylan watched her fight to hold on to the feeling. He'd never seen her look more beautiful. Her hair fanned across the pillow, her face expressing the myriad of sensations she was experiencing as he brought her to climax. His only regret was not being able to bury himself inside her and release his own explosion of passion.

In the aftermath she became shy with him, burying her face against his chest to keep from having him see her face. He held her for several moments, but desperately needed to attend to his own needs without alarming her. "Sleep now," he whispered and kissed her temple.

"You're leaving?"

"We both need some sleep," he said as he pushed her hair away from her face. "If I stay that won't happen." In spite of himself he could not resist one last searing kiss. "And I won't be responsible for keeping my promise not to compromise you," he added as he got up and found his clothes. "Good night, Caitlin." He closed the door softly behind him and the room was black.

She lay there for a long time reliving in detail what had just happened. She'd been a fool to think she could be satisfied with one taste on which to build a lifetime of memories. The truth was she wanted him more than ever— and she wanted all of him. With a disgusted sigh she turned onto her side. Had she no pride? The man would do what she wanted—especially when it came to this—but it meant no more to him than a momentary pleasure. He did not love her. He had talked every night at supper about going to California. No doubt there would be women out there, beautiful women, young and adventurous. Women who would know what a man like Dylan wanted, would know how to pleasure him. She thought of her own fumbling touches and buried her face in the pillow. How on earth was she ever going to face him in the morning?

Nine

If Dylan had thought the night of lovemaking would change things he was wrong. The following morning she acted as if nothing had happened. She was fully dressed when he entered the kitchen, wearing only his pants. He had fantasized an early morning tumble. Had imagined waking her, peeling off the nightgown that covered her from head to toe to reveal the naked pleasures awaiting him beneath those yards of muslin.

"Good morning," she said but did not look at him. "Sit down and I'll start your eggs."

He reached for her as she poured his coffee, but she evaded him. "I have a very full day," she said. "School, of course, and then Molly wants me to help her select fabric for her wedding gown. This evening Mother and I will be meeting with the ladies of the church to plan the wedding and reception. I was thinking, it will probably be so late when we finish, why don't I just stay the night?"

"It's less than ten blocks," he said. "I'll come get you. We can walk home."

She was so nervous she almost dropped the plate she had prepared for him. It clattered to the table as she hurried to move away from him lest he try and touch her again. "Molly would be disappointed if I didn't stay. We haven't had much of a chance to talk lately, and you know how she likes to chatter."

The only person chattering was Caitlin. Dylan attacked

his breakfast. "Do as you please," he muttered. "You will anyway." He gulped down the last of the coffee, scraped back his chair, and left the room. He'd thought they had finally made some progress. He had dared to hope that she might care for him. Instead he felt like a damn science experiment.

Before she had cleared and washed the dishes she heard the cottage door open and close and caught a glimpse of him rounding the house and heading out for the mines.

That evening Dylan considered stopping off at Heathcote's, but he really wasn't in the mood for bantering with his cronies. Instead he headed home. The cottage was dark, and he hated the emptiness of it without Caitlin's familiar presence. He lit a lamp and sat alone at the kitchen table, eating the cold supper she'd left for him. He was strangely disappointed that she hadn't also left a note. What was he expecting? he wondered. An apology? A promise to be home by eight? Of course, since she thought he couldn't read, she would not leave a note.

He washed his dishes and attended to the evening chores. He moved with familiarity through the dark house and had decided to retire to the loft and his journal for the night when he passed the open door of the bedroom. Carrying the lamp, he entered it.

The scent of Caitlin filled the air. It had become as familiar to him as the scent of the cedar trees in the surrounding woods. The bed was perfectly made, and her personal things were lined up on the dressing table in neat little rows, the various bottles arranged in decreasing size from tallest to smallest, the silver-backed brush, comb, and hand mirror rigidly aligned in the exact center of the small table.

He walked to the wardrobe and opened it. Everything was perfectly hung and organized. Her hat boxes were stacked and labeled on the top shelf. Her shoes sat matched and pointed forward in rows that looked as if at any minute

they might march off to battle. Suddenly it became impera-
tive for him to find some sign that she was capable of
distraction, capable of losing control the way she had in
his arms the night before. He searched the bedside table
and found nothing. He moved back to the parlor, where he
rummaged through the desk at which she sat every night
reading, correcting papers, or teaching him. Nothing.

He picked up the book of poems she'd been reading the
night before and opened it. There pressed between the
pages was a scrap of paper. He opened it and turned up
the lamp to read her small neat handwriting. It was dated
three weeks earlier, and she'd used it to mark the poem
he'd completed for her a few nights ago.

Dylan was written at the top. His heart leapt and he
hurried to read the rest, certain that she had poured out
her true feelings for him one night while sitting alone and
waiting for his return from the mine. His heart hammered
as he read the words that would finally reveal her true
feelings.

> *This man has a surprising ability to learn for one
> of his background and station. It is a pity he was not
> taught in his early years, for surely he could have con-
> sidered so many possibilities other than the backbreak-
> ing work of mining. I had doubts when he first came
> to me, but I find him a joy to teach. Ours is a strange
> bargain, but one I think has repaid each of us in ways
> that will enrich our lives for years to come.*

He refolded the paper and returned it to the book. He
thought about the outpouring of words that filled his own
journal lying upstairs now with his things. He'd been a
fool. She thought of him as her inferior—"one of his background and station." She had told him once that she would
never marry because in Mineral Point there was no one
she could bring herself to even consider loving for all her

days. *No one good enough,* he thought. She had said repeatedly that she preferred to be alone. At least then she could make a life of her own choosing. It would be lonely but she had family and friends and of course, her teaching. It was more than many people had in their lives, she'd said. What on earth had ever possessed him to think he might woo and win her? He replaced the book on the arm of the chair and slowly climbed the stairs to the loft.

When Caitlin returned to the house after school the following day, everything was the same. Dylan had obviously eaten the cold supper she had left him. She imagined him here alone, walking through the rooms of the small cottage. She walked through the place, looking at it from his point of view for the first time. She realized that everything in sight was something of hers or her family's. Even his clothing was out of sight. No coat hung on the peg in the kitchen. No hat on the hall tree by the front entrance. Nothing of his was in the bedroom. She thought about her parents' bedroom, the way her father's things were part of it, his collars starched and waiting in the drawer of his bureau, the fact that he had a bureau. She climbed up to the loft determined to bring at least some of his things down where they would be more accessible to him and more a part of the house.

His daily clothes, personal toiletries, and bedroll were gone. Only his Sunday clothes and the items she had insisted he place in the loft for his comfort were still there. Caitlin experienced a sense of panic unlike any she had ever known. He was gone. She felt bereft. Abandoned. She ran back downstairs and looked around, trying to decide what to do. She left the cottage and then wondered where she should go.

"Your mister coming in tonight?" Her neighbor called across the low stone wall as she waved her white cloth toward the mines, continuing the tradition of calling the miners home for supper. " 'Cause when he headed out last night, my Frank wondered what he was doing going out there after dark like that and all. Maybe he hit a strike?"

"He's doing some extra work." Caitlin knew her excuse for his absence was lame, but it was the best she could do. She shielded her eyes against the setting sun and studied the horizon now caught in the shadowy dusk. There on the hillside she spotted the campfire.

"Don't look like he's coming in yet," her neighbor remarked, then herded her children back inside.

Caitlin swallowed her pride and waited for the other miners to come down the street. "Excuse me, Mr. Paynter, I was wondering if you spoke to my husband today." She smiled in what she hoped was a charming manner and continued. "You see, I was at my mother's last night and we missed seeing each other this morning. I think he may have told me he was working extra, but . . ." She shrugged and smiled.

"Didn't speak to him today, ma'am. Saw him last night and he said something about spending some time at his old camp." The miner glanced toward the hillside. "Looks like that's where he might be."

"Yes, thank you."

He could have gotten word to me. She fumed as she went back inside the cottage and closed the door. *It's only ten blocks.* She recalled his words of the day before when she'd said she would stay over at her mother's house. She planned to have a word with him about that when he returned—except he didn't return. Not that night or the next. By the third day the town was buzzing with rumors about the young couple's obvious argument. Her students shared the rumors they overheard from their parents in whispers that were neither hushed nor subtle.

Caitlin ignored them for the first two days, but by the end of the week they had reached dangerously scandalous proportions. She had heard everything from the idea that she had driven him out to that he had a mistress and she had discovered them in bed together one day when she returned from school. Her father and brothers were bent on confronting Dylan themselves, upset with the innuendo surrounding Caitlin, and them by association.

"I'll handle this, Father," Caitlin said when her father took her aside following a very strained Sunday dinner and asked her what she needed.

The piteous looks and murmurs that had followed her as she had taken her place in church and throughout the week as she went about her shopping had been the final straw. Dylan had no right to do this to her, to place her in this position. She could not fathom what had made him so angry other than the fact that she had left him for one night. Perhaps he had hoped to make a regular habit of their night of lovemaking, but that was simply impossible. He certainly must understand the dangers of that. What if things went too far? What if she became pregnant? He had said he would protect her, not leave her in the lurch. She had waited for almost a week for the man to come to his senses, but for all his charm, Dylan Tremaine was stubborn—possibly more stubborn than she.

After lunch she put on her heavy shoes and set out across the hillside toward the mines. She stalked across the rocky ground that had been hardened by several nights of heavy frost. She resolved not to think about her concerns for him lying up there night after night while the wind howled and the icy rains pelted the windows of the cottage. She had deliberately prepared a large basket of food on the off chance she might be observed by prying eyes. It would seem as though she had simply headed out to bring him provisions like any good wife.

She spotted him from several yards away, sitting hunched under his moleskin slicker, his hat pulled low over his eyes. He appeared to be writing something, more likely making marks in the ledger he kept. She sighed wishing she'd helped him more with his sums and figures.

"Dylan," she called and had the satisfaction of seeing that she had taken him completely by surprise. He hastily packed away the small notebook and stood up. He did not come to meet her, and when she reached the campsite, his face was hard with fury.

"You'll catch your death out here," she reprimanded as she paused to catch her breath. "It's freezing already. By tonight it will be quite unbearable."

He turned on her, his eyes flashing with anger. "As I have told you before, I am not one of your pupils, Caitlin. I'm a grown man and I know what I'm doing."

"Well, perhaps you could do me the courtesy of explaining it to me, because I can tell you now that neither I nor anyone in town understands."

"Are people talking?"

"Of course. Gossip and speculation run wild under the most normal of situations in a town the size of Mineral Point. This is hardly normal."

"And that gossip upsets you." It was a statement, but she answered as if he had posed a question.

"Of course, it's upsetting—for me, my family. . . ."

"Oh, that's it, isn't it? That's what has brought you traipsing out here. You don't care what I think or feel, but let your precious family have some concerns and that brings you out here double quick, does it?"

"I never said . . . I have no idea . . . I cannot imagine. . . ." She sputtered, unable to decide which direction to take first. She closed her eyes and willed herself to regain control. "Dylan, whatever has upset you we need to discuss it. This is not a good situation for you or for me. I will not have us be the topic of common gossip."

"You! You! You!" he shouted, flailing his hands about in frustration. "You don't want to be seen with me except in circumstances you arrange. You drag me into your little scheme and then expect me to be content to hide away in the attic of that damned cottage of yours until you need to put me on display. You give yourself willingly to me one night and then act as if we've committed the seven deadly sins in the morning. You slink away to Mommy and Daddy the minute things get a tiny bit out of your control. You . . ."

Blessedly he seemed to have run out of accusations. He threw up his hands and stalked away from her.

"Will you please end this foolishness and come home?" she asked after giving him a few minutes to compose himself.

"This is my home," he muttered, refusing to look at her. "I believe you've gotten what you wanted from me—and perhaps a bit more." His bold perusal of her body left no question of his meaning. He shouldered his pickax. "Now if you'll excuse me, I have ore to mine so I can put together the rest of the money I need to get the hell out of this town and away from you."

"Dylan Tremaine, you are the most exasperating man!" she shouted at his retreating back.

He paused and then turned. "And you, *Miss* Pearce, should learn to come down off that high horse of yours once in a while. No wonder you can't find yourself a real husband. I pity you that you're willing to settle for a life full of loneliness and seclusion when there's so much more to be had." Satisfied to have had the last word, he stalked off.

When Caitlin got back to town, she first assured her family that all was well. "Dylan has struck a good vein," she said. "He's afraid to leave it lest what he's been able to accumulate be stolen. He'll be home soon. Until then we'll just have to endure the gossip."

By the time she got to her cottage she felt as if she might be physically sick. The tears she had held at bay by sheer force of will since he'd flung that last comment at her came as soon as she had entered the cottage and latched the door. She ran to the bed and cried herself into exhaustion.

She slept fitfully for an hour and then got up to stoke the fire and force herself to eat some broth. She thought about Dylan's parting remarks. She didn't want his pity. She wanted his love, and because of him the life she had thought would be perfectly satisfactory now loomed ahead bleak and empty of meaning.

In the past year she had come to terms with the fact that she would probably never marry. She had thought it through quite carefully. Her teaching would give her the contact with the children she loved so much. It would be nice to have children of her own, but that was clearly not to be. While she was still young she would no doubt miss being in love, but as the years passed good friends, the life she made for herself, her family would all fill in the gap left by the absence of a husband. Then Dylan had walked into her life, his boyish grin setting her heart afire.

At first she had simply been excited by the fact that with Dylan in the picture she could not only achieve her goal for Molly, but have the life she had planned for herself as well. During those first days and weeks she had thought of little else than finally being able to establish herself in the cottage, surrounded by her books and the things she had collected. She envisioned her best students stopping by for tea and, later in life, coming back to Mineral Point, grateful to her for the small part she would have played in making their lives a success. Then she had fallen in love with Dylan.

Honestly, that man is playing havoc with my life, she thought as she rinsed out her dishes and wandered aimlessly into the parlor. There might be no personal item belonging to Dylan to be seen, but she felt his presence everywhere she looked. She thought about how during those first days after they'd come to the cottage he had filled the small room with laughter and conversation . . . and his passion.

She walked to the door of the bedroom and stood there for a long moment, letting the memories wash over her. This doorway was the exact spot where they had stood the night he took her to bed. She relived every moment of that wonderful night. Desire overcame her to the point that she had to sit down, and she found herself facing the open door of the bedroom, recalling how he had undressed her, touched her, held her. Her body ached with longing for him, and she knew that she must do whatever possible to bring him back under her roof. Whatever time there was left before he had enough saved to head for California, she must use every hour to try to convince him that his assessment of her was wrong. Failing that, she would do whatever it took to get him back in her bed and create the kind of memories she knew would sustain her for the rest of her days. Pride could no longer play a part in this, for once Dylan left she would have only the memories she could make now.

Late into the night she sat at her desk, writing up a plan for wooing Dylan Tremaine. The following day she set the plan in motion. Her first move was to head straight for Gar Heathcote's saloon the minute school was out.

"Mr. Heathcote, I've come to invite you to join Mr. Tremaine and myself for supper tomorrow evening. Of course, Rob is welcome as well."

Heathcote simply looked at her as if she had suddenly begun to speak in a foreign tongue. "You want me to come to your house?" he asked.

She nodded. "And Robert, too. Is tomorrow evening convenient for you?"

"Yes, ma'am. It'll be a slow night here. I can close up for an hour, I suppose." He continued to regard her with open suspicion.

"That's wonderful. Please come at six if that is convenient."

"Yes, ma'am."

Next she walked across the street to Gribble's market. "Mr. Gribble, I wonder if I might have a word with your wife," she inquired.

"I'll get her," the startled man replied, and he stepped behind a curtain where Caitlin could hear hushed whispering until the man reappeared with his wife after a few minutes.

"Good day, Mrs. Gribble. I've come to ask for your help. You see my husband is of Cornish ancestry—as are you—and he's often talked about a special saffron cake his mother used to prepare for him back in Cornwall. I was wondering if you might be able to share a recipe with me for that dish?"

The older woman beamed with delight. "Why, bless your heart. I guess you've heard the old saying that the way to a man's heart is surely through his stomach," she teased. "You come on back here with me, and we'll just get you that recipe. I'll even lend you my special pan. Howard, pull together the ingredients for Miss . . . Mrs. Tremaine's saffron cake," she ordered as she escorted Caitlin into the living quarters the couple shared with their four children. "Don't you worry, honey, we'll get that stubborn man of yours to come home."

The rest of the evening, and after school the following day, Caitlin spent preparing the meal and setting the table in the tiny dining room just off the kitchen. She used her grandmother's best lace cloth and a set of fine china her parents had given them as a wedding present. She worried about what to serve to drink with the meal and finally decided to serve milk. She couldn't very well serve spirits with young Rob coming.

At four-thirty she stood out in back of the house and waved the bright pink kerchief Molly had given her. Up and down Shake Rag Street a few of the other women were also waving cloths to signal their husbands that it was suppertime. She watched anxiously for Dylan to come across the field.

"Tremaine!"

Dylan heard one of the miners who worked up at the zinc mine calling for him.

"Tremaine!" the man bellowed, as another took up the call. Soon there was a chorus of men calling his name and laughing in between.

"What's the problem?" he asked when he topped the rise and met them coming toward him on their way back to town. They were covered with dust but smiling. Dylan thought they must have hit a strike and wanted to invite him to join them at Heathcote's. Well, he might just do that. Truth was, it was getting pretty lonely out at his camp. He hated to admit it, but he'd gotten to like sleeping inside, having somebody put a hot meal on the table for him, having her waiting for him all clean and smelling good at the end of a hard day even if the lady did think of herself as much too good for the likes of him.

"You might want to take a gander down there at the street," his friend said. The others just grinned and smirked, punching one another with their fists or elbows.

Dylan turned to follow their gaze down the hill toward town. "Yeah?"

"Seems to me there's a new rag being shook," his friend said, which brought a fresh wave of guffaws from the others.

Dylan looked again. *Impossible,* he thought, but there it was, bright pink and waving lustily. *What is she up to now?*

"Looks like all is forgiven, Tremaine," one of the men teased. "If I was you I'd waste no time standing here gawking. The little lady just might change her mind. I'd imagine it gets a mite lonesome, not to mention cold, sleeping up there in that badger hole of yours."

Dylan grinned. "You don't know the half of it, gentlemen," he replied. "See you in town," he called as he headed over the rise and straight toward the fluttering pink cloth. *Whatever scheme you've cooked up now, Cait, you'd best be prepared to play by my rules,* he thought as he marched purposefully toward the cottage.

When she finally spotted him, her heart lurched. When he got within sight, she noticed that he looked tired, and she was glad that she had taken the time to heat the water and fill the copper bathtub in the kitchen. When they were face to face he said nothing but pulled her hard against him and kissed her thoroughly. Somewhere behind him, she was aware of the sound of male laughter and cheering. Then he swatted her on the bottom and headed for the house. "What's for supper, woman? I'm starved," he announced.

"We have company coming. Hurry and clean up," she said excitedly, relieving him of his lunch pail the way she had observed the other wives doing when their husbands returned from the fields.

Dylan stifled a groan and walked stoically into the cottage. He was in no mood for Molly and Geoffrey tonight. He had spent an exhausting day with little to show for it, working out his anger on the hard rock of the mine, trying to break through to the subsurface where he knew he'd find more ore. His work today had been as fruitless as making love to Caitlin.

Inside he was assailed by a potpourri of delicious smells. He noticed that the table was set for four so at least her parents wouldn't be coming as well. He walked straight back to the kitchen and spotted the tub and the kettles of water steaming away on the stove.

"I'll get you fresh clothes," she called, and it took him a moment to realize she had gone into the bedroom, not up to the loft. He heard the wardrobe door open and close and then a bureau drawer. She returned with a complete change of clothes and left it for him on a chair. "I'll just go change myself," she said shyly. "You go ahead and bathe." Then she went into the bedroom and closed the door.

He poured the water into the tub, undressed, and eased himself into the water. It was like a tonic for his weary muscles. He used the soap and shaving supplies she'd provided. "Who's coming?" he called to her, and felt more interest in the answer than he had a few minutes earlier.

"Gar Heathcote and Rob," she replied as she stood before the mirror, redoing her hair. It occurred to her that married people would talk to each other this way. She heard the splash of the water as he stood up. She closed her eyes as she imagined the water droplets clinging to his naked body.

"I'm decent," he called. "You don't have to hide out," he added as he opened the bedroom door.

"I wasn't hiding," she said and finished fixing her hair.

"Then look at me," he commanded in a voice that was dangerously quiet.

She put down her brush and turned to him. He looked wonderful, freshly scrubbed and dressed in the clothes she'd worked half the night washing and ironing for him. He strolled into the room and pulled open a drawer in the bureau in which she had placed a fresh supply of extra shirts and underwear, purchased from her father's store, no doubt.

He made no comment, but shut the drawer and walked over to the wardrobe. Her cheeks flamed as he slowly took stock of his suit and the other clothes he'd left in the loft hanging next to hers. "I have to finish supper," she said and left the room. *What have I been thinking? What is he thinking now about the blatant message the moving of his clothes to the bedroom sent?*

He came back into the kitchen and leaned against the

door frame watching her. Her hand shook as she stirred the stew.

"If what I just saw in there was an invitation, Cait, I accept."

Caitlin turned to retrieve a bowl from the cupboard. Dylan blocked her way, pinning her between the stove and himself. Either way she moved, she was sure to get burned. She was saved by a tentative knock at the front door. "That'll be our guests," she said and wiped her hands on her apron as she sidled away from him and went to answer the door.

The evening was a disaster from beginning to end. It quickly became apparent that Gar Heathcote thought they had been invited so that she could talk to him about Rob. This had made him angry with Rob, and the two of them had clearly had words and barely spoke during the meal. The food was a catastrophe. The saffron cake was a glutinous mess, completely inedible, though all three men tried valiantly. What conversation there was came in broken sentences or single word responses to Caitlin's questions. Rob risked the wrath of his father by announcing immediately after dessert that he had homework and leaving the table and the house. Dylan invited Heathcote outside for a cigar as much to calm him down as to enjoy the smoke and night air.

When Caitlin broke one of her best china cups while clearing the table, she sat down on the nearest chair and buried her face in her hands. The dinner had been a farce. If she weren't so personally involved she was sure she would be able to see the humor in it. No doubt Mr. Heathcote and Dylan were laughing their heads off out there in the yard.

She stiffened her spine and stood up, determined to have things cleared away and properly greet the men when they came back inside. It was hardly her fault that there had been such discomfort. She had certainly made every effort at conversation. She had introduced any number of topics she thought might be of interest, all to no avail. Of course, she shouldn't have attempted so many new recipes. The saffron cake definitely needed work, and she would have done better to stay with tried and true dishes she knew well. Under normal circumstances, she was an excellent cook.

It was probably to be expected that Rob and his father would be uncomfortable using good flatware and eating off fine china. But how was the boy to learn there were finer things in life? How was he to realize his potential if all he knew was what he heard and saw in that saloon? He had no mother to teach him, and in spite of his troublemaking, he was a clever boy with promise.

Caitlin rinsed the last dish and removed her apron. She checked her hair to make certain she was presentable and went to the parlor to await the return of the men. After several minutes she crossed to the window and lifted the curtain, expecting to see the two men resting against the low stone wall smoking their pipes. The yard was empty. The men were nowhere in sight. Caitlin returned to her rocking chair, determined not to take offense. Two hours later she was still sitting there—alone. Holding her emotions strictly under control she extinguished the lamps, undressed by the light of the moon and went to bed.

Ten

Dylan walked up the street toward the dark house. He knew he should have told Caitlin he was walking Heathcote back to town, knew he shouldn't have agreed to having one beer that turned into four with his cronies, knew she'd probably sat there waiting for him and Heathcote to come back inside, planning some entertainment as she liked to call it, probably reading to them or perhaps playing the small melodeon in the corner of the parlor.

The truth was he couldn't have dragged Heathcote back inside with a team of horses. The man was practically twitching when they stepped outside. Dylan suspected if he'd had to spend one more minute in Cait's house, he would have exploded.

"How do you stand it?" he asked. "All the books and fancy doodads and such? And she's a talker, ain't she?" he continued, clearly not looking for an answer. "Lord almighty, that woman can talk, and the thing is I didn't understand half of what she was talking about. Do you understand that stuff, Dylan? I mean, does the woman talk . . . you know, all during . . . well, you know . . . when the two of you—"

"None of your business, Heathcote."

They smoked in silence for a minute.

"I'll tell you this much, I'll be easier on the kid. I had no idea he was putting up with this every day."

"Caitlin's a good teacher," Dylan said defensively. "She

says Rob has real promise. It'd be a shame to put the idea in his head that he didn't need schooling."

"I'll send him to school, but I'm telling you if the kid needs to blow off some steam I'm likely to be understanding of that. No offense toward your lady, Tremaine."

"None taken. Come on, I'll walk back to the tavern with you."

Heathcote glanced at him with surprise. "That'll be okay with her?"

"Anything I do is okay with her, Heathcote. Now, you coming or not?" Perhaps he'd stayed so long at the tavern to prove his point.

Three hours later, Dylan stood inside the gate for several minutes, looking at the cottage. Her little show tonight had both touched and irritated him. He could not help but wonder what she was up to. Given what he had read in the note she'd written about him, no doubt her main concern was to get him back inside the cottage so he wouldn't be embarrassing her or her precious family anymore.

He'd gone with Heathcote to teach her a lesson, to make it clear that he called the shots going forward. If he decided to move back to the cottage, it would be on his terms. If he decided to go off with one of his cronies, he didn't need to check with her first. She was a woman playing the part of his wife. It was high time she understood there were things she needed to do to be convincing in the role. He took a deep breath and reached for the latch on the door.

Once inside the house, he made little effort not to wake her. He was spoiling for a fight, needed just once to have the upper hand with her. He pulled off his boots and started to undress as he went into the bedroom and watched her for a minute. She was lying on her side facing out, curled into a tight little ball, and he knew she was only pretending to be asleep.

He took his time undressing knowing she was following the sounds, enjoying the thought. When he had stripped naked he got into bed with her. He decided to take a firm tone with her. "Cait, I'm sorry if you're upset. I walked Heathcote back to town and lost track of the time, but you've got to learn that in my circles men do such things. They make the decisions. They . . ."

This wasn't working. All was silent on her side of the bed, much too quiet and still for her not to have heard him. He decided to take another tack.

"All the same, it was a good supper, Cait. Even the saffron cake wasn't that bad—just needed a bit more time in the oven is all."

Silence.

"And nobody cared what they were eating anyway—you had the three of us looking at you all night. You're real pretty sometimes, Caitie," he said softly, caressing each word. "Real pretty."

He sensed the tension leaving her coiled body and smiled. He kept talking, reaching over to stroke her hair as he continued. "I was thinking how proud I was that Heathcote actually thought I could win somebody like you—get you to agree to marry me, you know. The man couldn't stop talking about you. That's why he wouldn't come back in. He was shy with you—the boy, too. The way he looks at you." He chuckled. "The kid's got it bad."

Gently, he eased his arm under her and rolled her toward him. She didn't resist. "Happened to me once. I was fourteen and head over heels in love with the baker's wife."

"I bet she made a wonderful saffron cake," Caitlin said softly.

Dylan laughed and tugged her closer. "I would have eaten the ashes from that woman's stove and thought they were the finest thing I'd ever tasted." He kissed the top of her head. She curled into him. She smelled like fresh flowers.

"What did she look like?"

He raised up on one elbow and looked down at her. "Red hair—like yours." He arranged the masses of her hair over the pillow. "Skin like the richest cream," he murmured as he bent and kissed her eyelids, her cheeks, her throat. "Breasts that drove me wild the way they pressed against her dress, begging me to free them." He opened the ribbons on her gown spreading back the fabric. "Touch them," he whispered as he cupped and fondled her. "Kiss them," he mumbled as he lifted one swollen nipple to his mouth.

"What else?" Caitlin gasped, her body moving restlessly.

He snaked one hand under the hem of her gown and followed the line of her thigh up to her bare hip. "When she walked, the way her hips would sway, it was like an invitation and I thought it was just for me." He pressed his erection against the thigh he'd exposed and heard her breath catch. "I wanted her night and day. Thought of nothing else," he whispered against her ear.

"And if you'd had the chance, what would you have done?" she asked as she tugged at him urging him closer.

"First I would have undressed her so I could see all of her in the moonlight." He turned back the covers and pushed her gown higher until it was bunched above her waist. When she made no protest he lifted her and pulled it off.

"And then?" She was lying back on the pillow now, her arms stretched above her head. The moonlight streamed across her. She felt as if she was playing a part. She had become his fantasy, and it gave her the courage to flirt with him.

"Then," he continued as he fought to steady his breathing and keep his own need from his voice, "then I would make love to her." He leaned close so that he could see her face in the light. "Really make love to her," he added.

She curled her fingers into the hair at the nape of his neck and pulled him closer. "Show me," she whispered and that was his undoing. He'd come to her bed intending to teach her a lesson, to show her once and for all who was in charge. His tender words had been a deliberate ploy to woo her, but somehow once again she had touched something deep inside him, made the tenderness real, the need overpowering.

There was no more talk as he covered her body from head to toe with kisses intended to arouse and brand her. Where he wasn't kissing her, he was touching her, stroking her, positioning her to his pleasure. She did not resist or lie passively. Instead she touched him back, kissed him using her tongue and teeth, copying his moves, a willing student as he taught her the art of lovemaking.

He fought against his need to bury himself inside her, using his fingers to bring her to climax, finding momentary satisfaction in the escalation of her audible gasps until she could no longer hold back and released her passion with a sustained cry of pure pleasure. Afterward, she curled into him, warm and satiated, her fingers splayed across his chest.

"I'll be back," he whispered after a moment, knowing he needed to attend his own needs or be in agony.

"Let me," she said pulling him back.

"Cait," he warned. "You're playing a dangerous game."

"I trust you, Dylan."

He groaned. *A man would have to be a saint to resist this,* he thought and knowing he was far from saintly he eased over her. "You're sure?"

She nodded.

"It will hurt for a moment," he warned as he pressed himself against her and urged her legs apart.

She gasped with the realization of what was about to happen and he smothered it with a kiss. He could feel that she was still wet from her own climax. Slowly he probed her, slid in and pulled back. As expected she stiffened immediately.

"Did I hurt you?" He prepared to pull back, but she grabbed his rear with both hands and held him.

This time he did not pull back. Once he had penetrated and felt her jerk with the pain, he was incapable of control. As he felt the passion peak, he barely remembered to pull out in time to keep from impregnating her.

"No," she protested when he left her and that single word added immeasurably to his pleasure.

"It's okay, Cait," he said as he held her close. "Get some sleep. I'm fine. Everything's all right."

They lay together, their arms and legs entwined for several minutes.

"Dylan," she said softly. "I don't know how to say this, but whatever happens between us I want to thank you for this night. I'll never forget it—or you."

The following morning he was the one who couldn't face her. He had lain awake for hours, thinking about the folly of loving her. A woman like her and a man like him? Impossible. Sure, she had played the willing partner, but he understood that it was an adventure for her. She still expected him to stick to their bargain. She was simply storing up memories.

"Cait," he said to her that night after they had made love. "I can't do this anymore. It's not fair . . . to either of us. I'll lie with you, but I can't make love to you again. Something's bound to go wrong and I don't want to leave you pregnant and alone."

Then don't leave at all, Caitlin thought, but aloud she said. "I suppose that's the wisest course. Good night, Dylan."

For the rest of the week, each of them left for work in the morning and returned late in the day. She always had dinner prepared for him and insisted they spend at least an hour working on his reading after the meal. After that she would sit at her desk, working on her lessons for the following day. He knew she would always wait for him to make the first move, to touch her or kiss her. He would grow restless and wander out to smoke or make an excuse that he needed to check his claim.

Some nights he would force himself to stay away until he knew she would be in bed and asleep. She worked hard. As much as she might want to wait for his return, exhaustion would eventually win out, and he counted on that. He wanted her so desperately that his only defense was to stay away. He would slip into bed late at night and lie there listening to her deep steady breathing. Sometimes she would turn to him in her sleep and he would gather her close, holding her through the night.

The letter from his brother Ty arrived late that same week. Rob Heathcote and his friend Timothy delivered it to him as he sat outside his mine eating the pasty Caitlin had packed for him that morning. She no longer asked if he would be home for supper or whether he would return to his claim in the evening.

Dylan wiped his hands on his soot-covered pants and opened the single sheet of the letter. "It's from my brother," he told the boys.

"In California," the Filbert boy told Rob Heathcote.

"I know that," Heathcote answered testily.

Dylan scanned the message.

Have seen the elephant's tracks. Everything gone. Need your help. Contact me through Daniel Clayton, Salt Lake.

"What's that mean about the elephant?" Rob asked as he read the short message over Dylan's shoulder.

Dylan folded the letter carefully and pocketed the thin paper. "It's an old joke," Dylan said. "Has to do with a farmer who set out to see a circus that featured an elephant. Along the way, he crossed paths with the circus parade which was led by said elephant. The farmer was thrilled, but his horses bolted in terror."

"What's that got to do with your brother?" Tim asked.

Dylan shrugged. "It's sort of a secret language among miners who've headed West in the last year. They say they're headed out there to *see the elephant*—find their fortune."

"Your brother found gold?" Rob asked, and his voice was filled with awe.

"Not yet. He saw the tracks, not the elephant—that means he's in trouble," Dylan replied and pulled the paper from his pocket to read it once again. "Knowing Ty, it's a lot of trouble," he muttered to himself. *What the hell is Ty doing in Utah?*

At supper that night Dylan watched Caitlin as she served him without really looking at him. These last several days she'd seemed resigned to the pattern they'd established. Tonight there was something different—a tension he couldn't explain. Instinctively he knew something had happened. He asked about her pupils and her day at school. She answered in the briefest possible terms. After supper, he helped clear the dishes, and his presence in the kitchen seemed to unnerve her.

"Don't you have to go check your claim?" she asked.

"No."

He wiped the last of the pans as she scrubbed the stove.

"Well," she said brightly, "that seems to be everything here. Shall we work on your lessons?" She was restless and edgy, and he wondered if he was the one who had set the tension between them in motion.

"Let's sit down for a few minutes. I have something to tell you," he said, leading the way to the parlor where he sat in the chair he had come to think of as his while she perched on the edge of her rocker, obviously curious to hear what he had to say.

"I got word today from my brother, Ty. I think he's in

serious trouble, Cait. I need to head West as soon as possible."

"How did you hear from him?" she asked.

"Letter. Rob Heathcote helped me read it," he added, quickly remembering that he would not have been able to read it himself.

"I see." She stood up and walked to the fireplace and back to her desk. "When must you leave?"

"As soon as possible." Her reaction was not what he had expected, not what he had hoped for. She seemed relieved.

"Then we must prepare," she said matter-of-factly and walked to the bedroom, where she began opening the bureau and laying out his clothes.

"I don't think I'll need my good clothes out there," he said with a smile.

"Of course." She abandoned the packing as if suddenly unable to understand why she'd begun it in the first place. "Why don't you pack and I'll sit here and read to you? I found a story I think you'll find most amusing."

There was nothing unusual about her offer to read to him. She'd often done so since they'd first moved into the cottage as husband and wife. And yet, there was something artificial in her tone, in the set of her smile, in the stiffness of her back as she went to retrieve the book.

He considered her initial reaction to his leaving. He had hoped that she would rush into his arms, burst into tears, beg him to stay or take her with him. She had done none of that. He opened the bureau drawer and continued packing his things.

"Ah, here's the passage," she said as she returned to the room and started to read. "The wager is made. If I win, I'll have shortened the time before I can leave for the gold fields by a considerable amount. If I lose, I will have to leave town anyway, for I cannot pay the bet without giving up a substantial part of what I've worked for these last several months. Therefore, I cannot lose and must find a way to persuade her."

At first Dylan had listened with only half an ear, concentrating on folding his clothes while he considered once again his disappointment that she had no feeling for him at all. But as she continued to read aloud, something about the tone of her voice brought his attention to her.

"I am skipping some incidental parts here," she said as she paged forward. "Ah, here we have the thread of it. October 17, he writes, I have it for sure. I will ask her for lessons—surely no teacher can resist the opportunity to teach. I'll go to the schoolroom she holds in the basement of the church tomorrow and offer to exchange chores for lessons. I am so confident of my plan that I should increase the wager with Heathcote. I've no doubt in the least that by the end of the month I will have kissed Miss Caitlin Pearce in full view of the entire town, and she'll be my willing partner in that kiss."

Dylan stood with his back to her holding the shirt he'd been folding. He heard her close the journal, stand, and walk the short distance across the room. "I believe this belongs to you," she said, her voice trembling as she handed him the diary.

He took it from her and looked at her. "But did you read the rest, Cait?" he asked.

She looked at him, and he saw the depths of her anger. "I hadn't the stomach for it," she said and turned on her heel and left the room.

He tossed the shirt and journal in the general direction of the carpetbag he'd been packing. The shirt hit its mark while the journal slid to the floor. He ignored it and went to find Caitlin.

She had gone no farther than her desk. She was sitting there, calmly marking the papers her pupils had handed her that very afternoon. Her back was ramrod straight, and her jaw was set. "You owe me no explanation," she said.

"Oh yes, here." She handed him an envelope. "I believe you have earned this."

He glanced inside the envelope and saw the money. "Your savings," he said. "I can't take this." He placed the envelope back on the desk.

His refusal infuriated her even more than her discovery of his journal. "You will take this part of the money and go," she said, her voice raspy with emotion. "As for tonight, everyone will understand that you have had to return to your claim to shut it down before leaving. You'll spend the night there, returning at dawn. The two of us will spend that time here in this cottage. I will ask not to be disturbed. Everyone will assume we are saying our passionate farewell. I will come with you to the stage you can take to Galena for the start of your journey West. Once you are gone, please remember that a part of our bargain was that I would hear from you up to the time when the news arrives of your untimely death. Perhaps under the circumstances, that could be sooner rather than later. I understand the trail West is bustling with unsavory characters of all sorts. I'll forward the balance of the money then." She turned back to her work. "No one will find my sending money at that time strange since it will be necessary to cover the funeral costs."

Her hand shook as she attempted to mark the paper before her. Her eyes misted over with tears and she could not focus on the work, but she was determined not to let him see how deeply he had hurt her.

"Caitlin." His voice was soft, and she felt his hand brush her hair.

"Don't," she whispered. "Just please don't compound this by making an even greater fool of me than you have already."

He stood there a moment longer, then picked up his hat and walked to the door. "No one knew of the wager, Caitlin," he said. "No one but Heathcote."

"As if that made any difference," she said stiffly, refusing to look at him.

"I'll be back later. I'll not spend such another cold wet night in the field. I'll sleep in the loft," he said.

She wheeled around to look at him. "Perhaps had you not elected to stay out half the night these past weeks, leaving me here alone, I would not have discovered your secret and you would not need to beg."

"I'm not begging," he replied, his own temper flaring.

"Do as you please," she said with a dismissive wave of her hand. "Just get out of my sight and do me the one favor of not compounding your past deeds by doing anything that might mortify me further. I have to live in this town after all."

As soon as the door closed she released the sobs she had held in check for the past hour. She had wanted him to tell her she had misunderstood. She had prayed that he might have come to care for her at least a little. She had wanted him to refuse her orders, to force her to listen while he declared his true love for her. None of that had even crossed his mind. She'd been right not to read the rest of the journal. There could only be more pain in it for her.

Her tears turned to fury as she marched into the bedroom and finished packing all of his things. Obsessively she searched every part of the wardrobe, bureau, and room to make certain she had missed nothing. She found the incriminating journal lying half under the bed and placed it on top of his bag along with the envelope of money he'd put back on her desk before closing it for good. Then she hauled the bag up to the loft, positioning the journal and the envelope on top where he was sure to find them.

Anger was a momentary balm for her deep hurt. Determined that she should go forward as she had always planned, she spent most of the evening scrubbing the kitchen and giving the bedroom a thorough cleaning. When that was done she got into her nightclothes, hooked a chair under the latch of the bedroom door to secure it, and went to bed. For the first time since they had moved into the cottage she did not leave a lamp burning for Dylan's return.

Dylan walked across the hills and down to the cottage and wondered if he would ever take the walk again. He felt pulled in two directions. It was clear from his letter that Ty needed him. The boy had always been headstrong and impetuous, and the tone of the message inferred that he might have come up against trouble he could neither solve nor run away from. Dylan could not desert him.

On the other hand, there was Caitlin. He loved her. In spite of her stubbornness and her refusal to allow him to explain, he could not deny his love for her. In these weeks they had been together he had tried in every way to tell himself that it was the unusual circumstances of their relationship that drew him to her. He had tried to convince himself that it was the farce of pretending to be married that had made him think he needed her in his life, desire her so. But his feelings for Caitlin went beyond physical need. A dozen times a day as he worked alone he would think of something he wanted to share with her, tell her about. He loved listening to her talking about her teaching and the students she clearly loved. More than once he had found himself fantasizing about the children they might have if they were really married.

He walked up the front walk to the dark cottage. The absence of the welcoming lamp did not escape his notice. He entered the cottage and walked directly to the bedroom door. "Caitlin," he said softly. There was no sound. He tried the handle and realized he was locked out. He stood there a moment longer then climbed the stairs to the loft.

The following morning he woke to the smell of coffee brewing. He dressed and went downstairs. She was in the kitchen, dressed in her finest gown, the gown she had worn home from Madison. The gown he had helped her remove that night in her room so her brothers would think they were making love. He closed his eyes against the flood of memories.

"There's oatmeal on the stove," she said as she moved past him and returned to the bedroom. The door closed behind her. He walked to the stove and filled a mug with coffee. He scooped up a large serving of oatmeal and pulled out his chair. On the table next to his place he saw a handwritten note. He opened it and found the cold details of how she expected him to complete his part of their bargain—where to write her, how often, not to forget to address the letters to her as Mrs. Dylan Tremaine. The second page of the instructions was a final note:

Dylan, I wish to thank you for your assistance in fulfilling my plan. Molly and Geoffrey will be married over the holidays, and they are magnificently happy. As for me I am settled here in the cottage and looking forward to a life filled with my teaching and my books. You know how much I love my life, and I do thank you for helping me attain my own dreams as well. While your wager with Mr. Heathcote was something I would rather not have had happen, I do understand that you needed the funds to attain your own dreams. Luckily, we have each achieved our goals. Godspeed, Dylan.

                                               Caitlin Pearce

"Caitlin, get out here," he bellowed as he crumpled the note in his hand and threw it across the room. "Get out here now," he shouted. He strode to the bedroom door and turned the handle, prepared to force the door open if need be.

To his surprise it opened easily and she brushed past him, pulling on her gloves as she walked to the hall tree and retrieved her cloak. "There's been a change of plans.

I knew my family would want to say their good-byes so I made arrangements for us to all meet at Father's store. We should go now. By the time we walk there, visit for a few minutes and such, it will be nearly time for the stage. I suspect you would also like to say your good-byes to a few friends in town. This way there will be time for that." She finished pinning her hat in place and turned to him. "Shall we go?"

"Will you stop ordering me around, running my life for five seconds while I talk to you?"

She looked up at him and gave him a radiant and totally false smile. "No," she replied and opened the door. "Coming? Because it will seem very strange if you don't."

He was momentarily defeated. "If you'd just read the journal, Cait. Ty needs me now but I will . . ."

She was already out the door and halfway down the front walk.

By now the whole town had heard that Dylan was leaving, thanks to the efforts of Rob and Tim. Those they passed greeted Caitlin and Dylan somberly and moved on, respecting their privacy and these last moments together before Dylan left. At the store, Caitlin's brothers solemnly shook hands with Dylan and wished him well. Her father took him aside and spoke to him in low tones for several minutes. Her mother kissed him and wiped tears from her eyes with a lace handkerchief, and Molly began blubbering from the minute they arrived and had not controlled herself by the time they left to walk over to the hotel and meet the stage to Galena.

"Stage'll be about an hour late, folks," the desk clerk announced as they entered the hotel lobby. "Time enough for a bowl of Mildred's hot stew to get you on your way with a full stomach," he added with a nod toward the hotel dining room.

"We might as well eat," Dylan said to Caitlin.

She shrugged and headed for the dining room, deliberately selecting a table away from the windows. "Tea, please," she said when the waitress came for their order.

Dylan ordered the stew and a small loaf of saffron bread. "Might not get a taste of that for some time to come," he said with a slight smile.

They sat in silence until the food came. Anyone observing them would think they were a married couple about to endure a long separation, Caitlin thought. She felt the tears well once again and touched her lace handkerchief to the corners of her eyes to stem them, praying Dylan would not notice.

He noticed. He reached across the table and took her hand in his. She tried to pull away, but he held on tight.

"Don't," she whispered.

"Cait, you have to let me explain. I never meant to hurt you. I have to leave, but I want you to understand. I intend to come back—if you'll have me."

Her eyes were huge with shock as she looked at him. "What?" Her normal voice sounded loud to her own ears. To her surprise he smiled—no, he grinned, that infuriatingly charming grin that always made her heart turn somersaults.

"Well, that surely got your attention, didn't it?" he said as he leaned back and gazed at her. "Now I'm sitting across from the woman I know, the one who can't hide her emotions when she's really feeling something."

"You know nothing about me," she said and picked up her teacup, then immediately put it down because her hand trembled so.

He leaned toward her, his face very near across the small table, his voice a caress. "I know a great deal about you, Caitlin. Admit it, I know how to make you feel things you never thought you would feel."

"You are the most egotistical man I have ever known," she said dismissively.

He laughed, which further infuriated her.

"Dylan Tremaine, you have lied to me. You led me to believe you could neither read nor write when you do both, and apparently quite admirably judging by the number of entries in that journal of yours."

Suddenly he was serious, his eyes filled with a mixture of hope and anxiety. "Did you read it all, Cait?"

"Of course not. I'm not a sadist. I only read enough to prove to myself that you had lied to me about your illiteracy. Unfortunately, the passage I selected further compounded the deceit you have perpetrated on me."

He looked disappointed. "You always pull out those two-dollar words when you're upset, Cait. Do you know how annoying that is? Is that why you do it—to keep people at a distance?"

"It must be time for the stage by now," she said and stood up.

"Cait, I know I have no right to ask anything of you, but I need to say this. When this started I'll admit I was out to win a wager—simple as that. But along the way, things changed. Read the journal. If you can find it in your heart to forgive me and give us a fresh chance, write to me. I'll ask for a letter in all the major stops along the way." He ticked them off. "If there's no letter by the time I reach Salt Lake and Ty, then I'll not ask more of you. I'll accept your decision. Do we have a bargain?"

"Stage is waiting, folks," the clerk called from the front desk.

"You have to go," Caitlin said.

"Read the whole journal, Cait," he pleaded as he pulled the diary from his coat pocket and pressed it in her hands. "Please. I don't lie to myself, and I never thought anybody but me would see what's on these pages. Promise me you'll read it."

"Folks, the stage is leaving," the clerk said, this time from the doorway of the dining room. "Got to make up for lost time, you know."

"Coming," Dylan assured him. He put on his hat and picked up his bag. He placed one hand at Caitlin's waist and ushered her out to the waiting stage. To their surprise, members of Caitlin's family as well as several townspeople were there waiting to see him off and offer their support to Caitlin after he had gone.

"Guess we'd better make this look good," Dylan muttered as he tossed his bag up to the waiting driver. Then he swept Caitlin into his arms and kissed her so passionately that she completely forgot her anger and disappointment and kissed him back.

When he broke the kiss, he held her against his chest for a long moment. "Now that just might get me through some of those long lonely nights, Cait," he whispered. Then he released her, climbed into the stagecoach, and closed the door. "I'll write," he promised as the stage pulled away. "Remember, Salt Lake," he shouted as the team picked up speed. "I love you, Cait," he yelled as the stage turned the corner and raced out of sight.

He's lying even now—saying what he thinks ought to be said to make this all look legitimate, she thought. She continued to wave her lace handkerchief for several seconds after the stage was out of sight. She was oblivious to the journal she held clutched to her breast or the tears that streaked her cheeks and plopped into the dusty street. He had played his part to perfection right down to the tender farewell, and now he was gone. It was high time she got on with her life, for surely Dylan Tremaine had just taken the first step to getting on with his.

Eleven

The letters started coming two weeks later. Once they started they came so regularly that everyone in town would ask her what news she had had from Dylan that day. At first the letters were brief—two or three sentences, mostly about the logistics and expenses of starting the trip. She had never considered how much there was to think about in making such a journey. After the first few letters she looked forward to his letters, convincing herself that it was because she could share the details of the journey with her students.

After a few days the letters stopped and then a few weeks later started again, coming now in bunches, one for each day, but sent whenever he reached a place large enough to send them. The news they carried was weeks old, but that did not dull the excitement with which each was received—by the townspeople, by her students, and most of all, by Caitlin.

Each letter ended with his declaration of love for her and his wish that she could write him. But the farther west he traveled, the more impossible that became. Someone would have to be traveling in that direction and actually pass him along the way, reaching the next stopping place ahead of him.

Her students waited impatiently for each new installment of Mr. Tremaine's adventure as did others in town. Rob Heathcote in particular was fascinated by Dylan's reports.

His attendance record at school improved dramatically, and more often than not, he stayed to help Caitlin clean the boards, dust the erasers, and take out the ashes from the stove. As he worked, Caitlin would grade papers, careful to make no comment on his presence and sudden change of attitude.

"Where do you think Dylan . . . Mr. Tremaine is today?" he asked one afternoon. It had been several days since they'd had any letters. The boy sounded worried.

"Well, let's see." She pulled down the map that hung above the blackboard, a map she had studied every day since Dylan left, tracking his movements westward.

"The last batch of letters was sent from Fort Kearney," Rob said as he moved closer to study the map. "That's right there." He pointed to the dot on the map and smiled at her.

"And the week before that he was here," Caitlin pointed to a second spot.

"If we look at where he was the day before that, do you think we could figure out where he is right now?" Rob asked, and his eyes glowed with excitement. "You know, if we figure out how far he gets each day, we might be able to tell when we can expect more letters."

"What a good idea, Rob. Why don't you work on that and report to the rest of the class tomorrow?"

"Sure."

Sure. Her heart sang with delight. Rob Heathcote had willingly, enthusiastically accepted an assignment to learn something on his own. *Just wait until Dylan hears about this,* she thought and immediately her high spirits were doused. Dylan would not hear of it. To tell him would be to open the door a little and believe his lies. Still, she wished there was a way she could tell him that Rob's temperament had improved remarkably and that his letters had been responsible for that.

She walked home with a lighter step that afternoon. She

smiled at several people as she passed through town and stopped a moment to visit with her neighbor, Mrs. Paynter, before going inside her cottage. She kept his letters in order in a cardboard box she had spent one entire evening covering with scraps of wallpaper. She didn't share everything in the letters with the class. Some things she didn't even share with Molly. Some things were just for her, like the closing of the last letter she had received.

I know you heard me, Cait, calling out that I love you. I may have lied to you in the past, but I'm not lying now. I love you. I miss you. I go to sleep every night imagining you're here in my arms. There was no letter when I arrived here. Don't be stubborn, Cait. Read the journal.

In an early letter, he had talked about the scene when he'd arrived in Council Bluffs—hundreds of people preparing for the trip West, some for the gold, others for the land, and a few purely for the adventure. And he wrote of seeing some people who had turned back, defeated by the infinite possibilities for misfortune on the journey.

A dozen times or more today alone I've wanted to turn to you, to see the look on your face as you saw what I was seeing, to hear your comments, to watch you taking it all in, thinking about it, putting it into perspective as only you can. I never thought I'd meet a woman whose mind was as much an attraction as her body.

She had actually blushed when she read that. Every letter after that had become increasingly amorous. He would write about the texture of her skin, how she looked while he made love to her, and the pure pleasure of watching her sleep. Sometimes he would quote poetry, reminding her of

the nights they had sat together while she read aloud to
him.

*That's one reason I kept on with the lie, Cait. I was
afraid if you knew I could read the books for myself,
you'd see no need to read aloud and that would have
deprived me of hearing your sweet voice.*

She kept herself from totally capitulating to the crafti-
ness of his words by placing the unread diary carefully on
top of the box where she stored the letters. Every time she
was tempted to reread a letter, she would have to first con-
front the diary that had revealed his deceptions, his true
motives. It kept her rational. She reminded herself that she
was a spinster schoolmarm, and men as handsome and
charming as Dylan fell in love with vivacious women like
Molly, not serious, studious types like her. In time she was
certain the pain would ease and she would be able to move
forward with the life she had so sensibly planned for herself
before meeting Dylan Tremaine.

When he continued to woo her with words, she told herself that his pride was wounded. The conquest had not been
complete. In the end, she had unmasked his chicanery and
had the will to reject him. She reminded herself that a man
like Dylan would be challenged by that. He would be determined to win her back, and then in time, he would be
the one to reject her. She replaced the letters in the box,
and set the unread journal firmly on top.

The next batch of letters arrived two weeks later. Rob
Heathcote delivered them himself, having waited patiently
for the stage to deliver the mail and Mr. Filbert to sort it.
After handing the letters to Caitlin, he busied himself with
chores around the schoolhouse, glancing over his shoulder
from time to time to judge her progress in reading each
missive.

Caitlin noticed immediately how the tone of the letters

had changed. Dylan talked not of the country he was passing through, but of his native Cornwall. There was a tone of longing and loneliness in his words that grew progressively stronger with each new letter. His only comments on his travels for this duration were that the scenery was boring, a never-ending sameness to it until he felt as if he must have passed the same tree a dozen times within an hour.

The terrain here is so much the same, Caitie. I long for the wooded ravines and rolling moors of my native land. I could always count on the mineral plant to lead me to a fresh vein. I think about the fields of Mineral Point, a blanket of blue-purple mineral flowers for me to lie on at night, and I think most of all of lying there with you, Caitie, when next they bloom again. We'll lie there and listen to the rush of the stream and I'll sing you songs my mother sang to me. Still no word from you.

The final letter of the series was brief and heartbreakingly forlorn.

I am now traveling alone, the others having taken the trail northwest toward Oregon. The loneliness is nearly unbearable. I sing or talk aloud to keep myself sane. I have stopped here for the night. The saloonkeeper promises to send these to you with the next rider headed east—there are more and more of them. No one could be prepared for this trip. Tell Heathcote that I long for an evening's conversation and socializing in his establishment. This saloon is like a tomb. The patrons are either headed West to find their fortune or headed home busted. Either way, there is a palpable atmosphere of mistrust and suspicion. I bought a beer for one poor soul who had sold everything to come

*West from Ohio. The poor bastard is going home with
nothing but the rags on his back. We talked for a while,
and he thinks he's had contact with Ty. If so, my
brother has fared better than most—at least by this
fella's reports. We shall see. Ah, Caitie, my love, I am
so weary and missing you. How can you doubt my
love after all this time? Please say that you have relented and read my journal by now. I know we had a
bargain, but you are the only treasure I want or need,
and would that I had followed the guidance of Mrs.
Browning when she wrote toward the end of her wise
verse "The Lady's 'Yes' "*

> *Learn to win a lady's faith
> Nobly, as the thing is high,
> Bravely, as for life and death,
> With a loyal gravity.*

> *Lead her from the festive boards,
> Point her to the starry skies;
> Guard her, by your truthful words,
> Pure from courtship's flatteries.*

> *By your truth she shall be true,
> Ever true, as wives of yore;
> And her yes, once said to you,
> Shall be Yes for evermore.*

A note had been scribbled at the bottom of the page,
clearly added to the letter on a later date:

*I have had news of Ty. A fellow miner returning East
had heard of him camped just outside of Salt Lake.
The news was not good—rumors of sickness and
thievery. I don't know details yet, but this is his location. By the time you read this, I will be there. I fear
the worst. If there's no letter from you waiting in Salt*

*Lake, I have heard your decision. As soon as I can
locate Ty and made certain of his safety, I will send
news of my "death." I do it for one reason—I love
you, Caitie, and if this will make you happy, then I'll
fulfill this last piece of our bargain.   Dylan*

Caitlin wiped away the tears that slid down her cheeks.
Dylan had begged her repeatedly to write to him in Salt
Lake, but she had stubbornly refused to be taken in by his
charm. She had refused to read the journal, stubbornly
holding it up as evidence of his betrayal. Now it was too
late. By now he had arrived in Salt Lake and there was no
message.

"Where is he now?" Rob asked.

She had forgotten he was still there.

"South Pass—its the way through the Rocky Mountains," she replied, thankful to turn away from him toward
the map so he would not see her crying. "Here." She
pointed to the place on the map, and her finger shook.
"Right there," she added softly.

On her way through town she stopped to tell Hubert
Filbert that she was expecting a message from her husband.
Since Hubert sorted the mail, he would be most likely to
receive the message first. "It may be a spoken message or
just a note, and it will seem strange," she reported. "It may
actually seem to say that he has been killed in an accident.
I don't want you to be alarmed at that. You know how
Dylan loves playing the practical joke."

Filbert looked up at her, unused to hear her prattle on
like the other females in town were prone to do. "Yes'm,"
he said.

"The fact is, Hubert. It's a coded message. It means he
has found his brother and they have made a strike. In fact,
the message itself will probably be signed by his brother
Ty—that's to let me know Ty is all right."

As she made up the details to intercept the letter Dylan

would no doubt send, she saw that she had Hubert's full attention. "So it'd be good news cloaked in bad," he commented.

"Exactly. And you can understand why I find it necessary to confide in you and why I must ask for your full cooperation in not revealing this news to anyone else. The letter may come tomorrow or it may be weeks, depending, of course, on Dylan's progress in finding his brother."

"You can rely on me, Mrs. Tremaine. As soon as the message comes, I'll personally get it to you and not say a word to anyone else about it. It'll be good news, but it's your good news—you ought to be the one to tell folks."

"Thank you, Hubert." With a sigh of relief, Caitlin headed for home. At least when the letter came it would not be all over town that Dylan had died.

That night she sat up until nearly dawn reading and re-reading his journal. She studied every nuance of the words, looking for proof that her original hypothesis had been correct. But all she found was proof that his love for her had grown from the seed of admiration at her original audacity in devising the plan, and later that admiration had blossomed into respect as he had observed her as his tutor and found himself wanting to share his thoughts and opinions with her and hear hers in return.

The passages describing their lovemaking brought back a flood of emotions she had thought were firmly under control. She yearned for his touch as she read the passages that extolled the beauty of their lovemaking. But it was the last several entries that touched her most. These had been written during those long nights he had spent at his campsite. They were filled with longing and told of looking toward the cottage throughout the day, hoping to catch a glimpse of a waving rag signaling him to come home.

They told of his aggravation with her willful, stubborn ways, and his frustration with not being able to keep himself from positioning himself in the woods near the school-house just to catch a glimpse of her. It was the last entry that won her over completely.

I love her—there I've said it in print, tantamount to shouting it from the rooftop. She fascinates me with her beauty and her shyness that she hides under that mask of stern propriety. It delights me to know that I and I alone know the true depths of passion of which she is capable. It obsesses me to think I might lose her to another. Now she has discovered my deceit at the worst possible time. I must help Ty, and yet I cannot leave her. At least not for good.

What am I thinking? It is what she wants. She's made that plain enough. Can I blame her? I've embarrassed her, deceived her, hurt her deeply. And now I must leave her, just when I've found my heart.

The journal ended there. Caitlin laid it aside and sat on the bed, staring out the window. It had snowed the night before. It occurred to her that Christmas had come and gone with barely a notice on her part. She had spent it with her parents and the focus had been on the nuptials of Molly and Geoffrey scheduled for New Year's Day. In some ways she was grateful for the distraction of Molly's wedding. While everyone was suitably sympathetic about Dylan's absence, they were far more interested in the gala parties surrounding Molly's wedding.

When the day itself came, Caitlin dressed in a gown of green to attend her sister as Molly and Geoffrey were wed. All she could think about as she dressed was that Dylan loved her in green—he had said so in his journal. At the ceremony all she could think about was what it might have been like to stand opposite Dylan and repeat those vows, to really be his wife. She fingered the ring he had given her.

When she had first read about his wager with Gar Heathcote, she had wanted to rip the ring from her finger and throw it away. All through the next days and hours until he left, the ring had been like a shackle on her finger, one she was obliged to continue wearing to keep up appearances. In those first days she had been so hurt and angry that she had longed for the day when she would receive the news of his faked death and she could put the thing away forever. She had even thought of sending the ring to him with the balance of the money she owed him.

As time passed and his letters started to come she had found the presence of the ring on her finger strangely comforting. It was a reminder of the good times, the laughter they had shared, the fun they had had. And finally, when she read the journal, the ring became a symbol of a missed opportunity—her opportunity for true love, for living out her days with a good man who respected and loved her. Her own pride and stubbornness had kept her from letting him explain himself, had kept her from reading the entire diary rather than the one incriminating passage, had kept her from confessing that she was so angry because she loved him with all her soul.

As Molly and Geoffrey left for their new life in Madison amid shouted blessings and best wishes, Caitlin thought of the night she and Dylan had spent in Madison. She stood with her parents and brothers and thanked everyone for coming, and then she went home to her lonely cottage and cried herself to sleep. For the first time in her life, she felt things were beyond her control. Dylan was gone, and though she had been fairly cavalier about the variety of dangers that might assail him and make his faked death believable, now she worried about the very real risks he had taken every day since leaving. The newspapers were filled with stories of the trials of making the trek West— Indian attacks, weather, turbulent river crossings, lack of adequate food, disease . . . the list went on and on. Caitlin twisted her wedding band as she tried to decide what to do.

There were no more letters from Dylan, and there was no letter announcing his accidental death. The silence was deafening, causing Caitlin's concern for him to grow daily. She read and reread his letters and the journal. She wrote long letters telling him of her love for him, begging his forgiveness for her stubborn pride that had prevented her from getting word to him, urging him to hurry home where they could make a fresh start. She sent the letters out daily and prayed that somewhere, somehow, one of them would reach him. She grew tired of answering everyone's daily inquiries as to whether or not there had been any news, and she worried endlessly about him, imagining all sorts of horrors might have befallen him, ranging from capture by wild Indians to death in an avalanche. By mid-March with no word for over six weeks, she could stand it no longer.

As soon as her pupils had left for the day, Caitlin put on her cloak and bonnet and walked to her father's store. "I must get to Salt Lake City as quickly as possible, Father. Dylan needs me."

"Have you had word?" her father asked. Her parents were well aware of the number of weeks that had passed with no letter. They had watched their daughter pine away for her husband and had had long discussions about how best to console her.

"No, but I must go to him."

"It's a long and hard journey, daughter. I can't—"

"I am not asking permission, Father. I am asking for your help. My husband needs me, and I will go to him," she said with determination. "Now, will you help me get there as quickly as possible?"

John Pearce studied his daughter for a long moment. "There was a time, Caitlin, when I doubted your love for this man, though I never doubted his for you. There was a way he looked at you from that first day in church. I understood it completely, for it was the same way I had looked at your mother when we first met. If you feel you must go to him, we'll find a way."

For the first time since coming to the realization that her only option was to go to Dylan, Caitlin allowed herself to experience the emotion she had kept in check by sheer will for the past several weeks. "Thank you, Father," she said softly as the tears welled and spilled over.

Pearce pulled her into his arms in a rare display of fatherly love. "It will be all right, Caitlin," he murmured as he comforted her. "We will get you there with all speed."

"I love him so, Father. What if I were to lose him now?"

The wheels were set in motion immediately. Geoffrey was contacted in Madison, and within a day he had organized travel plans for Caitlin designed to get her to Salt Lake City as quickly and safely as possible. Mrs. Filbert was tapped to take over in the classroom for the remainder of the school year, for Caitlin's trip, even with all of Geoffrey's connections, would take weeks and who knew what she would find once she reached Dylan?

She packed lightly, assuring her mother and Molly that she would not need much and, if need be, she could purchase additional clothing once she arrived. Her father and both brothers gave her money, insisting she take it *just in case*. Her pupils gave her notes to carry to Dylan, thanking him for his letters and urging him to come home with her so they could hear the story of his adventure in person. Their actions touched her deeply, and she realized that her family and the entire town had come to care for Dylan. In less than forty-eight hours after she had decided to take action, she was on her way.

As she waited for the stage to take her to Galena and

the train, Hubert Filbert came running across the street waving a piece of paper. "Mrs. Tremaine, this was in the mailbag."

Caitlin's heart stopped as she read the words.

Dylan killed in avalanche. So sorry. Tyrone Tremaine

Hubert grinned at her. "I think that's pretty much the news you were expecting," he said.

Caitlin forced herself to smile at him as she folded the message written in Dylan's hand and slipped it in her pocket. "Yes, Hubert. It is the news I was waiting for." She hoped Hubert would not notice the devastation she felt at finally holding the promised conclusion to their bargain in her hands. The message meant only one thing—Dylan had given up and decided to go forward with his life without her.

Twelve

Tyrone Tremaine had gotten a good start on his personal fortune in California. He had staked a claim, worked it religiously, and gleaned several ounces of gold for his efforts. He'd also gotten caught up in the fever that was rampant throughout the area—the fever that deluded men into believing they had tapped a wellspring that would never run dry. After working hard for several weeks Ty heard about a place farther north where the precious ore was easier to find. He'd had enough of the backbreaking work of digging and shoveling for what to him seemed like minuscule amounts of gold compared to what he kept hearing others were reaping up north.

He abandoned his claim and decided to treat himself to a night in town before leaving. San Francisco was booming with activity. Buildings seemed to go up overnight and a man could find just about any kind of entertainment he wanted with the exception of the company of a woman. Women were scarce in California, so scarce that Ty and the other prospectors occasionally resorted to holding a "miner's ball," where men would dance with men and think nothing of it.

Ty loved San Francisco. He loved the energy and the newness of the place. He liked that every man here was coming from somewhere else, and nobody much cared what your life had been back in that other place. This unimaginable sense of complete freedom made him feel completely in charge of his own destiny. That night he strode into a local gambling house and enjoyed the attention and respect of the other patrons as he played the table games using gold nuggets to cover his bets.

He'd only intended to have some fun, to show off a bit, to enjoy the admiration of the other men. He knew how much he was willing to risk when he walked in, but he did not reckon with the intoxicating power of knowing the next throw of the dice or deal of the cards would double or even triple his money. By morning he had risked everything he had and lost it all. In the bright light of day he felt physically sick. How could he have so easily thrown away everything it had taken him weeks to gain? How could he have risked his future on a deck of cards or a pair of dice?

That morning Ty packed up and headed north. Along the way he was able to recoup a small portion of his losses helping others work their claims, but he wanted something of his own. He felt a burning compulsion to make amends for his disastrous mistake in San Francisco. In the back of his mind had always been the goal to be a rich man by the time his older brother Dylan joined him. Once and for all he needed to prove himself to Dylan, prove that he was a man now, capable of making his own way in the world.

The landscape in northern California was dotted with the camps of prospectors and the rough settlements they had established near those camps. It seemed to Ty as if every possible claim had been staked. He was feeling especially discouraged one night as he rode into one of the rough settlements, hoping for a handout and perhaps some information that would lead him to his fortune.

A saloonkeeper took pity on him and hired him on for the week to take the place of a man who had left just that afternoon to find his fortune. The saloonkeeper shook his head sadly and muttered something under his breath about the foolishness of young men. Ty was just glad to have some work, a place to sleep and solid food for a change.

On his third night working in the saloon, two men took their place at the bar and ordered beers for the house. A cheer went up and Ty served everyone the free round. Then he returned to the bar and engaged the men in conversation, knowing they must have hit a fresh strike. The pair were reluctant to talk at first, but several beers later their tongues loosed and they spoke in low confidential tones about the place they had discovered their gold.

Looking around to be certain no one else could overhear they asked Ty if he'd like a piece of their action. Ty had the good sense to be suspicious. Why should they cut him in? The men admitted that they were Easterners with no idea at all about how to work a claim. On top of that they had no equipment, and with the prices being charged for tools and such they'd use up the gold they'd found just outfitting themselves. Ty told them all about his mining background. He even bragged a little about the strike he'd made farther south carefully leaving out the part about gambling it all away.

The strangers told him he had every reason to be suspicious of them and offered to take him to the claim the following morning so he could see for himself. They said that with his trained eye and experience they'd no doubt at all that he would spot the gold at once.

Ty agreed. The following morning he met one of the men at the edge of town. The stranger said his partner wasn't feeling so good and would not be coming along. They headed north for an hour or more. When they reached the part of the stream the men had marked as their claim Ty found traces of gold right away. He tested several parts of the stream, finding gold dust in some parts but not others. Without revealing what he was seeing he asked the man what he and his partner were suggesting.

The man offered him a full third partnership for two

hundred dollars and the use of his equipment. Ty knew he didn't have two hundred dollars, but his employer did. He thought about how the saloonkeeper had entrusted the business to him while he went down to San Francisco on business. Ty knew where the extra cash was kept. He could borrow the money and replace it and no one would ever be the wiser. He accepted the deal.

That night the two men came into the saloon, and Ty gave them the money. They all agreed to meet at daybreak the following morning to head out to their claim. The men bought another round of drinks for the house and winked at Ty as they left the saloon. When morning dawned the men had disappeared; so had all of Ty's prospecting equipment he'd had stored in a shed in back of the saloon.

Ty rode out to the claim and checked it more carefully. After working the stream most of the morning he had to admit he'd been taken again, and this time it was somebody else's money that was gone. That afternoon Ty rode away from the bogus claim heading east. He had no way to pay back the saloonkeeper, and if he stayed around he was likely to be hung as a thief. Ty did the only thing left for him, he ran away.

"Glory be, son, when's the last time you had yourself a solid meal?"

Ty squinted up at the older man towering over him. He'd wandered into the settlement at Salt Lake sometime before dawn and collapsed in exhaustion in the alley behind a mercantile store.

"Sir," he said, and it came out a raspy whisper, "could you spare some bread?"

"I'll do a lot better than that," the man boomed and stooped down to help Ty to his feet. "Let's get you inside here. Your eyes are almost swollen shut. You just come across that desert, did you?"

Ty nodded and leaned heavily on the man as he helped him through the backdoor of the store.

"You sit yourself down here and stay put. My name's Daniel Clayton." He stuck out his hand.

"Tyrone Tremaine," Ty answered with a weak handshake.

Over the next few days Daniel Clayton cared for Ty as if he were one of his own family. Ty had never felt less worthy or more fortunate in his life. Clayton and his daughter Sarah fed him, provided him with fresh clothing and set up a cot in the back of the store for him to sleep on. Embarrassed at needing to depend on strangers for the very food he put in his mouth, Ty swallowed his pride and sent word to Dylan that he was in trouble and needed his brother's help. He had hoped Dylan would send money, but he was sure Dylan would come himself.

When Ty was stronger Clayton put him to work doing odd jobs to earn his room and board. When he realized Ty's talent as a stonemason he spread the word, and soon Ty had more work than he could handle in the town.

"What is this place?" he asked Sarah one afternoon when she brought him lunch as he worked on one of the community buildings down the street from her father's store.

"It's our Zion," she replied as she swept her hand across the vista of the town set neatly in the valley of the Great Basin surrounded by the stone fortress of the mountains.

"I mean who are you people? Brother-this and Sister-that and Elder-whatshisname?"

Sarah laughed. "We're the Saints," she replied. "Mormons. We follow the teachings of our Prophet Joseph Smith, the Bible, and the Book of Mormon."

"How'd you get to this place?"

"Our president, Mr. Brigham Young found it. He and several settlers came here a few years ago from the place we had to leave in Illinois after our leader was assassinated. Just like the Book foretold, our people wandered in the wilderness for days and weeks. When President Young saw this place he knew God had led him here. God showed us the way. He showed us how to use the water at hand so that we could start our farms and gardens. God cares for us. We simply need to do his bidding and we shall be protected and provided for."

Ty considered the way she spoke about God as if she had some sort of personal conversation with him every day. He turned away from her, concentrating on his work. "Then you'd best stay clear of the likes of me, Sarah Clayton, for no greater sinner ever walked the earth."

Sarah was silent for a moment, then she placed her hand on his shoulder. "There is redemption, Tyrone," she said softly, and seeing he was not yet ready to hear her she left him.

Ty was determined to repay the saloonkeeper he'd stolen from in California. He wanted not only to repay the money he'd taken but to add to it. Every penny he could spare went into a tin box. Each night he would sit on the back steps of the Claytons' store and count the coins. At the rate he was going it would take the rest of his life to pay off the debt. Depressed, he would stare out at the mountains that surrounded the community. One night he began to think about those mountains, the canyons they concealed, the streams at the bases of those canyons.

There's ore in rock, he thought, *so why shouldn't it be possible that there'd be gold somewhere in those mountains.* The more he thought about it the more sense it made to him. He used the free time he had to ride up into the foothills and along the rims of canyon walls. One day he saw it. A narrow deep canyon just like the ones he'd seen in California. He made his way down a trail to the base of the canyon. He examined the stream which was deep and fast-running. *There could be gold,* he thought excitedly.

The following day he went to Daniel Clayton and told him of his theory.

"Son, there's treasure within you. You've only to recognize it. You should concentrate on that and stop this fool's quest. The Saints came here to farm, to find wealth in the land and each other. You'd do well to think on that."

Daniel often spoke to him about repentance and embracing the one true faith. It was amazing what they had accomplished—these Mormons. The town was beautifully laid out, its fields of bounty stretching across the plain of the great Salt Lake. Ty was tempted. In Cornwall he had often dreamed of the day when he might have a spread of his own, land as far as the eye could see, all belonging to him. But first, Ty was determined to make his way, to prove himself worthy of the respect with which Daniel and the others in town treated him. To him that meant repaying his debts and earning enough so that he never had to rely on the charity of others again. It also meant being able to meet his brother with his head held high and enough money for the two of them to head back to California, where Ty was determined to redeem himself.

When Daniel saw his mind was made up, he agreed to loan Ty a wagon and sell him the supplies he needed to set up a camp. Several times over the next few weeks he rode out to the canyon himself, spending the night after helping Ty build a rough shack and furnishings before heading back to town the following day.

For his part Ty insisted on paying for everything in cash. When he ran out of cash he moved back into the back of the store and worked until he had the wherewithal to buy his next load of supplies. Then he would head back to his camp and stay until those supplies ran out.

The one regret he had was leaving Sarah each time. When he'd first met her he'd dismissed her as too young, too innocent for the likes of him. As time went by and she sought him out, talking to him, asking him questions, telling him about the Mormon faith he began to look forward to those times he spent with her however brief they might be.

He was also frustrated by having to go back and forth.

The small amounts he could earn doing odd jobs did not buy enough supplies to last him for very long even with Sarah adding extras to his order when he wasn't looking. Just when he'd made a start prospecting, he'd have to head back to town to find work.

"I've sold my mule," he told Sarah one afternoon as they took a long walk out into the country together.

"How will you get to and from town?" she asked, and for the first time since he'd met her he heard an expression of alarm in her usually calm serene voice.

He shrugged. "I'll walk when I have to. The thing is I'm going to use the money from the sale of the mule plus whatever I can earn over the next two weeks to put together enough supplies to keep me for at least a month. I have to do it, Sarah. It's no good this coming back and forth, back and forth."

She was quiet for a long time. "I wish I could understand why this is so important to you," she said finally. "I wish I knew why you are so driven by the need to make an earthly fortune. I wish I could persuade you that through the faith you will find the material and emotional wealth you seek."

He envied her that she could find such satisfaction in believing, but that was Sarah. Ty viewed his life as far more complicated than Sarah's. He had a great deal more to achieve and repent for than she would ever have. "I have to do this, Sarah," he said stopping her from walking on by taking her shoulders and turning her to face him. "There are many reasons, reasons I haven't told anyone. I stole money back in California, Sarah."

Her eyes widened, but she made no comment.

"I thought I was merely borrowing it and would be able to repay it without the owner ever knowing it was gone, but I was wrong. I owe that man a great deal, and intend to repay him."

When she did not turn from him in disgust, Ty continued.

"There's more. I've sent word for my brother to come here, not because I want to see him—although I do—but because I was weak and afraid, and all my life my brother has been there to make sure I was all right. This one time I would like him to come and find me better than all right. I want to be able to offer him the stake he needs to go with me to California and make our fortune."

"You are determined to return to California," Sarah commented, and her eyes brightened with unshed tears. "Why? California was nothing but loneliness and heartbreak for you. You have said so yourself. Why is it so important to you?"

"Don't you see, Sarah? I need to return there to prove to myself that I can."

She looked confused. "You don't want to go for any other reason?"

"No."

She turned away. Ty gently turned her back to face him and was surprised to see that she was angry.

"Well, it's a stupid reasoning you have, Tyrone Tremaine. My father has given you everything you could need or want to make a fresh start here, to be a success right here, and you think nothing of it."

"That's not true. Your father has been wonderful to me. *You,* Sarah, have saved my life. Every time I think of you it warms my heart, gives me such a feeling of peace and contentment . . ."

"And yet, it is not enough. We are not enough. Only California."

"I had hoped that in time we might be closer, Sarah. I had dared to dream that in time you might come with me."

She was speechless with surprise. "How could you think I would leave this place? I have told you what we went through to get here. Why would I leave?"

"Because, though it is too soon to be certain, I think in time that we might come to love each other, Sarah."

"If that were so, then why wouldn't you stay?" she asked softly.

He had no answer for that, and the rest of their walk was finished in silence.

Dylan quickly discovered that Tyrone Tremaine was well known in Salt Lake City where he had earned a reputation as a prospector haunted by past mistakes and obsessed with a drive for redemption as he worked the streams that cut through the foothills of the Rockies to the east. Those who knew him in Salt Lake knew he hoped to make enough to return to California and start fresh. When his prospecting wasn't going well—which was a great deal of the time—he did odd jobs in town in exchange for food and other supplies. His expertise as a stonemason was especially renowned. But no one in Salt Lake could recall seeing him for the past several weeks before Dylan arrived and began asking questions.

To make matters worse, there was no word from Caitlin. At each major stop on his journey, Dylan had hoped to find her letter of forgiveness waiting for him. Until now he had always been able to persuade himself that she was only following instructions to reach him in Salt Lake. The letter would be there, he had told himself through the hundreds of miles he had traveled.

When there was no letter, at first all he felt was sadness and disappointment, but the more he thought about it the angrier he became. *Damn the woman and her stubbornness. Would it have killed her to read the journal? But no, she'd judged me purely on the basis of something written early on, before I'd gotten to know her, to love her. Well, to hell with her.*

At first he had refused to satisfy her by sending the letter she had dictated as the final piece of their cursed bargain. Let her figure out how to explain to everyone in

Mineral Point why he wasn't coming back. Let her sit and stew for a while, wondering when she might finally be free of him. Let her explain again one day when he showed up because not even Caitlin Pearce could keep him from heading back there if he was of a mind to do so. Determined to get on with his life, he went to buy supplies for his trip back into the foothills and canyons to find his brother.

"Good day, sir. How can I assist you?" The young woman behind the counter smiled at him. She was like many of the women in this friendly town, welcoming without being forward, friendly without being brazen. She was the prettiest thing he'd seen in months. In another time, another place, Dylan would have been interested in seeing where things might lead. But Caitlin had ruined that for him. Instead he pulled out a list of items and thrust it toward the young woman. "I need these supplies," he said gruffly and turned his back on her.

Undeterred by his rudeness, the clerk smiled and went to work filling the order. "My heavens, you must be planning to be out for some time," she commented as she scanned the list.

Dylan grunted.

"Are you heading on to California or staying around here? I only ask because recently we've seen more men making the decision to stop here. Of course, part of it is there's been rumors of gold here, too, though frankly I think they miss the point. Our treasure here in Salt Lake is not of the mineral sort. It's the community, the life, the faith that makes us wealthy." She moved up and down gathering the supplies, humming to herself, completely unruffled by his stony silence.

"You say some believe there might be gold here?"

"East of here in the hills and canyons. I haven't heard of any, but we've had one young man staying around for several months now. He worked here in town doing odd jobs to get money for supplies and equipment. I never met a more determined soul. I just hope he's not disappointed. He's such a nice person, but Tyrone Tremaine is the stubbornnest soul I have ever met."

Dylan dropped all pretense at disinterest. The woman knew Ty. "Tyrone Tremaine is my brother. Do you know where he went?"

"I can show you. My father helped him set up camp, though we don't believe in what he is doing. There are no easy ways in this world, Mr. Tremaine." She pulled out a piece of paper and drew a surprisingly detailed map. "That is the canyon he has set his sights on." She shook her head. "He's so determined to find gold to make up for . . ." She shrugged her thin shoulders and smiled apologetically as she returned to gathering items for his order. "It's none of my business really."

"But you care," Dylan said, studying her more closely.

She paused, and he saw that she was blushing. "Your brother is a very . . . charming man, sir. He stops by the store here from time to time when he's in town. We talk. We have walked together. I tried to persuade him that God's treasure is of far more value than man's. Your brother doesn't like to hear about God."

Dylan smiled. "My brother is a fool, Miss . . . ?"

"Sarah . . . Sarah Clayton," she replied.

"Well, Sarah Clayton, I'm pleased to make your acquaintance. My name's Dylan, and if my brother gave up a chance to go walking with you in order to run off to those hills and peck around for a tiny bit of gold, he's a much bigger simpleton than I thought."

Sarah blushed again. "You're very kind," she said shyly.

Caitlin had said that about him in the days before she'd found out about the wager and his pretense to be illiterate. He doubted that she thought of him as kind these days. Apparently, she didn't think of him at all. He took out his money and paid the bill. "When I see my brother I'll tell him you asked about him," he said, and smiled when the color once again flushed her cheeks.

"I do hope he's well," she replied in the same calm even tone with which she had conducted the entire conversation, but her expression showed she was worried. "It's been several weeks since he was in town."

"So I understand from others I've spoken to. Don't you worry, Sarah. If I know my brother, he's gotten engrossed in his prospecting and forgotten to take note of the passing days. When he runs out of food he'll come on back to town."

"Thank you, Mr. Tremaine," she said with a radiant smile. "I wonder if you would like to join my father and me for supper this evening? My father and Ty worked together on some projects. Perhaps he can tell you more."

"It's Dylan, Sarah, and if you're offering a home-cooked meal and your company, believe me, you don't need to ask twice. I'd be pleased to come to supper."

His spirits were much improved as he left the store. With women like Sarah around, why on earth should he hold on to the idea of making a life with someone as obstinate and headstrong as Caitlin? *Because no matter how many times you try, you cannot get her out of your mind.* Well, maybe it was time he tried. If Ty was fool enough to pass up an opportunity to get to know Sarah, Dylan decided he wouldn't make that same mistake. Even if things did work out between Sarah and Ty, she'd shown him there were definitely possibilities other than Caitlin.

He finished his preparations and returned to the boarding house to clean up. Just as he prepared to leave his room, he scribbled the required note to Caitlin and asked the landlady to see that it was sent with the next rider headed East. He was not one to hold resentment, and it was time he got on with his life as Caitlin clearly had decided to do with hers.

As he walked the short distance to the Clayton house

he felt better than he had in weeks. He didn't know where things might lead with Sarah, if anywhere at all. It was a sure thing, though, that spending time with her could help dull the pain of remembering Caitlin and the passion they had shared.

Sarah's father was a distinguished older man who clearly doted on his only daughter. A skilled craftsman, he had worked with Ty, doing some stone work on several of the new buildings and houses going up in the thriving Mormon community. It was comforting to hear him talk about Ty, about Ty's talent and genial personality. He also hinted that Dylan's brother had been through some tough times, times he chose not to talk about much, but which clearly were the driving force behind his determination to find gold and make his fortune.

After supper Dylan sat with Sarah for a long time after her father had excused himself to tend to his chores and retire for the night. As they talked he realized that she was a lovely caring woman—a simple woman who would see her life's purpose as seeing to the happiness and health of her husband and children. He also saw that she was in love with Ty. A common thread ran through her conversation, and that thread was Ty. In her polite inquiries into Dylan's family history and the Tremaines' immigration to America, she was always listening for references to Ty.

At one point it occurred to him that if his brother was fool enough to miss a chance to woo and marry her, then Dylan and Sarah could probably build a safe, comfortable life together. Each of them would have a past love they would never forget, but each of them would be kind enough and practical enough to recognize the value of their own union. A man could build a good life with a woman like Sarah.

"I have to go," Dylan said, shaking off the thought as ludicrous. After all, he had only met the woman this day. "I'll be heading out early tomorrow to find my brother."

Sarah frowned. "I hope he's all right," she said softly. "As I mentioned, it's been longer than usual since he came to town."

Dylan saw that the words were all she had to show her concern, her fear that something terrible had happened to the man she loved. He gave in to the natural urge to give her comfort and put his arms around her. He was surprised to find that the feel of her against him gave him solace in return. Perhaps his thoughts had not been so far-fetched after all. Perhaps the smartest thing he would ever do would be to find somebody like Sarah Clayton to spend the rest of his days with.

"Good night, Sarah. Thank you for supper." He kissed her lightly on the top of her head and released her. When she looked up at him she was smiling even though tears glistened in her large dark eyes.

A miner Dylan had met outside Salt Lake said the last time he'd been in town Ty had talked of working the Sweet-water River. The map Sarah had drawn confirmed that. Dylan headed back to the foothills. It took him three days to find his brother's camp in a narrow deep canyon just west of South Pass. It amazed him to think he'd been within a mile of his brother when he came through the pass.

As he worked his way down the steep banks of the hill-side toward the stream and campsite, his uneasiness increased. There was no sign of life at the camp. No wisps of smoke rose from the shack he assumed Ty was living in. No mule stood hobbled near the stream. He saw no sign of his brother anywhere.

He resisted the urge to call out. Instead he checked his Colt revolver and looked for the way into the camp that would attract the least attention. His heart hammered against his rib cage as he imagined all the terrible things that might have befallen Ty. For the thousandth time since leaving Wisconsin, he thought about how much he wished he'd persuaded him to remain in Mineral Point. They could both be safe now. He'd be married to Cait and living a quiet normal life in that small stone cottage on the edge of town.

He saw movement behind the blanket that served the ramshackle structure as a door as if someone had brushed against it. He crept closer. Someone was definitely inside his brother's shack. Whether or not it was Ty was the only question. He moved close to the canvas door and pushed the barrel of his pistol against the man's back. "Cornishmen are like the turf," he said gruffly, then nudged the man with his pistol. "Finish it," he commanded.

"Cornishmen roam the earth," Ty replied. "Now put down that bloody pistol before you shoot somebody, brother."

"Ty?" Dylan lowered the pistol and pulled aside the blanket, whereupon his brother greeted him with a huge grin and a bearhug.

"You came," the younger man said as he hugged Dylan hard. "You actually came," he said again, and this time his voice cracked on the words.

"I told you all you had to do was let me know you needed me. It took awhile—you're not exactly across the street, you know," Dylan replied, sustaining the hug long enough to give his brother the time he needed to compose himself. "What's the trouble?"

Ty sniffed loudly and broke the hug. He gave a nervous laugh and moved a couple of steps backward. His eyes were bright with fever, and his shirt was soaked with sweat. "I'm busted, Dylan," he said softly. "Lost everything out in California. I was headed back when I stumbled across this place. Sold my mule last time I was in Salt Lake to a miner heading on to California. I actually tried to talk him out of going. Been able to do some work in exchange for food up until a few weeks ago—then this." He indicated his leg, which was heavily bandaged.

"What happened?"

"I fell. Some loose rock on that cliff up there." He waved a makeshift crutch toward a bluff high above them. "Musta laid up there for a day and a half before I made it back here." He staggered a bit and grabbed onto Dylan for support. "I think I'd better sit down," he said with a grimace of pain.

Dylan helped him ease himself to the cot in the corner of the cramped shack and took a good long look at him. "You look like hell," he observed.

"You're no beauty yourself," Ty replied testily. "Hand me that bottle yonder."

"How long since you ate?" Dylan asked as he retrieved the bottle of cheap whiskey his brother had indicated.

Ty shrugged. Then his eyes welled with tears again.

"You need that leg looked at. I'll head back over to Salt Lake in the morning and bring a doctor."

"No need to go for the doc. It's broke," Ty said with a disinterested slap at his thigh. Then he stared out toward the rushing stream as he took a long swallow of the whiskey. "The thing of it is, I know there's ore here, Dylan. Not a lot. Not like California. But enough to get us back on our feet, and then we can head on to California. They're making big strikes there. Thousands of dollars in one day," he murmured dreamily as he closed his eyes and rested his head against the post of the cot that doubled as a place to hang his clothes. "But the easy stuff is gone," he continued. His eyes were closed, but it was clear to Dylan that he was talking about California. He couldn't remember the last time he'd heard his brother talk about anything else. "The ones who'll make it out there now are men like us who know what they're doing—Cousins Jack, that's us, brother. Men of Cornwall who can find the tiniest bit of ore in the most obscure places." He lifted the bottle in a toast and took another swig. "But time's running out, brother. We got no time for you to run back to fetch a doctor. We've got to start right now, find the gold here and then head on West." His eyes were wild with fever and panic.

"Stay put," Dylan ordered and climbed up the hill to where he had left his own mule hobbled while he made sure it was safe to enter Ty's camp. Leading the beast, he carefully worked his way back down to the campsite. The trail was narrow, and loose rock made it slippery. Along the way he passed a patch of brush that was broken and flattened. He looked up at the steep cliff above and wondered if this was the spot where his brother had landed when he fell. If so, it was a wonder he wasn't dead.

Back in camp he unloaded the supplies he'd brought and then persuaded Ty to let him take a look at his leg. He tried not to show how the look of it worried him. He'd seen any number of injuries in his work as a miner—this one was bad. He bathed and cleaned the open cuts around the broken bone telling Ty about meeting Sarah as he worked; then he handed Ty the almost empty bottle of whiskey.

"Take a big swig," he said, "but don't swallow 'til I tell you. Got that?"

"Sure." Ty gave him a big grin and then emptied the bottle, holding it to his lips until the last drops ran out of his full mouth and down his cheeks.

"That Sarah is one good-looking woman, brother. You could do a lot worse." Dylan grabbed Ty's foot and yanked it hard at the same time he ordered Ty to swallow the whiskey. Ty let out a yell.

"What the hell did you do that for?" he demanded.

"I can't promise it'll heal right and proper, but this'll at least help." Dylan examined the alignment of his brother's leg and gave a grunt of satisfaction. "Now hold still." He used two boards he'd salvaged from the pile of scrap outside the shack to make a splint, then wrapped it with strips of canvas. "There." He looked on his handiwork with satisfaction. "Now, how about something to eat? After supper, we'll see what we can find to make a crutch for you."

Dylan set about building a blaze in the small corner fireplace and cooking some buffalo jerky, potatoes, and onions for the two of them. He could imagine Caitlin sitting across from him, trying the strange meat—tough on the outside but remarkably sweet and tender under that natural crust. Her beautiful eyes would light with wonder, and she would smile. She always smiled when she unearthed a new bit of knowledge or tried something different. He loved that smile.

Ty was still complaining about his leg when Dylan handed him a plate piled with the cooked jerky. "Tell me about this place," he said, casting about for any topic that would take Ty's mind off his leg. For the rest of the evening Dylan kept Ty talking about how he'd worked the stream—the tools he'd used, the methods he'd picked up from other more experienced miners. Dylan knew Ty was in no mood for a lecture. He also was in no shape to travel. They might as well settle in for a few weeks until Ty's leg could heal enough for him to make it back to Salt Lake.

The thing of it was, Ty wasn't the only one short on funds. Dylan's money was almost gone as well. Although he had been careful of every penny since leaving Mineral Point, he'd even had to dip deeply into the part of Caitlin's stipend she had insisted he bring along. That bothered him. He was determined to repay that money as soon as possible. He wanted no ties to the woman. He certainly didn't want to be beholden to her, even from thousands of miles away.

Ty seemed to rest easier after supper. Dylan helped him wash up and positioned him on his cot so that he could get some sleep. Throughout the evening to kill the pain, Ty insisted on dosing himself with hefty swigs from a fresh bottle of whiskey. When he finally slept—or passed out—Dylan sat by the fire, thinking about how he was going to get his brother out of this mess. Out of habit, he pulled out paper and pencil and started writing down his observations of the last few days. He'd written several pages before he realized that he was writing to Caitlin. He told himself he was doing it purely as an exercise to help him think things through. It was routine, and it worked for him so why change just because he'd never mail the letter and there was no more Caitlin in his life?

Thirteen

Caitlin's journey began in earnest when she took a steamer up the Illinois River to St. Louis. The boat was filled with all manner of activity. There were families headed West to homestead as well as prospectors hoping to make their fortunes. All of these hopeful people shared the cramped space with wagons and livestock. The noise and the stench were overpowering, and Caitlin could not wait for their arrival in St. Louis where at least she would be able to escape the crush of people for a little bit. Everyone was talking about gold. The newspaper accounts had fired their imaginations, and tales of finding nuggets the size of a man's fist were rampant throughout the voyage.

The scene that greeted them as they docked in St. Louis was one of even more activity. Up and down the levee business of one type or another was being conducted. Here, families were approached as they left the steamer to join this group or that for their trek West. Farther down, there were men shouting orders as African slaves unloaded huge bales of cotton or bundles of sugar cane onto waiting wagons. The shops along the side streets were crowded with customers, and Caitlin thought about her father and how he would love to have so many customers demanding to be served. She felt her first twinge of homesickness, but she knew she had made the right decision. If she and Dylan were to have any chance at happiness, going to him was exactly what was called for. His letters had made his feelings clear. She needed only to reassure him of her own love for him and they could finally put the silly bargain behind them and start a real life together. She only hoped she would not be too late.

She took a tighter grip on her carpetbag and crossed the street to what appeared to be a respectable hotel. Inside, the lobby was filled with people, some of them guests, others there to offer goods or services to those headed West. Caitlin paid the purveyors no mind as she strode directly up to the desk and waited to be served.

"A room please," she said as soon as the harried desk clerk glanced at her. "And I'll need to hire someone to collect my things. I've just arrived on the steamer there." She motioned toward the front window, where the now-empty steamer was docked.

"You and about fifty-eleven other folks," the clerk muttered. He pushed the register toward her and reached for a key while she signed it. "I got one room left."

She hesitated for one minute and then wrote Mrs. Dylan Tremaine with a flourish.

"That'll be two dollars, ma'am." He saw her surprise at the price and smiled. "It's the times, ma'am. I'm figuring you'll be wanting a bed to yourself. Truth is, I can get two bucks for a bed shared by three others. Folks'll pay a lot for anything they need for the trip West, and that includes a night's sleep." He grinned up at her, and she saw that his teeth were yellowed with tobacco. "Tell you what I'll do for you, seeing as how you're prettier than most who comes through them doors. I'll throw in the cost of delivering your stuff. The room's on the top floor, up them steps 'til you can't go no further, then down the hall, last door on the right, front street view." He pounded a bell next to the guest register. "Boy, get Miz Tremaine's things. Steamer there that just come in," he directed. "I'll take care of it, ma'am," he assured her as he handed her the key.

Caitlin noticed how he made sure he placed the key in her hand in such a way that his own fingers could graze hers. She shuddered slightly and forced a smile. "Thank you."

The stairway narrowed with each flight, and there were times when she was forced to flatten herself against the wall just to let other guests pass. It occurred to her that she was ill prepared for this adventure and it would do her well to take some time to think through her next course of action.

The room was cramped, with barely space for the single cot and the small washstand. Caitlin went immediately to the window and forced it open. The street sounds that had been muffled before filled the tiny space. There was a light knock at the door, and she opened it to find a young boy doubled over under the weight of her trunk.

"Good heavens, child, put that down immediately and let's slide it inside here," she ordered. He did as he was told, nodded once, and was gone. Caitlin sat on the edge of the trunk and took a long look at her surroundings. Never in her life had she felt more unsure of herself than she did now. For a moment she could not think what her next move might be, and she was not above admitting that she had seen men down on the docks, not to mention the desk clerk, who had looked at her in such a way as to make her distinctly uneasy.

The first thing she did was to slide the trunk against the door and then lay out the considerable amount of money she had brought with her. It seemed to her that her best course was to hide it in various places so that should she be robbed she would still have some resources. Once she had accomplished that, she took the pitcher from the wash basin and went in search of water and a towel so she could refresh herself before supper. The desk clerk sent the boy who had delivered her trunk scurrying to pump the water and handed her a piece of toweling that was little more than a rag. For this he charged her an additional fifty cents.

In the hotel dining room the O'Donnells, a family she had met on the steamer, invited her to join them at their table. They instructed her about what she would need to purchase for the trip now that she had arrived in St. Louis and shared information they had learned about the best places to make those purchases. Eliza O'Donnell showed her the guidebook they would use as they traveled. It certainly appeared to be thorough in its advice.

> *We will leave you to choose your own starting point, simply stating that Westport, Independence, and St. Joseph have facilities peculiar in themselves for the outfitting of the Emigrant. Every requisite for comfort or luxury on the road can be obtained at either of those places, on nearly as low terms as at St. Louis.*

The O'Donnells invited her to travel with them and others in their group, which was leaving in two days, and offered the services of their eldest son, Jack, to drive her wagon for her. She thanked them profusely, agreed to give their four children lessons along the way in exchange for their son driving her wagon, and insisted on paying for their supper since they had been such a help to her.

Wearily she climbed the four flights to her room, using the lantern the desk clerk had provided for an additional nickel to light her way. When she had once again barricaded the door, she undressed and lay down on the narrow cot. The docks were quieter now. The harmonies of the slaves singing as they rested after their long day of back-breaking work lulled her to sleep. In a few days they would head back South while she headed West. Their journey was routine. Hers was sure to be the grandest adventure of her life.

The following morning she was up and out early. She

spent the morning preparing for her trip, buying the provisions the O'Donnells had advised. Staples—of bacon, flour, coffee, tea, and sugar—and something called *hardtack*. There were crackers, cornmeal, and dried meat and fruit to be purchased. Caitlin had never imagined she would need to carry so much with her. In addition to the food supplies she would also need soap, candle wax, lanterns, washbowls, pots and pans, and blankets. Finally as she handed over a list of standard medicinal supplies, the shopkeeper advised her that she would need 2 quarts of #6 extract of cayenne pepper and a gallon of the best brandy for *medicinal purposes*.

"You'd best have one of these as well, ma'am," he added as he removed a revolver from a glass display case and placed it and a box of ammunition with her other supplies.

"I . . . that is, there's no need. . . ." Caitlin stared at the gun as if it might go off in her face at any moment.

"Ma'am, there's all sorts of possibilities for trouble on a trip like this—both from outside and *inside* the company when you're a female traveling alone, if you get my meaning. You take this along, and don't be afraid to use it. Here, I'll load 'er up for you and show you the fundamentals."

The shopkeeper also advised her where to go to be outfitted with a horse, a yoke of four oxen, and a wagon, then offered to have her supplies, including feed for the livestock, delivered to the outfitter by the end of the day.

"The wagon'll run you about seventy-five dollars, four oxen about two hundred dollars. Mules are good too, but they cost about twice as much and they're stubborn as all get-out. For a lady like you the oxen'll be the best."

"Thank you, sir," Caitlin replied, relieved to have found at least one merchant in town who appeared to consider the customer rather than the amount of the profit. At that her money was going faster than she had imagined. "I'll go attend to the purchase of the wagon and livestock and stop back to settle my account."

"Beggin' your pardon, ma'am," he said as he tallied the bill. "You'd be a sight better waiting another four weeks to go. The rains'll slow you down now, and there might not be enough tall grass to keep the livestock fed along the way. It'd go a good bit easier if you was to wait for another month."

"Thank you for your good advice, sir," Caitlin replied. "The problem is I have waited too long already. My husband needs me, and I must get to him as quickly as I can."

By the end of the day she was the proud owner of a fully outfitted covered wagon, a team of oxen to pull it, and a small homely gray horse named Buster.

"He might not look like much, ma'am," the blacksmith told her, "but I'll wager you two weeks pay he'll make it to where you're going. You can't say that for them fancy, pampered Eastern horses there." He glanced at a team Caitlin had shared the steamer with—a team that had already made the trip from Ohio. Buster looked as if he'd need to think twice about making it across the street.

The following morning Caitlin climbed onto the high wooden seat of her wagon and checked it once again to be sure everything was in place. Because, unlike the others, she was not moving furnishings and other household possessions, there was plenty of room for her to set up sleeping space inside the wagon. Young Jack O'Donnell greeted her with a shy smile and climbed aboard to take the reins. "Once we get out of town a ways," he said, "you might find it easier to ride Buster there or walk alongside," he advised. "Riding in the wagon can make a body sore in a hurry." As if to drive home his point, they hit a rock protruding from the road and Caitlin bounced high off the seat, landing with a hard thud on her backside.

With the sun rising at their backs the small parade of wagons set out. Their destination was Council Bluffs, Iowa, and they hoped to be there by the end of the week. "Do you think we'll make it in a week, Jack?" Caitlin asked more to make conversation than anything else.

"Aye, if the rains don't come and the creeks don't rise," he said.

Ty's leg had been badly infected when Dylan first treated it and although bathing the open sores and rewrapping the limb helped, Ty's fever was so bad for the rest of the week that Dylan was afraid to leave him. So instead of heading back to Salt Lake for the doctor, he did the best he could to make his brother comfortable and to get liquids down Ty's throat. During the daylight hours when Ty fell into a fitful sleep, Dylan spent his time examining the variety of tools his brother had built or collected for working the streams. At night he would have Ty explain their workings. Once he was sure it was safe to leave Ty alone for a while, he set to work.

At first he worked the area of the creek closest to the shack. When the weather was decent he'd set Ty up outside the cabin to watch him and call out instructions about his technique. It seemed to lift Ty's spirits to see Dylan working the stream, panning for gold. As the days went by he urged Dylan to move farther upstream. Dylan gave Ty no argument. He did not try to talk him out of his fool's mission to find gold. Dylan's plan was simple. He would methodically work every foot of the creekbed and report back to Ty each evening. When Ty realized there was no ore, then maybe he'd come to his senses and give up his senseless search for instant wealth.

The scrubby vegetation and freestanding rock formations were so thick in places he often lost sight of the creek as he made his way along the shore, although the canyon was so deep and narrow it was impossible to get lost. He didn't see any other people until the fourth day. He first heard the voices through the thick scrub. Something about the tone of the conversation warned him not to make his presence known. Instead he moved as close as possible, staying behind rock formations so he could get a look at what the men were doing. Just as he pushed aside one scrubby bush for a better look at them, one of the men fired a shotgun and the sound ricocheted up and down the canyon.

"Now over there," the other man said, urgency making his voice shake with excitement. "Hurry up."

A second shot.

"That oughtta do it," the shooter said.

"I'll be the judge of that," his partner replied as he bent down and dipped his hat in the stream scooping up a hatful of water and sediment. He fingered through the sediment, then gave a satisfied chuckle. "It's good, Jed, real good. Looks plum natural." He pulled a small leather sack from his belt and placed a couple of pieces of the gravel in it. Then he washed out his hat and turned to his cohort. "We'd better git, Jed. No telling if anybody heard them shots." He glanced around nervously and seemed to look right at the spot where Dylan was hiding. "It's too damn quiet down here," he muttered as he and Jed headed up the trail and out of the canyon.

Dylan waited for some time before leaving his hiding place and walking into the creek to check the area where the unnamed man had scooped up the creekbed sediment. Following the same routine, he examined the dregs once he'd poured off the water and discarded the obvious and larger stones. What was left was a mixture of creekbed sandstone and pebbles and traces of *gold dust.*

That night he told Ty what he'd witnessed and showed him the flecks of dust he'd recovered.

"They're saltin' a claim," Ty said angrily. "I'm embarrassed to say I fell for the same scam out in California. It's how I lost everything. Those two you saw today are probably hightailin' it back to Salt Lake right now. I heard tell of a couple of scoundrels like that working in Colorado.

The Riley brothers—Jed and Mick. They mighta made their way up here."

"One of them called the other Jed," Dylan said.

Ty nodded. "It's probably the same guys. In the next couple of days—as soon as they can find a willing sucker—they'll be back showing off the claim and then offering to cut him in or even sell him the whole thing."

"The shotgun was loaded with gold dust?" Dylan asked.

Ty nodded. "It's the best way to scatter the dust—makes it look random and natural."

"How can we stop them?" Dylan asked.

Ty looked alarmed. "Stop them? Dylan, you don't want to mess with these guys. They'd as soon shoot you as look at you. You'd best work the creek south of here for the next several days."

Dylan frowned. "It's not like you not to want to help a fellow miner, Ty."

"You don't know these fellas, Dylan. They're a new breed of bad. What's the point of trying to help a fella if I end up dead and so does he? At least the other way he just loses his money."

"Maybe you've got a point, brother," Dylan said, but he didn't sound convinced.

In spite of the rains, Caitlin's group made good time, and it took only three extra days to reach Council Bluffs. The sight that greeted them there took their breath away. Everywhere they looked they saw wagons headed West. When they left they were part of a long line of "prairie schooners." Indeed the wagons did look like so many ships sailing on the sea of the grassy plain.

It was another two weeks before Fort Kearney came in sight. Along the way several families had livestock stolen by the Pawnee. The thefts only served to alarm the travelers more than the constant barrage of printed circulars being passed from wagon to wagon on the train. The circulars warned travelers to beware of the Indians and reported all manner of dreadful deeds befalling those who had traveled this way before.

It was near Fort Kearney that Caitlin came face to face with her first Indian. She returned from relieving herself in a cluster of bushes near the camped wagons and came face-to-face with a tall, wild-looking man, wearing nothing more than a blanket tossed over one shoulder and a scrap of cloth to cover his loins. He wore a headdress of feathers signifying that he was among the leaders of the tribe. He was in the process of stealing the pancakes she'd left cooking over the fire.

"You there," she said in what she hoped was a voice that would command respect. "Stop that this minute."

The Indian glanced at her, gingerly plucked the pancakes from the skillet, and casually strolled away, eating one as he went. His demeanor told her clearly that as a woman she was beneath his notice.

Caitlin picked up the skillet and followed him, holding the skillet aloft. "Give back those pancakes," she ordered.

The Indian glanced at her and upon seeing the skillet she wielded in a threatening way, his eyes widened.

"I do not know how things are done in your culture, sir, but in mine thieves are tried and sometimes shot. I resent your taking my property. I especially resent your doing so in broad daylight and without any obvious remorse. You can redeem yourself in only one way—return the remaining cakes and we will forget the entire incident." She held out the pan and indicated by gestures of her head and free hand what she expected him to do.

The Indian considered her for a long moment, then placed one cake in the skillet.

"All of them," she said and once again brandished the skillet, realizing too late that the action sent the returned pancake flying.

With a snort of disgust the Indian threw the other pancakes on the ground as well and stalked off.

Caitlin thought about the incident while she made more pancakes. Perhaps the man was simply hungry. Perhaps he had a family he was trying to feed. In the end she piled a stack of pancakes on a plate and covered them with molasses. She saw the Indian and several of his cohorts in conversation with the trailmaster. She walked over and presented the platter of pancakes to the trailmaster. "Perhaps our guests are hungry," she said and glanced directly at the Indian who had stolen her pancakes before walking away.

At Fort Kearney she left letters for her parents and for Molly, describing the trip in detail. She also enclosed one for her students, along with a special note for Rob urging him to continue his studies and telling him what places to locate on the map for the younger students. Their next great challenge would be crossing the Platte River she told Rob, but first they must cross the Great Plains where the trail wound west as clear as the streets of Mineral Point. After years of hauling supplies to the forts strung across the plains, the rutted path was there, parallel wheel ruts cutting through the plains. All they had to do was follow it. She knew that every person on the wagon train had a different hope for what would be at the end of that trail.

It took weeks to cross the plains. Hour after hour, day after day of the same flat and undisturbed terrain. Most of the time it was dry, but when the rains did come they were merciless, accompanied by a high howling wind that buffeted the wagons, causing them to moan and creak. Sometimes it rained through the day and night, and the heavy wagons would become mired. They would have to stop or go around a disabled wagon, hoping its owner could make the necessary repair and catch up with them by nightfall.

At this rate it would be autumn before they reached California, Caitlin feared, as day after day they traveled what appeared to be the same trail. The scenery never changed only the weather. Tempers flared as the days dragged on. Sickness was rampant though no one in their small group died. Her spirits dropped. Perhaps she'd been foolish to even attempt the trip. If she'd stayed in Mineral Point and sent letters to Dylan, surely eventually one of them would have reached him. Instead she was here in the middle of mile after endless mile of flatlands with no town in sight and no opportunity to send or receive word. She did not want to contemplate how his feelings might have changed in all this time.

"Buffalo," the trailmaster shouted and the word was passed back from one wagon to the next.

Caitlin shielded her eyes and looked out toward the west. What she saw at first was a long dark line that seemed to stretch from one side of the horizon to the other. It looked like a legion of soldiers. Then as the wagons came steadily closer she was able to make out the huge animals. "There must be a thousand of them," she said excitedly to Jack.

Dylan had written her about the buffalo—"an unbelievably huge beast who appears to be clumsy and lumbering yet is surprisingly quick." Now seeing them for herself brought home the full force of his description. She took the reins of her wagon as Jack mounted Buster and eagerly joined his father and the other men on the ride out to bring down enough of the huge animals to supply every wagon with meat for days to come. Cait was struck by the great clouds of dust the horses raised as they galloped across the prairie. She realized they had left the rains far behind and were seeing less and less greenery in this new drier terrain. What if the shopkeeper in St. Louis had been right? What if they had left too soon and the grass was not high or plentiful enough to feed the livestock?

She wiped away the trickle of sweat that streaked her face and concentrated on keeping the wagon in line. She realized how used to the noise of the daily trek she had become. Whips cracked and men yelled as they urged the animals onward. Here and there a baby wailed, someone laughed, a wagon spoke splintered. Her hands were starting to freckle, and she thought about how horrified Molly would be to see her not protecting her creamy skin with gloves. The thought made her smile. The idea of Molly on a trip like this made her laugh out loud. She would be a trembling mass of hysteria if she were here now, surrounded by the dust and the distant thunder of a thousand buffalo on the run, interrupted by the shouts of the hunters and the occasional pop of a rifle. Caitlin found it all thrilling, and her only regret was that Dylan was not by her side. There was no turning back now, she realized. She had set her course. She needed only to remind herself that every mile they traveled brought her that much closer to a reunion with her beloved. She simply refused to consider the fact that she might be too late.

At night she wrote her parents and Molly and then treated herself to rereading one of Dylan's old letters before going to sleep. At this point she was able to read letters that described the same scenery she had witnessed that very day. She felt closer to him knowing they had now shared experiences, even if they were still separated by hundreds of miles and many weeks of misunderstanding.

Two days after crossing the Platte they had to navigate a steep rocky hill. The road ascending the hill was crooked and uneven and the wagons tilted crazily as they negotiated the narrow treacherous trail. On the other side they came upon a sudden turn where the road narrowed even more. One wagon attempted to take the turn too fast and overturned. The young boy who had been driving the wagon fell beneath the team of mules scrambling to regain their footing as the weight of the wagon dragged them to the edge of the narrow road. The boy was pulled from the rubble, but died within the hour.

It was the first death among their group, and everyone took it especially hard. Camp was quiet that night with people speaking in hushed whispers as the sobs of the boy's mother permeated the night air. Caitlin lay in her wagon and thought about the terrible realities they had faced that day. For the first time since leaving home she was frightened, not for herself but of the unknown. What if Dylan had met a similar fate in crossing that particular passage? And how could she be sure she herself wouldn't die farther along the trail?

Outside Fort Laramie the trailmaster called for everyone to pull the wagons into a circle for the night. The fort itself was more of a trading post than a military installation, but it boasted a saw mill, a store, and a blacksmith. The travelers were able to resupply their stocks, have wagons repaired and horses shoed. Once they had restocked their supplies, the travelers spent the rest of the afternoon and evening butchering the buffalo the men had brought into camp from the morning's hunt. A group of friendly Indians who had also set up camp outside the fort showed them the best way to preserve the meat. Jack brought Caitlin a slab of it for herself.

"They call it jerky," Jack reported as he showed her how to cut the meat into long strips and then helped her run string along the sides of her wagon from front to back so she could hang the strips on the wagon. "They need to cure for a couple of days," he instructed. "The Indians said they sometimes do that over a slow fire, but since we need to keep moving, they said it'll work just as good to dry the strips in the sun as we travel."

"You're a very good teacher, Jack," she complimented him. "Thanks for your help. I have a small gift for you." She handed him a big package of candy sticks she had bought at the store. "You can share them with your brothers and sisters," she suggested.

He gave her that same shy grin with which he'd greeted her that first morning. "Thank you, ma'am. You know, when I was little I thought I might maybe be a teacher one day." He shook his head as if the very idea was ridiculous.

"I think that's probably one of the most noble professions you could aspire to, Jack. It's a wonderful dream and one I hope you realize someday."

Jack smiled at her. "I hope you get your dreams, too, Miz Tremaine," he replied. "I hope you and your mister are together real soon."

Dylan had headed out every morning toward the south end of the canyon, to satisfy Ty's fear that he not tangle with the Riley brothers should they return. But as soon as he knew he was out of Ty's sights, he doubled back and headed north. Whatever happened, he wasn't going to let those two scoundrels take advantage of some poor unsuspecting dreamer. Maybe he felt bad about not having been there when Ty needed his help, but he was now determined nobody else was going to get conned out of his life savings if he could help it.

To pass the time he worked the stream above and below the spot where he'd observed the two men salting the claim. Each night when he returned to camp, he brought with him the evidence of his day's work. It was hard watching his brother's dream die in bits and pieces, but he would soften the blow by talking about the life the two of them would share working the land. He would remind Ty that he'd once had another dream. Before gold fever had taken over, Dylan knew his brother had dreamed of the day when he would own land—lots of it, where he could roam and ride to his heart's content. Ty hated the underground work of mining. Dylan mentioned Sarah from time to time and was pleased to see that talking about the girl always lifted Ty's spirits.

On his third day out he whiled away the time by panning in the stream while he waited for Jed and his partner to return to the salted claim. Mostly he enjoyed the rhythm of the process. He really didn't expect to find anything. If there was gold in this stream surely one of the hundreds of prospectors trampling through here on their way to California would have found it. But it was a good way to spend his days while he waited for Ty's leg to heal enough for them to travel, and the work kept him from thinking too much about Caitlin.

Using Ty's iron pan, he scooped up the soft dirt he found at the edge of the stream. Then he stepped into the icy cold creek and stooped down, swirling the pan under water and slowly raising it out of the stream, the way Ty had shown him. This was how he spent most of every day, knee-deep in icy water, panning for gold that he was certain wasn't there. He was beginning to feel pain in his legs at night long after he'd left the stream and stretched out to sleep. He'd heard others talk of rheumatism and figured that's what it was. He kept the swirling motion going, slowly, rhythmically, every so often jerking the pan quickly into and out of the water, which served to rid the contents of the lighter sand and other residue.

Nothing as usual.

He repeated the exercise, his ears attentive for the sounds of men's voices. He stepped out into the center of the creek. The water was still cold from the snow melt and runoff. As he dunked the pan and started the familiar routine yet again, he spotted a single cluster of blooming mineral plant. The sight of the blue-purple flower made him homesick, and he realized he was not thinking of home as in Cornwall. His thoughts were of home in Mineral Point—with Caitlin.

He glanced down at the pan's contents as he dipped it in and out of the creek several times. By now he paid little attention to the actual gravel and rock in the pan. It was an exercise, something he did to pass the time. From time to time he would glance down to see what was left in the pan before stooping to fill it again. It was backbreaking and boring work, but that was what mining was. No wonder most miners thought of it as a means to a better end.

Something half buried in the black dirt and debris left in the pan caught his eye. The stone was no bigger than half his smallest fingernail, but as soon as he pulled it free he knew this pebble was somehow different. Could Ty have been right? Was there gold in this canyon, and had he found it?

He knew at once that this was no case of additional salting. Ty had explained that salters rarely placed anything more than dust at the site—it was all that was needed to get the attention of a potential sucker. If this thing was gold, it had been here all along and chances were there was more of it. His heart hammered.

What he was holding in the palm of his hand was not dust. It was more pebble than stone, but it was solid and he was becoming more and more convinced that it was gold. His first instinct was to run all the way back to camp and share the news with Ty. His second was to protect the site from anyone else who might come along and start the same kind of random panning he'd been doing for days now. Complicating any decision were the sounds of men's voices coming from the trail that led into the canyon.

Dylan checked his revolver and moved quietly into a cluster of rocks on the opposite side of the creek from where he knew the men would pass. He was about a quarter of a mile north of where the men had salted the creek. He watched as Jed and the other con man led two other men to the creek. They were talking excitedly to the pair as they led the way down the creek.

"Mick, I think it was farther down," Jed said.

Mick and Jed, Dylan thought. Ty had been right. The Riley brothers were working this area now.

"Yep. We marked the spot," Mick assured the two strangers.

Stealthily Dylan tracked them down the creek.

"Here's my mark," the one called Mick yelled to the others. Dylan had noticed the marks left by the two thieves on trees and brush surrounding the fake claim. "Test for yourselves, gentlemen," he added with an expansive sweep of his hand to encompass the creekbed and its shoreline as the rest of the party caught up to him.

The two strangers glanced at one another and then at Jed and Mick. These guys looked like they had it bad—gold fever. Here was their chance to be rich without having to face the dangers of making the rest of the journey to California. The two tried hard not to show their excitement, but it was plain on their faces.

"What do you think?" Jed asked anxiously when one of the men had panned several loads with no apparent success. "Maybe it was more in that direction we hit paydirt," he instructed, clearly apprehensive that the men were too inexperienced to recognize what was right under their noses. Mick gave his partner a look of warning, and Jed backed off.

" 'Course there might be nothing here more than what we found," Mick commented with an attitude of nonchalance. "Just wish we hadn't got word of Mama doing so poorly back home. Just hope me and Jed can get there before she goes."

The two strangers remained silent, but their faces spoke volumes. Clearly they had seen the dust in more than one place as they'd checked the stream. Their only decision was how to gain the claim for the minimum amount of cash. Dylan shook his head in wonder. Being played out before him were two different con games, and he wondered if it was worth it to try and help the strangers. On the other hand, stepping forward now would assure that none of them would accidentally stumble across the bonanza he'd just discovered farther upstream.

"Fifty dollars," one of the strangers muttered as he

rinsed out his hat and slapped it back on his head. He fingered the revolver at his hip.

Jed and Mick glanced at each other. "Two hundred," Mick countered. Then he gave the men a sad smile. "Come on, fellas, we been working this stream for months, and just when we've hit paydirt we got to leave."

"To bury our sweet mama," Jed added, whipping off his hat and placing it over his heart in a gesture of respect.

The strangers conferred. "One hundred and one fourth of everything we find—final offer," the one said.

Mick fingered the phony claim papers in his vest pocket. Dylan watched as he considered his options. To insist on cash on the barrelhead instead of part of the claim was to as good as admit the claim was phony. "How do Jed and me know we'll ever see any of that extra?"

The man who'd been quiet throughout the entire transaction pushed his hat back on his head and looked Mick square in the eye. "You're just gonna have to trust us— same way we're trusting you now," he said.

Dylan grinned. Maybe these guys didn't need his help after all.

"Make the deal," Jed urged Mick.

Mick removed the papers from his pocket. "Let's see the cash," he ordered.

The quiet man and his partner both drew their guns. "Hands up, boys," the quiet one ordered while his partner moved quickly to relieve Jed and Mick of their weapons. "Maybe I should introduce myself. I'm the law in these parts, and we don't take kindly at all to folks trying to con innocent people out of their hard-earned money even when they're willing."

"You can't prove nothing," Jed argued.

"Shut up, Jed," Mick ordered. "Hold on. I'm sure we can work something out. After all, we never said for sure there was gold here."

"That's true enough. Then you won't mind if I take this

off your hands," the lawman said as he plucked the claim papers from Mick. "Now why don't you boys head on outta here, and don't let me see you around these parts ever again. Are we clear?"

"Yessir," Jed sniveled.

"We'll be needing our guns," Mick said testily.

"I'm sure you've got at least a shotgun back with your things in town. I'd really recommend you boys get going before I change my mind about arresting you. Seems I heard tell of some swindling going on in Colorado a few months back." He waved his gun in the general direction of the trail and waited.

Mick stalked off, with Jed not far behind. The two lawmen followed them, leaving Dylan alone once again. He waited only long enough to be sure he wouldn't be noticed before racing back to camp to share his news with Ty.

Fourteen

There was never any end to the work to be done along the trail, yet Caitlin relished the chance to do her part. She felt as if every time she did a chore, she was learning something new, something that would make her a better wife for Dylan. On top of that every day she felt stronger. In those early weeks, she had gone to sleep early every night and had wakened every morning with aches and pains she hadn't thought she could endure. She had never in her life done so much physical labor, but as she performed the work, she felt such a sense of accomplishment. By the time she reached him, she wanted to be strong and fully prepared to take her place at his side as a full partner.

She was also glad for the opportunity to teach the children. It made the time pass, and it made her feel connected to home. On top of that, she knew that her willingness to do her share, plus teach the children, had earned her the respect of her fellow travelers. Since beginning the trip, Caitlin had seen the development of more close friendships than she had ever known in her life. At the start she realized several of her fellow travelers had looked upon her as odd, but before the first week had passed, she was simply one of the group—someone to laugh with, help with the work, and share stories of home. The children's parents repaid her with milk from their cows and a helping hand if she needed repairs to her wagon. Eliza O'Donnell had shown her how to let a bucket of milk hang off the side of the wagon as they bounced along the rutted trail. By evening she had butter.

Jack talked all the time about his plans once they reached California, confiding in her his deepest thoughts and dreams for the future. In the long hours they had spent together along the trail, he had lost all his shyness with her. It was like traveling with a younger brother and Caitlin knew she would miss him dearly once the day came to go their separate ways.

One day they spotted the famous landmark of Independence Rock. Caitlin told him the story of how it was named by Colonel Fremont on the Fourth of July. Jack rode out with his father and several of the other men for a closer look at the awesome monument. As the wagons got closer, Jack came riding back alone, pushing Buster hard and shouting something unintelligible.

Caitlin's heart pounded and she prayed there hadn't been an Indian ambush or an accident. Throughout the trip they had been on the lookout for Indians. They had encountered a few, mostly around the forts where they stopped to replenish supplies, and all of them had been helpful and friendly. Still, the fear persisted.

"Miz Tremaine," Jack yelled, "you gotta see something. Come on. You gotta see this."

"Jack, what on earth has gotten into you?" His mother who had been walking alongside Caitlin's wagon looked up at her eldest son.

"Ma, take the reins for Miz Tremaine, please. She's just gotta see this," he pleaded.

"Jack, what is it? You're scaring your mother—and me, for that matter," Caitlin said.

"It's your name. It's there on the rock. The trailmaster says people leave their names or messages for those who come along, and your name is there. I bet Dylan did that, don't you think?"

Caitlin pulled the reins hard and stopped her wagon.

Eliza O'Donnell was aboard almost before the wheels stopped turning. "Well, go on," she urged. "You can't miss this."

Caitlin accepted the hand Jack offered to pull her onto the saddle in front of him. "Hold on," he said and dug his heels into Buster's sides.

The rock that had seemed impressive in the distance was no less than majestic up close. "It must cover ten acres or more," Jack reported. "That's what Pa thinks. Ten acres for one rock." He shook his head in wonder as he halted Buster and helped her down. "Come on."

He led the way over the massive rock, climbing higher and higher. Caitlin followed, her attention focused on the ground to be sure that she had solid footing. Only after she had hurried to keep up with Jack for several minutes did she pause to catch her breath and look up. There before her was a vista such as she never could have imagined seeing for herself. The mammoth rock on which they stood was bare of all vegetation and rose directly out of the ground, independent of any other elevation. The plains spread out below them on all sides.

After taking a moment to look around, Caitlin eagerly followed Jack the rest of the way to the top where she turned slowly in a circle, awed by all she saw below her.

"Imagine it, Jack," Caitlin said. "Imagine how far we've come."

"Come over to this side," Jack called as he scampered to the far side of the rock.

Caitlin saw that he was pointing to dozens of names and messages that had either been painted or carved into the stone. If it was true that her name was there and Dylan had carved it, then he had been thinking of her, loving her.

"There," Jack said, pointing to a place high on one side.

Caitlin was the simple inscription carved into the rock, and below it in smaller letters were Dylan's initials. There was no date or message, just her name and his initials, but it was more than enough. "Thank you, Jack," Caitlin whispered, and her eyes welled with tears of joy. "Thank you."

After they had passed the rock, they faced the mountains—the giant Rockies that loomed along the horizon in a solid jagged but unbroken line. It had taken two months to reach this point. The peaks towered over and around them and seemed insurmountable, but the trail was well worn and the ascent so gradual that the travelers hardly realized how high they had climbed until they stopped to look behind them. When they reached the summit, Caitlin gathered the children and showed them how water pouring down one side ran east toward the Atlantic while water pouring down the other ran west to the Pacific. She wanted to have each child scratch his or her name into a loose stone and pile them together at the summit marking their presence there, but there was not a single stone to be found, or a stick or branch. That as much as anything made her consider the full magnitude of their crossing these awesome mountains. Once they descended on the opposite side their lives would be changed forever.

When the party entered the Colorado Valley they found the streams rife with alkali that poisoned the water. The pasture for the livestock was equally venomous. To find safer water and feed as quickly as possible they slept in shifts and traveled through the night. When they occasionally stopped to rest the animals they herded them into a makeshift corral where they could monitor what they ate and drank.

They were making exceptionally good time. It had been less than ten weeks since they'd left St. Louis. At this rate they would reach Salt Lake by week's end. The weather was beginning to warm, and there was every indication that as soon as they crossed one more river the worst of their trip was over, at least for the time being.

Then it started to snow.

Caitlin wondered what else could delay them. The trailmaster ordered the wagons pulled into a tight circle on the banks of the Green River and all of the horses and other livestock were corralled inside. Caitlin joined the other women in searching for buffalo chips to use in place of wood for fires while they stayed in camp and waited out the storm.

It snowed for two days before the skies cleared and the sun came out. The trailmaster checked every morning to see if they could make a safe river crossing. Twice he decided it was too dangerous; then, on the third day, the camp awoke to find that they had neighbors. A large contingent of Shoshone Indians had set up camp just across the river. The trailmaster stared across at them, scratching his beard.

"I'd thought we'd go this morning," he told those gathered along the shore with him.

"What has changed your mind, sir?" Caitlin asked. Her patience was wearing thin. They had had to wait for days for the storm to subside and the weather to clear enough for them to proceed. At this rate she'd never find Dylan.

"Ma'am, we've been most fortunate with the savages up 'til now, but we've also been within a rifle's scope of a fort or armed forces. This is different. We're on our own here. I'd just as soon not push our luck."

Caitlin looked across the river. What she saw was a mirror image of the activity going on in their own camp. The women and older children were cooking and doing the ordinary household chores associated with being on the trail. The younger children played in the melting snow. The men sat close to the riverbank and studied the wagons on the opposite shore. "They appear to be perfectly harmless," she announced.

"Well, ma'am, you being a teacher and all, I'm sure you've got all the answers," the trailmaster said testily. "I say we wait them out. Better to be safe on opposite shores than sorry on the same one, if you get my meaning."

Caitlin was aware of the snickers of some of the men

and boys, but when she looked at the faces of the other women, she knew they were as weary as she was of the delays enforced by the elements. Like her, they were running out of patience with delays imposed by the trailmaster. Like her, they looked across the river and saw families trying to make do, just like their own.

"We'll wait 'em out," the trailmaster said looking across the river, but clearly delivering his message to Caitlin.

"That could take days," Caitlin argued.

The trailmaster shrugged. "Yes'm. Could even be weeks if they don't make a move," he muttered, and then covered his grin by spitting a stream of tobacco juice into the river.

Caitlin turned on her heel and returned to her wagon. She spent the next hour with the other women melting snow for doing the laundry. She insisted on helping Jack's mother with the myriad of chores that came with caring for a large active family. The two women worked in comfortable silence.

"Injuns coming," one of the men shouted, and all eyes turned toward the river where a small band of Indians were, indeed, crossing, working their way slowly across the fast-running waters that had kept the river from freezing solid.

The women herded the children into the safety of the wagons. By now the youngsters knew the drill: lie down and stay down until it was safe. The men armed themselves. Everyone in camp went silent as they watched and waited.

Three Indians halted their horses several yards off shore. "It could be a trap," the trailmaster warned.

"For heaven's sake," Caitlin said with an exasperated huff. She stood between two of the wagons and shouted to the leader. "Can we help you?"

The proud brave scanned the tightly circled wagons for the source of the voice. He seemed momentarily surprised to see the slight, redheaded woman waving to him. "I said, can we be of help?" she repeated through cupped hands.

"You're determined to start something, ain't you, lady?"

the trailmaster muttered, but he moved next to her, his gun at the ready.

"Go now," the brave replied.

"Like hell we will," the trailmaster started to say.

Caitlin shushed him with an impatient wave of her hand. "Go now?" Caitlin responded, her voice rising in question.

"Now," the brave urged and indicated the river. "You go now," he repeated motioning from one shore to the other. To emphasize his point, he and the others rode a few yards toward their own shore and back again. "Now," he demanded.

"He's telling us to cross the river now," Caitlin told the trailmaster.

"All of a sudden you understand Injun talk?" he replied in exasperation.

"The man is speaking English," Caitlin replied patiently. "It would probably be wise to talk to him calmly and see why he is suggesting we cross now. I'll be happy to go with you."

The trailmaster looked from her out to where the Indians waited. When the leader saw he had their attention once again, he shouted, "River," then used sign language to show it would rise.

"He's saying the river will rise," Caitlin translated.

"I can see that, and I already know that. The other piece of that is that the river will also go back down."

"Shush," Caitlin ordered shading her eyes from the sun. "He's trying to tell us something more."

The leader rode close enough to shore to bend down and scoop up a handful of snow which he threw into the river, then another. Then he made a slow sweep of the hills surrounding them and repeated the action of throwing the snow into the river.

"I think he's trying to make the point that the snows will melt, probably especially fast since the days are warmer now, and the river will rise and possibly flood," Caitlin said with a satisfied smile.

The trailmaster frowned. "He's got a point," he said to the other men as if Caitlin were nowhere in sight. "I'm going out to talk to him. Cover me."

Caitlin threw up her hands in exasperation and moved aside to let him pass. At least he was willing to take action even if he did need to take the credit for making that decision.

It took them three days to move all the wagons across the river, even with the help of the Indians. If they had waited, it would have taken weeks. The Indians showed them how to follow a current instead of trying to go straight across. They pointed out sandbars to make the crossing easier, but sometimes the weight of a wagon caused it to break through a sandbar. Then everything would plunge into the water and everyone would scramble to rescue what they could, further delaying the crossing.

When they were finally across, everyone in camp helped prepare a feast to thank the Shoshone and then settled in for the night. Caitlin had dressed in dry warm clothes and had begun to reread Dylan's journal when she heard a knock at the back of her wagon. She loosened the pucker ropes that closed either end of the canvas-covered top, offering her privacy when she needed it. The trailmaster was standing outside. He held his hat in both hands and looked anywhere but at her.

"Ma'am, I just wanted to say . . . well, I guess I owe you an apology. . . . You know, about the matter with the Injuns."

"You were only doing what you thought best," Caitlin replied.

The trailmaster nodded and continued to stare at his feet.

"Was there anything else?"

"Just wanted you to know you did a hel—heck of a job

out there these last three days. You've pulled your weight on this trip, ma'am. We all respect you for that."

"Thank you." Caitlin was inordinately pleased by the compliment. "I appreciate that you took the time to—"

"Good night, ma'am," the trailmaster said and stepped around the side of the wagon and out of sight.

When Dylan showed his brother the pebble he'd discovered, Ty was unexpectedly suspicious. "Looks like gold," he muttered as he turned the stone over and over in his hand.

"It's not part of the salted claim, Ty," Dylan assured him.

"One way to check it," Ty replied and reached for a box of lye on the shelf above his cot. "Boil it in this for five or six hours. That'll tell the tale."

"But what do you think, Ty? Could it be gold?"

Ty studied the rock for a long time. "I think I don't want to get my hopes up, brother," he said quietly.

The two men were quiet throughout supper and after. From time to time they would glance at the pan in which the lye mixture was boiling over the campfire. Each found routine chores to occupy him while they waited out the hours. Dylan couldn't help noticing that Ty was getting around a whole lot better than he had been.

"Your leg's coming along pretty good," he commented.

Ty smiled. "There was a time there when I thought your cure was worse than the pain, but I think you mighta saved me, Dylan. A couple of times while you were gone I took off the splints and put some weight on it. Last week I took my first walk without the splint. I'll limp a little, but maybe that'll make the ladies sympathetic, you know?"

Dylan laughed. "You don't need to limp to have the ladies all over you, little brother. You never did. 'Course you might not be able to outrun a determined one anymore," he teased. "Like Sarah Clayton."

"Might not want to," Ty said. "Might be nice to get caught. You'd know all about that now, wouldn't you?" He took a long swallow of his tea. "You ain't talked much about her, Dylan," he said quietly. "I got your letters, and that's all you did talk about. Since coming here, though, you've been awfully quiet."

Dylan considered telling his brother the whole incredible ale of the bargain he'd first struck with Caitlin and then now he'd fallen in love with her—and lost her. Maybe one Jay he'd tell Ty about it, if for no other reason than to save his brother from making a similar mistake. But for now it was too fresh and hurt too much for sharing with anybody else, not even his own brother. "I'm a lucky man," was all he said, and he turned away to tend the fire.

"Well, you gonna tell me about her, or do I get to guess?"

Dylan answered Ty's outburst with silence.

"You could at least tell me what she looks like," Ty fumed.

"Picture fiery red hair hanging all the way to her waist, green eyes that sparkle like precious metal, skin that's the color of fresh morning cream. And on top of that she's about the smartest person I ever knew—man or woman."

"And just why would this paragon choose you?"

"I've asked myself that a thousand times," Dylan said quietly. And he had questioned the rightness of his love for Caitlin; in the long nights or as he worked alone panning for gold, he wondered what in God's green earth had ever given him the gall to think she might return his love. "What about you? No perfect woman out there in California?"

Ty laughed. "No women period in California—least not anybody you'd want to spend eternity with." Then he sobered and stared at the fire. "But California is something special all by itself, Dylan. A man's free to be or do anything he wants out there. There's nobody calling the shots, bossing you around. Everybody's the same—starting out. I loved it out there," he said dreamily.

They both fell silent. Ty continued to stare into the camp-fire flames. Dylan readied his equipment for the next day's search. They had each been seduced, he thought as he worked. Ty by the totally uncompromised life he might lead in California and Dylan by the emerald eyes of a certain prim and proper schoolmarm.

"Should we check it?" Ty asked after an hour, nodding toward the pot where the pebble boiled in the lye solution.

"You're the expert," Dylan replied. "Has it been long enough?"

"Yep. Let's see what we've got." He knelt by the fire and used his crutch to push the pot away from the flames. Using his shirttail as a hotpad he poured off the hot scalding liquid. Then he dumped the pebble into the spoon they'd used to stir their supper of beans and onions. Dylan moved closer as Ty brought the spoon into the light of the fire.

It caught the light and held it, reflecting it back. "It's a nugget," Ty said reverently. "An honest-to-God gold nugget, maybe as much as a quarter of an ounce."

Dylan just stared at the tiny rock. It came by its name honestly, for he'd never seen anything as shiny and gold as this. "Do you think there's more?"

"Yep," Ty said as they both remained mesmerized by the nugget.

"You ready to go to work and help me find it?" Dylan asked.

Ty grinned. "Yep," he said again and laughed.

That night was the first one since Dylan had found him that Ty did not use whiskey to help him sleep.

"Ty?" Dylan called to him in the dark of the shack.

"Yeah?"

"I'd like to keep that nugget—if that'd be all right with you."

"For Caitlin?" Ty asked.

"Maybe. Would it be okay? I'll pay you your half," Dylan assured him.

Ty laughed. "You found it. It's yours, brother. Now get some sleep."

Dylan lay on his back, listening to the sounds of the night. He was going to send that nugget to Caitlin to repay what he owed her for using the money she'd paid him. He needed to show her that he'd made something of himself after all.

The next day the brothers were up well before dawn. Dylan helped Ty load the mule with equipment and showed him where he'd found the nugget. Carefully the two brothers marked their claim, staking out the entire area between their shack and well beyond the point where Dylan had hit paydirt. Ty set to work reassembling the equipment and setting up a camp for them to work from while Dylan headed into town to file their claim. When Dylan had tried to get Ty to come with him, his brother had adamantly refused.

"Out in California, if you leave your claim unworked for a week or so, it's fair game. I expect there's not much difference here."

Dylan had never seen Ty so happy, and for the first time he understood that for Ty it was as much the adventure of the search as finding the strike that made it all worth the effort.

Caitlin could recall only a handful of lighthearted moments as they continued their trek through the solid and unyielding mountains. One came when they reached a small canyon late one afternoon. The children were the first to discover that it was possible to talk in a normal voice and hear three repeats. Laughing and giggling, they called out to friends three wagons away and carried on whole conversations. Then the men got caught up in the fun of

it, calling out directions and orders that echoed and rever-
berated against the narrow canyon walls. Up and down the
length of the parade of wagons there was the welcome relief of laughter.

At Eliza's urging, Caitlin stepped up to take her turn.
"Dylan," she said in a normal voice. *Dylan . . . Dylan . . .
Dylan.* The sound ricocheted off the canyon walls. Caitlin
smiled and repeated his name, shouting it this time. Up
and down the canyon, the name resounded. For the first
time in days, Caitlin laughed.

The relief of laughter, of enjoying themselves, was like
a tonic. Overnight their moods shifted, spirits were revived,
and the determination to see the trip through was renewed.
In recent weeks they had witnessed horrible things. They
had seen personal articles abandoned along the way as people had evidently attempted to lighten the load in order to
make the trek over the mountains easier. There were deserted wagons, broken beyond repair. Then they had come
across the carcasses of livestock—mules and oxen who had
simply collapsed from exhaustion and lack of food and
been left to die. And finally they had seen the graves,
mounds of rocks piled high and marked with rustic wooden
crosses, sometimes a name and a date or age. With each
passing day morale had plummeted. Arguments were more
common, and a few families turned back, afraid to go on.

They camped at Fort Bridger. One more ridge of mountains loomed before they would enter the Great Basin Valley. Once they crossed through the pass the trailmaster told
them they would see a sight they would long remember—
the beautiful Salt Lake valley. When they saw that they
could be assured that the worst was behind them, at least
until they reached the desert. He advised them that the
route was the most precarious of their travels, and they
would climb to an altitude of over seven thousand feet.
Caitlin looked up at the snow-covered heights and won-

dered if, even in late summer, the mountains were entirely free of snow and ice.

It took three days to cross. Every night Caitlin read the same letter, the one in which Dylan had talked about seeing the great Salt Lake for the first time.

It glistens, green and beautiful like your eyes, beloved Cait. I have heard that Ty might be there. I pray that it is so, for that would shorten my search by weeks. But the other side of that is that if he is in Salt Lake, why? Something terrible would have had to happen to make him leave California, and I pray that he is safe. I love you, Cait, and I long to gaze into your eyes and tell you so even as I stand here at this mountain pass and gaze down on this beautiful lake. I only pray I will find your letter waiting there.

But, of course, there had been no letter from her waiting for him. She pulled out the message Hubert Filbert had handed her as she'd boarded the stage to begin her journey. What had caused him to decide to fulfill his end of the bargain after weeks of professing to love her? She could no longer suppress the doubts that enveloped her when she was alone with nothing but her thoughts and the evidence that he had decided to let her go. Caitlin lay awake far into the night, wondering where Dylan was and if he thought of her at all these days.

The next day she and the rest of the party trudged on through narrow mountain gorges and crooked turns that were sometimes so close the wagons were barely able to negotiate them. Then, suddenly, the road turned, leading them through an opening that framed the valley and the beautiful Salt Lake spread out below them. Caitlin stood with the others and looked out over the valley hundreds of feet down, with nothing to obstruct her view for miles.

Against a background of mountains the beautiful lake

did, indeed, glimmer in the distance. The town was a welcome sight as well. Laid out with wide tree-lined boulevards, it boasted dozens of neat small houses and larger community and business buildings. There were gardens and trees, and she understood why the emigrants spoke of this as being like the Promised Land. In the thin clear air of the mountains everything took on a clearness and distinctiveness that made the view seem unreal.

It amazed Caitlin to see how much had been accomplished since the Mormons had left their home in Illinois less than two years earlier. She had read about Joseph Smith as well as the current head of the movement, Brigham Young, and she had to admit that she was intrigued by the prospect of learning firsthand about this revolutionary religious movement. Caitlin stood a moment longer than the others, wondering if Dylan and Ty were still down there, wondering if it could be possible that her long journey was almost over.

By the time Caitlin and the others pulled their wagons into the town of Salt Lake City they had traveled over thirteen hundred miles and had witnessed a landscape that changed almost daily. But that was of little significance when Caitlin thought of the changes in herself. She was not the same woman who had left Mineral Point. She was physically stronger and mentally wiser for the experience. Whatever happened between her and Dylan, she knew this had been the right decision. She would never regret these past months, and she would never forget the people with whom she had shared this experience.

Fifteen

In the settlement at Salt Lake, the people were inordinately kind and eager to welcome the travelers and make them comfortable. The women were especially good-hearted, concerned that the women on the wagon train take full advantage of the hospitality they offered them in their homes. Caitlin enjoyed her first bath in weeks and reveled in the clean fresh clothing provided. The Mormons were different in many ways from any people Caitlin had ever known, yet they were alike in all the important ways.

"I understand that you are seeking your husband," one of the older women commented as she helped Caitlin and the other women wash clothes.

"Yes, the last letter I had from him before I left on my own journey indicated he might stop here for a time. Perhaps you have heard of him—Dylan Tremaine?"

The woman thought about the name. "There was a young man, Tyrone Tremaine, who was in town for a time."

Caitlin's heart pounded. "That would be my husband's brother. Is he still here?"

"I really haven't seen him in some time. Perhaps you should ask Daniel Clayton at the supply store. I know Tyrone worked for Brother Daniel and bought supplies there when he could afford them."

Caitlin went immediately to the store. The young woman behind the counter greeted her with the same friendly open smile she had encountered throughout the town. "How may I help you, miss?"

"Is Daniel Clayton here?"

"Not just now. I'm his daughter, Sarah. Perhaps I could help?"

"Do you know Dylan Tremaine or his brother, Tyrone?"

Sarah smiled. "I've had the pleasure to meet them both. Dylan was here several weeks ago. He is so very kind, a wonderful man," she added, and then blushed. "My father and I both enjoyed his company."

Caitlin's heart stopped. In a moment she imagined the meeting. Dylan with his smile and charm meeting this beautiful young woman. How could she have imagined that Dylan would simply assume she loved him even though he found no letter of forgiveness when he arrived in Salt Lake? How could she have been so stupid to have thought that in all the weeks and months it had taken her to cross half a country to find him, Dylan would not have found someone else. Someone far more beautiful than she. Someone who would think of him as wonderful and tell him so. Someone like Sarah Clayton.

"Do you know the Tremaines?" Sarah asked.

"Yes. I've come to . . ." She paused. *To what? To claim my husband who isn't my husband at all? To proclaim my love*— far too late to do any good at all?

"Are you all right, miss?" Sarah had come around from behind the counter and taken Caitlin gently by the arm. "Why don't you sit over here for a minute? You're quite pale."

"I'll be fine," Caitlin assured Sarah.

"Dylan came in search of his brother, Tyrone," Sarah explained as she exited through a curtain and returned with a glass of cool water. "Isn't it wonderful that he would be concerned enough to travel from who knows where just to help his brother? I'm afraid people aren't all that caring especially during these times." She motioned for Caitlin to drink more. "I mean this gold fever seems to have infected people in strange ways. I only hope that Dylan is able to talk some sense into his brother."

"Do you also know Tyrone?" Caitlin asked.

"Yes. Ty is also a good man, but he lacks Dylan's maturity and reason, I'm afraid. Ty is one who has been affected by this gold fever, and it has made him a person obsessed. In the end I fear it will leave him a most unhappy person." It was hard to imagine someone as sweet and composed as Sarah Clayton could ever lose control, but she certainly appeared on the edge of doing just that when the subject of Tyrone Tremaine arose. Perhaps she was upset because Ty's whimsy had put Dylan in danger unnecessarily.

There was no doubt in Caitlin's mind that Dylan had worked his magic on Sarah Clayton. Nor did she doubt that when he'd arrived in Salt Lake and found no message from her, he'd decided to move forward with his life and forget her. With women as beautiful and nice as Sarah it wouldn't take long at all.

"I could show you how to find them," Sarah offered. "The truth is I've been concerned myself. It was weeks ago that Dylan left to search out his brother. A couple of miners came through town not long ago trying to sell a claim, and we later learned they'd salted the claim. They were caught working an area at the upper end of the canyon near the Tremaine camp."

"What is 'salting'?" Caitlin asked.

Sarah explained, then laughed. "Isn't that ridiculous? What men will sometimes do to find riches when all they really need to be happy is peace of mind."

"Is there gold there?" Caitlin asked. "In the canyon where Dylan is?"

Sarah shrugged. "Maybe. Anything's possible, but it's doubtful. My father says that when a man's got the fever, he sees gold everywhere." Sarah replied; then she looked sad. "Dylan will have trouble convincing Ty that there isn't gold there somewhere. He has about the worst case of fever I ever saw."

"I have to find him," Caitlin pleaded. "Will you help me?"

"Why?" Sarah asked. "Are you related?"

"I really can't explain that. I know them, and I've come all the way from Wisconsin to find them. Please, won't you help me?"

Fortunately for Caitlin, Sarah was a trusting soul. Caitlin's heartfelt plea moved her, and she agreed to give Caitlin the directions she needed to find the camp. She also suggested two or three men in town who would be good guides to accompany her. Caitlin thanked her profusely and left the store. She did not say that she had no intention of using one of the guides Sarah suggested. Instead she would persuade Jack to accompany her until they found the camp; then he could return to town and go on to California with his parents. Whatever Caitlin found in that camp, she had reached the end of her journey. She would not be going on with the others.

For days, Dylan had insisted on standing in the icy cold stream, pouring water over the dirt he and Ty took turns shoveling into the hopper. As he scooped and filled the hopper, Ty would "rock the cradle" by working the handle that rocked the hopper causing the sediment to filter through the perforated bottom where it got caught in the apron and was dispersed out the lower end. Any gold-bearing sediment would be caught behind one of the crossbars called riffles that lined the base of the contraption.

For hours on end the two brothers worked their claim. At the end of the first day they had less than an ounce of gold, but they were elated. At the end of the first week, they had gleaned four ounces. As they worked Ty talked excitedly of building a sluice so they could dig deeper into the soil and process more of the dirt in a shorter time.

"We're doing fine as we are, Ty," Dylan replied. It concerned him that his brother's lust for gold seemed insatiable. "There's no rush. The object was to find gold. We've found it."

Ty frowned and turned back to rocking the cradle.

"You know, little brother," Dylan said, trying to change the mood, "that Sarah Clayton is sweet on you."

Ty continued to scowl, but the hint of a smile tugged at his lips. "What makes you think a fool thing like that?"

"As soon as she found out who I was, the woman was off and running, telling me all about you, singing your praises, talking about taking some long walk with you." Dylan shook his head and shoveled another load of rock into the hopper. "I swear I couldn't get her to shut up long enough to find out where you were."

"She's not like that," Ty commented. "She's so quiet. I have to do most of the talking."

"Sounds like the lady likes what you have to say," Dylan said and leaned on his shovel, closing his eyes against the blinding pain of the headache that had come on the night before and had escalated steadily through the morning. "You know you could do a lot worse than take your share of what we dig out of this canyon, buy a good piece of land, and settle down right here with Sarah. You always dreamed of owning your own hunk of land, Ty."

Ty gave a mirthless hoot of laughter. "Yeah, right. A girl like Sarah Clayton has her pick of the men in Salt Lake and you think she'd choose me?"

"I think it's worth your best shot," Dylan replied, but he didn't pursue the conversation. The truth was it was all he could do to hold up his end of the work. For the past few days in addition to the headache, he'd experienced a disturbing numbness in his legs and he'd noticed the beginnings of a rash on his wrists and ankles. He'd told himself

it came from the long hours spent standing in the cold
stream and sleeping in his still wet underwear every night.
Back in camp he massaged his legs and sat as close to the
fire as possible, but the chill that cut all the way through
his bones would not leave him. This morning he'd tried to
shake off the double vision that came and went as he followed Ty up the stream to their stake. He bent down to
scoop another shovelful of rock and sediment.

"Ty?" The shovel fell from his hands.

"Lord, almighty, Dylan, what is it?" Ty was next to him,
holding him as he slumped to the ground. "Dylan?"

"Caitlin . . ." The single word was whispered before
Dylan slipped into unconsciousness.

Ty sat on the ground holding his brother and looking
wildly around. What could he do now? He couldn't leave
Dylan here while he went for help. It could be weeks before
anyone came this way. If he did leave to go for help, it meant
there'd be nobody to keep watch on their claim. He glanced
around, assessing the possibility of intruders being able to
come in and jump the claim while he was off fetching the
doctor. The odds were good that nobody would come, but
what if they did? What if the Riley brothers came back? All
the backbreaking work would be for nothing.

Dylan moaned and curled into a ball as if cold or in
pain. Ty backhanded the sweat that rolled down his forehead. "Come on, Dylan," he urged as he stood and dragged
his brother onto the rocky shore. "We got to get you back
to camp, then I'll figure our next move."

He hefted his brother onto the back of the mule and headed
back to the shack. Trying desperately to think what might
be the best medicine, he settled Dylan onto the cot, wrapped
him in every blanket he had, and then poured a generous
helping of whiskey into a tin cup. He lifted Dylan's head
with one hand while he tried to force-feed him the liquid
with the other. "Come on, Dylan, take it," he urged as the
precious whiskey passed his brother's slack lips.

Dylan coughed and swallowed, then mumbled something more about Caitlin.

"Yeah, buddy, I wish she was here too, but you're stuck with me for now." He forced a little more of the whiskey into Dylan's mouth, then polished off what remained in the cup himself. "I got to get back to our stake, Dylan," he said as he eased his brother back and readjusted the covers. "Soon as I figure out how to secure the place I'll go for help, I promise. In the meantime you just sleep—best thing for you." Ty wasn't sure whether he was trying to reassure Dylan or himself.

Caitlin made plans to part company with her fellow travelers who would strike out on the last leg of their journey to California the following morning. She was able to sell her wagon and team of oxen to other travelers who had lost theirs in crossing the mountains, and she gave what remained of her other supplies to Jack and his family, keeping only what seemed practical for her stay in Salt Lake, which she hoped would be brief.

She spent the rest of the day outfitting herself to head back into the foothills and find Dylan. She was relieved when Jack offered to stay and go with her, catching up with the wagon train later. She'd been reluctant to ask this of Eliza, realizing that Jack was not much more than a child himself.

"I'd appreciate that," she replied. "Is it all right with your parents?"

"It was Ma's idea. I shoulda thought of it myself, but the good thing is somebody thought of it. We can't have you heading off into back country all alone. Ma says if you run into any Indians or bad sorts you'll need somebody to protect you." He grinned at her and Caitlin smiled.

"I'll accept on one condition," she added. "As soon as we have located the camp you'll head back here to catch up with your family. I mean it, Jack," she added when she saw that he was about to protest. "I won't have you wasting precious hours coddling me when your family needs you."

Jack frowned. "If that's the way it has to be," he agreed reluctantly.

"Thank you. We'll leave in the morning at first light."

Ty decided to check the claim once more and then wait for morning before leaving to get the doctor. Dylan was restless and hallucinating throughout the night. Ty kept him calm with frequent doses of the whiskey, but he didn't like the way things were going. On the occasions when Dylan was conscious he was talking wildly about Caitlin, morose that she had abandoned him one minute and then swearing at her for her lack of faith in him the next. Ty was determined to go for the doctor, but wondered how he could leave his brother in this shape for the time it would take to get to town.

To make matters worse when he checked the claim the following morning there were telltale signs that someone had been there. *Had the Riley brothers returned?* Ty nervously fingered the gun he carried in his belt and scanned the high walls of the surrounding canyon. *Somebody could be watching right now,* he thought. *Watching and just waiting to pick us both off.* That meant he couldn't leave. He'd just have to doctor Dylan as best he could and keep watch on the claim as well.

For the next two days and nights Ty divided his time between the cabin and the claim. He was exhausted from lack of sleep, but he refused to close his eyes for more than a few minutes at a time. Once when he went to check on Dylan and found him wandering around the camp, delirious with fever, he decided more drastic measures were needed. He force-fed his brother enough whiskey to make sure Dylan passed out, then used rope to tie him to the bed before he returned to the claim.

All was as he had left it, but that didn't mean there wasn't trouble out there somewhere. He decided his best bet was to set traps around the camp and the claim—tripwires and such—and then find a hiding place up in the rocks with a vantage point for watching both locations. By now he knew every inch of the canyon and could move easily from one place to the next without detection if he were so inclined.

He returned to the cabin, made a big show of preparing to head into town and then started up the trail. If anybody was watching they would think he'd gone for supplies or the doctor. This would flush them out for sure. Ty smiled to himself as he turned off the trail and headed down a narrow path to a point where he could observe everything without being seen himself. For the first time in two days he permitted himself to close his eyes. If somebody tried to slip into camp or the claim site they would trip one of the traps and Ty had no doubt their shriek of shock would reverberate off the canyon walls and wake him.

Jack and Caitlin were fortunate enough to spend the night in the barn at a small farm close to the trail that would take her to the canyon where Dylan and Ty had last been spotted. She had deliberately disguised herself as a man, and when the farmer and his wife kindly invited Jack and her inside their small cabin, she insisted the barn was good enough and bid them good night, insisting on paying them for the night's lodging.

They were up and gone before sunrise, following the map Sarah had provided and grateful for the lone trail that led down into the narrow canyon. At mid-morning she spotted the shack and the campsite. She could also see the place where Dylan and Ty had set up their equipment to work the stream, but she saw no signs of life at either location.

"I'll be fine from here on, Jack," she said, trying hard to keep the quaver of concern from coloring her words.

Jack looked skeptical. "Why don't you let me go with you at least until you rouse somebody? It looks awful quiet down there."

"They're prospectors, Jack. One wouldn't expect to see them lounging about in the middle of the morning like this. I have no doubt that they're off at some other part of the canyon, looking for gold. I'll go down to camp, prepare a proper meal, and surprise them when they return at the end of the day."

Jack was clearly torn. "If you're sure—"

"I'm absolutely sure. See for yourself. The camp is there, and nothing's amiss. Now, please don't make me feel any more guilty than I already do for taking you away from your parents. They need your help, Jack. They depend on you a great deal."

Finally Jack agreed and turned his horse back toward town. Caitlin watched him go, realizing that while she might exchange letters with Eliza from time to time, she would not see the family again. She thought about Eliza's stories of her parents and in-laws and brothers and sisters, all left behind in Kentucky. She recalled how Eliza's eyes had never failed to glisten with unshed tears as she told those stories. It was perhaps the greatest hardship of the journey, the leaving of loved ones and with no idea when, or if, you would ever see them again.

Caitlin waved at Jack as he turned back once before heading over the rise where they had first looked down on the valley. Tears rolled unchecked down her cheeks as she slowly swung her arm from side to side in a gesture of farewell. Urging her horse Buster to move on, she slowly wound her way down the steep path toward the camp.

Ty awoke with a start, his senses on alert. He rolled on to his belly and looked out over the terrain below. By the sun's position it was about noon. All was quiet, but he knew from experience that didn't necessarily mean all was well. He squinted into the bright sunlight reflected off the clear stream. *There,* he thought and drew his gun from his belt. He'd spotted something or somebody moving toward the shack. He hurried down the narrow path that wound through the rocks to the rear of the campsite.

He arrived just in time to see the intruder trip the wire he'd run from the entrance to the shack to the edge of the creek and go sprawling with a yelp of surprise. Ty grinned and stepped out from behind the rock, gun drawn and cocked.

"Git up," he ordered as he brandished the gun and stepped carefully over the wire. Just then there was another loud shout of surprise from up the creek at the claim. Ty glanced in that direction and the intruder on the ground before him rolled over and bit his leg, causing him to drop his gun. The pistol fired as it hit the ground.

The intruder's hat had come off in the fall, and Ty found himself face to face with a very angry, very beautiful red-head. "You could have killed me," she said as she retrieved her hat and struggled to her feet. "I must assume that you are Tyrone since you favor Dylan a great deal. Where is your . . . ?"

"Shut up, would you? Somebody's jumping my claim, lady, and I got no time for the likes of you," Ty answered as he bent to retrieve his pistol and then headed at a limping run toward the claim site.

Caitlin scrambled to her feet and watched him go. She observed two other men hightailing it up into the hills as her attacker chased them, yelling and firing his gun at them. She sighed and turned toward the shack. Inside she heard the guttural sounds of someone trying desperately to catch his breath. She pushed aside the filthy blanket that served as a door and entered the filthy, dark cabin. The stench practically drove her out, but she waited a moment for her eyes to adjust to the low light.

She was standing in a single small room. Two cots, a square table and two handmade chairs were the only furnishings. Some shelves had been tacked to two of the walls to hold supplies. There was a small fireplace, cold now, but clearly of use for the chilly nights and for cooking when the weather turned foul. A rope had been strung to serve as a clothesline, though it was empty of any fresh laundry at the moment. On the table were a small weighing scale, a log book, and a lantern.

She lit the lantern and moved quickly to the man lashed to the cot.

"Dylan," she whispered as she stared at him in shock. He was thrashing about, fighting the restraints that held him, his eyes wild and unseeing, his hair lying in dank sweat-dampened strings on his forehead and neck. He had a full beard and clearly had not bathed in several days, if not weeks. "My heavenly stars, what has happened to you?" Caitlin cried as she put down the lantern and knelt next to the cot. She worked feverishly to release the ropes that held him down.

Immediately, Dylan relaxed a little. "Sarah? Is that you?" he croaked. He blinked and tried to focus. He'd been dreaming about Ty, worried about his thirst for gold and wanting him to find a nice girl like Sarah and settle down. Was he awake or still in the dream. "Sarah? Where's Ty?"

"Sh-h-h," the woman came closer and eased the bands about his chest that had held him. "I'm here," she said softly.

"Thank you for coming, Sarah," Dylan murmured and drifted once again into sleep.

Caitlin stood beside the cot for a long moment, looking down at the man she loved. The man who apparently no longer loved her. She had no idea what she should do—leave now? Send Ty for Sarah to nurse him? Stay? It was impossible to say just how sick Dylan was. Clearly he was running a high fever and his strength was gone. There

was an ugly rash over much of his body. The restraints
indicated that even Ty, strong as he was, had had some
problems containing his brother. She glanced around the
shack and shuddered.

"Who the hell are you?" Ty demanded as he thrust aside
the blanket over the door and entered the cabin. He planted
his long legs in a stance of authority and leveled a rifle at
her head.

Caitlin gathered her wits and went into action. "I am
Caitlin Pearce—perhaps your brother mentioned me. And
I assume you are the recalcitrant Tyrone who has left your
gravely ill brother lying here strapped to this filthy cot
while you are off who knows where chasing gold. Well,
let me tell you, young man, there will be some changes
around here now that I've arrived. You won't like them,
but that's too bad. Our concern must be for your brother
at this time."

Ty stared at her openmouthed as she picked up a pan
from the rough-hewn table next to the cot and brushed past
him on her way to the stream. "Please do something about
keeping that blanket flap open so Dylan can have a bit of
fresh air and if you think it's possible, find me anything
that resembles a clean cloth with which to bathe your
brother."

"Now see here . . ." Ty began, but he got no further.
Caitlin turned and fixed him with the look she had perfected for use on rebellious and disobedient young people,
and he threw up his hands and turned back to the shack
where he lifted the blanket and looped it behind the warped
board that served as the portal for the doorway. "There,"
he said with a satisfied smile.

"It will do," Caitlin replied as she walked back to the
shack with a full pan of water and inspected his work.
"And now that cloth, if you please."

He started to loosen the sweat-soaked kerchief he wore

around his neck and was pleased to see her eyes widen in repulsion. "It's all I got, lady," he said.

"For heaven's sake. Go up that trail and collect my horse. I left him tied to a small sturdy bush over to the side. In the bag on his right haunch you will find some clean linens. Please be quick about it."

Ty muttered something under his breath, but he did as he was told. In the short time he was gone the woman had carried out most of the contents of the small shack and piled them in a heap. Ty hobbled her horse and went inside. "What the hell do you think you're doing, lady?"

She wheeled around and pulled herself to her full height which was still considerably less than his own. "Now see here, Tyrone. I would have hoped we might have met under better circumstances and gotten off to a more amicable start. However, that was not our fate. Your brother will tell you that I do not tolerate profanity under any circumstances. If you cannot find other words to make your point, then I expect you to keep quiet. In case you haven't noticed, your brother is extremely ill. Why you have elected to leave him here and not at least go for a doctor is beyond me. The man is completely dedicated to you, talked of little other than you while we were . . . when I knew him in Mineral Point. The least you could do—"

Suddenly Dylan sat bolt upright on the cot and cried out in an indistinguishable gibberish as he tore at his clothing.

"Oh, my stars," Caitlin murmured as she rushed to his side.

Ty was right beside her, and she saw that he was as scared as she was. "What are we gonna do?" he asked.

He's so young, she thought as her eyes met Ty's terrified gaze across the narrow cot. *Not much older than Jack.* She took a deep breath and tried to speak calmly.

"We've got to get him to a doctor or get a doctor out here. Until then we've got to do whatever we can to bring down his fever. Have you given him any medicine at all?"

"Just this," Ty said, holding up an almost empty bottle of cheap whiskey.

Caitlin frowned. "Do you think you could carry him outside to the stream and bathe him while I clean things up here and make some stew? Our first task must be to make him as comfortable as possible. Then we'll try to get some nourishment down him."

Ty nodded.

While Ty stripped the clothes off Dylan, who had now lost all energy as suddenly as he had become hysterical, Caitlin used her own blankets to make up the cot. It was clear to her that Dylan was in no shape to travel. His fever was high, and he seemed to be in pain, probably an indication that the whiskey had worn off. She retrieved the bottle of brandy the shopkeeper in St. Louis had advised her to carry. It was dusty and unopened, and she stared at it for a long moment.

The day she'd bought this brandy seemed so long ago, and the woman who had reluctantly accepted the shopkeeper's advice no longer existed. Caitlin had changed so much. She glanced toward the stream where Ty was trying his best to bathe Dylan. How much had Dylan changed over the long months since they had parted? How foolish all that had transpired between them in Mineral Point now appeared. She had spent these past months struggling with life and death issues, watching people make the most difficult choices for themselves and their loved ones. How could she have been so foolish as to think her worries related to Molly were of any consequence at all?

She opened the bottle and poured a small amount of brandy into her own tin cup. At least she knew that cup was clean. She really wouldn't vouch for the sanitation of a single item inside the cabin. She walked down to the edge of the stream, carrying a blanket and the brandy. "Wrap him in this and try to get him to drink," she said as she set blanket and cup on a flat rock near the stream.

She tried to hide her shock at seeing Dylan in the light. He was so pale and thin, and the rash was even more prominent in the light of day. "How long has he been like this?" she asked.

"Must be a little over a week now," Ty replied as he spread the blanket and carefully wrapped his brother in it. "What do you want done with those?" He nodded toward the pile of filthy clothes Dylan had been wearing.

Caitlin resisted her first thought which was to burn them. "Leave them. I'll wash them in the morning along with the bedding. Do you need help carrying him back to the cabin?"

Ty's raised eyebrows told her that he found the idea of her helping him carry his brother ridiculous. "Nope. I've got him." He hoisted his brother high in his arms and staggered up the slight rise toward the shack.

"I'll start some supper," Caitlin said as she followed him.

Supplies in the shack were meager at best. Had they not had Caitlin's fresh stock, she wasn't sure if there would have been enough food left to last another day. "Tyrone, tomorrow you must go into town for the doctor and more supplies."

"Can't do that," he mumbled as he used his teeth to tear off another chunk of buffalo meat.

Caitlin's eyes widened. "You must do that," she replied.

Ty glanced at her, gave a heavy sigh, and set his plate aside for a minute. "I can't leave our claim right now," he explained patiently. "I know you see that as selfish, but believe me, I'm doing this as much for Dylan as for me. Somebody was there just today. I'm pretty sure it was the Riley brothers, and I'm pretty sure they'll be back. You coming in here and triggering that tripwire and the pistol going off and all scared them off today, but they're out there." He scanned the surrounding blackness. "You can bet on that."

"Your brother needs a doctor, Ty. He is extremely ill.

You tell me he has been this way for over a week. He has a high fever, and—"

"Oh, that part just started a couple of days ago," Ty said, and returned to his eating.

Caitlin tried hard to hold her temper, but failed. "Are you seriously suggesting that your little rock pile up the creek is of more importance than your brother's life? Do you have any idea at all what that man in there has gone through for you? Have you no gratitude? No loyalty?"

Ty looked at her across the dancing flames of the fire for a long moment. She saw that he might be young, but he was unintimidated by her. He had seen too much in his short life. "Ma'am, I appreciate your being here and all that you're doing for Dylan. If you hadn't showed up today I don't know what I woulda done, but the fact is, Dylan would be the first to say we need to watch our *rock pile* up there, so here's an idea, why don't you go for the doctor and I'll handle things here?"

"I'm not leaving Dylan," she said with quiet determination. "It's taken me too long to find him. If he is dying, he will die in my arms, but before he does I will do everything I can to save him. So I suggest we come to some sort of compromise before morning, because I am staying here and you are going for the doctor, do I make myself clear?"

"I don't reckon that's much of a compromise," he said.

"It's the best I have to offer," she replied, her eyes meeting his.

Ty stood up and glared at her. "I gotta go check the claim," he said as he drank the last of his coffee and tossed the remaining few drops on the fire, causing the flames to spit and flare.

Caitlin went inside to check on Dylan. He was burning up and had tossed the blanket aside. She knelt next to him. "Dylan," she said softly. "Dylan, I'm here. You're going to be all right, I promise you that. Everything will be all right." She tried to recall what she had learned about medicine and treating illnesses on the long trip overland.

The nights were still cold, and wind whipped through the open doorway. With a weary sigh, Caitlin lit a lantern and pulled the drop across the door to block out most of the wind. Ty had laid wood in the small fireplace, and she lit it. Then she wet a cloth in the pan of water she'd carried up from the stream and sat on the side of the cot to bathe Dylan's face as she hummed an old hymn. After a while she felt a draft and knew Ty had returned.

"I'll bed down out here," he said.

"Take the other cot. I'll sit with Dylan," Caitlin said and continued humming and stroking Dylan's brow.

"Is he gonna be all right?" Ty asked.

"We'll be fine, Tyrone. Now get some rest."

Ty settled in, and the only sounds were the howling wind and Caitlin's soft humming.

"I'll go for the doc in the morning," Ty said, his back to her.

"Thank you," Caitlin replied. "Good night, Tyrone."

"Good night, ma'am."

Sixteen

The following morning Ty saddled Dylan's mule and packed enough supplies for two or three days on the trail. He kept glancing at the sky, assessing the potential for snow. It was late in the season, but in the mountains anything was possible. He made Caitlin demonstrate her expertise with the revolver and the shotgun he kept inside the cabin. "Not bad," he commented, and she could see he was pleasantly surprised. Over breakfast he had told her there were Indians in the area, but she had nothing to fear from them. "Just don't trust any white man who comes snooping around."

"Be sure to tell the doctor everything about Dylan's illness," she instructed as she helped him pack. "I'm going to try the cayenne powder today. Perhaps that will break the fever." When Dylan's fever had spiked again just after breakfast she had sent Ty to fetch the small sack of cayenne from her bags. Ty showed her how to make it up as a tea for Dylan and to use it as a poultice on his chest. She glanced nervously at the gray, cloud-laden sky. "You should get started."

"If the Riley brothers come, you know what to do?"

She smiled at him. "Shoot first and ask questions afterward," she said, repeating the instructions he had drilled into her again and again over breakfast.

"They're dangerous, ma'am." Ty was not smiling.

"I'll be fine," she assured him. "Now go before the rain starts."

Ty looked up. "More likely snow. At least that'll keep the Riley boys away—they'll stay put so as not to get lost."

"What about you?" Suddenly Caitlin was worried about the boy. "What if the snow causes you to lose your way?"

For the first time since they'd met, he smiled. "That won't happen, ma'am. I know every inch of the country between here and Salt Lake, and other than that little bonanza up there, I'm pretty sure there's not an ounce of gold in any of it." He jerked his head in the direction of their newly staked claim as he tightened the cinch on the mule's saddle.

"Just be careful and hurry back," Caitlin said, then surprised both of them by kissing Ty on the cheek.

After she had given Dylan a dose of the cayenne concoction and covered his chest with a poultice made of the same ingredient, she spent the rest of the morning kneeling at the shore of the creek and scrubbing the bedding and Dylan's clothes. She used a bar of lye soap she'd brought with her. The rocks along the shore served as washboards. She hefted the heavy wet fabric and spread it on rocks and scrub bushes to dry, wishing the sun were stronger. The snow started just after noon and continued through the long afternoon and night.

At noon she had gone back inside and tried to force-feed Dylan some broth. He had been sweating profusely and tearing at the covers, throwing them aside. She decided to bathe him in cool water. Perhaps that would bring down the fever. Then she had seen it. An area of the rash more prominent than the rest. It had a dark center.

"Tick," she whispered, remembering all at once the time on the trail when Jack had been bitten by a tick. She tried hard to remember how Eliza had handled it. Jack had been very ill, but Eliza had removed the tick and Jack's improvement had been almost miraculous.

Caitlin brought the lantern close and propped Dylan's leg up with some extra blankets so she could have a better look at it. She looked around for something sharp but fine. A knife was too thick and heavy. She thought of her sewing kit and quickly retrieved one of her darning needles. She held the point of the needle in the flame for a minute as she had seen Eliza do. Then slowly, cautiously she worked at the skin around the dark center. She knew she had to remove the tick imbedded in the sore. Only that would give Dylan a chance to recover.

When she had managed to open a small flap of skin near the core, she looked around for something she might use to grasp the tick and pull it out. Her eyes caught the glimmer of Ty's scale where he weighed his findings at the end of the day. There, next to the small balance plates, was a long narrow tool that looked like a pair of tweezers. Caitlin reached for it and carefully practiced squeezing the two points closed and holding them tight. It might just work.

She stuck the end of the tool under the flame for a minute, then, anchoring Dylan's foot between her legs, carefully maneuvered the end of the tool under the flap of skin. Dylan moaned. Caitlin knew the danger lay in having the tick burrow even more deeply under Dylan's skin. Slowly she positioned her operating tool to either side of the dark center. Taking a deep breath and holding it, she made her move, squeezing the points quickly and holding on.

She'd never been so happy to see blood in her whole life. She held up the tweezers, still clutched so tightly in her hand that her knuckles had turned white, and smiled as she saw the tick caught between the points. Quickly she thrust the end of the tool into the flame of the lantern until she was satisfied that the beast was dead.

Then she turned back to Dylan, bathed the open sore in brandy, and dressed the wound. Dylan slept through it all.

She could only pray that she had found the cause of his illness and removed it in time.

Afterward, Caitlin gathered the still-soaked clothes she'd washed earlier in the stream and spread them over every available surface after she had filled the crude clothesline. By pulling one chair close to the fire and letting the heat dry the clothing on it, she managed to dry enough items to dress Dylan in long flannel underwear and a flannel shirt. The cabin was stiflingly hot, so she stood at the open doorway to catch a breath of fresh air, watching the snow fall and worrying about Ty. She'd mentioned the kind farmer and his family, and she hoped Ty had taken refuge with them for the duration of the storm.

Bathing and dressing Dylan had taken a great deal of physical and emotional effort. It was impossible not to look at his naked body as she struggled to pull the clothes on. Impossible not to touch him, not to recall every detail of those nights when they had shared the bed in their cottage at Mineral Point. By the time she'd finished Caitlin was crying from exhaustion, loneliness, and fear that she had come too late.

She was standing at the door watching it snow and drinking a cup of tea when Dylan stirred. He'd been so quiet throughout the long afternoon and evening that she had worn herself out running back and forth from her washing to him, to make sure he was still breathing.

"Cold," he mumbled. "So cold."

She pulled the blanket back over the doorway and rushed to his side. He was huddled under the blankets and shivering. "Cold," he murmured again and pulled the blankets tighter.

Caitlin looked around for extra covers. It was indeed a cold night. The wind was howling, and the snowstorm had reached blizzard proportions. She regretted having sent Ty out in this weather and prayed he was all right. "Here," she said softly, and piled on the blankets she'd used to make a pallet for herself on the floor next to Dylan's cot. Then she poured a cup of tea. "Drink this," she instructed as she sat beside him and helped him to a half-sitting position.

"Cait?" His eyes strained to focus.

"I'm here, Dylan. Now drink some of this."

Caitlin. Impossible. Then it's true. I'm dying. Dylan released a shuddering sigh that seemed to rattle the very depths of his soul. He had no idea how long he'd been here. He had vague memories of Ty carrying him from the stream where he'd fallen. They'd been talking about Sarah, and then he'd thought Sarah was there in the cabin. Or had that been a dream as well? It was hard to know what was real and what was the fever. The last several days were a blur to him. He recalled bits and pieces, but nothing seemed to fit together.

"Cait?" His voice was barely a whisper, and his throat felt as if it would explode. He stretched out his hand, certain that as soon as he touched what appeared to be her, she would disappear. But she was real. He grasped her hand and held on.

"I know you're cold, Dylan. There are no more blankets." She sat on the side of the cot and considered what to do. Over and over he murmured, "Cold, cold, cold." Telling herself there was no other choice, she lifted the covers and got into bed with him, pulling his weakened body close to her own, feeling her own warmth seep into him.

"Cait, Cait, Cait," Dylan whispered to himself. She was a mirage he knew, but just thinking of her calmed him. In his delirium he imagined her in bed with him, holding him, her breath fanning his neck the way it had back in Mineral Point. He relaxed and let the darkness overtake him once more.

When Cait woke, it was already light outside. Dylan was breathing easier than he had since she'd arrived, and his fever seemed to have broken. Caitlin eased herself from the cot and took a bucket to collect fresh water. The scene that greeted her as she stepped outside was in total contrast to the morning before. More than a foot of snow covered the ground. The sky was still a bleak gray, and the wind continued to howl. It was hard to tell whether it was still snowing or simply the wind working its will on the already fallen flakes. The drift outside the entrance to the cabin was up to her knees.

Caitlin filled the bucket with snow and stepped back inside. She would melt the snow over the fire, but first she had to rebuild one and she would use the last of the wood to do it.

"Caitlin, it's you." Dylan's voice was still weak and hoarse, but his eyes were clear and focused.

She took his outstretched hand and held it. "Well, at last," she said, trying hard not to show that she was so relieved she wanted to burst into tears and then find solace in the warmth of his arms. Instead, she moved briskly to the fireplace where she had started a pot of stew cooking. She scooped some of the broth into a tin cup and brought it to him. "You need to get some nourishment in you, Dylan. Sit up and drink this."

"What are you doing here?" he asked, still unable to grasp the reality of her presence.

It was a question she was unprepared to answer even though she'd known it would be asked. If indeed he had moved forward with his life, had struck up the beginnings of a relationship with Sarah, what was she to say? Was she to swallow all of her pride and tell him the truth? Knowing Dylan, he would feel obligated. After all, he was one of the kindest most decent men she had ever known. He might abandon the budding friendship with Sarah and return to her out of some misplaced sense of duty or loyalty. Caitlin couldn't bear that. She didn't want his pity. She wanted his love.

"Cait? I asked you a question."

"We can talk about that later. Drink this before it gets cold." She held the cup for him, noticing that his hands shook as he tried to bring the cup to his lips. He coughed and choked. "Not too fast," she instructed, using her shirt-sleeve to wipe his face.

He caught her wrist and held it. "Caitlin, why did you come?"

Her mind raced. How could she admit she had come to declare her undying love when he had found Sarah in the interim?

"Did you get my letters?" he asked before she could form a reply.

Caitlin nodded. "Yes, and they were quite wonderful, Dylan. In fact they were so descriptive that I found myself wanting to see the very sights you outlined."

"You traveled over a thousand miles to see the sights?" He barely got the words out before he was forced to lie back and catch his breath.

She nodded and tried to force back the tears that threatened. She resisted the urge to gather him to her breast and soothe him until he was once again breathing normally. Instead she stood by his bedside and waited for him to catch his breath. "Drink some more," she urged, placing the cup in his hands. "I have to check on my horse and gather some firewood, or we'll surely freeze tonight." She wrapped her shawl around her head and shoulders as she rushed from the cabin.

The air was clear and cold, and the wind had died down some. But the drifts were high, so it took her some time to work her way around the side of the cabin to the place where Ty had stored a supply of wood. Then she had to work to clear the snow and find some logs several layers down that were not soaked and stood a chance of burning. As she worked she tried to think about her next move. With the snow, it would be days before Ty returned—days *and nights* where she would be alone with Dylan. The best course seemed to be one of nonchalance. His letters had intrigued her. There was no reason not to travel and see the West for herself. Imagine her surprise when she'd heard he was also in Salt Lake.

She piled the logs high in her arms and carefully worked her way back to the cabin. To her relief, Dylan was sleeping again. She stacked the wood near the fireplace, added two small logs to the fire, and tiptoed out to check on Buster. Assured that her faithful horse had weathered the storm, she repaired the canvas shelter Ty had constructed for the horses, then collected several pails of snow to use for water. When she could find no more to do outside the cabin and had to admit her feet and hands were nearly frozen, she went back inside. Blessedly Dylan appeared to be napping.

"You can't hide from me forever, Caitlin," he said quietly, his eyes still closed, his hands folded across his chest. "Why didn't you answer my letters?"

"I . . ."

"You admit that you received the letters?"

"Yes."

"Well, I didn't just write about the scenery or the trip, Caitlin."

"I know." Exhausted, she sat on the edge of one of the chairs, but she did not look at him.

"I told you I loved you. I told you repeatedly."

She nodded and by sheer force of will held the tears at bay.

His tone shifted, and she heard him struggle to a sitting position. "I know you had feelings for me once, Caitlin. I counted on your sense of fairness to forgive me for the deception. I counted on those feelings to carry you past your anger."

She was starting to come to terms with the complete folly of her coming here. She was tired and cold, and she would kill for a long hot soak in a real bathtub. "It's true.

There was a time . . . I . . . thought I might love you, Dylan, but—"

"But what? There is no *but*, Caitlin, unless you never loved me." He was incredulous, bordering on anger.

"Oh, for heaven's sake, Dylan, be reasonable," she wailed as she stood and paced the small confines of the cabin, her hands flailing dramatically as she ticked off her arguments. "We had a business arrangement. There were moments to be sure when it perhaps went a bit beyond that. But you were the one who laid the ground rules. You said if there was no letter when you arrived here, you would have your answer. Was there a letter? Of course not. And before you get all upset, let me assure you that I have read your journal. I know your deception was something you put into effect well before we began to . . . to . . . share a friendship—a friendship I assure you I cherish a great deal."

As she made yet another pass by his cot, he caught her wrist and pulled her into his arms. "Shut up, Caitlin," he muttered just before kissing her into silence. She did not resist at first, only after a moment, only after beginning to kiss him back did she push him away.

"Dylan, I will excuse that because of your illness. It's clear to me that you have suffered some delirium and confusion as part of your fevered state, but this is not at all why I am here and we will not do this." She took advantage of another of his coughing jags to move off the bed and across the room, where she busied herself mixing a fresh batch of medicine for him to drink. "Here," she said as she thrust the concoction at him. "Drink it all."

He sniffed it suspiciously. "What the hell is this stuff?"

"Just hold your nose and drink it, and don't for one minute think I will tolerate your swearing simply because you are ill."

"I'll drink it on one condition."

She sighed wearily. "I'm in no mood for making deals, Dylan. Drink your medicine."

"I thought you liked making bargains," he said with a sly grin. "You tell me the truth of why you're here, and I'll drink this down to the last drop." He held up the cup in a mock toast.

"I am here because the wagon train I was with stopped for a few days in Salt Lake. I recalled that you had indicated in the last letter I received that you had had news of Tyrone here. I was curious to know the end of the story— that you had been reunited and both of you were all right."

The cup wavered slightly and she could see he was struggling with disbelief. She sighed and pressed on. "When I learned that neither of you had been seen or heard from in some time and that both of you were last seen in town, I became concerned. As you well know there's a new group of wagons in town practically every two days so I knew I could join up with a fresh group for the remainder of my journey, should I decide to go on."

"To California?"

"Of course The news is quite incredible coming from there these days. I'll admit that having come so far it seems a shame not to make the entire journey. But despite what you may think, I am not so heartless or so callous that I would leave a friend in need. Your friend, Sarah, was kind enough to provide me with information. Following her instructions, I was able to make the trip here where I met Tyrone and found you."

"Sarah who?"

Sarah who! Sarah who thinks you walk on water. "I believe her last name is Clayton. I met her when I went to get supplies. Oddly enough you thought I was Sarah the other day when I first arrived." She walked over to him and nudged the cup. "Drink up, Dylan," she said softly and went to prepare supper.

The dwindling supplies worried her. If Dylan regained

any semblance of a normal appetite there wouldn't be enough to last them two days. She'd have to do something about that in the morning.

"What kind of wildlife have you seen around here?" she asked him as they ate.

He gave her a skeptical look. "You don't have to force conversation, Caitlin," he said and swallowed another spoonful of the broth she'd placed next to him.

"I'm serious. I thought I saw some rabbit tracks in the snow."

"Jackrabbit? Maybe. There's probably some black-tailed deer. Why are you so interested? Don't tell me you plan to go hunting?" He grinned.

She smiled sweetly and relieved him of his empty dish.

He watched her wash out the dishes and throw the left-over water out into the snow with an expertise that came only with practice. "Tell me about your trip out, Cait."

She told him the story as she prepared dough and kneaded it into bread for the following day's meals. She covered the pan with a cloth and set it near the fire to rise overnight. Their conversation was easy and familiar. He asked questions. They shared observations of the terrain they had each traveled. He laughed at her stories of the trailmaster and crossing the river.

"You should get some sleep," she said when she saw him fighting to stifle a yawn. "It's been a long day for you, and you're still running a bit of fever." She pressed the back of her hand to his cheek.

He caught her wrist and held her hand next to his face, turning it so he could lightly kiss her palm. "I'm glad you're here, Cait."

She pulled her hand away and busied herself straightening his covers.

"Where are you sleeping?" he asked.

"There," she said and nodded toward the other cot. "If you need anything—"

"Funny. I dreamed last night that you shared the bed with me." Her startled glance was all he needed to confirm his suspicion. He smiled. "Good night, Caitie," he said, and slid under the covers.

The shotgun blast brought him fully awake. He half walked half crawled to the doorway and lifted the canvas. Caitlin was striding back up the rise from the stream. In one hand she cradled Ty's shotgun. In the other she carried a thoroughly dead jackrabbit by its long ears. She was dressed in men's canvas pants and a woolen jacket. Her hair was haphazardly tucked under a wide-brimmed felt hat. The snow was up to her knees as she followed her own tracks back to the cabin. When she glanced up and saw him leaning against the doorway, she raised the rabbit triumphantly and smiled. "Dinner," she called gaily. Dylan thought he had never loved her more.

"You should be in bed," she chastised him as she brushed past him, bringing a breath of cold clear air with her.

"I can't stay in bed forever," he replied. *Although if you would agree to stay there with me I would happily spend the rest of my life there on that cot.*

"Nevertheless, you have to be careful. We've no idea what your sickness is. It may be that the worst has passed. Yet there may be a recurrence." She thought of the stories they had heard along the trail of cholera and other illnesses killing entire families sometimes. Her mood, which had been so high, shifted. "Please get back into bed, Dylan," she said and went to check the bread she'd left baking on the fire.

Only because his legs promised to fail him completely if he stood for another minute did Dylan do as she asked. He hated his weakness, hated having her see him this way. He ran his hands over his face and felt the full and scraggly beard that covered his cheeks and chin. "Cait, do you think you'd have time to help me shave today?"

She seemed pleased and surprised. "Of course. We'll do it after breakfast. The sun is out, and it promises to be a mild day. I'll bundle you up, and you can sit outside for a bit. The sun and fresh air will do you good."

"How many days has Ty been gone?" Dylan asked as she carefully shaved the last of the hair from his chin and neck.

"Three now," she replied. She sounded worried.

"He'll probably make town today. I wish there were some way to get word that there's no need to bring the doctor. I'm feeling much stronger."

"That's good." Caitlin did not tell him she wished Ty would return that day. When she'd been stalking the rabbit, she'd seen footprints in the snow across the creek. They were coming from the direction of the claim. She hoped it was the trail of the Indians Ty had mentioned and not the Riley brothers. Either way, she planned to check on things there once she got Dylan to agree to an afternoon nap. If someone was poaching the claim she would find out soon enough. Ty had set certain traps that were intended to discourage the presence of any intruders at the site, but with the snow the traps might not work.

To her relief Dylan willingly lay down on the cot following their lunch of rabbit stew. Caitlin was heartened to see that his appetite had returned. She was sure he would sleep the afternoon. After checking to be sure Buster had food enough, she pushed her revolver into the belt she wore around her coat and set out.

The trail Ty had shown her was slippery, but she realized that it kept her hidden from view. The series of rocks and bushes formed a solid path of cover as she worked her way toward the claim.

Dylan lay on the cot and waited. Caitlin had been unusually anxious during their lunch. She'd clearly been relieved when he'd gone willingly to bed right after the meal. He'd heard her go out to check her horse and then nothing. He struggled to his feet and found a pair of trousers, his boots and jacket. It took longer than he liked to dress. He was still so damned weak. He looked around the cabin and saw the crutch he'd fashioned for Ty. Using it as a walking stick, he made his way to the door.

There was no sign of life when he looked out. He could hear the horse moving around in the shelter, but there was no sign of Caitlin. He thought of calling out, but something about the quiet told him not to do that. Instead he went back inside and got the shotgun she'd used to shoot the rabbit. He'd reloaded it for her while she'd skinned and prepared the rabbit as if she did such things every day.

Her tracks led directly from the horse's shelter up the hill and along the trail that rimmed the campsite. He knew she had gone to the claim even when her tracks were no longer visible in the melting snow. Slowly he worked his way along the trail, cursing the need to stop and gasp for breath after only a few steps.

Caitlin stealthily crept down the trail. There was no sign of disturbance around the claim, but she intended to check the traps to be sure they were still in place. Ty had assured her that the Indians would immediately recognize and avoid each trap since they were the ones who had shown him how to set them in the first place. Only white men, greedy for instant wealth, would ignore the signs and blunder into the camp.

Everything was as she and Ty had left it. Caitlin licked her lips and realized how dry and chapped they'd become as a result of her exertion and her fear. She worked her way carefully to the edge of the stream. The water was icy cold and clear. Using her hands as a cup she leaned down to quench her thirst and soothe her chapped lips and cheeks.

Just then two men stepped out of the brush on the opposite side of the stream. Caitlin's hand went instantly to her pistol.

"Whoa, hold it there, sonny," one of the men said, raising his hands in mock surrender. "We're just passing through. No need for us to have any trouble here."

Caitlin realized that because her hat disguised her hair the men thought she was a boy. That was good. She was also relieved to see they were leading a fully loaded burro. Clearly they had followed the trail into the canyon without knowing anyone else was there.

"You having any luck?" one of the men asked.

Caitlin shrugged and stood up slowly. She tugged her hat more firmly in place. It was safer if these men continued to mistake her for a boy.

"Well, Jed, guess we'd best be moseying on. Looks like we'll have to head further south. This young fella 'pears to have everything in these parts sewed up tight."

Jed. Ty had called them the Riley brothers— Mick and Jed. Her heart hammered.

"I kinda like it here, Mick," the other man said, eyeing Caitlin as he started slowly across the stream.

"Well, you got a point there, Jed. It's a fine-looking setup. Looks like it's been here awhile. That's a sure sign of success if you get my meaning." He also started across the shallow stream, but she noticed the brothers had spread out, one to her left and one to her right.

Caitlin fingered her revolver as she backed away, trying to keep them both in sight. "I think you fellas oughta go," she said gruffly. "My partners will be coming along any time now."

Both men continued to advance. She kept backing away and too late remembered the tripwire. In an instant she was falling backward, landing hard in a cluster of shrubby bushes. Her hat fell off and her hair tumbled out.

"Well, well, well," Mick muttered with a leering grin.

Jed gave a low whistle of surprise and pleasure. The two brothers grinned at each other and advanced.

Caitlin struggled to stand but kept losing her footing on the loose rocky soil. She had never been so terrified in her life. She resorted to the only tactic she knew—the strict schoolmarm reprimanding unruly children.

"Now see here," she said firmly as she finally regained her balance and stood with her back to the canyon wall. "You are trespassing and that is against the law. I've heard of you young men being in trouble before. What do you think your mother would say if she knew you went about harassing innocent hard-working people? I'm sure she didn't raise you to become common criminals. Listen to me, Jed and Mick Riley, I want you to cross back over that stream, take your mules, and leave."

At first she thought she had miraculously gotten through to them. When she brought up their mother she was relieved to see the brothers look ashamed. Perhaps she should have stopped there, for the last part of her lecture seemed to have simply provided the time they needed to refocus their attention on her.

"I don't think so, missy. It's been some time since me and Jed's seen anything close to as pretty as you. I think we'd like to stay awhile and get to know you."

Jed snorted and laughed. "Yeah, we'd like to get to know you *real* good," he agreed and once again both brothers made their move. Mick grabbed her hand as she reached for her revolver.

Caitlin looked him straight in the eye. "I want you to leave," she said and tried without success to keep the tremor in her voice from betraying her. "I want you to do that right now before my partner returns and shoots the both of you."

"Ah, come on, Cait, let me shoot 'em and put 'em out of their misery."

Dylan.

Never in her life had Caitlin been happier to see him even if he was barely standing, leaning for support on a rock formation about twenty yards from where she stood surrounded by the Riley brothers. "Step away, gentlemen," he said softly and revealed the shotgun he carried.

Mick had his back to Dylan. Jed was standing behind his brother and Caitlin. "Look out, Mick, he's got a shotgun," he shouted and went for his pistol. Mick tossed Caitlin aside and went for his own gun. Both men fired at the same time. Mick's shot went wild as he stepped in front of Jed and was struck down by his brother's bullet.

Jed dropped his gun, and his face was ashen as he raced to his fallen brother. "Mick? Mick? Talk to me." He started to cry as he cradled his dead brother in his arms, Mick's blood soaking his canvas pants and shirt. "Mick?" he repeated again and again.

Dylan hobbled over and helped Caitlin to her feet. "Are you all right?"

She nodded shakily and as they leaned against each other it was hard to say who was giving the most support. "He's just a boy," Caitlin whispered after a moment as they stood watching Jed sob over his brother.

Dylan nodded, then stood by in stunned silence as Caitlin moved to Jed and knelt next to him. "Jed? Mick's gone. I'm so sorry, but you mustn't blame yourself."

The boy continued to whimper, but her words seemed to calm him. She put her arm around his shoulders. "Come on," she said kindly. "Mr. Tremaine and I will help you bury your brother."

Dylan couldn't believe his ears. This was the same kid who'd not fifteen minutes ago been licking his chops and planning to rape her, probably murder her for the hell of it. Now she was treating him like one of her students. "Cait, I . . ."

She silenced him with a look as she eased Jed away from Mick's body. "It's all right," she crooned gently.

Dylan rolled his eyes and leaned heavily on the home-made crutch as he hobbled over to Mick's body. "We can bury him over there," he said, using the crutch to point to the far side of the stream.

"That'll be a good place, Jed. See, he'll be under that lovely spruce tree there."

The kid backhanded his tears and nodded as he glanced at the grave site. "We'd best get started," he said and trudged across the stream to get a shovel from the supplies strapped onto the mule's back.

Caitlin watched him go. She thought about Jack and Ty and now Jed—so young, all of them and yet they had seen more of life's harshness than many people ever knew in their entire lives.

Dylan helped Caitlin wrap Mick's body in an old piece of canvas. "I'm going to get my Bible," Caitlin told him. "You help Jed and I'll come back. We should read a passage and say a few words."

"Caitlin, you do remember that the both of them would have ravaged you and then killed you just for the fun of it?" Dylan squinted up at her as he pulled the last of the ropes tight to hold the canvas in place around Mick's body.

Caitlin's eyes flashed with impatience. "And Mick paid a terrible price for that. So will Jed since he'll have to live with the fact he shot his own brother. I think a little charity is in order here, Dylan."

Dylan glanced back at the body, more to hide the smile he couldn't suppress than anything else. "Just wanted to check," he muttered.

Caitlin turned on her heel and headed back to the cabin.

By the time she returned, Jed and Dylan had completed the burial. Mick's final resting place was a pile of rocks under a small blue spruce tree in a narrow canyon in Utah. Jed stood staring down at the fresh grave. "He's a long way from home," he muttered.

"Only his physical remains," Caitlin said quietly.

Jed started to cry again. "All we wanted was our share of the riches they all said was here for the taking," he said.

"It's a common mistake." Caitlin opened her Bible. "Would you like me to read something, Jed?"

The boy nodded.

Caitlin turned to the Twenty-third Psalm and read it aloud. Toward the end she realized Jed had joined in, softly repeating the words from memory. Her heart ached for him. When the psalm ended, the three of them stood in silence for a long moment. "Come on, Jed," Caitlin said. "You can stay with us until you decide what to do." She saw that Dylan was prepared to protest and silenced him with a look. "I trust you've learned a painful lesson today and there will be no further trouble."

Jed nodded in agreement to her terms, and the unlikely trio made their way back down the stream to the cabin. Dylan watched as Caitlin prepared a light supper, all the while keeping up a one-sided conversation with the boy. He realized this was more than teaching. She was mothering the lad. He thought as he often had about what a good mother she would make. He looked at her with Jed and imagined her with children they could have had together. Maybe it wasn't too late for them after all.

No one seemed all that interested in eating, so supper was a brief and silent affair. Afterward, Jed refused her offer for him to sleep inside and insisted on bedding down outside by a small campfire. Dylan was up several times during the night. Caitlin heard him go over to the canvas doorway and look out, checking on Jed. It was nearly dawn before he settled into a deep sleep. When they woke the following morning, Jed was gone. When Dylan insisted on checking the claim before breakfast, he found a roughly fashioned wooden cross that had not been there the day before planted at one end of Mick's grave.

Seventeen

"Was anything missing?" Caitlin asked as she dished up breakfast for him. He knew she was mad at him for being so suspicious of Jed. With his brother's death, the boy had become a veritable paragon in her eyes.

"I just went to do a routine check of my business, Caitlin. I didn't expect there would be anything missing."

She pursed her lips in that way she had when she was upset about something and poured herself a cup of coffee. "When do you think Ty will return?" she asked as she paced the perimeter of the cabin, sipping her coffee.

"Could be today. By the end of the week for sure." It annoyed him that she was so anxious for Ty's return.

"We need to make plans," she announced as she ceased her pacing and took her place on the chair across the table from him.

He had a brief moment when he dared to hope she might mean plans to set everything to rights. Plans to get married for real, to make a life together finally. He saw by her concentrated scowl that he was wrong. "Plans?"

"Of course. I mean everyone in Mineral Point will want to know why you aren't returning with me."

"Doesn't everyone in Mineral Point think I died in an avalanche?"

She could feel him studying her closely. "Oh, that. Your message arrived just as I was about to begin my trip. At the moment I suppose everyone thinks you'll be coming home with me."

"And why am I not?" he asked, trying hard to keep his rising temper at bay.

She gave an exasperated sigh. "That's what we have to decide. How did you die? Yesterday's incident gave me an idea. I mean I assume that claim jumpers like the Riley brothers are relatively common. They come upon us while Ty is away. There are two of them and only one of you. They take us by surprise. You're determined to protect me from harm. There's a fight. You're shot. You die in my arms. Ty returns just in time to chase the Rileys away, but he's too late to save you. Together, your brother and I bury you; then he heads on to California and I start back home." She paused as if considering the details of the story. "I'll need to shop for some clothes," she said, more to herself than to him. "They'll expect to see me in mourning. And I should write to them, describe the whole horrible incident so the details are well known before I return and I won't be expected to tell the story over and over."

Dylan pushed back his chair and strode out of the cabin with more vigor than he had felt in days. *Damn the woman,* he thought angrily as he hobbled off to the claim. He needed some relief from spending every minute with her, wanting her, wanting to strangle her when she talked foolishness like this. He reached the claim and started to work. The physical activity felt good even though he was still very weak from his long illness.

As he worked, he thought about Caitlin. It was clear that she had made up her mind to return to Mineral Point without him. The question was *why*. Why had she come in the first place if she didn't have feelings for him, and if that was the case, why had she now changed her mind? He certainly didn't want to believe that tall tale about reading his letters and wanting to see the sights for herself.

He worked the area where he and Jed had taken stones

from the creekbed to cover Mick's grave. The sediment and stones there were looser and easier to pan. Slowly he swirled the pan of silt and gravel as he tried to recall every detail of what had happened since Caitlin arrived.

His first memory was of her kneeling next to the cot. He'd thought it had to be Sarah—that soothing voice, comforting him, assuring him all would be well. The gentle hands applying cool cloths to his fevered brow. But the woman he thought was Sarah had said something that had confused him, made him think he was dreaming or hallucinating or both. Suddenly it became very important that he remember what she had said while she was wiping his brow and comforting him. Somehow he knew it was a clue to Caitlin's actions.

He studied the dregs in the pan—black sand and water, no sign of gold. He dumped the remains and scooped up a fresh load. He thought of those long days when the fever had been with him and she had been there. It all seemed like one endless night, and there had been so many times he'd thought he would die without ever seeing her again.

Don't you die on me now, Dylan Tremaine.

He paused, remembering. She'd said that repeatedly and more.

I didn't travel halfway across the country to have you die before I could tell you how much I love you.

Had she said it or did he simply want it to be so? He emptied the pan and bent to fill it once more. He glanced down and there under the water, just at the toe of his boot, he saw it. A nugget the size of his thumbnail. He plucked it from the stream, his hand trembling with excitement. He knew at once that it was real. He knelt, oblivious to the cold water soaking his pants. Using his fingers, he carefully sifted through the layer of pebbles where the nugget had been. He found two more, much smaller but no less impressive.

He wanted to shout. He wanted to tell Ty that the strike

was far more than either of them had believed. He needed to share his news. He held the nuggets to the sun and thanked God for their good fortune. Then he saw Caitlin standing on the opposite side of the stream, a puzzled expression on her face.

"Caitie, come quick," he shouted as he tried to get to his feet, but he slipped and fell back into the stream where he lay on his back splashing water with both hands and feet and laughing like a madman.

Caitlin dropped the bucket of stew she'd brought as a peace offering and ran to him. *Oh, my stars, the fever's back,* she thought as she tripped and stumbled over the rough terrain to reach him before he drowned himself. *Please, God, don't let it be so. Not when he's just come back to me. Not now.*

She reached him and he sat up and caught her by the hand, pulling her down into the water with him. "We're rich, Caitie," he said, grinning broadly. "Look at this. Ty is going to be ecstatic." He opened his hand to reveal three small stones. Three small *gold* stones.

Having no idea of their value, Caitlin smiled at him. Her mood was bittersweet. She was happy that he and Ty had finally struck their fortune, sad that it meant for certain he would leave her. "That's lovely, Dylan. Now please get out of this cold water before you catch your death."

He tugged her back down. "Caitie, this is not the fever talking. I hold in my hand a small fortune, and there's more right over there. I kept thinking we'd gotten lucky and found the little bit of gold that was here, but Ty was right. There's more—maybe a lot more. I don't know how much there is, but whatever there is, it's ours. This alone is enough to give us a comfortable start on the rest of our lives."

Caitlin looked more closely at the nuggets. "They're worth that much?" *Can I dare to hope that he will be*

*satisfied with what he finds here? That he will have no
need to go on to California?*

He nodded.

"You sure they aren't part of the salting that Jed and his
brother did?"

"They use dust for salting, Cait. These are nuggets." He
placed them in her hand and closed her fingers around
them.

"Oh, my stars," she murmured as the reality of what he
was saying began to register.

"Exactly," he replied with a broad grin. "We found a
few pebbles and some dust before I got sick, but nothing
close to this. I think Ty and I should be able to find however much is hiding in this stream."

His excitement was contagious. She started to smile. She
handed him the nuggets, and he put them in his shirt
pocket. They rested on their knees in the middle of the
stream and scooped up the sediment letting it sift through
their fingers back into the clear water. They were like children. It had been such a long time since they had shared
such happiness, such pure joy. They laughed and shouted
as they repeatedly scooped up the debris and let it slide
back to earth. Finally, exhausted they rested their palms on
their knees and looked at each other, their expressions so-
bering as they leaned closer. Their lips met, tentatively at
first, the pain of the last months flashing across their
minds.

Then he pulled her against him and kissed her with all
the hunger and passion he'd held in check since her return.
"Ah, Caitie," he murmured softly as he feathered kisses
across her cheeks and temples, pulling off her hat and toss-
ing it in the general direction of the shore. "Thank God
you came," he whispered, and his voice cracked with emotion.

Caitlin was surprised to feel tears dampen his cheeks.
She loved him so, and she was so happy for him. He had

found the treasure he'd set out to find. He and Ty would be able to mine this area and make enough to take them to California, where they would no doubt find riches beyond their wildest imaginations.

"Come on," she said softly, permitting herself the indulgence of burying her face in his thick dark hair once more. "We need to get back to the cabin and into dry clothes before you have a setback." She stood up and looked down at him, and her heart filled to bursting. How was it possible to love a man so much, she wondered. She turned to go.

"Caitlin?" He caught her hand. "Have you forgiven me? You know, for what happened in Mineral Point?"

She did not look back at him, but she nodded. "Of course. Now come along. This water is freezing, and Ty will never forgive me if I lose you now."

They walked back to the cabin together. To keep from dealing with the horde of emotions that threatened to overwhelm her, she questioned him at length about what was involved in recovering whatever gold there might be from the stream. He explained the process and told her that until Ty returned he was going to need her help working the claim. It pleased her to hear him say he needed her, even if it was only to fill in for his absent brother.

When they reached the cabin, she sent him inside to get out of his wet clothes while she fed Buster and busied herself with other chores, stalling until she was certain she had given him enough time to clean up and change.

By the time she finished, the sun was setting and she was cold and tired. Dylan was waiting just inside the door.

"Please come in," he said with a devastating smile.

Inside the small room was lit by a blazing fire and several miner's candles placed about it. He took her hand and led her near the fireplace. "You're half frozen," he admonished as he helped her out of her coat.

She shivered, but knew it was less the cold than being alone with Dylan. He'd changed into dry clothes and carefully brushed his wet hair. There were two large kettles of water beginning to steam over the fire and a washtub stood on the earthen floor next to the hearth.

"What's all this?" she asked and could not keep the nervous tremor of excitement from her voice.

"You need a warm bath," he said quietly as he began opening the buttons of her shirt. "We haven't a bathtub so we'll have to make do." The shirt was open. He left it on her as he reached for the waistband of her trousers.

"Dylan," she said, and her tone was a husky warning as she placed her hand on his knowing the simple act was all that was necessary to stop him.

He sighed and paused in the act of undressing her. "Caitlin, I want to make love to you. I want us to celebrate. I want us to have this night for ourselves, to remember for the rest of our lives. I don't know what the future holds for either one of us, but I do know that we care for each other and that we have tonight. Tomorrow or the next day Ty will probably return and we will have lost the chance. Please don't deny us this." His gaze met hers as he waited for her answer.

She thought about the night he had asked to make love to her at the cottage. She thought about how the memory of that night had sustained her across the plains and mountains and through the hardships of the trip to find him. She thought about having this night to sustain her on the journey home. "Yes," she said softly and opened the first button of her trousers.

It was a long time before either of them said anything aloud, but they spoke volumes in their touch and their response to each caress. He finished undressing her, and when she stood naked before him, he led her over to the washtub, holding her hand as she stepped over the edge of the wide shallow pan and stood in the center of it. He retrieved the hot water from the hearth, and she realized he had scented it with the pungent berries of the cedar shrub that grew near the cabin. He scooped up a tin pitcherful of water and slowly poured it over her shoulders, using his fingers and palms to massage it over her breasts and back, refilling the pitcher and repeating the action until every inch of her had been anointed and touched by him.

He had her sit in the washtub, her legs crossed in the fashion of the Indians she had observed on the plains. As he washed her hair, he hummed.

"What's that song?" she asked.

"A Cornish lullaby. My mother taught it to me."

"Tell me about her. Tell me about your family, Dylan."

Slowly he told her of the hard times his parents had endured, of his father's death in the mines, of his mother's insistence that her boys come to America for a better life. "I never saw her again," he whispered, and his voice cracked.

Caitlin reached up and stroked his cheek. "Teach me the lullaby, Dylan," she said softly.

As he taught her the words and melody, he helped her from the makeshift tub, dried her carefully, and wrapped her in a blanket. He brushed out her hair as they sat together by the fire, singing. She felt as if he had cast a spell. She was mesmerized by the dancing flames and the rhythm of his hands working the brush through her long hair. She felt closer to him than she ever had before. She felt she knew him now, and that made her love him even more.

After a time he stood and undressed. She watched without shame, enjoying the ploy of the candlelight and firelight over the hard plains of his body. When he was naked she saw that his desire matched her own and she stood up and went to him, dropping the blanket as she walked straight into his arms.

He lifted her and instinct told her to gather him closer by wrapping her legs around him. Her breasts were even with his face, and she arched her back inviting him to touch her there. He covered one swollen nipple with his open mouth, and she locked her fingers in his hair urging him closer. He used his tongue and teeth to tease her until she cried out in frustration; then he released that breast and ministered to the other.

She bent to kiss his hair, his temple, his ear. She gently thrust her tongue around the inner edge of his ear and thrilled to his murmured gasps of excitement that matched her own. She felt him pressing against the opening at the apex of her legs and realized how easily she could take him inside simply by sliding down onto him. She considered the boldness of such a move and then willingly abandoned all caution. She did not care what he thought of her. She loved him, wanted him. If he thought of her as wanton and shameless, so be it. She positioned herself to take him inside her.

"Cait." Now his was the voice of warning, but it was smothered in a low growl of pure desire as she followed her intuition and pulled slightly away before lowering herself again, taking him deeper into her body.

Dylan let out a low cry of pure pleasure and tumbled with her onto the cot. He positioned her on top of him, his eyes bright with desire in the flickering candlelight that surrounded them. Using only his fingers and hips, he instructed her how to ride him to bring them both to the pinnacle of ecstasy. When he tried to pull out at the moment of his release, she dug her knees into his sides and held fast. If she could not have him, perhaps she might have his child to love and cherish for the years to come. When he surrendered all control and cried out his pleasure as he exploded inside her, Caitlin rejoiced, exulting in the moment. If it was all they had, it would be enough, she decided.

Their bodies were covered with a fine sheen of sweat as they fell against each other in the aftermath of their lovemaking. She lay on top of him, and he covered them with a blanket. They slept lightly. He woke and eased out of bed to extinguish the candles and tend the fire. When he returned he looked down at her, her hair fanned over her bare shoulders, her mouth partially open as she breathed in the soft even rhythm of sleep. He wanted her again. He could not imagine a time when the sight of her would not cause him to want to make love to her.

"Caitlin," he whispered as much to hear her name on his lips as to wake her.

She opened her eyes immediately and, seeing that he was all right, smiled, and held open the covers to welcome him back. He was right. They might not have forever, but they had this night. In minutes their bodies were entangled as they explored new rhythms of the primitive dance of their lovemaking.

The following morning there was none of the discomfort that had always followed their lovemaking in Mineral Point. Caitlin hummed happily to herself as she prepared their breakfast. Dylan weighed out the nuggets and told her the value combined with everything he and Ty had found previously was probably close to three hundred dollars.

While they ate he explained the process of using the cradle and as always was astounded and pleased by her insightful questions, her insatiable curiosity for learning new things. Once again he thought about her as the mother of his children. Today they might be closer to that than he had ever imagined. Not once during their lovemaking had she allowed him to pull away. He had not wanted to argue with her, but now he was more determined than ever to make her his wife.

After breakfast they headed for the claim. Caitlin fretted about his overdoing and insisted on taking her turn loading rock into the hopper while he worked the cradle. He saw how strong she had gotten enduring the trip West. He regretted missing that and resolved she would make no more trips without him at her side.

"Caitie?" He leaned on his shovel and watched the rhythm of her as she bent to shovel a fresh load of stone into the hopper.

"Hmmm?"

"Did you ever think we might have been able to make a go of it? I mean if we'd been married for real?"

She paused, her back still to him, but he saw her muscles tense.

He continued watching her intently for the slightest sign that would give him his answer. "I mean, I know we both were determined to live the single life when we first met, but I'm wondering—after your trip and all—if that idea has changed for you?"

"You mean philosophically?" she asked and seemed relieved. She turned and shaded her eyes from the sun as she looked up at him.

He shrugged and waited for her to say more.

"The last few months have changed the way I look at a great many things," she admitted, still watching him closely. "I suspect you have come to some new ideas about your view of life as well."

I love you, Dylan Tremaine. Dylan knew he had not imagined the words.

"What if I were to suggest we reconsider our original plan? Certainly last night proved that we have feelings for each other. In time . . ."

Don't spoil what we shared last night! She wanted to shout it. *Don't take that away from me.*

She straightened and came to stand toe-to-toe with him. "Now you listen to me, Dylan Tremaine," she lectured. "I know you. You are a good and decent man, and I suspect you are having second thoughts about what happened last night. You want to do your duty by me, but I am here to tell you right now that there is no need. We are both adults and can take full responsibility for what happened—as well as for any consequences there might be."

His temper flared. "I won't have you bearing my child without me," he argued.

She threw up her hands in exasperation. "There is no child," she shouted as she tried hard to keep from bursting into tears.

"How can you be so sure?" he demanded.

"I'm sure," she retorted, "and that is my final word on this subject." She turned back to her work and refused to speak to him. Of course, she couldn't be sure at all, but she would not have him stay with her out of pity or duty. They worked in a strained silence. After a while she told him that she thought they had done enough for one morning.

He did not argue. They returned to the shack, where she prepared lunch for him and then insisted he rest while she did some laundry. He slept for over an hour and when she woke she acted as if nothing had happened, chatting conversationally about seeing a black-tailed deer across the stream as she scrubbed the clothes.

As Dylan had predicted Ty arrived that afternoon, but it was Daniel Clayton, Sarah's father who drove the buckboard the two men eased down the narrow trail into the canyon. "Doc was out delivering babies several miles north when the blizzard hit," Ty explained as he and Daniel halted the wagon and climbed down. "Dan Clayton, meet my brother Dylan Tremaine."

Daniel and Dylan shook hands. "It's good to see you again, Mr. Clayton," Dylan said. "I don't believe you've met Caitlin."

"My daughter Sarah spoke of you. She was glad to hear you had reached the boys here safely. It's a pleasure to meet you." Dan Clayton removed his hat and nodded politely at Caitlin. "Tyrone tells me you worked a minor medical miracle on this one," he said, jerking his head toward Dylan. "Probably the mountain fever. We see it from time to time. He looks pretty good for one who was as sick as Ty described."

"I'll say," Ty agreed. "The both of you look like you're bursting."

Dylan and Caitlin looked at each other and laughed. "Tell him. Show him," Caitlin urged.

Ty's eyes widened in anticipation. "What is it?"

Dylan dug around in his pocket and revealed the five new nuggets he and Caitlin had found during the day's work.

"Well, I'll be," Dan Clayton said in a hushed tone as he bent down to examine the treasure.

Ty was practically speechless. "When . . . where . . . I mean . . ." He paused and then started to smile and hoot and holler. "We're rich. Rich, rich, rich." He made a song of it to accompany his impromptu jig of joy.

Caitlin, Dylan, and Dan Clayton stood by and laughed with him. "Come, I'll show you," Dylan said after a few minutes. Caitlin went back to the cabin to prepare the evening meal while the three men went to examine the claim site. She could hear Dylan telling them about the Riley brothers. "Caitlin was incredible," she heard him say, and her heart sang.

When they returned to the cabin, Dylan looked tired, and during supper he had a coughing spell that racked his entire body and left him gasping for clear breaths of air. It was decided then and there that Daniel would stay and help Ty work the claim while Dylan and Caitlin went back to town. "Doc should be back by the time you get there, and this is nothing you should leave to fate," Dan Clayton advised. "The only reason you appear to be up and about at all is by the grace of this good woman."

The fact that Dylan readily agreed to the plan gave Caitlin cause for concern. He had seemed so much better. She chastised herself for being so selfish, for letting her emotions rather than her head guide her. She should have forced him to return to the cabin sooner the previous day when he'd found the gold. He'd been wet and cold and had worked himself to exhaustion. Then he had been awake most of the night, and today they had worked long hours filling and refilling the hopper, each new discovery restoring their energies.

Dylan lay down on the cot right after supper and was soon sound asleep. Caitlin cleared the supper things while Jed and Daniel set up a tent outside and prepared to camp there for the night, leaving the second cot for Caitlin. When she went out to dump the dishwater, Daniel had already retired for the night and Ty was smoking his pipe as he settled the mules and checked on Buster.

"I'll hitch the wagon for you first thing tomorrow and drive you out of the canyon. Once you get up top you'll be fine the rest of the way," he said without looking at her.

"I appreciate that," Caitlin said. "I'm glad Dan will be with you," she added.

"Dan's a good man." Ty finished his chore and leaned against the edge of the cabin, looking up at the stars. "I like it here, Caitlin. This place suits me, so I won't be going back to Wisconsin with you and Dylan. I hope you understand that and can help me make Dylan understand as well," he said quietly.

"What makes you think Dylan wouldn't want to stay here as well?"

Ty let out one of his trademark hoots of laughter. "The man has not stopped talking about Mineral Point since he got here. If I have to hear one more time how beautiful it is there and how great the people are, I think I'll punch him. Not to mention how many times I heard about you before you showed up. Stars above, the man was downright poetic, and I figured you couldn't possibly be as pretty or as smart as he talked." He glanced her way. "But you are," he added, "and I understand why he loves you so much."

Caitlin peered at him through the darkness, trying to read his expression. "He told you that he loved me? In those words?"

"He didn't have to, but yeah, he said it." He sounded puzzled. "Why? Is it supposed to be some kind of secret? Does your family disapprove of Dylan?" Now he sounded a little defensive.

"My family loves Dylan," she assured him, "as do I." There was no sense trying to explain things to Ty.

Ty nodded and tapped the ashes out of his pipe. "Well, I'll be turning in now. Good night, Cait," he said, and he bent to kiss her cheek as he passed her on his way to the tent.

The following morning, as promised, Ty rode with them to the canyon rim. Just before leaving them, he handed Caitlin a letter. "I'd appreciate your giving this to Sarah Clayton," he said, and Caitlin noticed that he blushed as he said it.

"I'll do that. You and Daniel take care now. We'll be back soon," she promised, but her confidence wavered as she glanced back at Dylan. Ty and Daniel had prepared a place for him to lie down so he could better endure the long hours of the trip into town. He was sitting up, leaning against the side of the buckboard as Ty took his leave.

"Save some of that glitter for me," he said as he reached up to shake hands with Ty.

"You just be sure you don't spend all the money you get for what you're carrying with you on loose women and gambling," Ty ordered, but he was smiling. He turned back to Caitlin. "You won't forget to take the letter?" he asked.

"I won't forget," she assured him.

"I wonder what Ty is writing to Sarah about," Caitlin said after he'd headed back down the canyon trail and she'd snapped the reins to get the wagon rolling.

Dylan chuckled. "Well, seeing as how Ty is heads over heels for the lady, my best guess would be that letter is my baby brother's attempt at a love note."

"You knew that?" she asked and listened for any hint of disappointment in his answer.

Again he laughed. "It'd be hard not to know. The boy talks about her all the time. He used to spend half the night telling me how it could never work out because he was heading back to California and she'd never leave her friends and family here."

"I see," Caitlin replied.

Ty and Sarah. Not Dylan and Sarah. Perhaps Ty had been right. Perhaps Dylan did love her. She smiled to herself and urged the team to pick up the pace.

Eighteen

Salt Lake was a beehive of activity as usual. The thriving community boasted the start of several more new houses and shops than had been under construction when Caitlin had stopped there before. It was dusk as they pulled up to the Claytons' store. Dylan was asleep in the back of the wagon. Sarah was locking the door, closing up for the night.

"Sarah," Caitlin called as she pulled hard on the reins and set the wagon's brake. "Hello. I'm not sure you recall but—"

"Caitlin, how wonderful to see you. Are you traveling alone?" Sarah hurried over to the side of the wagon.

"No, Dylan's here in the back." She lowered her voice, hoping not to wake him. "He fell asleep about an hour ago after trying hard to show me that he didn't like all this pampering Ty and I were giving him. Your father sends his love, and this is from Ty." She handed Sarah the letter and recognized the look of anticipation and delight with which the woman regarded it. Sarah's reaction confirmed Caitlin's hope that she returned Ty's love and had not fallen for Dylan instead.

"Then you've just arrived," Sarah said as she hastily pocketed the letter and turned her attention back to Caitlin. "Why don't you come home with me? We've got plenty of room. You can get Dylan settled, and I'll go for the doctor." She glanced at the form in the back, and her brow furrowed with worry. "Is he very bad?"

"I resent that," Dylan replied, his eyes still closed. "I happen to be a very decent sort of fellow."

Sarah giggled and Caitlin rolled her eyes. "You may as well make up your mind here and now, Dylan Tremaine. A doctor is going to examine you before the night is over."

"I'd rather be closely examined by you," Dylan muttered.

Caitlin blushed and hoped Sarah had not heard that. "He's still running a bit of a fever," she said quickly. "Sometimes he just mumbles incoherently."

"Let's get him to our house," Sarah said, and climbed aboard for the short ride to the edge of town and the small adobe house she shared with her father.

Along the way the two women chatted easily about Caitlin's trip from the camp to town. Caitlin realized that before now she had respected Sarah as a rival and had regretted she would not have the chance to know the woman better. Now, if Sarah and Ty were to marry and she and Dylan married, they would be sisters. She found that she liked that idea very much. Spontaneously she reached over and covered Sarah's hand with her own. "Thank you, Sarah, for everything you and your father are doing for us."

Dylan walked into the house with Caitlin and Sarah's help. As soon as Sarah saw that he was settled on her father's bed, she left to get the doctor.

"Alone at last," Dylan said with a sly grin as Caitlin bent to cover him with a blanket. "Come here, woman."

He pulled her onto the bed with him, kissing her slowly and thoroughly as he explored the contours of her body with his hands.

"Dylan, stop it," Caitlin protested, but she could not deny the thrill of having him hold her.

He moved over her and she saw that his expression was more serious than his teasing would have indicated.

"Caitlin, I have something to say to you, and I want you to hear me out."

"Dylan, they'll be plenty of time for us to discuss whatever it is . . . Dylan!"

He had started opening the neckline of the dress she'd chosen to wear into town in place of her camp outfit of pants and a man's shirt. "Now," he insisted, "or the good doctor and fair Sarah will return to find you naked as a newborn."

"You're impossible. Now stop it this minute." She slapped at his hands and tried to sit up.

He caught both her hands with one of his and pinned them above her head as he continued working the buttons until her dress was open to the waist. He fingered the ribbon ties of her camisole and paused, watching her expectantly.

"All right. Say what you have to say, but be quick about it," she said.

To her surprise, he released her hands and helped her sit up on the bed. When she began refastening her dress, he pushed her hands away and did it himself, all the while delivering the speech he'd been working on from the time they'd left camp.

"Caitlin, I know we have our differences—backgrounds, upbringing, family and all. But with my part of the gold we've found I can provide a good life for us. It's true I won't have the same standing in the community of someone as respected as your father, but we can build a good life, Cait, for ourselves and our children. I know you love me. I heard you say it when I was out of my head, but that was real. I'm asking you to consider marrying me for real."

Caitlin studied him for a long moment. "This isn't because you're worried that you may have impregnated me when we . . . the other night?" she asked. "I mean you really want to do this? I can be very difficult sometimes as you know. These last few days have been somewhat idyllic for the two of us and—"

He kissed her to shut her up. "Yes or no," he growled as he broke the kiss and they heard Sarah's buggy pull up to the house.

"Dylan, we need to—"

"Yes or no, Cait? Right now. Decide."

She had decided months ago. She loved him. She would be his until eternity whether or not they spent a life together. She lowered her lashes and studied her hands.

His heart sank. He'd been so sure . . . so certain. How could she have made love with him like they had unless—

"Yes," she whispered so softly he at first thought what he had heard was the front door opening and Sarah's distant voice talking to the doctor.

He looked at Caitlin and she was smiling at him. She cupped his face with her hands. "I love you, Dylan," she said. "My answer is yes. Now please let me up before Sarah and the doctor walk through that door."

He kissed her once more, a quick kiss that promised everything, then pushed her to a sitting position on the edge of the bed while he assumed a pose of exhausted repose, the back of his hand resting dramatically on his brow, his eyes closed.

"You're quite an actor," Caitlin said as she covered him with a blanket. "I'll have to remember that."

The doctor pronounced him to be in miraculous health considering the fever he had endured. He then suggested that perhaps Dylan might wish to rely on a cane for a few days until his strength returned. "Can't have you falling on your face just now when you've practically been brought back from the dead by this pretty lady here," he said as he snapped his black bag closed and took his leave.

Sarah brought a cane that her father had carved for himself when he'd broken his ankle two years earlier. Dylan tried it out the next day when he and Caitlin went into town with Sarah. Clearly, he enjoyed the attention using the cane garnered for him from sympathetic females up and down the street.

Their first stop was a meeting with Brigham Young whom Dylan promised to give a tenth of the gold for the work of Mormons if Young promised that he would not broadcast the find. After all, Ty would be becoming a member so he might marry Sarah.

"It may be that there's more," Dylan said, "but that canyon is narrow and too small to handle the influx of even a dozen more men. One fella already died trying to get something without working for it. Ty deserves the chance to work his claim in peace."

Young agreed.

Dylan took Caitlin's hand and drew her forward. "I'd also like your help in something else, sir," he said.

Young smiled.

"Miss Pearce and I would like to marry—the sooner the better. Will you secure a minister for us? My future wife is a Methodist."

"It would be my pleasure and honor," Young replied.

Before Caitlin knew what was happening, they had selected the day and time, and Dylan was pulling her back down the street toward the shops. "Come on, Caitlin, let's celebrate."

Caitlin soon discovered that Dylan's idea of celebrating was to buy gifts. First they selected a beautiful hand-woven shawl for Sarah and a new pipe for Daniel. Then he ordered boots for himself and Ty from the cobbler. He bought gifts for everyone in Caitlin's family as well as for Gar Heathcote and Rob. When Caitlin protested that they had no assurance the gifts would ever be delivered, he paused and his expression turned serious. "We're going to deliver them, Cait. You and me—we're going home."

"But I thought you'd want to stay here. I mean, what about Ty? What about the claim?"

Dylan laughed. "Ty will eventually marry Sarah. Daniel will help him work the claim, and when it's worked out he'll see that Ty and Sarah are settled in a place of their own right here in Salt Lake. We have enough, Caitlin. We have wealth beyond anything we would have imagined. We have each other, and I don't know about you, but I want to go home to Wisconsin."

Ever since the night before when they had finally confessed their love for each other she had not permitted herself to think about home. She had told herself that Dylan was all that mattered. Where they lived was not an issue, only that they never lost one another again. Now, to find out that he, too, dreamed of going back to Mineral Point— that he thought of that as his home. . . .

"Here, here, there's no reason to cry, Caitie," Dylan said, his voice tinged with distress. "Don't you want to go home?"

She nodded and sniffed back the tears. "More than anything," she mumbled.

Dylan frowned. "Then let's get married and get going. It's a long trip in case you forgot," he teased.

Caitlin smiled up at him. "You've made me so happy, Dylan," she said.

"I've just barely gotten started," he replied with a mischievous wink.

He was true to his word. In the next several hours, he insisted that he move out of Sarah's house until after the wedding. Caitlin was actually disappointed at that, but he told her he intended to court her properly from that moment until the hour of their wedding two days hence. And court her, he did.

The flowers started to arrive that very evening. Over the next forty-eight hours there was a new bouquet every morning, noon, and night, with a handwritten note from Dylan accompanying each one counting down the hours until their vows. He had the finest seamstress in town come to the house to take her measurements and show her designs for a gown. He ordered bolts of fabric brought for her to select not only her wedding gown but a full trousseau, and put additional seamstresses to work making her new wardrobe. Deliveries of fancy hats to match each gown followed. And then there was the jewelry—a locket engraved to his favorite teacher, a small gold watch to pin to her lapel embellished with small emeralds, earrings of pearl and filigreed gold. She began to worry that he had melted down every ounce of the treasure he had worked so hard to extract from the hard rocky soil.

That evening as they sat at dinner together in the local restaurant, she gently chastised him for his extravagance. To her amazement, he laughed.

"My darling Cait, do you have any idea what we have found in our small claim? Everything I've spent, even the donation to Young's temple has barely made a dent. And think of what Ty and Daniel are finding as we sit here. I can afford to be generous, Cait, and there's no one I would rather shower with gifts than you. Please indulge me, and trust that I won't jeopardize our future security."

She hardly knew what to say. "It's worth that much? You're rich?"

"*We're* rich, my love. When we return to Mineral Point you can choose any house you want and we can buy it. Or we'll build a new one."

"That would be lovely," she replied. She thought of the cottage, cozy, small, the place where she had first fallen in love with him. She knew it was impractical, but she loved that cottage.

"Do you think the land surrounding the cottage might be available?" Dylan asked.

It was as if he could read her very thoughts. "The cottage is at the end of the row," she replied. "I don't really know who owns the woods next to it. Why?"

He shrugged and glanced around the dining room as if

what they were talking about was no more than idle chatter. "I was just thinking. I mean knowing how you wanted so much to live in that cottage, but it being small even for two of us, well, the thought occurred to me that we might build onto it."

"Oh, Dylan, could we?" She reached across the table and clasped his hand. "It would make me so happy."

He turned his gaze on her, and his eyes sparkled as he saw her smiling at him, loving him, happy to be with him. "For the rest of my life, Caitlin, making you happy is my purpose. We will have our hard times and our sorrows, but I will do everything in my power to see that when they come, they don't last. I love seeing you smile, and love knowing it was I who put that smile on your beautiful face."

Caitlin blushed. No one had ever called her beautiful before, but when Dylan said it she believed it. She felt beautiful when she was with him, and the fact that she would share the rest of her days with him made her happy beyond anything she had ever known. "I love you, Dylan," she said softly.

He seemed surprised to hear her say it aloud, especially in public surroundings. His heart swelled with pride that he had won her love. "And I love you, Caitlin." He pulled his pocketwatch out and smiled. Then he plucked the single flower from the vase on their table and handed it to her. "Only twelve hours to go."

She carried the flower to her room and pressed it carefully in the pages of the journal she had kept from the day she'd left Mineral Point on her journey West.

They were married the following morning at ten o'clock in the parlor of the Clayton home, by a Methodist minister Brigham Young had retained for them. Sarah and Ty attended them, and Daniel and others they had befriended in the neighborly community witnessed the ceremony. Caitlin wore a gown of cream lace. It was the most beautiful dress she had ever owned. As she walked down the stairway and into the parlor toward the fireplace where Dylan waited, she could not help but wonder whether or not some day the two of them might watch their own daughter wearing this same dress at her wedding and then their daughter's daughter in the gown and so on for generations to come.

The idea that she was actually imagining a grown grand-daughter before she and Dylan had children of their own made her smile. Only she suspected the idea was not so far-fetched, for with each passing day she was more convinced than ever that she and Dylan had made their first child that night in camp. She glanced up as she traveled the last few feet to the altar and saw him looking at her with such adoration she thought her heart would burst.

Ty and Daniel left right after the ceremony to return to camp. They would work the claim until it yielded no more. Both men agreed that while there might be more canyons with undiscovered gold to explore, they were not interested. Daniel told Dylan that for the past few days Ty had talked longingly of owning a spread of his own and seemed to have abandoned any intention of returning to California.

"You're a good influence on my brother," Dylan told Daniel as he bid the older man farewell. "Thank you."

"I'm in hopes your brother will be my son-in-law one day soon. What I do for him, I do for my beloved Sarah," Daniel replied. He hugged Caitlin. "You're just about the prettiest bride I've seen," he said softly. "Be very happy. Dylan is a good man."

Daniel went to finish loading supplies from his store while Dylan and Caitlin went in search of Ty. They found him with Sarah, the two of them oblivious to their sur-roundings as they shared a passionate kiss.

Caitlin tugged at Dylan's sleeve. "Let's leave them alone," she whispered.

"Daniel will be waiting," Dylan replied, but he also seemed reluctant to intrude. "If they don't get started soon, it'll be too late to make camp tonight and they'll either need to camp on the trail or wait until morning."

"Surely, it wouldn't be so terrible if they spent the night here," Caitlin said.

"Ty's worried. In spite of everything the word has spread about the strike. There are others around like the Riley brothers who'd take advantage of any opportunity they could to jump the claim. Unfortunately if it's left unattended for too long, someone could do that legally."

Caitlin glanced at Ty and Sarah. They had broken the kiss and were talking softly to each other, but they were still clinging to each other as if they wanted never to part. Dylan took Caitlin's hand and pulled her forward. "Daniel's waiting, Ty," he said.

Sarah looked stricken. Ty nodded, then turned back to her, taking her by the shoulders. "One month," he promised. "Then we'll be married and settle. Will you wait for me?"

Sarah was crying in earnest now, but she managed a weak smile and nodded.

Ty kissed her hard one last time and then released her. "Coming," he muttered. He turned to Caitlin and hugged her. "Thank you for loving my brother," he said softly. "We're proud to have you in the family."

Caitlin hugged him back. "Be careful," she said. "I mean it. I want you and Sarah to come see us one day. I have grand plans for all of us so don't go getting yourself hurt."

Ty released her and grinned. "Yes ma'am," he replied.

The two brothers first stuck out their hands for a manly farewell, but then abandoned that gesture and fell into each other's arms. There wasn't a dry eye to be found among the four of them as Dylan and Ty promised to stay in touch, promised to visit, and urged each other to take care. Each one of them knew that this could well be the last time the two brothers would see each other in spite of their idea of exchanging visits. The truth was the distance was so great, and both men knew their lives would probably not permit them to take time for extended travel.

When Ty released Dylan, he pulled a small bulging sack from his vest pocket and handed it to his brother. "Your wedding present," he said with a grin. "I didn't have time to do any shopping."

Dylan hefted the weight of the sack and looked at his brother. "We can't take this," he said. "It's too much. You've no idea how much more is out there. Ty. Don't be foolish."

Ty frowned and then fumbled in his other pocket. When he pulled out an identical sack from that source and held it triumphantly aloft, the two brothers laughed and then fell into each other's arms again, hugging and dancing and pounding each other on the back. Then they grabbed Sarah's and Caitlin's hands and began dancing with them until the four of them were breathless with laughter and celebration. Caitlin knew that each of them would think of this moment often over the years, and she loved Ty for giving them the gift of this memory.

"You coming, young fella?" Daniel called from astride his horse.

"Coming," Ty called and turned to give Sarah one last kiss. "One month," he repeated as he dashed off to take the reins of his horse from Daniel.

Caitlin and Dylan left Salt Lake late the following morning. While Caitlin had been having fittings for her wedding gown and trousseau, Dylan had been outfitting a wagon and selecting a team for the trip home to Mineral Point. They would join a small party of other wagons headed East. Some had come West to find gold or the answer to their dreams and been disappointed. Others had come to settle the new frontier, but found themselves miserable and homesick for family and friends. A very few had found what they came for and had never had any intention of staying.

The group was getting a late start. It was already August, and by September there would be snow in the mountains. The first part of the journey promised to be the most difficult. Mountain paths were sure to be wet and slippery. Autumn rains would swell the rivers and make crossings more hazardous. The rains would also soak the rutted trail winding endlessly across the plains, causing wagons and livestock to become mired in mud.

On top of that Dylan had heard reports of Indian attacks on wagon trains as the Indians began to understand the magnitude of the sheer numbers of white people coming through their lands. To make matters worse, there were increasing outbreaks of cholera among the emigrants coming West. The number of dead escalated every week. He could protect Caitlin from Indians and natural disasters, but he could not save her from such a dreaded disease. As he stocked the wagon, he considered the wisdom of staying in Salt Lake for the winter and heading home in late spring. But he had promised Caitlin that they could be home for Christmas, and he had no intention of starting their marriage by going back on his word.

He leaned against the doorway of the Claytons' store and watched her and Sarah selecting the household supplies for the trip. *My wife*, he thought. He still couldn't believe that she had come all this way, risking everything to find him. She stretched to retrieve some canned goods from a high shelf. He watched the pull of her cotton dress against her breasts. It didn't take much for him to drift into a memory of their night of lovemaking. . . .

After Ty and Daniel left, Sarah had told Dylan that she would be spending the night with friends and wanted them to make themselves at home. The newlyweds had shared the supper Sarah had left for them and then had sat outside, looking up at the stars and planning their future. After a while they had gone in and up to the bedroom Caitlin had occupied for the past few days.

Dylan had stretched out on the bed and waited for her to finish her nightly preparations. He watched her take down her hair and remove her outer garments. He waited as she stepped behind a folding screen and removed the rest of her clothing. He closed his eyes and thought about the days and weeks ahead of them, difficult weeks. He wished it were over already and they were safely back in Mineral Point in their own cottage, in their own bed.

"Dylan?" Caitlin had stood next to the bed in nothing more than her simple muslin nightgown, its ribbons left undone revealing a hint of her naked breasts. She had undressed him as he lay on the bed. Then she had stood next to the bed and slipped the gown from her shoulders, allowing it to fall to the floor around her feet. In that moment he had thought his heart would hammer its way right out of his chest. His breath came in heaves as he reached for her, pulling her into bed and taking her without preamble. She had been moist and ready for him, and lifted her hips to receive his every thrust, her fingernails raking his back as he poured himself into her.

Later he had taken the time to teach her the many ways a woman used to satisfy a man, and vice versa. He had been delighted to find that her insatiable curiosity for learning had opened her mind to trying whatever he suggested. He smiled now as he recalled how he had begun a trail of long wet kisses at her mouth and pursued them down and over her breasts, her stomach, her inner thighs. Hesitatingly he had used his tongue and breath to moisten the triangle of hair at the apex of her legs.

She had gasped and stilled as if awaiting his next move, but she had not pulled away. He had paused and then moved lower, his mouth over her opening, his tongue gently probing. She had cried out, then grasped handfuls of his hair and pulled at him, urging him to relieve the building explosion of her desire.

"What on earth are you thinking about?" Caitlin asked him now, but when she saw the expression on his face, she knew. She blushed deeply and turned back to her work hoping Sarah had not noticed.

Dylan had made love to her repeatedly through the night. There had been the unabandoned wildness of that first coupling after she had undressed him. Then there had been the slow, sweet torture of his refusing to take her until she had been little more than a quivering mass of passion in his hands. On that occasion when he had finally plunged deeply inside her, she had thought she would faint from the sheer magnificence of his filling her.

They had slept a bit after that, their bodies slicked with sweat and entwined. He woke her just before dawn, his mouth open over hers, their tongues engaging in a waltz of passion. When he had broken the kiss, she had cried out until she realized his plan to kiss every inch of her. She had cooperated with his every signal, arching, turning to give him access. When she had felt his mouth and tongue probing between her legs, she had been shocked. Surely this was indecent, even for a married woman. But the sensations she felt were incredible.

"I want you," he whispered. Caitlin gave a startled shriek as canned goods went flying. She had not heard him come up behind her.

"Dylan," she chastised him, but the truth was if he'd wanted to take her there on the shop counter she could not have refused him.

"Sarah, can you finish up here?" Dylan asked as he scooped Caitlin high in his arms. "My wife and I have business."

"Dylan!"

Sarah smiled. "Go on," she said. "I'll finish the order."

"Put me down this instant, Dylan," Caitlin protested as

he carried her outside the store and down the street toward the Claytons' house. "It's the middle of the day. People will be scandalized."

"And in an hour we'll leave here and probably never return. Let's give them something to talk about, Cait, something to remember us by."

"You're impossible," she replied, but she could not keep the smile from her lips.

When he saw that she would cooperate he put her down and grabbed her hand running with her toward the house. They were both laughing as they ran past startled shopkeepers and townspeople out doing their chores or visiting with neighbors. They reached the house laughing and out of breath. The door was barely closed before they were in each other's arms. They did not bother undressing any more than was absolutely necessary. They fell onto the floor and smothered their cries of release in more kisses.

Afterward they lay together as Dylan filled her head with dreams of all the days and nights to come. "Tonight we'll make love under the stars, Caitie. Someday we'll tell our children about this."

"We can't talk about such things to the children," Caitlin scolded him.

"After they're grown," Dylan said. "When we're old and they can't imagine us in bed together doing anything more than sleeping."

Caitlin giggled, then stilled as she felt Dylan's fingers tracing a path up her inner thigh. "There's no time," she whispered but her voice caught as he found the one spot he seemed to know would drive her wild.

"There will always be time, Caitie," he said softly as he pulled her on top of him and positioned her to receive him.

Caitlin lowered herself onto him, taking him inch by inch more deeply inside, pulling away and then taking him again. She felt his hands on her naked hips beneath the voluminous fabric of her cotton dress, and there was something very scandalous about that, the bright sunlight streaming through the windows as they made love on the floor, as if they were doing something indiscreet. She rested her palms on his shirt and thrilled to the heat of him soaking through the fabric. She watched his face contort as he came inside her and she felt a moment of such power, such triumph as she collapsed against him, their bodies still joined.

"Mrs. Tremaine?"

She didn't want to move. "Hm-m-m?"

"Let's go home," he said softly.

Caitlin smiled. *Home. More to the point home with Dylan. Could anything be more wonderful?*

Nineteen

In the novels I read for pleasure our story would have ended happily ever after right there, Caitlin thought just a month later as she watched Dylan and the other men ferrying wagons and livestock across the fast-running river. But this was real life, and the reality was that they had started their marriage on a dangerous journey on which weather and Indians and disease all conspired to destroy their happiness.

Already they had faced unusually early ice and snow in the mountains; Indians who came in the night and stole or ran off their livestock, forcing them to delay their journey until the strays could be rounded up; and the dreaded cholera which had struck their group hard. Five travelers, including the trailmaster, had died of the dreaded disease that struck suddenly and sometimes took its victims in a matter of hours.

A doctor in a wagon train headed West advised them to disinfect everything whether or not it had been touched or used by the deceased. They camped for two days by the Sweetwater to wash everything thoroughly, air all the bedding, and repack the wagons. During this time the men met to decide who might be designated to take charge, at least until they could reach Fort Laramie and hire a new guide. Dylan was the unanimous choice.

Caitlin was proud and worried at the same time. The trailmaster was expected to take the risks, make the decisions, lead the way. If there was danger from Indians or other unknown enemies Dylan would likely be the first to encounter such danger. On top of that she had not been feeling well for several days now. She had kept her symptoms to herself, terrified that they were the first signs of cholera. She knew it was unfair to her fellow travelers, and she tried as hard as she could to keep her distance, making excuses about needing to attend to a chore or write a letter when the women gathered in the evening to visit with each other. During the day she insisted that Dylan ride his horse so that he would have the freedom to move up and down the wagon train, giving directions and encouragement. She drove the wagon and that further isolated her from the others. At night she sent Dylan out to take his turn on watch, knowing he would sleep in the tent outside the wagon rather than disturb her sleep in the middle of the night when his watch was over. She had to protect him until she was certain it was not cholera.

"Caitie, you've hardly eaten a thing," Dylan commented one evening as he wolfed down his normal generous portions of the food she'd prepared for their supper. "As a matter of fact you haven't been eating much for the past few days."

She tried to laugh it off. "I eat. I just don't need the amount of food you do."

He frowned and dropped the subject, but she knew he was watching her closely.

The following morning she slipped away from the camp as had become her habit after breakfast. Anyone seeing her would think she had gone to relieve herself. She felt the wave of nausea as she hurried away from the wagons and barely made it to a secluded spot before she was sick. She fell to her knees, the sickness sending mighty heaves through her as she threw up the tiny amount of food she'd forced herself to eat, knowing Dylan was watching her.

As she gasped for air and waited for the next wave to

come, Dylan knelt next to her. "Why didn't you tell me?" he asked, his face contorted with worry.

She shrugged and then turned away as the next wave hit.

Dylan held her head and his cool hand was like a balm on her brow.

"Is it over?" he asked after holding her for several moments and waiting with her.

She nodded. "For now."

He helped her back to the wagons and brought her a cup of cool water from the stream. He also brought Lizzie Johnson, the nearest thing to a nurse or doctor available. Lizzie had overseen the disinfecting of the wagons. She had been the first to diagnose the illness among the travelers as cholera. She covered her mouth and nose with a handkerchief and climbed into the wagon where Caitlin rested.

"Caitlin, what's the trouble?" she asked in her eternally cheerful voice.

Caitlin explained the course of her illness to the older woman who had ordered Dylan to go about his business until she called him. As Caitlin talked about the nausea, the lack of appetite, the exhaustion she felt beyond what should be normal, Lizzie slowly lowered her makeshift mask, and when she did she was smiling broadly.

"It'd be my guess that you've not got the cholera, young lady. What you've got is a baby growing in your belly— that'd be my guess."

Caitlin blinked. She had hoped she was pregnant when they left Salt Lake, but with all the misery they had endured on the trail she had forgotten all about the idea. "I'm with child?" she said in an awed tone.

"Sure showing all the regular signs—no appetite, can't keep nothing down. Why with my first five I was sicker than a dog for the first three months. The last three I ate anything I wanted and never felt a minute's upset. It'd be my guess you're about two months into it. Does that make sense?"

Caitlin nodded. Then she started to laugh and cry and hug Lizzie.

"Here, here, missy, you'd best be saving your celebrating for that man of yours out there," Lizzie instructed. She patted Caitlin's hand. "You're gonna be just fine," she assured her and then lifted the flap of the wagon. "You can come on in now, Tremaine," she called.

Dylan was inside the wagon almost before the words had left Lizzie's mouth. "I'll be going now," Lizzie said. "You call me if you need anything at all. I'll send my oldest up to help you drive partway. You can take a little nap. And start eating," she ordered as a parting shot.

Dylan barely heard anything Lizzie said. "You're all right?" he asked anxiously.

"Yes. Oh, Dylan, we're going to have a baby."

His eyes widened. "A ba . . . That's why . . . you mean . . . a baby?"

Caitlin nodded and caressed his cheek. "Our first child," she said softly.

Dylan threw back his head and let out a whoop of joy.

There was a tentative knock on the side of the wagon. "Captain?" The other men had taken to calling him that since they had elected him their leader. "Everybody's all hitched and ready," the man said.

Dylan lifted the flap of the wagon and stuck his head out. "We're having a baby," he said giddily. Then he shouted it, "A baby!"

Caitlin laughed. "Be quiet. You'll make them think I'm having it this minute. Now go on. Get this train moving. We need to make time, *Captain* Tremaine. I want to have this baby at home in my own bed."

She was successful in persuading him to mount his horse and take his position at the head of the wagons, but she had to enlist Lizzie's support when he rode back later and found her in her usual post, driving their wagon.

"Now you listen to me, Dylan Tremaine," Lizzie ordered as she walked alongside Caitlin's wagon. "Your wife is having a baby. She's not dying. She's not even sick. She needs to do what she normally does if you want that child to be strong and healthy. I take no stock in this business of a woman taking to her bed just because she's got a bun cooking in her oven."

Dylan blushed purple and rode on ahead on the pretense of checking their forward progress. Caitlin and Lizzie held their giggles until he was out of earshot and then laughed until tears ran down their dust-streaked faces.

They made good time all the way to Fort Laramie where they were able to replenish supplies and offer advice to new emigrants headed West. That night they joined the soldiers in the fort for a welcome night of square dancing, singing, and storytelling. Dylan had never seen Caitlin look more radiant then she did that night. She had taken to tying her hair back with a ribbon which gave her a girlish look that he found irresistible. She wore a soft cotton housedress that accentuated the roundness of her expanding belly. Every soldier in the place could not take his eyes off her, but Dylan felt no jealousy. If he had ever doubted her love for him, those doubts were gone. From the day they had learned of her pregnancy, a bond had been formed between them, and it seemed indestructible.

That night as they lay together in their wagon, she reached over and gently placed his hand on her stomach. He felt a slight shudder under his flattened palm that she held pressed to her naked flesh. He pressed harder and felt movement, a stirring that was faint but undeniable. Tears welled as he gently laid his cheek where his hand had been. *My wife. My child.*

* * *

The Platte ran yellow with churned-up clay and mud. It appeared almost to be boiling, it was so agitated and high. There was no way to determine its depth, and it would be foolhardy to risk its currents. Still, though there were trees to shade them from the oppressive heat and choking dust of the late September weather, the ground was completely barren of vegetation. There wasn't a blade of grass for the livestock to eat. The growing numbers of emigrants headed West, combined with weeks of drought followed by torrential rains, had exhausted any possible food supply for the animals.

Caitlin sat on the high seat of the wagon and listened to Dylan and the other men discussing their options. Tempers were short. It had been a discouraging and exhausting week. Along the way they had witnessed horrors such as they could not have imagined. Along with the thick dust that clogged their lungs and made breathing difficult, they had passed an astounding number of carcasses of oxen and mules that had died on the trail, the carcasses left to rot in the hot sun. The odor was repugnant, the sight of the dead animals was grisly. In addition the landscape was now littered with the splintered remains of abandoned wagons that had clearly broken down on the trail and been irreparable. Caitlin wondered what their occupants had done. How much of their hopes and dreams had been left behind with that wagon?

"Caitie?"

Dylan sat astride his horse alongside their wagon. She smiled at him, knowing he was weary of the responsibility thrust upon him as their leader, hoping he would see in her eyes that no matter what he did, she believed in him, in his ability to take them home.

"Some of us are going to ride out a ways and see if there's pasture. We'll drive the animals with us except for a few. If we find pasture, we'll camp for a day or so to let them eat their fill, then come back and go on. By that time maybe the river will calm a bit as well."

He looked so tired, and Caitlin longed to touch his face, to hold and comfort him. "Be careful," she said.

"Some of the older men and the ones with young children are staying behind," Dylan continued as if she hadn't spoken. "They'll watch out for you." He glanced at her growing belly. "You'll be safest here," he added as if he were trying to convince himself.

"I'll be fine," Caitlin assured him.

Dylan nodded and nudged his horse with his heels. Caitlin watched him ride as far as a couple of wagons and then abruptly turn around and ride back. "I love you," he said huskily as he reached up and pulled her toward him for a farewell kiss. Caitlin resisted the urge to cling to him, and it was she who broke the contact.

"Go," she said, "and hurry back."

He smiled at her and tipped his hat. Then he was off, calling out orders as he and three others rode off. They would go searching for pasture. The others would circle the wagons, unhitch the teams, gather the livestock, and then drive them in the direction Dylan and the others had headed. The rest of the party would remain camped along the banks of the raging Platte and wait for word.

Dylan and his scouting party found pasture about twelve miles north. They sat on the rise of a hill and looked down at the most beautiful grassy valley they would ever see; then they let out a whoop of joy and rode hard to meet the drovers and the livestock. The following morning one rider was dispatched back to camp to let everyone know of their success and to expect their return in three days.

"Give this to my wife." Dylan handed the young messenger a letter he had written the night before. It was the

first letter he had written her since they had truly become
man and wife, and in it he had poured out his heart to her
and his unborn child. They had made the worst of the trip,
he told her, and once he returned and they crossed the
river, he had no doubt that they would make good time the
rest of the way.

Crossing the river was also on the mind of Jake Eldridge.
Jake had signed on as a teamster with the train back in
Salt Lake. When the first trailmaster had died, he had
thought he would be elected boss. After all, he was the
most experienced, having traveled the trail numerous times
with various groups over the years. But the people had
chosen the Cornishman—a foreigner who knew less than
nothing about trailblazing. When Tremaine had gone riding
off with the others to find pasture, he'd finally made his
first good choice as far as Jake was concerned. He'd left
Jake in charge.

Early on the morning of the first day after Tremaine and
the others left, Jake rousted three or four of the men he
knew had favored him to take charge of the trip. "We're
crossing today," he said. "Round up the animals we've got.
We'll pull each wagon to the edge, take off the wheels and
undercarriage and float them across one by one. By the
time Tremaine and the others return, we'll be ready to roll
as soon as we get the livestock across."

It sounded like a good plan especially to men who were
restless and bored and who were weary of their wives and
children constantly asking when they might move on. Word
spread from one wagon to the next as the emigrants woke
and set about their early morning chores.

"Mr. Eldridge, do I understand correctly that you have
decided to cross before my husband and the others return?"

Jake looked down at the Tremaine woman. Even with
her belly swollen with a youngun she was the prettiest thing
in camp. More than once he'd stood outside her wagon
when he knew Tremaine was pulling sentinel duty and

watched her shadowed movements as she prepared for bed. Trouble was, she was also a most opinionated creature. Jake had thought more than once how he'd like to take her down a peg or two off her high horse.

He deliberately looked at a point over her head and spit a stream of tobacco juice out of the corner of his mouth. "Yes'm. That's the plan all right."

"I'm not sure that's wise, Mr. Eldridge. My husband distinctly told us to remain where we are until he and the others return."

"Your husband put me in charge, ma'am. I say we go."

"And I say we put it to a vote," she challenged, planting her feet and folding her arms defiantly across her chest.

"Take your vote, missy," he said as he leaned within an inch of her face. "You'll lose," he said gruffly, and then he laughed.

His putrid breath fanning her face rivaled the stench of the dead animals they had passed on the trail. Caitlin moved a step back in revulsion. She saw immediately that her action had angered Jake.

He grabbed her upper arm and squeezed hard. "You thinking you're too good for the likes of me, missy?"

"Let me go this instant," she demanded.

He squeezed harder and then released her. "You'd just best be remembering who's in charge here, Mrs. Tremaine. That husband of yours ain't here, and nobody else has the time to care much what happens to you." He turned and walked away, shouting orders as he went.

Caitlin remained where she was and folded her arms, holding at bay a shiver of revulsion and fear as she watched Jake organize people for the crossing. She could not deny that he was right. People were anxious to get home now that they had made the decision to head East. They were bored with waiting and any action that seemed designed to give them a headstart at getting back on the trail would be applauded. She watched the camp become a beehive of activity. Spirits were high as everyone made quick work of breakfast and prepared their wagons for the crossing.

"Jake's got 'em crossing the river," the messenger called as he rode hard to carry word back to Dylan and the others.

Dylan checked the darkening sky for the third time that morning. A storm was brewing and he knew from experience it could come up sudden and fierce. His main concern had been how to contain the animals so they wouldn't stampede. Now his focus shifted. "He's what?"

The breathless rider pulled his lathered horse to a quick stop next to Dylan and the other scouts. "Crossing," he managed to gasp out. "He's floating the wagons across. Three were in the water when I left."

The first bolt of lightning split the dark sky, and the men brushed away the first large drops of rain. The livestock shifted restlessly. A horse whinnied in alarm.

"What're we gonna do, Captain?" one of the men asked.

"Herd the stock over to that hillside there and keep them as close as you can. Use every man to circle them. When the storm passes, if there's daylight, start back to camp." He rode off just as the storm broke. No one needed to ask where he was headed.

Caitlin had stood on the banks of the river and held her breath as she watched Jake Eldridge orchestrate the crossing of the first wagons. She would grant him that his organization was expert. He had dispatched one group of men to the opposite shore to pull each wagon to safety as it completed the crossing. Then they would work as quickly as possible to reinstall the undercarriage and wheels and hitch a team of oxen to pull the wagon to high ground.

She knew it wasn't an issue of whether or not the wagons were capable of crossing. They had been designed for just such a purpose, their seams expertly sealed against moisture, their bodies specifically shaped for floatation. The spirits of the people on either shore rose with the safe crossing of each wagon. Jake was their hero of the hour. But Caitlin had noticed the darkening sky. True, the black clouds were in the distance, but she knew how quickly a storm could come and how dreadful it could be. So did the others, but their attention was focused solely on the activities of the crossing. They cheered each wagon as it was pulled to high ground on the opposite shore even as they backhanded the first drops of rain that pelted their faces.

"You're next, missy," Jake said softly. He had come up behind her as she had busied herself with securing her wagon for the storm.

"I'm not going," she said defiantly, refusing to even acknowledge his presence. "You are endangering the very lives of these people unnecessarily and I will have no . . ." Her sentence hung in the air unfinished as Eldridge picked her up and strode toward the river.

She was mortified to hear the laughter of her fellow travelers as she kicked and pelted Eldridge with her fists. The crossing had been going well for much of the day, and they were ripe for some entertainment.

"Got us a bit of a scaredy-cat here, folks," Jake called out. "Can't say as I blame her, being with child and all. Now just calm down, missy, before you hurt that baby of yours."

Helplessly Caitlin watched as the men pulled her wagon to the edge of the river and removed the undercarriage. It was raining harder now and the drumbeat of thunder played out an ominous cadence as a background to the noise of the men shouting back and forth to each other as they guided each wagon across.

Caitlin assessed her situation. There were five wagons in the river now, winding their way in a serpentine line to the opposite shore. The wind had picked up and the second wagon from the end tipped crazily from side to side. Caitlin saw that it contained the Carson children. Their mother had died of cholera on the trip out, and their father had decided to turn back before he lost any more of his precious family. Ben Carson was with Dylan. He'd left the children in the charge of his oldest daughter, Amelia. Amelia was ten years old.

Caitlin saw Amelia watching her. The child's eyes were wide with fear, and she was holding her baby brother in one arm while her other was wrapped around the shoulders of her six-year-old sister. With each flash of lightning and crack of thunder she seemed to tighten her grip and shrink farther into the bed of the rocking wagon.

"It's going over!" one of the men shouted as he made a futile grab to prevent the wagon from capsizing.

Caitlin saw Amelia still holding the baby get carried away from the overturned wagon by the current just as one of the men in the water grabbed her sister and pulled her to safety.

"Do something!" she shouted above the din of the storm at Jake.

Unceremoniously he dropped her to the ground and ran into the river. His eyes were wild with fear as he reached for the children, caught the baby but missed Amelia who was swept farther away from help by the current. Caitlin looked around for anything that might help rescue the girl who could be seen bobbing in and out of the rushing water as she floated farther and farther away from the opposite shore and toward Caitlin. In the middle of the river she bumped up against a rock and wrapped her arms around it as she fought to hold her head above water and cried hysterically.

Grabbing a tent pole the men had been using, Caitlin lay on her stomach on the rain-slicked shore and stretched the pole out to the child. "Hold my feet," she ordered others who stood on the shore in stunned disbelief. They rushed to do her bidding.

"Amelia," she shouted, "grab the pole."

The terrified child refused.

Caitlin inched farther out over the water. She could no longer tell the difference between the rain and the spray kicked up by the wind and rushing river. "Grab on and we'll pull you in," she called. "Come on, Amelia. That's a brave girl."

After what seemed an eternity Amelia took the pole. "Hold on," Caitlin called as she turned to the others, entreating them to help. Two women lined up behind her and pulled the pole in inch by inch as Caitlin brought Amelia closer. When she was within a few feet of safety two men stepped into the stream and lifted her out of the water. Everyone gathered round as the three children were reunited. Caitlin struggled to her feet and smiled, then gave a shout of surprise as the muddy bank caved in and she fell backward into the water.

Dylan was less than ten yards away when he saw the land beneath Caitlin's feet give way, and he watched helplessly as she tumbled into the wild river. He reined his horse in hard and leapt from the saddle as he heard her shout of surprise above the crashing storm. His heart pounded against the wall of his chest as he waded into the river and worked his way toward her. Her face surfaced and he saw her gasp to fill her lungs with air before she sank again. The current fought against his every move, and his legs felt like lead weights as he struggled to reach her, screaming her name to let her know he was there. She surfaced and seemed to look directly at him before the water washed over her again.

Other men had joined him in the river, working their way out as far as they dared, swinging ropes in Caitlin's direction, but she either did not see them or was too paralyzed with fear to reach out for them. The water was chest high, and Dylan knew it would soon be over his head so he began to swim, fighting the treacherous current and reaching toward her with every stroke. At last his fingers closed around her sodden skirts and he pulled her to the surface. Her eyes were closed, and her body was lifeless in his arms.

No, he screamed inwardly as he examined her face and saw the bluing of her lips. "No!" he shouted to the heavens.

"Dylan, take the rope," someone called.

He secured the rope around himself and Caitlin, and permitted the onlookers to pull them to shore as he spoke softly to her, tears streaming down his face. When he could feel solid ground under his feet he stood up and carried her the rest of the way. On shore the first face he saw was that of Jake Eldridge. Dylan paused for a moment and stared directly at the teamster. Then, without a word, he moved on to a wagon that had not yet been stripped down for crossing.

From the back of it, hands reached for her lifeless body. Dylan was barely aware of the women who reached for her and lifted her carefully into the wagon, laying her out on the straw bed. "Turn her over," Lizzie Johnson instructed, and then she knelt and began to press hard and repeatedly on Caitlin's back until she stirred and coughed up water. "She's breathing," Lizzie reported and moved aside as Dylan jumped into the wagon and cradled his wife's head against his chest as they moved her to a half-sitting position that permitted her to breathe more easily as she coughed up more water and phlegm.

"Caitie," he said softly, "come on back to us. Come on," he urged.

After what seemed an eternity Caitlin opened her eyes. She reached up and stroked his cheek, then let her hand drop back to her side.

"We'd best get her into dry things," Lizzie said. "Pearl, look in that trunk yonder and fetch me that flannel gown." She began stripping off Caitlin's sodden garments.

"What about the baby?" Dylan asked. The question had been uppermost in his mind since the moment he realized Caitlin was alive.

Lizzie shook her head. "Time will tell," she said. "Why don't you go on out and let folks know she's going to be all right?"

Reluctantly Dylan left the wagon. The storm had settled into a soft steady drizzle without the fireworks of the thunder and lightning. The wind had died down and an eerie stillness had settled over the camp on both sides of the river as everyone waited for news.

"She's alive," Dylan reported as he walked past them straight to the river. He looked across at the other side where half the emigrants waited. He considered the five wagons still in the river. Then he looked directly at Jake Eldridge. "Get those wagons to one bank or the other. We'll make camp and wait for the drovers to bring the stock." He started to walk back to the Johnson wagon to check on Caitlin.

"Tremaine, I'm—"

Dylan turned to face Jake and permitted himself the relief of anger. "You're a fool, Eldridge. I thought you were to be trusted. I thought you were the most experienced man among us. That's why I wanted you here. You almost killed three children and my wife today. You may well have killed my child. Get out of my sight. Don't let me cross paths with you again."

Dylan lay next to Caitlin through the night. Lizzie Johnson came by every hour or so to check her. Of the three of them Caitlin was the only one who got any sleep. Toward morning Dylan dozed, his hand protectively cra-

dling Caitlin's stomach. He was awakened by a twitch and
thought at first that Caitlin was trying to turn over, but she
was in a deep sleep, her breath coming in long even drafts.

He flattened his palm against the flannel fabric and
pressed. He felt movement. He scrambled to the opening
of the wagon. "Lizzie, come quick," he called.

Lizzie hauled herself into the wagon, her eyes red from
lack of sleep.

"The baby moved," he told her, and he smiled for the
first time in hours.

"You're sure?"

He took Lizzie's hand and pressed it against Caitlin's
stomach. "Wait for it," he whispered, and they held their
breaths.

After what seemed an eternity, there was a slight but
definite kick. Lizzie smiled and nodded as she moved her
hand slowly around the area. "The kid's a kicker all right,"
she muttered, but she was grinning as well.

"What's all the fuss?" Caitlin asked sleepily.

Epilogue

Tillie Polkinghorn opened her hat shop as she had every weekday morning for the past ten years. As always she went inside and quickly retrieved the broom she used to sweep the spotless boardwalk in front of her shop. Sweeping was her excuse for being out on the street to see what was going on, who was passing by, who looked a bit the worse for wear from having spent too much time and money in Gar Heathcote's establishment the night before.

On this particular morning she was hoping to see anyone with whom she could share the latest gossip. She was fairly bursting to tell the limited details she knew and gather additional particulars she might have missed. The object of her interest was none other than Caitlin Pearce. Well, Caitlin Tremaine. Tillie had been studying the details of Caitlin's actions over the past year and had found several issues that she felt warranted closer attention. Especially now that Caitlin and Dylan had rolled into town bigger than life earlier that month and announced their intention to settle in that ridiculous little cottage on Shake Rag when she was clearly expecting any minute and they could certainly afford a decent house.

"Elsie!" she called out, waving to the owner of a neighboring shop who was opening her doors for the day. Elsie returned her wave, and signaled that she would be right with her.

A few minutes later the two women were leaning on their respective brooms and debating the latest news they had been able to gather on Caitlin.

"One of the wives down on Shake Rag was in yesterday," Elsie reported in a low voice that could barely be heard above the din of passing wagons. "Her husband told her that Dylan and his brother struck it rich out West."

"In California," Tillie added, nodding knowingly.

"Oh, but it wasn't California. It was in Utah, near where those Mormon folks that had that trouble a few years ago down in Illinois picked up and went."

"You don't say," Tillie tittered. This was indeed news. Everyone had assumed the handsome young miner had headed for California. Certainly that was where Caitlin had said she was headed when she left town so suddenly.

"Do you think she was already . . . that it, could she possibly have been *with child* before she left?"

"What does that matter?" Elsie snorted derisively. "They were married. Besides she would have had to be showing at her sister's wedding and if anything, she looked like she needed a decent meal."

Tillie searched for another avenue. "Well, if you ask me they certainly don't act like decent married folks. If they've been married all this time, how come they still conduct themselves like they do?" She glanced up and down the street and moved a step closer to her friend. "I saw them last night, walking home after he called for her at school. You could not have wedged a table knife between the two of them from shoulder to hip, if you get my meaning."

Elsie nodded, eager to add her own news. "One Sunday just after they came back to town, I heard tell they was out in their buggy parked back in the woods. Now I'm not at liberty to say who spotted them, but suffice it to say neither one of them was completely dressed, if you gather my meaning. Will you tell me why, even if you wanted to indulge in that sort of thing, you wouldn't do so in the privacy of your own home?"

"Good morning, ladies. Glorious day, isn't it?"

Both shopkeepers spun around quickly as Caitlin marched past them on her way to her classroom. They nodded and smiled and watched her in embarrassed silence, wondering what she might have overheard.

"And that's the other thing," Tillie hastened to say as soon as she felt it was safe to resume the conversation. "Caitlin used to be such a stuck-up thing, wouldn't give you the time of day. Now she's all sunshine and howdy-do."

Elsie nodded vigorously in agreement. "My nephew tells me she's the same way in school, laughing with the children, taking them on outings in the middle of the day for no good reason."

"It's a pure scandal the way she flaunts that pregnancy of hers. Any decent woman would take to her bed until the child comes," Tillie fumed.

"On the other hand, my nephew has certainly improved his attendance since she returned, and he's getting higher marks as well."

"You almost sound like you approve," Tillie objected. "I'm telling you there's something improper about those two, her and that miner of hers, and one of these days I'm going to figure it out. I've thought it from the start—that rush marriage of theirs and then they did all that fighting. Oh, they tried to hide it, but a man does not sleep outside unless he's been forced there by his woman."

"I'll say one thing," Elsie commented wistfully as she watched Caitlin proceed up the street, "if acting lovesick makes you look that radiant and happy, I'd be willing to give it a try."

Tillie pursed her lips and resumed her sweeping. "Elsie! That's scandalous," she chastised.

Elsie chuckled. "Maybe so. But you mark my words, it

ain't Dylan's money that makes her look so happy like
that—it's Dylan."

Dylan had seen Caitlin off for school as he had every
morning since they'd returned to Mineral Point and she'd
insisted on resuming her teaching in spite of her advanced
pregnancy. He smiled as he recalled how her mother and
Molly had broached the subject one Sunday after the family
had shared their first Sunday dinner in months.

Mary Pearce had initiated the discussion. "Caitlin, dear,
I know you love your teaching and your students, but—"

"It's unseemly," Molly had finished for her mother. "I
mean, for heaven's sake, Cait, look at you. You're as big
as a house. What on earth are you telling those children?"

Caitlin smiled. "I suspect there isn't a child in my classroom who isn't familiar with the way babies come to this
world, Molly. I've had no complaints from the parents
either."

"Begging your pardon, Caitlin, but your pupils come
from families who are . . ." Her brother Edward fumbled
for words as he became aware that Dylan was studying
him intently. "That is to say, you have a certain . . ."

"Oh, come out with it," Molly protested. "Caitlin, you
are embarrassing the family."

"Molly, dearest, I am sorry for that, but I will not hide
myself away when I feel perfectly well and can make a
contribution to the education of these children while I wait
out my time."

"Father," Molly wailed.

John Pearce had remained uncustomarily silent during
the exchange. "Times are changing, Molly. Dylan, I'd like
to see those plans you've drawn up for expanding the cottage." And with that, he ended the matter once and for all.

The truth was John Pearce was so relieved to have his
eldest daughter home safe and sound he would have per-

mitted her almost any indiscretion. In a rare moment of candor he had confided to Dylan that until she had left, he had never realized how much he looked forward to his debates and discussions with the well-read Caitlin, how much he enjoyed sharing a new book with her or having her bring one to him.

"I thought we had lost her," he had admitted in a voice that was barely audible.

"Sir, you should know that our intent was always to come home. Caitlin's family means too much to her. I would never ask her to leave this place," Dylan assured him.

"Thank you, son," John replied and gave Dylan an awkward pat on the shoulder.

As the women cleared the table, Caitlin reminded Molly of her own indiscretions when she and Geoffrey were courting, and of how Caitlin had respected those even though it wasn't until she fell in love herself that she understood. Perhaps one day when Molly and Geoffrey had their own children, Molly would understand.

Dylan could not deny he wished Caitlin would stay at home where he could have someone watch over her properly while he went about his business, but he would not ask that of her. Instead he had given Rob Heathcote the task of watching over her—unbeknownst to Caitlin, of course. She would never stand for it.

Tillie Polkinghorn was standing outside her shop as Dylan made his way up the street to his office. Since returning to Mineral Point he had set up a business, investing his new wealth in property and projects around Mineral Point and all the way to Madison. "Good morning, Miss Polkinghorn." Dylan tipped his hat to the milliner.

Tillie blushed purple as she always did when he spoke to her. Caitlin insisted that Tillie and the other women in town had terrible crushes on him. He smiled as he passed Tillie and continued up the street. Then he stopped.

"You know, Miss Polkinghorn—or may I call you Tillie?—I do believe my wife needs a new hat," he said as he retraced his steps and peered in the shop window. "Do you suppose you might do something special—something that would be just right for her hair and coloring?"

Tillie was nothing if not a shrewd businesswoman. "Well, I'm not sure, Mr. Tremaine. I have a number of orders just now and—"

"I'll need something for Caitlin's mother as well. Oh, yes, and there's her sister. I can't very well forget Molly." He chuckled as he ticked each order off on his fingers.

Three hats, Tillie thought. *Three special orders.* She could charge top dollar.

"Of course, I'll want only the finest materials," Dylan continued. "And I wonder, if you might also design something that would be appropriate for a child, an infant?"

Tillie's heart melted. *No wonder Caitlin can't keep her hands off the man,* she thought. *He's utterly delicious.* "I'm sure I can meet your expectations," she assured him as she gazed up at him adoringly.

"Splendid," Dylan replied with a devastating smile. "Shall we go inside and write up the order?"

Rob Heathcote pretended to work the long columns of sums before him, but in truth he was watching Mrs. Tremaine. She didn't look so good that day. Something was different about her. She seemed distracted, and more than once through the morning he'd seen her place her hands on her waist, kind of massaging it and then her back as if she was in pain. At lunch he was going to slip away and go find Dylan.

"You know, children," Caitlin said with a bright smile. "It's such a lovely day. Why don't we take the rest of it off? You can use the time to work on your nature projects. We'll reconvene tomorrow."

She certainly didn't have to ask twice, Rob noted as the rest of his classmates quickly exited the room. They could be heard clambering up the church stairs, their voices growing louder and more excited as they went.

"Rob?"

"You need some help?" he asked without preamble.

She grimaced and held up her finger as if asking him to wait for the pain to pass. "I think I may. . . ." Then she cried out and doubled over.

"I'm getting help," Rob called and bolted from the room. He raced down the street to his father's saloon. "Pa! It's Miz Tremaine. I think the baby might be coming. I think she's in trouble." He grabbed his father by the shirtsleeve and pulled him physically into the street.

"Hold on. You go for the doc. I'll go get Miz Tremaine," Gar Heathcote said.

Rob nodded and took off at a run for the doctor's office and home three streets over. He was relieved to see that the doctor was in his office. The waiting room was filled with patients, but Rob burst right through the closed office door. "You gotta come," he demanded. "Caitlin's having her baby."

"Coming, son," Doc replied as he calmly finished dressing the cut on the patient in front of him.

"Now," Rob urged. "She don't look so good."

"Hold your horses, son. Babies come in their own good time."

"Well, this one's coming right now."

Caitlin sat on the edge of her chair, clutching the edge of her desk. The first wave of intense pain had passed and nearly five minutes had elapsed before the second wave came. *This is it*, she thought excitedly. *Our baby is coming.*

She glanced around the room, wanting to record every detail of the experience in her mind. When Gar Heathcote rushed in, she was smiling.

"Hi, Gar," she said as if these were the most normal of circumstances under which to see the saloonkeeper. "Is Dylan with you?"

"No. Haven't seen him. I sent somebody to check his office, but he's not there."

Caitlin nodded. "He's out at the mine. He can't stay away. Will you help me get home?"

"We'll wait for the doc. Shouldn't you be lying down or something?" He hovered about her like a mother hen, his hands fluttering around her without actually touching her.

"I won't break, Gar," she said with a chuckle; then the pain gripped her again and she gave an involuntary shout.

"What!" Gar shouted in return.

"Ah, here you are," Doc said as he hurried forward and took hold of Caitlin, supporting her until the contraction had passed. "Is that the first one?"

Caitlin shook her head. "Another one about five minutes ago."

"Well, let's get you home and get this baby born." Doc instructed Gar and Rob on how to carry her out to his buckboard, where he had laid out blankets for her in the back. "Ready?" he asked as he climbed onto the driver's seat.

"You gonna make it?" Rob asked anxiously.

Caitlin smiled. "Go get Dylan," she said just as the next contraction grabbed her.

One of the first investments Dylan had made when he and Caitlin had come back to town was a full partnership in the new mine that had started up shortly after he left town. His partners were businessmen from Madison who knew next to nothing about mining. They were happy to have the Cornishman in their midst. For his part, Dylan was delighted to have the opportunity to put to work many of the ideas he'd fashioned through the long years of mining on his own. The men respected him because they knew he had experience and understood what they had to face every time they went down into the bowels of the earth. They trusted him to care for their welfare at the same time he was taking care of his own profits.

Three of his miners were standing with him, showing him the operation of a newly delivered piece of equipment when Dylan heard Rob Heathcote's shout. He turned slowly, his heart beating fast as he scanned the valley below for the boy.

But before he saw Rob, he saw something else. There was Molly, leaning out of the bedroom window and gaily waving a bright pink rag. "Dylan," she shouted, "come quickly. It's time."

Dylan let out a whoop of joy and took off running pell-mell down the hill toward the cottage. His shouts of excitement and celebration could be heard up and down the streets of the town, and everywhere they were heard people stopped and smiled and nodded knowingly. The badger and his proper schoolmarm were having their baby. It was indeed a glorious day.

FROM ROSANNE BITTNER:
ZEBRA SAVAGE DESTINY ROMANCE!

#1: SWEET PRAIRIE PASSION   (0-8217-5342-8, $5.99)

#2: RIDE THE FREE WIND   (0-8217-5343-6, $5.99)

#3: RIVER OF LOVE   (0-8217-5344-4, $5.99)

#4: EMBRACE THE
    WILD LAND   (0-8217-5413-0, $5.99)

#7: EAGLE'S SONG   (0-8217-5326-6, $5.99)

ROMANCE FROM ROSANNE BITTNER